Royalty and the Crown:
P...

ROYALTY AND
THE CROWN:
LEILA & GAGE

Two captivating stories of regal romance
from two fantastic favourite authors

ROMANCING THE CROWN: LEILA & GAGE

Virgin Seduction
KATHLEEN CREIGHTON

Royal Spy
VALERIE PARV

◎™ MILLS & BOON®
Pure reading pleasure™

This collection is first published in Great Britain 2008.
Harlequin Mills & Boon Limited,
Eton House, 18-24 Paradise Road, Richmond, Surrey TW9 1SR

ROMANCING THE CROWN: LEILA & GAGE
© Harlequin Books S.A. 2008.

The publisher acknowledges the copyright holders of the individual works, which have already been published in the UK in single, separate volumes as follows:

Virgin Seduction © Harlequin Books S.A. 2002
Royal Spy © Harlequin Books S.A. 2002

Special thanks and acknowledgement are given to Kathleen Creighton and Valerie Parv for their contributions to the ROMANCING THE CROWN series.

ISBN: 978 0 263 86108 2

064-0908

Printed and bound in Spain
by Litografia Rosés S.A., Barcelona

ROMANCING THE CROWN

*The crown prince of Montebello is home at last.
Now the Montebellan royal family extends its
hand in friendship to the Tamiri sheikhdom
and journeys to Tamir to celebrate a royal
wedding – or is that **weddings**?*

Leila Kamal: The youngest Tamiri princess's
impulsive actions have stirred up a hornets' nest.
But what stings most is that her new husband has
yet to make love to his wife!

Cade Gallagher: This brash American knows
he's all wrong for a pampered princess. Still he's
never seen anyone so lovely...or wanted a woman
so much.

Virgin Seduction

KATHLEEN
CREIGHTON

THE KAMAL FAMILY

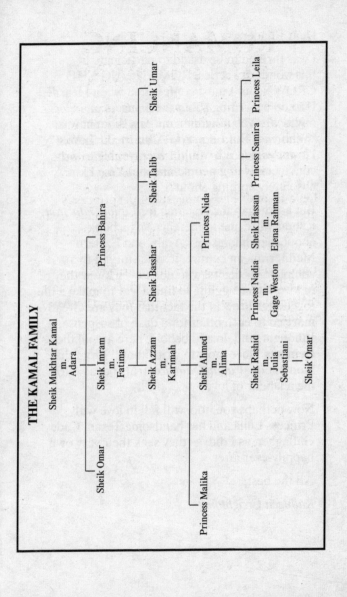

Dear Reader,

I was thrilled to be asked to participate in this wonderful series, ROMANCING THE CROWN, but I must confess that when I learned I would be writing about the princess of a mythical Arab kingdom, my first thought was, "Who, *me*? But I don't *do* Arab sheikh books!" How, I wondered, would I ever be able to write convincingly of a people and a culture I knew absolutely nothing about?

But as I began the research for *Virgin Seduction*, it suddenly came to me: this isn't a book about sheikhdoms and Arabs and Eastern Mediterranean culture, it's the story of two complete strangers, who don't even know they're in love yet, struggling to find a way to make a life together. Throw in the fact that they are already married to each other for a dash of suspense, I thought, and, lo and behold, here are all the elements I love most to write about! From that moment on, *Virgin Seduction* truly became for me a labour of love.

Now perhaps you, too, will fall in love with Princess Leila and her handsome Texan, Cade Gallagher, as I did, as they seek their very own happily-ever-after.

All the best,

Kathleen Creighton

Prologue

Sheik Ahmed Kamal, absolute ruler of the Mediterranean island kingdom of Tamir, had reason to count himself among those whom Allah has richly blessed. Indeed, he was the happiest of men as he stood in the modest but beautifully appointed mosque that was his family's traditional place of worship and prayed for divine guidance and blessings for his youngest son, Hassan, on the solemn occasion of his marriage.

Before him were the bride and groom—at this moment, at least, appropriately separated—with eyes downcast as befitted such a solemn and worshipful occasion. Today the bride—as well as many of those assembled for the *Nikah* ceremony, and Sheik Ahmed himself—was modestly veiled and dressed in the traditional costume of her husband's people. In Ahmed's opinion, it was a much more pleasing mode of dress to both the eye and the spirit than the Western styles he'd grudgingly adopted in recent years.

A fine woman, Elena Rahman, Ahmed thought to himself. Hassan had chosen well—or so Ahmed had been assured by Alima, his wife, whose judgment in such matters he had learned to trust. To be honest, he'd had reservations about the girl at first—she was, after all, an American. And the daughter of a terrorist! But as Alima had pointed out, she was at least a true believer by blood and birth. And it must not be forgotten that Elena Rahman was CEO of one of the most prosperous oil refining companies in the American state of Texas. Yes, thought Ahmed, who had ambitious plans for his country's own oil resources…Hassan had made a very good choice, indeed.

As he began the first of the required Quranic verses, Ahmed's gaze expanded to include the two people standing with the bride and groom as witnesses, and his heart grew near to bursting with pride and thanksgiving. His eldest son, Sheik Rashid, and Rashid's wife, Princess Julia of Montebello, were only recently wed themselves, and parents of Sheik Ahmed's first grandchild, Omar—already the apple of his grandmother's eye, and, it must be confessed, of his grandfather's as well.

As serene and happy as the couple appeared today, the truth was that Rashid and Julia's union had come about only after much intrigue and extreme peril. In the end, it had brought about the reconciliation of a century-old feud between their respective countries, and as a result, prospects for a future of prosperity and mutual cooperation between Tamir and Montebello had never been more promising.

It was time now to conclude the ceremony with the traditional prayers for the bride and groom, for their families and friends and for the community at large. As he intoned the beautiful and time-honored words, Ahmed raised his head and his arms to encompass them all: his two sons and their wives; his own beloved Alima, still as lovely as the day of their own *Nikah* ceremony; their three daughters, Nadia, the eldest; gentle Samira; and Leila, the youngest and secretly his favorite—and most vexing—child.

The ceremony was almost concluded. Quickly, Ahmed's eyes continued their sweep of those assembled inside the mosque—a small, select group, for the most part close family and friends, according to the traditions of his people. There in the back, he caught sight of Butrus Dabir, his trusted advisor and—who knows?—perhaps soon-to-be son-in-law, if only Nadia—stubborn daughter!—would see fit to accept him.

But that small cloud over the sheik's happiness passed quickly.

Also among the guests assembled in the mosque were the bride's two guests, from Texas—that rather outspoken woman who was Elena's friend—what was her name? Oh yes, Kitty. And the tall and somewhat mysterious man who had come as the bride's guardian and protector. According to Elena, the man was her adopted brother and only family, although, since there was no actual blood tie between Cade Gallagher and Elena Rahman, and Ahmed being a suspicious and extremely traditional man by nature, he thought it a strange relationship.

Near the front of the assembly, dressed in well-tailored Western-style suits, was the contingent from Montebello. Several, including Ahmed's new ally and in-law King Marcus Sebastiani and his firstborn son, Prince Lucas, stood with heads respectfully bowed. The day after tomorrow, to conclude the weekend's festivities, there would be a state dinner and reception to celebrate the joyous occasion of the prince's miraculous return from the dead as well as the new alliance between the two countries as personified by the marriage of Rashid and Julia.

But first…tomorrow would be the *Walima,* the feast given by Hassan to celebrate the consummation of his marriage to Elena Rahman. The palace would be ablaze with flowers and light and alive with laughter and music. There would be an abundance of good food, good friends and good conversation, all of which Ahmed most especially enjoyed. It would be a joyous occasion. On this day, all was well with the Kamal family. Tamir was at peace, and prospects for its future prosperity were bright.

Yes, thought Sheik Ahmed as he uttered the final words of the *Khutba-tun-Nikah,* life is indeed good.

Allah be praised.

Chapter 1

From a balcony overlooking the palace gardens, Leila watched the man in the dove-gray cowboy hat stroll unhurried along tiled pathways. She'd watched many people traverse the garden that morning, but she particularly liked the way this man moved—confidently but without arrogance. The way he seemed to study everything around him—the flowers, the fountains, the colorful mosaics at his feet—with unselfconscious interest reminded her of a child at the zoo.

She laughed out loud as a brightly colored bird flitted across the man's path, startling him. He lifted his head to follow the bird's flight, revealing a deeply tanned, hard-boned face, cheeks creased, teeth bared in a smile. For several seconds he seemed to look right at Leila, and her breath caught, stifling the laughter. Oh, she knew he couldn't really see her. She was well concealed behind the balcony's intricately carved screen. It was just that he had such a *nice* smile.

''That one,'' she said in a conspirator's whisper to the

woman beside her. "Who *is* he—the one in the hat? I saw him yesterday at the wedding. He *must* be an American."

"Oh yes, Princess, he is—and not only that, but from *Texas.*" The servant Nargis threw a guilty glance toward the divan where her mistress, Leila's sister Nadia, had her nose—and her attention—safely buried in her sketchbook. She lowered her voice anyway. "His name is Cade Gallagher. The princess—er...Mrs. Elena invited him. Salma heard her tell Madam Alima that he is her guardian."

Leila made a derisive sound, forgetting to whisper. "Do not be silly. Elena is an American. In America women don't have guardians." She couldn't keep a note of envy out of her voice. Her new sister-in-law was only four years older than Leila, but so smart and sophisticated, and the head of her own company! And still she had managed to attract and win the love of a handsome and powerful man like Hassan.

Nargis shrugged. "It is what I heard."

"Perhaps Elena only wished to honor the customs of our country," said Leila's sister Samira in an appeasing tone, laying aside the needlepoint she'd been working on and coming to join them. "You know that since the death of her father, she has no family of her own. This man may be a distant relative, perhaps a friend or even a business associate. Anyway," she added, gently chastising, "if Hassan has agreed to have him here as a guest, there can be nothing improper about it. You should not gossip, Leila."

Leila hooked her arm through her sister's, not in the least chastened. "Oh, but look at him, Sammi—do you not think he is handsome?" But at the same time she was thinking that the word "handsome" really did not suit the tall man in the gray suit and cowboy hat. It seemed too pale and feminine a word, somehow.

"He seems very...rugged," said Samira after a moment's consideration, voicing Leila's very thoughts. "Quite imposing, really.'' She tilted her head sideways as she thought about it. ''It would be difficult not to be intimidated by such a man.''

''Oh, I know,'' Leila teased, rolling her eyes, ''you'd prefer someone more suave…someone smooth, someone sophisticated—'' she pointed ''—like that one there—the dark, beautiful one with the impossibly gorgeous eyes.'' And much too aware of how gorgeous they are, she thought with disdain. She didn't know quite why, but she found something about the man vaguely unpleasant. Rather like food that had been cooked in too much grease. ''And…is he not the one I saw talking with you yesterday?''

''That is Desmond Caruso, Princess,'' Nargis interrupted eagerly, pleased to be the bearer of information that would make her once more the center of attention. ''He is one of the Sebastianis—you see, that is Duke Lorenzo with him. And the woman with the red hair is Duke Lorenzo's new wife, Eliza. She is an American, too, you know.'' Her voice dropped to a gleeful whisper. ''A *newspaper* reporter.''

''Really?'' As always, Leila's interest perked up at the mention of America, and she did not stop then to wonder why Samira had suddenly gone so pale and silent.

''*Really*—you three are the worst gossips,'' said Nadia, making a tsk-tsking sound. But she said it good-naturedly as she, too, came to join them at the screen.

There was a little silence while the four women watched the shifting patterns below in the gardens…people gathering, greeting, moving on. Sounds drifted up to them on the balcony…the tinkle of water in the fountains, snatches of laughter and the murmur of conversation.

''Well,'' Leila said flatly, ''I do not trust a man who is that handsome.'' A small, involuntary shiver surprised her. Funny—the same thing had happened to her when she had seen him talking with Samira yesterday in the corridor near the great hall. Something about the man was definitely off,

but Leila did not mention it. No one would take her seriously anyway. She smiled with lowered lashes and added
in a voice like a purr, "I much prefer the tall American.
Do you not think he looks like a cowboy? Even dressed in
a business suit?"

Samira smiled indulgently. "Oh, Leila, you just like
Americans. You have a fascination with that country."

"Why not?" said Leila, tossing back her long, black
hair. "America *is* fascinating."

"How do you know?" Samira asked with a trill of
laughter.

Leila could feel her cheeks growing warm. "Hassan evidently thinks so. And Elena has told me about America—
especially Texas. Since Elena is from there, it must be a
very wonderful place, must it not? She is so smart, so..."
She caught herself before she could say the word in her
mind—*free!*—and instead turned her back on Samira and
addressed the sister on her other side. "Nadia? Wouldn't
you like to visit America?"

Nadia gave an indifferent shrug. "What is so special
about America? It is just...very, very *big*."

"But," said Leila eagerly, "that is what makes it special." She threw her arms wide. "It *is* so big. And
Tamir—" she brought her hands almost together "—is so
small." She finished with a sigh. "It is hard to imagine a
place so enormous."

Oh, but Leila could imagine it. If she closed her eyes
she could see herself mounted on one of her brother
Rashid's polo ponies, riding like the wind across the green-
gold fields of his farm on the outer island of Siraj, with the
wind blowing back her hair and the sky cloudless and blue
above and all around her and the land seeming to go on
and on forever.

Only it did not go on forever, of course—how could it,
on Siraj or even Tamir? Very quickly the land ended and

there were the cliffs, and below them the white sand beaches and blue-green water. Someday, she thought with a sudden and intense yearning, I want to go to a place where the land does not stop.

"Where would you like to go in America, little sister? What would you want to do there?" Nadia was looking at her, smiling in that tolerant, affectionate way she had, as if Leila were a particularly appealing, perhaps even moderately amusing child. "Shopping, I'm sure. Perhaps…New York City?"

Leila had shopped in London boutiques and Paris salons; her shoes were custom-made in Italy. What, she thought, would New York City have to offer her that those fashion centers did not? But she only said with a shrug and a superior smile, "I was thinking more of Hollywood. Maybe…Rodeo Drive?" But images of endless desert vistas and ranges of snowcapped mountains remained wistful and golden in her mind. Like memories, except—how could she have memories of places she had never seen?

Nadia laughed. "Hollywood? Oh, Leila, you are a dreamer."

Stung, Leila said, "Why is it so impossible to think of going to America?"

"You have no reason to go," Samira answered in her matter-of-fact way. "Father would never allow you to make such a trip just for fun, and what other reason would you have, when Europe is so much closer?"

Leila had to bite her lip to keep from mentioning the fact that Hassan had attended college in America. Her own education had been restricted to an all-female boarding school in Switzerland, capped off by a year in England, and her brother's engineering degree from M.I.T. was a source of envy to her.

"What about business?" she said after a moment. "Now

that Hassan has married Elena, and she is head of an oil
company—''

''But that is Hassan's business. It has nothing to do with
you. No, Leila, dear—'' Samira gave her arm a not unsym-
pathetic squeeze as she turned away from the screen ''—I
am afraid the only hope you would have of visiting America is if, like Hassan, you were to marry an American.''
She and Nadia exchanged laughing glances. ''And for that,
you must first wait until Nadia and I have found husbands.''

''I will be old and ugly before that happens,'' Leila
grumbled.

Never one to entertain a dark mood for long, she straightened, dimpling wickedly as she peered through the screen.
''Speaking of prospective husbands—guess who has just
arrived. Look, Nadia, it is Butrus Dabir.'' She slid her eyes
toward her oldest sister, lips curving in an innocent smile.
''Is it true he has asked Father if he may marry you?''

Her teasing was rewarded by a most satisfactory gasp of
dismay from Nadia. ''Where did you hear that?'' Hands on
her hips, she rounded on her servant. ''*Nargis?* How many
times—''

Nargis was already making a hasty retreat, after sneaking
Leila a delighted wink. ''Yes, Princess—I am going to prepare your bath now. Did you wish the jasmine scent, or the
rose? Or perhaps that new one from Paris...'' She ducked
through the draperies and disappeared into the princesses'
sitting room.

''She is *such* a terrible gossip,'' Nadia said crossly,
snatching up her sketchbook from the settee and preparing
to follow. In the doorway she paused to give her sisters a
piercing glance. ''I have *not* said I will marry Butrus.''

''She will, though,'' said Samira with a shrug when Nadia had gone. ''I am almost sure of it.''

Still gazing intently into the garden, Leila could not repress a shiver. ''I wish she would not. Even if it means we both must wait longer before we can marry.''

''You do not like Butrus?'' Samira looked at her in surprise. ''He is very handsome, in his way. And he has been almost a member of the family for so many years. Father trusts him.''

''It is just that…he seems so cold. I do not see how Nadia can possibly love him.''

''Perhaps,'' said Samira thoughtfully, ''there are other reasons to marry besides love. Not,'' she hastened to add, ''that I would ever do such a thing. But…who knows what is in another person's heart? Nadia's, after all, has been broken once already. Perhaps she does not wish to risk such pain again. And I suppose if the other reasons were important enough…''

Leila said nothing. Once again she was watching the man in the dove-gray suit and cowboy hat stroll along the tiled pathways. This time she did not take her eyes off of him until he had disappeared from view beyond a stone archway thickly entwined with climbing roses.

In the shaded promenade beyond a rose-covered archway, Cade Gallagher paused to light a cheroot—a small sin, and one of the few vices he allowed himself. He was alone, for the moment, in this secluded part of the palace grounds, and he relished the solitude and the quiet, pulled it into himself along with the honey-sweet smoke of the cigar. As he exhaled, the chatter of strangers' conversation receded to background noise. Nearby he could hear the twitter of birdsong, and the musical ripple of water. The air was cool and fragrant, misty with breeze-blown spray from distant fountains.

Not quite the juniper and live oak-covered vistas of his Hill Country ranch retreat back home in Texas, he thought, but not at all bad.

Admittedly, he hadn't seen much of Tamir so far, save for the mosque and the royal palace and gardens. Thanks to the usual flight delays, he'd arrived late yesterday afternoon, just barely in time for the marriage ceremony. He found it all interesting, though frankly he was already beginning to feel cooped up and restless. He was more than ready for all this partying and celebrating to be over with so he could get on to his real reason for flying halfway around the world to this remote little island kingdom— business.

More specifically, oil business. In the beginning he'd resisted Elena's invitation to attend the wedding as her honored guest, and to stand up for her as her guardian—ridiculous idea, he knew of no one on earth less in need of guardianship than Elena Rahman—in place of nonexistent family. At first. Until she'd mentioned that Sheik Ahmed Kamal, her father-in-law to be, was interested in refitting his country's oil refineries, perhaps even building new ones. Cade was in the business of building and refitting oil refineries. The opportunities had seemed too promising to pass up.

There was very little in this world that impressed him, certainly nothing having to do with wealth or title or positions of power. But the old sheik—Sheik Ahmed—he'd made one hell of an impression on Cade, even after only one brief meeting. He was sharp, that one. Silver-haired and carrying the weight of a little too much good living, but still crafty as they come. Surprisingly unpretentious, too. The man was the absolute monarch of his country, yet he'd elected to use the title of sheik—a general all-purpose title of respect, was the way Cade understood it—rather than king. Cade liked that.

He liked the sheik's son, Hassan, too, though he wasn't ready to admit as much to Elena. Cade was beginning to think Elena hadn't completely lost her mind after all, marrying into a Middle Eastern royal family. Hassan seemed westernized enough, and Elena was just hardheaded enough, as he well knew from personal experience, that they might actually make a go of it.

All at once he was remembering the unheralded softness in Elena's voice on the telephone when she'd called to tell him of her plans to marry Hassan. He was remembering last night, and the way her eyes had shone when she'd lifted them to her new husband's face as he'd drawn aside her veils... Twinges of unfamiliar emotions stirred in his chest—envy and longing were the only two he recognized. Annoyed, he drew deeply on the cheroot, his motions momentarily jerky and disconcerted.

It was at that moment when a low murmur of voices reached him from beyond the rose-covered archway. Glad of the distraction, he hurriedly composed himself, preparing to make polite small talk with intruders on his private corner of Eden. Instead, the newcomers—two of them, from their conversation—halted just on the other side of the arch. About to step through and join them, Cade hesitated. Something—the sneering quality of the speaker, perhaps—made him go still and alert and stay right where he was, hidden from view by a lush bank of hibiscus.

"...*joyous* occasion!" Suddenly raised, the voice was sharp, sarcastic and clear. That was followed by a distinct snort.

"You seem less than pleased, Desmond," the second voice remarked in a mildly surprised tone. "Lucas is our cousin. Even if he were not family, I would have thought King Marcus's joy would be reason enough for us to celebrate. After all, he had all but given his son up—"

"Now, don't get me wrong," the first speaker broke in hastily, his voice now smooth as oil. "I'm as thankful as anyone that Prince Lucas has turned up alive and...*apparently* none the worse for wear." There was a

pause, and then in a decidedly unctuous voice, "I'm thinking of *you*, Lorenzo."

"What do you mean?" The question was curt, a little
wary.

"Oh, come now—don't pretend you don't know that in
the crown prince's absence, King Marcus had been groom-
ing you as his heir. Now that Lucas is back in the picture,
your position in the royal court can hardly be the same."

There was an ambiguous sound that could have been
amusement or reproof. "It's never been my ambition to
govern a country, Desmond. I'm happy with the position I
have, thank you." And after a pause… "In any case, I
really don't think it's *my* position you're concerned about."

The reply was blustering. "Look, I'm thinking of my
own future, too—sure I am. I'm not going to deny having
ambitions."

"My God, Desmond, are you that mercenary? That
you'd wish Lucas had *not* returned, for the sake of your
own—"

"How can you think such a thing of me, your own
brother?" Whoever he was, Cade thought, this Desmond
had apparently really stepped in it, and was now backped-
aling so fast he was almost sputtering. "I only meant—I
was referring to our future in service to King Marcus. My
only ambition is to serve His Highness, in any way I can,
as he sees fit…"

As the voice babbled on, Cade almost snorted out loud.
This Desmond guy was slippery as a snake oil salesman.

Apparently his companion was starting to have some
doubts about the man's character, too, brother or not. There
was a formidable chill in his voice when, after a marked
silence, he suddenly said, "I see my wife is looking for
me. Excuse me."

Footsteps quickly retreated. A moment later Cade heard
the hiss of an exhalation followed by some mutterings that

sounded mostly like swearing, and then a second set of footsteps moved off aimlessly along a tiled path, fading finally into the general noise of mingling guests and whispering water.

Cade released a breath he'd not been aware of holding, then took a quick drag on the cheroot he'd all but forgotten. Cautiously, casually, he stepped around the clump of hibiscus. Interesting, he thought as he watched two men in white dinner jackets move off in different directions. Apparently all was not entirely rosy after all in this Garden of Eden.

Back in the crowded main courtyard, he snagged a waiter, resplendent in white brocade and saffron yellow turban.

"Excuse me—uh, do you speak English?"

Balancing a tray of fruits carved to look like flowers, the waiter dipped his head respectfully. "Of course. How may I help you, sir?"

Cade smiled in mild chagrin. The man sounded as if he'd stepped right off the campus at Oxford—or wherever it was those British lords went to school.

"Uh...yeah, I was wondering if you could tell me who that gentleman is—the one with the lady with red hair. I was just talking with him, and didn't catch his name."

"That would be his lordship, Duke Lorenzo Sebastiani of Montebello, sir. The lady is his wife—an American. I believe her name is Eliza."

"Ah—of course. And that gentleman over there—the dark one? I think he said his name was Desmond...."

"Yes sir—that is Duke Lorenzo's brother, Desmond Caruso, an advisor to King Marcus."

"Ah," said Cade. "Yes...thank you."

"I am happy to be of service, sir." The waiter bowed and went on his way.

Interesting, Cade thought again. But, since it didn't have

anything to do with Tamir or Elena or her new in-laws, it
didn't concern him, either.

He winced as a piercing "Yoo-hoo!" rose above the
pleasant chuckle of a nearby fountain. "Cade—oh, Cade!"

He groaned and glanced around in hope of finding cover.
Seeing none, he rolled his eyes and fixed what he hoped
was a welcoming smile on his face as, with one last fortifying puff of his cigar, he went forth to greet Elena's other
guest, her loud and annoying friend, Kitty.

Leila was bored. The wedding banquet had been going
on for more than three hours, and showed no signs of con-
cluding any time soon. The parade of waiters bearing trays
laden with an incredible variety of delicacies seemed endless, even though Leila—and, she was sure, most of the
other guests—had already eaten as much as they could possibly hold. The food had been wonderful, of course, befit-
ting a royal *Walima*—chicken simmered in pomegranate
juice and rolled in grape leaves, veal sauteed with eggplant
and onions and delicately spiced with tumeric and carda-
moms. And for the main course, Leila's favorite—whole
lamb stuffed with dried fruits, almonds, pine nuts, cracked
wheat and onions, seasoned with ginger and coriander and
then baked in hot ashes until it was tender enough to be
eaten with the fingers. Leila had eaten until she felt stuffed
herself—which was, she supposed, one advantage in being
forced to wear the gracefully draped but all-concealing
gown that was Tamir's traditional female costume. At least
she didn't have to hold her stomach in.

The trays now were offering a variety of fruits, as well
as an amazing assortment of sweets—cakes, pastries and
candies, even tiny baskets made of chocolate and filled with
sugar-glazed flower petals. Ordinarily Leila had an insatia-
ble sweet tooth, but tonight she was too full to do more
than nibble at a chocolate-covered strawberry.

She had also drunk much more of her country's traditional mildly fermented wine than she was accustomed to, and as a result was becoming both sleepy and cross. Not to mention frustrated. It was such a beautiful evening—stars were bright in the cloudless spring sky that canopied the palace's Great Courtyard. The *Walima* was being held outdoors in order to accommodate the great number of guests, as, according to tradition, everyone in the immediate vicinity was invited to a marriage feast, rich and poor alike. Tiled in intricate geometric patterns and flanked on both sides by stone colonnades, the Great Courtyard was a formal rectangle that extended from the palace to the cliffs, where arched portals framed a spectacular view of the sea. Tables draped in linen and set with fine china and crystal had been set up on both sides of a chain of fountains and narrow pools that divided the courtyard down the middle and reflected the stars and hundreds of flickering torches. A light breeze blowing in from the sea was heavy with the scent of night-blooming jasmine and moonflowers. It was a beautiful night. It might also have been—*should* have been—a very romantic night.

Except that Leila had been trying all evening without success to catch the eye of the man she would very much have liked to share such an evening with—the man she had noticed that morning in the garden, the Texan in the dove-gray suit and cowboy hat. As luck would have it, he was sitting at a table almost directly across the reflecting pool from hers. Tonight the hat was absent, and, like many of the other male guests present, particularly those from Montebello and America, he wore a white dinner jacket. Though in Leila's opinion, none of the other guests looked so lean and fit and dangerous in theirs, or boasted such broad and powerful shoulders. She could see now that his hair was thick and wavy, a rich dark blond. It gleamed like gold in the flickering light of the torches. She would like to know what color his eyes were, but they were set deep in his rugged face, and masked in shadows.

If only we could dance like Americans do, she thought wistfully as she watched a line of professional performers of the traditional Tamari dances, faces veiled and torsos cleverly concealed, undulating their way down the length of the courtyard, weaving in and out among the tables to the rhythmic keening of native flutes and sitars. Jewels flashed from their ankles, wrists and hair as they performed the intricate hand movements and kept time to the music with tiny finger cymbals. Like most girls in her country, Leila had learned secretly as a child how to dance the traditional dances, though of course it would not have been proper for a princess to actually perform for anyone—except, perhaps, for her husband, in the privacy of their marriage chambers. If I ever *have* a husband, she thought moodily, as without her realizing it, her body began to move and sway in time to the music.

On her right, Samira nudged her and hissed, "Leila—stop that. Someone will see you."

Leila rolled her eyes. *So what?* she wanted to say. It would not be the first time. Many people had seen her dance in Switzerland and England, and the world had not come to an end. When she was in boarding school she had learned to dance the western way, to rock and roll music, and in England she had even—and she was sure her father would have a heart attack if he knew—danced with boys the way westerners did. *Touching* one another. And nothing terrible had happened then, either. She was still, alas, very much a virgin. And likely to remain one for the foreseeable future.

"I am *bored,*" she whispered back. "I have eaten too much and I want to lie down. When is this going to be over?"

"Hush," Samira scolded. "This is Hassan and Elena's night. Remember your manners."

"I wish we could at least mingle with the guests—talk to them," Leila said, wistfully eyeing the golden-haired man across the reflecting pool. But his head was bowed as he listened, apparently with close attention, to the frizzy-haired woman seated next to him. Leila sighed. And before she could stop it, her mouth opened wide in a blatant, jaw-popping yawn.

"I'm sorry?" Cade politely lowered his head in order to hear what the woman at his side was saying above the discordant wailing these people called music.

Kitty repeated it in a loud, hoarse whisper. "I said, that girl across the way over there has been tryin' her darndest all evenin' long to catch your eye. I believe she'd like to flirt with you."

Cade's glance flicked upward reflexively. "Oh yeah? Which one?" Anything, he thought, to relieve the tedium. He wasn't accustomed to spending three hours over dinner.

"That one—the real pretty one in the aqua blue dress...long black hair with gold thingies in it...looks like something out of *The Arabian Nights*. See her?"

Cade looked. He'd already noticed the girl, since she was drop-dead gorgeous and he was a man and only human. Now, though, he felt a shiver of silent laughter ripple through him. "You mean, the one who looks like she's about to swallow herself?"

His amusement blossomed into an unabashed grin as the girl's bright and restless glance collided suddenly with his. Her eyes went wide with horror and she slapped a long, graceful hand over her mouth in a belated and futile attempt to cover up the yawn. Next, he watched, fascinated, as a parade of expressions danced across her face like characters in a play: dismay, chagrin, vexation, arrogance, pride, irony…and finally, to his delight, a dimpled and utterly winsome smile.

Kitty gave a little crow of triumph. "There, you see? I told you she was flirtin' with you."

"Kind of young, don't you think?" Cade drawled. "Not to mention," he added, as the significance of that circlet of gold medallions on the girl's head sank in, "if I'm not mistaken, she's a princess."

"Really?" Kitty gasped before she caught herself, then added with a lofty sniff, "Well, so what if she is? Hassan's a prince. That didn't stop Elena." She gave an excited little squeal. "Oh—I just realized—that would make her Elena's sister-in-law, wouldn't it? I'll bet she could introduce us— uh, you."

"I wouldn't count on it," Cade said dryly. "Looks to me like they keep those princesses pretty tightly under wraps."

Pretending disinterest, he watched out of the corner of his eye as an older woman flanked by a cadre of female servants suddenly appeared beside the princesses' table across the way. This woman he knew. He'd been presented to Tamir's first lady—Elena's new mother-in-law—along with her husband, Sheik Ahmed, following the wedding ceremony last night. Alima Kamal—who, he'd been told, preferred not to use a royal title—was dressed in the same gracefully draped style of gown as were her daughters, this one deep royal blue liberally trimmed with gold. Like her daughters, she wore a circlet of gold medallions in her still-raven black hair. They glinted in the torchlight as she grace-fully inclined her head. Without a word, all the occupants of the princesses' table rose and were swallowed up by the royal entourage, which then moved away in the direction of the palace, veils fluttering, like a dense flock of brightly plumed birds.

"Wow," breathed Kitty. "It really *is* like something out

of *The Arabian Nights*. Do you think they keep them in a harem?''

Cade gave a snort of laughter. ''I'm sure they don't. For starters, the sheik only has one wife. And, if Hassan is any indication, they're pretty westernized here. All this native costume stuff tonight—the turbans and veils—I'm sure is just for this occasion. Some kind of wedding tradition, probably.''

''Umm-hmm...'' Kitty was thoughtfully chewing her lip. ''Well, I'll still bet Elena could introduce you to that cute little sister-in-law of hers, if you asked her to.''

''No, thanks.''

''Why not? She's *very* pretty, and she was definitely interested in *you*, Cade.''

''Not on your life.'' Cade's grin tilted with grim irony. A knockout she might be, but not really his type and way too young for him, anyway. Not to mention that the very last thing he needed was to get tangled up with some royal pain-in-the-ass princess, when what he was really hoping for was to close a nice, lucrative business deal with her father, the sheik.

Chapter 2

Eight horses thundered in close formation down a grassy plain on what appeared to be a collision course with disaster. Long-handled mallets flashed and winked in the bright morning sunlight to the accompaniment of guttural cries, grunts of effort, and shrill and imperious whistles, while on a sideline shaded by olive trees that looked as though they might easily have dated from biblical times, Cade watched the proceedings with an interest that could best be described as ambiguous.

He wasn't a polo fan—in fact, he knew next to nothing about the game. He considered it a rich man's sport. And while there were some who'd place Cade in that category, *he* certainly never thought of himself in those terms. As far as he was concerned he was just a hardworking businessman who happened to have made a lot of money, which put him in an altogether different class than those who had nothing better to do with their time than gallop around a field on horseback jostling one another for the chance to whack a little ball with a big mallet.

"Snob," said Elena teasingly when he voiced that opinion to her. "I knew it. You, Cade, are a working-class snob. Come on—polo is the sport of kings."

"I rest my case," Cade said around the stem of his cheroot.

"*And,* it's one of the oldest sports, maybe the first ever invented." She shot him a mock-piercing look. "What's this prejudice you have against royals? Seeing as how I'm now one."

"Prejudiced? *Me?*" he countered in mock outrage. "I don't even know any royals—except Hassan, I guess."

"That's what prejudice is," Elena said smugly. "Forming an opinion without personal knowledge." Her eyes went to the riders on the field, seeking and fastening on one in particular. "Anyway, you've met a few more in the past couple of days. Hassan's parents… What did you think of them, by the way?" Her tone was carefully casual, but Cade heard the question she was really asking: *Do you like him…my husband, Hassan? Please like him.*

He glanced down at the woman he'd thought of as a sister for most of his life, arguably the only family he had left. He said gruffly, "I had my doubts about your husband for a while. You know that." His voice softened. "But as long as he does right by you, that makes him okay in my book." He paused. "So…are you? Happy?"

She drew in a deep breath and let it out slowly, then smiled up at him, and he read her answer in her shining eyes before she spoke. "Yeah, Cade…I am."

Cade took a quick sip of his cheroot, surprised again by that sudden fierce ache of envy. "Then that's what counts."

Elena shot him a searching look. "So…what *did* you think of them—Hassan's family? The old sheik?"

He took a moment to consider, though he didn't need to. "Ahmed's a sharp old fox," he said finally. "Knows what he wants for his country, and won't give an inch until he

gets it. He'll drive a hard bargain, but he'll be fair.'' He
gave a dry chuckle. ''I'm looking forward to doing business
with him.''

''What about his wife—Alima?'' Elena smiled ruefully.
''My mother-in-law.'' She paused, shaking her head. ''Boy,
I never thought I'd say *those* words.''

''She seems very nice—warm.'' He didn't tell her that
for some reason the sheik's wife had reminded him, in ways
that had nothing to do with physical resemblance, of his
own mother. What he remembered of her, anyway.

''And Rashid?'' Elena's eyes were once more on the
field of play, watching the swirling mélange of men and
horses. Sunlight glinted off helmets and goggles and sweat-
damp horsehide, while brightly colored jerseys tangled together like ribbons. Eyes sparkling, she answered herself
before he could. ''He does raise some fine ponies, you've
gotta admit.''

Cade grinned. ''He does that.'' He'd been admiring
Rashid's own mount in particular, a dapple gray stallion
with the Arabian's classic dish face and high-arched neck,
graceful, delicate lines and, it appeared, the courage of a
lion. He was hoping to find an opportunity to talk horse
breeding with the prince…maybe discuss an exchange of
bloodlines—

His thoughts scattered like dry leaves as several ponies
thundered down the field in tight formation, close to the
sideline and only a few yards from where he and Elena
were standing, shaking the ground beneath their feet. A
gasp went up from the spectators, followed by shouts—
mostly of triumph, intermingled with a few moans of dismay. Apparently the Tamiri team, jubilant and easily dis-
tinguishable in bright gold and black, had just scored on
the scarlet-clad Montebellans.

Distracted by the celebration on the playing field, it was
a few seconds before Cade noticed the woman running—

no, dancing—along the sideline, keeping pace with the ponies galloping barely an arm's length away beyond the low board barrier. He had an impression of slenderness and grace as unselfconscious as a child's, of vitality as voluptuous and lush as Mother Earth herself. The unlikely combination tugged at his senses—and something else, some cache of emotions hidden away, until that moment, deep inside him. His breath caught. Protective instincts produced electrical impulses in all his muscles.

She's too close. She'll be trampled!

The alarm flashed across his consciousness, there one second, gone the next. Cynically, he thought, *She's a grown woman, she's got sense enough to stay out of harm's way.* His heart was beating fast as he settled back to watch her. He realized that, incongruously, he was smiling.

She was dressed all in earth tones—shiny brown leather boots to the knee, a divided skirt in soft-colored camel suede that hugged her rounded hips like kid gloves, and a cream-colored blouse made of something that looked like— and undoubtedly was—silk, with long flowing sleeves cuffed tightly at the wrist. The skirt was belted at her waist with a silk scarf patterned in the Tamari team colors— yellow and black. She wore a hat to shade her face from the blistering Mediterranean sun, the same soft suede as her skirt with a wide brim and flat crown, like those Cade associated with Argentinean cowboys. A hatstring hung loosely under her delicate chin to keep the hat from blowing off in the unpredictable sea breeze. Beneath the hat, raven-black hair swept cleanly back from a high-cheekboned face to a casually wound coil at the nape of a long, graceful neck.

Entranced, Cade thought, *I wonder who she is.* And following that, clearly, distinctly, *I want her.*

He acknowledged the thought unashamedly but with a wry inner smile. He was fully grown-up, no longer a child,

and years ago had learned that *wanting* did not necessarily
mean *having*.

Shouts of outrage and a shrill whistle interrupted his appraisal of the woman. He almost chuckled aloud as he
watched her express her own dissatisfaction with what was
happening on the field, whirling in fury and stamping her
foot like an angry child. Moments later she was in motion
again as the horses and riders careened back down the field,
once more dancing along the sideline, completely caught
up in the action, her body bobbing, jerking and weaving in
unconscious imitation of the players. As if, Cade thought,
she longed to be one of them, rather than just a spectator.

And then…he caught his breath. As she moved directly
in front of him, a gust of wind caught her hat from behind
and tipped it neatly forward off her head. She gave a little
shriek of dismay and grabbed for it, but it was already
tumbling across the trampled grass, directly into the path
of the oncoming horses. Cade felt his body lurch involuntarily, before the thought had even formed in his mind.
*She's so damned impulsive! My God, is she crazy enough
to go for it?*

As if she'd heard his thought or maybe sensed his forward lunge, she stopped herself abruptly and spun toward
him, delightfully abashed, like a little girl teetering on the
edge of the curb, preparing to earnestly swear, ''I wasn't
really going to run out in the street, *honest.*''

Perhaps loosened by that movement, her hair came out
of its sedate coil, unwinding like a living creature, something sleek and sinuous awakening to vibrant life. As it
tumbled down her back in a glorious black cascade, at that
precise moment she locked eyes with Cade. Catching her
lower lip between white teeth, she gave him a winsomely
dimpled smile.

Recognition exploded in his brain even as desire
thumped him in the groin. The double whammy caught him

off guard. Breath gusted from his lungs as if he'd taken an actual blow.

"Don't even think about it."

Cade jerked toward the quiet voice, mouth open in automatic denial. One look at Elena's face told him protest was pointless, so instead he laughed and wryly shook his head. "Let me guess—one of the princesses, right?"

She nodded. She was smiling, but her eyes were grave. "Leila—the youngest. I'm serious, Cade. If the sheik catches you laying so much as a finger on that girl, all bets are off. He watches her like a hawk."

"Evidently not today," he murmured out the side of his mouth as the princess approached them, stepping gracefully up the slight incline into the shade of the ancient olive trees.

Holding out her hand to Elena and, for the moment, ignoring Cade completely, she cried out in obvious delight, "Elena—hello!" And then, her expressive face scrunching with chagrin, "You saw what happened?" She had a charming accent, more pronounced than Hassan's—the result, Cade surmised, of having had much less contact with westerners. The quality of her voice was low and musical but with a huskiness that caressed his auditory nerves like coarse-textured fur.

"Oh, I did," Elena said with a moan of feminine commiseration. "I'm so sorry. It was such a beautiful hat."

The princess pursed her lips in a brief but charming pout, then smiled and gave a little shrug. *C'est la vie.*

She turned to Cade, finally, her eyes emerging from under thick sooty lashes like mischievous children peeking out from behind a curtain. "Hello. I am Leila Kamal." The way she held her hand out made him wonder if she expected him to kiss it.

Which was probably why, out of pure contrariness, he did nothing of the sort, but instead took her hand in a good old Texas American-style handshake. A moment later he wondered if that had been a mistake as well. Her hand was smaller and at the same time firmer than he'd expected. It left an impression on his senses of both strength and vulnerability, and he found himself holding on to it for a lot longer than was probably sane, while his mind filled with images and urges that had nothing whatsoever to do with sanity.

"This is Cade," said Elena. "Cade Gallagher—my friend and, uh, guardian."

"Of course." Lashes lifted; eyes gazed at him, somehow both dark and bright, mysterious as moonlit pools. He had a sudden sensation of leaning slightly off balance, as if his internal gyrocompass had been knocked out of kilter. "And also your brother—but not *really*." The dimples flashed. "For that I am glad, because if you were truly Elena's brother, and she is now my sister, then you would be *my* brother, as well." Her laugh was low, a delightful ripple, like water tumbling over pebbles. "And I most certainly do *not* need any more brothers. Two is quite enough!"

Cade found himself floundering in unfamiliar territory, at least when dealing with a beautiful woman. Not that he considered himself suave—far from it—but he'd never found himself utterly at a loss for words before, either. At least, not since about seventh grade. He was muttering something unintelligible when a discreet cough from Elena reminded him that he was still holding the princess's hand. He released it…laughed…and felt as awkward and abashed as the twelve-year-old Cade he painfully remembered.

"Are you enjoying the game, Mr. Gallagher? Exciting, is it not? Especially since Tamir is winning." Her eyes held a gleeful sparkle.

He wondered suddenly if the reason he felt so young was simply because *she* was, and the thought helped restore him to sanity. That, and a calming sip of his cheroot. "I am, very much," he drawled, gazing over her head to where the action was taking place now, at the far end of the field. "Especially the horses. That gray stallion of Rashid's—"

"Oh, but they are all Rashid's ponies. He raises them, you know, on one of the other islands. Siraj—it is just south of Tamir. Perhaps you would like—"

"Cade raises horses, too," Elena interrupted. "Arabians."

"Really? But that is wonderful!" In her eagerness and enthusiasm she seemed almost weightless, like a bird, he thought—a blackbird one sudden motion away from taking flight. "How I wish that I could see *your* horses, Mr. Gallagher."

"Maybe someday you will," Cade murmured, and felt a strange little shiver go through him—some sort of primitive warning. He coughed, glanced at Elena and gruffly added, "When you come to Texas to visit your brother."

And he watched the light go out of the girl's eyes as if someone had thrown a switch, shutting off all circuits. Her lashes came down and her smile faded. Her body grew still.

"Yes," she said softly. "Perhaps…" She turned away, one hand going to her forehead. "Oh—I see the play has been stopped. Someone has fallen off. I think now it is safe to get my hat. Please, excuse me—"

Maybe it was because she'd looked so sad—Cade had no other rational explanation for doing what he did. He shot out a hand and caught her by the arm. The feel of her flesh beneath the silk fabric of her blouse sent impulses tingling along the nerves in his fingers as he gruffly said, "Here—I'll get it."

With that, he strode past her down the slope, stepped over the low barrier and scooped what was left of the hat out of the trampled grass. Grimly ignoring the smattering of applause from nearby spectators, he whacked the hat once against his thigh, then retraced his steps to where Elena and the princess were waiting for him under the trees.

"There you go," he said as he handed the hat over to its owner. "For what it's worth. Looks in pretty bad shape."

"It is only a hat," Leila said, smiling but without a trace of the sparkle that had lit her eyes before. Cade was conscious of a vague disappointment. It was like watching the sun set without colors. "It is not important. But it was very kind of you to retrieve it for me. Thank you.

"Well—" She looked quickly, almost guiltily, around. "I must go now. Someone will be looking for me. Elena, I am so glad to have had a chance to see and talk to you. And Mr. Gallagher, it was very nice meeting you. Thank you…goodbye…." Cade watched her disappear into the crowd like a doe in dense forest.

"Cade," Elena said in a warning tone, "I mean it—she's absolutely off-limits."

He pulled his gaze back to her, covering the effort it cost him with a snort and a wry smile. "Hey, she's too young for me. Besides," he added after a moment's contemplation of the end of his cigar, "she's not really my type."

Elena gave a derisive hoot—not very ladylike, but pure Texas. "Oh, yeah, I know all about your 'type.' Whatever happened to that Dallas Cowboys cheerleader, by the way?"

"She was a nice girl," Cade said with a small, reminiscent smile. "We…wanted different things, is all. She was thinkin' in terms of wedding bells and baby carriages, while I—"

"I *know* what you were thinkin' about," Elena said dryly. "The same thing you're thinking right now, which is absolutely out of the question. You promise me, Cade—"

Laughing, he held up both hands in a gesture of surrender. "Hey—you've got nothing to worry about. Like I said earlier, and like I told your friend Kitty last night—where

is she, by the way? Haven't seen her around this morning."
He looked around furtively, half expecting to see a fuzzy
brown head bobbing through the crowd, to hear that gawd-
awful, *"Yoo-hoo!"*

Elena grinned. "I think maybe she overdid a bit on the
rich food last night. She was planning on taking it easy this
morning, getting all rested up for this evening's festivities."

Cade made a sound somewhere between a groan and a
sigh.

Leila ran across the courtyard, the patterned tiles smooth
and warm under her bare feet. She had taken her boots off
in her chambers, but had found it impossible to stay there.
She felt too stirred, too restless to stay indoors—which admittedly was not an uncommon way for Leila to feel.

But this was different. Today the pounding of her heartbeat was only an echo of the thunder of horses' hoofbeats.
The breeze from the sea tugged gently at her hair, but she
longed to feel it whipping in the wind as she raced wild
and abandoned across fields without boundaries. Today,
every flower and tree and shrub in the gardens, every fountain and vine-draped arch and pillar, seemed like the bars
of a prison to her. A very beautiful prison, it was true, but
a prison nonetheless.

And something else. Today as she ran, she thought of
the way a garden feels when it rains—a contradiction of
freshness and excitement and anticipation, but also a bit of
gloom and sadness, a yearning for the sun's familiar
warmth. And all of her insides seemed to quiver like the
leaves of flowers and shrubs and trees when the raindrops
hit them.

The palace gardens were vast, and Leila knew every inch
of them, including hidden nooks and bowers where she
occasionally sought refuge from turbulent thoughts like
these. Today, though, it wasn't refuge she wanted. After

this morning, she very much needed to confront those disturbing thoughts, face them head-on, and then, if at all possible, decide what she was going to do about them. For this she had chosen a spot she was almost certain would be empty at that hour—the private terrace adjacent to the family's quarters where she sometimes took breakfast with her sisters, or her mother and her mother's faithful servant, Salma, who had once been Leila's nanny. The terrace faced northeast and overlooked the sea. Now, approaching midday, it would be shaded, with a nice breeze from the sea to cool her burning cheeks while the gentle trickle of the fountain and the heady scent of roses would, she desperately hoped, help to calm her fevered thoughts.

Never had Leila so desired to be alone with those thoughts! Oh, such humiliating, embarrassing thoughts. And so she was dismayed to find, as she plunged headlong through the arched portal that was the garden entrance to her retreat, that someone was there before her.

Worse, a stranger. A woman with drab brown hair—rather frizzy—was sitting in a chair beside the fountain, reading a paperback book.

Leila's headlong plunge had already taken her several steps onto the terrace before she realized it was already occupied. She lurched to a halt, arms flung wide, body tilted forward, and uttered a soft, disappointed, "Oh!"

The woman quickly set aside her book, a romantic novel, by the looks of the cover. She smiled, and Leila recognized her then—the woman who had been talking with Cade Gallagher during the banquet the night before. She felt a jolt of excitement, then an alarming twinge of jealousy. But it was fleeting. The woman wasn't very pretty, and besides, Leila told herself with a mental sniff, she's old. At least forty.

"I'm sorry," the woman said, and Leila noticed that she

had an accent just like Elena's. "Gee, I hope I'm not where I shouldn't be. I was looking for someplace cool and quiet, and...well, the roses just smelled so good...."

"No, no, it is quite all right." Leila had been raised to be polite to her elders. She advanced, hand outstretched. "I am Leila Kamal. Please—do not get up."

In spite of Leila's assurance, the woman half rose and at the same time managed to execute an awkward sort of curtsey. "I'm Kitty." And oddly, it was she who sounded out of breath, though it was Leila who had been running. "Elena's friend."

"Yes, I saw you last night at the banquet. You were talking with Mr. Gallagher." Leila spoke slowly, absently. An idea was beginning to take shape in her head.

"That's right!" Kitty looked pleased, perhaps flattered that Leila had noticed her. Then her pleasure changed to concern. "My, but you look warm. Would you like something cold to drink? There's a lot more here than I'll ever need." She indicated a water-beaded pitcher and several glasses sitting on a tray on the glass-topped table an arm's length away. "It's some kind of fruit juice, I think—got a little bit of a bite to it. It's not quite up to sweet tea, but it's pretty good."

"Thank you," Leila said with an absent sigh, then gave the plain woman a friendly smile. "I have been watching the polo match. You do not care for polo?"

She sat down in a chair beside the table and only then realized she was still holding what was left of her hat. She glanced at it, frowning.

"Well, you know, it's not really my sport. I'm more a Dallas Cowboys fan," Kitty began apologetically, then gave a gasp of dismay as she, too, noticed Leila's hat. "Oh, my goodness, what in the world happened? That's a real shame."

Leila shrugged and placed it on the tabletop. ''The wind blew it onto the field and the horses trampled it,'' she explained matter-of-factly as she poured herself a glass of the blend of pomegranate and grape juices. She sipped, and found it nicely chilled and just slightly fermented. She lowered her lashes, veiling her eyes, and casually added, ''Elena's friend—Mr. Gallagher—got it back for me.''

Kitty chuckled and rolled her eyes. ''Oh yeah, that sounds like something Cade would do.''

Leila flashed her a look of what she hoped was only polite interest. ''You know this Mr. Gallagher—Cade—very well?''

''Not *real* well, no—mostly through Elena.'' But then Kitty gave a little smile and sort of waggled her shoulders as she settled back in her chair, reminding Leila so much of her favorite source of gossip, Nargis, that she almost laughed out loud. ''He is a good-lookin' man, though, isn't he?''

''He is handsome,'' Leila said in a considering tone, then made a brushing-aside gesture with her hand as she picked up her glass. ''But surely such a handsome man must be married.''

Kitty shook her head, looking gleeful. ''Uh-uh—he's not.''

Leila glanced at her in surprise. ''Really? Then…surely, someone special—a girlfriend?''

''Not that I know of.'' The expression on Kitty's face reminded Leila now of the palace cats—she all but purred. ''Lots of girls, I imagine, but, nope—no one in particular. Elena would have told me if there was.''

''But that seems very strange,'' Leila said, frowning. ''What do you suppose is the reason? There must be some reason why a man of his age—he is what, thirty?''

''Thirty-six,'' Kitty promptly supplied. ''I know, because Elena told me he's six years older than she is.''

Thirty-six…ten years older than I am. But that is good—

Startled by the thought, Leila guiltily slammed it into a drawer, hidden far away in the back of her mind.

''Perhaps,'' said Leila with a sniff, ''he is not a good man.''

''Cade?'' The other woman looked taken aback, even mildly affronted. Then she chuckled. ''I'm not sure how you mean that, honey, but if you mean 'good' like in decent, honorable—that sort of thing—then I can pretty much tell you there's probably not a better man alive. Cade Gallagher is so honest it's scary. Oh, I hear he's tough when it comes to business, but judging from the way I've seen him with Elena—'' She interrupted herself to lean forward like a conspirator. ''His parents are dead, you know, just like Elena's—they're all the family each other's got.'' She sat back with a little wave of her hand. ''Anyway, as far as I can see, the man's got a heart like a marshmallow.''

''Marsh…mallow?'' The word was unfamiliar to Leila.

Kitty laughed. ''It's a kind of candy—real soft and gooey, you know? And sweet.''

Sweet? Leila chewed doubtfully on her lower lip. ''Sweet'' was not a word she had ever heard applied to a man before. Certainly not to one as rugged-looking as Cade Gallagher.

''Well,'' said Kitty with an air of finality, ''I know Elena thinks the world of him—that's enough for me.''

And, Leila realized suddenly, *I think Elena thinks the world of you, too.* She must, to have invited the woman to her wedding. This woman—Kitty—seemed like a kind person. A bit of a gossip, maybe, but Leila saw no real harm

in that. The important thing was, she was Elena's friend.
Elena trusted her.

Leila took a deep breath and made a decision. She sat
forward, hands earnestly clasped. "Please—tell me about
America. What is it like, between men and women? How
is it when they are..." she waved a hand in a circular
motion, searching for the word. "I am sorry, I do not
know—"

"You mean, dating?"

"Yes." Leila let out a breath. "Dating." She had learned
a little about the customs of Europe and England from
classmates in boarding school, but what she knew of America came mostly from movies and very old television pro-
grams, and she was, she feared, badly out-of-date. "You
must understand, here we have no such thing. What is it
like? How, exactly, is it done?" And without her realizing
it, her heart had begun to beat faster.

"What's it like?" Kitty gave a dry little laugh. "Not that
I've had much personal experience lately, you understand,
but from what I can recall, it can be anything from fun and
exciting to downright awful. As for how it's done—honey,
there've been about a bazillion books and magazine articles
devoted to *that* subject."

"Oh, but please," Leila cried, "you must tell me. For
example, must the man always be the one to...to..." Frustrated, she paused to frown and gnaw at her lip. She was
not accustomed to feeling so awkward, and she did not like
it one bit.

"Make the first move?" Kitty said kindly.

"The first move—yes!" Leila was almost laughing with
relief. "Must the woman always wait for the man to do it?
Or may the woman be the first one to speak?"

Kitty gave a merry laugh. "I guess that depends."

"On what?" She leaned forward, intent with purpose now.

"Oh, well…on your generation, for one thing. Now, *my* generation, they're pretty much stuck on the 'leave it to the guy to make the first move' tradition. Men my age seem to feel threatened by pushy women, for some reason." She sighed.

Leila wasn't exactly sure what was meant by "pushy women," but she forged on, eager to get to what she really wanted to know. Breathlessly, she asked, "And…Mr. Gallagher?" It was hard to imagine such a man feeling threatened by anything, much less a mere woman.

"Cade?" Kitty had that look again, the one that made Leila think of the woman's animal namesake. She leaned forward as if she were about to reveal a great secret. "Just between you and me, I think that man focuses entirely too much on business. I think maybe if a woman wanted to get his attention, she might *have* to be a little bit pushy."

"Pushy?" Leila frowned. That word again. The pictures it brought to her mind didn't seem appealing to her.

"You know," Kitty said, lifting one shoulder just slightly. "Give him a little…nudge in the right direction. A *push.*"

"Ah," said Leila, feeling as if a light had come on in her head, "you mean, not a real push, but a suggestion. And this is…permissible in America?"

"I don't know about all of America, but in Texas it is."

"Thank you," Leila breathed. "That is what I wanted to know." She placed her glass on the table and rose to leave, preoccupied and just in time remembering her manners. Turning back to Kitty, she said automatically, "It was very nice talking with you. I hope I may see you tonight at the reception?"

"Oh," said Kitty, looking solemn, "you can count on it."

As Leila was turning away, she saw the other woman pick up the paperback book she had laid aside when Leila interrupted her. She thought it must not be a romance novel after all, but perhaps a very funny one instead. Because, as she found her place and began to read, Kitty was laughing to herself, and the smile on her face stretched from one ear to the other.

Chapter 3

The hum and clatter of sound from the reception hall receded as Cade strolled deeper into the gardens, and was gradually usurped by the quieter conversation of the fountains. The music followed him, though, carried on the soft evening air like a sweet-scented breeze. At least it was western music tonight. Not *country* western, that would have been too much to hope for—but the classical stuff, something vaguely familiar to him. Mozart, he guessed, or maybe it was Beethoven. He never could keep those guys straight.

He had the gardens to himself tonight. Everyone seemed to be inside the grand ballroom, nibbling fruits and exotic Middle Eastern tidbits and awaiting the arrival of the king of Montebello and his entourage, including the recently restored crown prince, Lucas, who not so long ago had been all but given up for dead. Elena had filled him in on that story, and thinking of it now, Cade could only shake his head. The whole thing sounded like something out of a spy novel to him.

He'd pay his own respects to the honored guests before the night was over, of course; he owed that much to Elena. But for now, he was seizing the opportunity for a much needed breath of fresh air. And some space—oh, yeah, that more than anything. There was something about this damned island, beautiful as it was, that gave him claustrophobia. He'd be glad when all the hoopla was over and he could get down to doing business with the old sheik. Hassan and Elena were postponing their honeymoon long enough to give him the intro he needed to smooth the way, but he was confident the negotiations would be easy sailing for all concerned.

As he stepped though the rose-covered arch that led to the promenade where yesterday he'd stood and listened to that strangely sinister conversation, he paused once again to light one of his cherished cheroots. This time, though, he didn't linger there but continued on down the tiled walkway, which was arrow-straight and flanked on both sides by rows of intricately carved columns and lit at regular intervals by torches. At the far end, through another arched portal, he could see where it opened out finally onto a cliff-top terrace overlooking the sea. Through the portal the sky still glowed with the last wash of sunset, and it seemed to Cade like the gateway to paradise.

He walked toward his destination slowly and with a pleasant sense of anticipation, savoring the taste of the cigar, enjoying the textures of the night and his aloneness in it, feeling the breeze curl around his shoulders like a cloak…stir through his hair like caressing fingers…

And something shivered down his spine. He'd felt something…something that wasn't really a touch. Heard something that wasn't *quite* a sound. And knew with absolute certainty that he wasn't alone in the promenade any longer.

He halted…turned. Froze. His heart dropped into his shoes.

Halfway between the archway and where he stood the figure of a woman paused...hovered...then once again moved slowly toward him. Tonight, she wore an evening gown of a delicate yellow-gold, something shimmery that seemed to glow in the light of the torches like a small pale sun. It had a high neck and long, flowing sleeves, a bodice that clung and skirts that swirled around her legs so that she seemed to float, disconnected from the ground, like a wraith or a figment of his imagination. Except that he knew she was only too real.

Strands of long black hair, teased by the same wind that made a plaything of her skirts, coiled around her shoulders and lay like a shadow across one breast. Something glittered in the twist of braids on top of her head...caught an elusive source of light and winked. He couldn't see her features in that purple dusk, but he'd known at once who she was. In a strange way, her body, the way she moved, seemed already familiar to him.

Leila almost lost her courage. The tall figure silhouetted against the evening sky and framed by gold-washed pillars seemed so forbidding, utterly unapproachable, like a sentinel guarding the gates of Heaven. But, oh, she thought as her heartbeat pattered deliriously in her throat, how commanding he looked in his evening clothes—how elegant, even regal.

And yet—the notion came to her suddenly, the way such insights often did to Leila—as elegant and at ease as he appeared, there was something about the formal dress that didn't suit him. As if his appearance of ease went no deeper than his skin...as if it were his soul that was being suffocated.

Almost...almost, she turned to run away, to leave him there with his solitude. For uncounted seconds she hovered, balanced like a bird on a swaying branch, balanced, she was even in that moment aware, between two futures for

herself…two very different paths. One path was familiar to
her, its destination dismally certain. The other was a complete unknown, veiled in darkness, and she had no way of
knowing whether it might lead her to the freedom she so
desired…or disaster.

She hovered, her heart beating faster, harder, and then,
somehow, she was moving forward again, moving toward
that imposing figure in evening clothes. She felt a strange
sense of inevitability as the figure loomed larger, as she
drew closer and closer to the American named Cade Gallagher. And it occurred to her to wonder if she had ever
had a choice at all.

They were only a few feet apart now, close enough that
one or the other *must* speak. But Cade only looked at her
and went on quietly smoking…something too brown to be
a cigarette, too slender to be a cigar. Reminding herself
what Kitty had said, that in America—in Texas—it was
permissible for a woman to speak first, Leila summoned all
her courage and sent up a small prayer.

"Good evening—it is Mr. Gallagher, is it not?" She kept
her voice low to hide the tremors in it. "May I call you
Cade?"

"I wish you would." *His* voice was a husky drawl that
shivered her skin as if someone had lightly touched her all
over. He gave a bow, and she wondered if he might be
mocking her. "Good evening, Princess—or is it, 'Your
Highness'?"

"If I am to call you Cade, then you must call me Leila."
She was glad for the shadowy torchlight that hid the blush
she could feel burning in her cheeks. On the other hand,
she hoped he *would* see the dimples there, and as she joined
him, she smiled and tilted her face toward him and the light.

He waited for her to reach him, then turned so that they
walked on together toward the terrace, side by side. Leila's
heart was beating so hard she thought he must hear it.

After a moment he glanced down at her and said, "Shouldn't you be at the royal reception?"

She hesitated, biting her lip, wondering just how "cheeky"—it was a word she'd acquired during her school days in England—she dared be. Hoping he wouldn't think her insolent, she looked up at him through lowered lashes and colored her voice with her smile. "Yes, I should. And...should not *you* be, as well?"

He acknowledged that with a soft and rueful laugh. Emboldened, she added, "You are certainly dressed for it." And after a moment, bolder still, "You do look quite nice in evening dress, but..." She counted footsteps. One...two...

She felt his gaze, and, looking up to meet it, caught a small, involuntary breath. *To get his attention, a woman would have to be a little bit...* She smiled and said on the soft rush of an exhalation, "But, I liked what you were wearing yesterday—especially your hat. You looked quite like a cowboy."

She heard the faint, surprised sound of *his* breath as he looked down at her. "Yesterday?"

"I saw you in the garden," she explained with an innocent lift of her shoulders. "I was with my sisters, on the balcony outside our chambers. I could not help but notice you. You stood out, among all the others. I thought you looked...very American—like someone I have seen in the Western movies."

He gave a little grunt of laughter, but she didn't think it was a pleased sound.

She conjured up a new smile. "But tonight...tonight you look very different—elegant, very sophisticated. And, of course, *very* handsome."

He laughed uncomfortably. "Princess—"

She laughed too, in a light and teasing way, and before he could say more, hurried on. "But, you have run away

from the reception and all the ladies who would admire
you, to walk alone in the gardens…'' She left it hanging,
the question unspoken.

Cade brought the slender cigar briefly to his lips before
answering. ''I needed some air,'' he said abruptly, and there
was a certain harshness in his voice now. They had stepped
onto the terrace that overlooked the sea. He made a gesture
toward the emptiness beyond the marble balustrade. ''Some
space.''

A breeze from the sea lifted tendrils of hair on Leila's
neck. She felt a shivering deep inside her chest. *Space…*

''Yes,'' she whispered, forgetting to flirt, for all at once
her throat ached and she no longer felt like smiling.

They stood together at the balustrade in silence, shoulders not quite touching, and she felt the ache inside her
grow. I shouldn't have done this, she thought in sudden
and unfamiliar panic. *This is terrifying. Perhaps I am not
cut out to be a pushy woman.*

Far below, waves collided gently with the rocky cliff,
sending up joyful little bursts of spray. The rhythmic
shushing sound they made was familiar and soothing to
her soul. She listened to it for several more seconds, then
lifted her eyes to the almost invisible horizon.

''I understand, I think,'' she said quietly, leaning a little
on her hands. ''I come here often when I am feeling…''
At a loss for the word, she gave a little grimace and shook
her head.

''Cooped up?'' Cade softly suggested, watching the horizon as she did. She looked him a question, not being
familiar with the expression. He glanced down at her.
''Walled up…fenced in—''

''Oh, yes!'' She turned toward him, her breath escaping
in a grateful rush. ''That is it exactly—walled up and
fenced in. But what is this…coop? I do not know—''

He shrugged and turned his gaze back to the sea. ''It's

an expression they use where I come from. A coop is a kind of pen. They keep chickens in it.''

''In Texas?''

''Yeah…'' He said it on a sigh. ''In Texas.'' After a curiously vibrant pause, one that fairly sang with unspoken communion, he jerked himself upright and away from the silence with a loud and raggedy attempt to clear his throat. ''Other places, too. Pretty much any place they have chickens.''

He couldn't believe he was having this conversation with a *princess*. One that, even in a designer gown, really did look like something out of *The Arabian Nights*. But talking about chicken coops, dopey as it was, seemed infinitely safer than that terrifying sense of…what in the world *had* it been? Affinity, concord…none of those words seemed adequate to describe what had just happened between them, between himself and this woman from an alien culture…a kind of *oneness* he'd never experienced before with another human being. As if, he thought with a shudder, she'd somehow found, and for that one brief moment touched, his innermost self. His soul.

''Texas.'' Her sigh was an echo of his. ''It must be very wonderful.'' Hearing a new lightness in her voice, he looked at her warily. Torchlight played mischievously with her dimples.

She's flirting with you, Cade. The thought made him almost giddy with relief. This was familiar territory, something he was pretty sure he knew how to handle.

He turned toward her and leaned an elbow on the balustrade, relaxed now, and casually smoking. ''Some parts of it are,'' he drawled, ''and some aren't.'' He was thinking about the West Texas oil country, and parts of the Panhandle that were so flat you had the feeling if you got to running too fast you'd run right off the edge of the world.

Even such a thing as wide open spaces could be carried too far.

Maybe because his thoughts were back home in Texas and he was feeling a little bit overconfident, it was a few seconds before he noticed the intensity of Leila's silence. By the time he did, and snapped his attention back into focus on her, it was too late. He thought it must feel something like this, the first moment after stepping into quicksand—a disquieting, sinking sensation, but not yet sure whether he ought to panic or not.

When had she come to be standing so close to him? The sea breeze carried her scent to him, sweet and faintly spicy. The word "exotic" came to his mind. But then, everything about her was exotic. Was that why she seemed so exciting to him? The fact that she was different from every other woman he'd ever met?

Don't even think about it. She's absolutely off-limits.

Or was it simply that she was forbidden fruit? Off-limits. Inaccessible. Except that, at this moment, at least, he knew she was entirely accessible…to him.

To think like that was insane. And insanely dangerous. He was dealing with a tiger out of her cage, nothing less.

Except that she didn't look much like a tiger at the moment, or anything even remotely dangerous. She looked soft and warm and sweet, more like ripe summer than forbidden fruit. Torchlight touched off golden sparks in the ornaments in her hair and in her eyes. Gazing into them, he felt again the peculiar sensation of not-quite-dizziness, as if his world, his center of gravity, had tilted on its axis. Clutching for something commonplace and familiar, he took a quick, desperate puff of his all-but-forgotten cheroot.

Her whisper came like an extension of the breeze…or his own sigh. For one brief moment he wasn't certain whether it was her voice he was hearing, or merely the echoes of his own thoughts.

"Do you want to kiss me, Mr. Gallagher?"

Cade almost swallowed his cigar. *Do you want to kiss me?*

What on God's green earth could he say to that? Jolted cruelly back to reality, his mind whirred like a computer through countless impossibilities, distilled finally down to two: Lie and tell her he didn't, which would be unconscionably cruel; or tell her the truth, which would most likely land him in more trouble than he cared to think about.

It was probably gut instinct that made him do neither of those things, but instead try to laugh his way out of it. To make light of it. A joke.

Tossing his cigar over the balustrade with an exaggerated, almost violent motion, he snaked one arm around her waist. The other he hooked across her back at shoulder-blade height, and laying her against it, arched his body over hers in broad parody of some old silent movie clip he'd seen recently, he couldn't recall exactly where—The Academy Awards, maybe?—about an Arab sheik in flowing robes and headdress seducing a wild-eyed maiden in a tassel-draped tent.

"Kees you?" he intoned in a ludicrous and excruciatingly awful mishmash of several different accents—he had no idea where he'd gotten that from. "Oh-ho-ho, mademoiselle…"

Startled eyes gazed up at him. He felt a sensation of falling, as if the ground beneath his feet had dropped away.

What now? He had no idea what he was supposed to say next. That was the trouble with those silent movies, he thought. They were *silent.* Short on dialogue, long on action. And he was pretty sure he did know what action was supposed to come next.

Don't do that. You can't. You'd be crazy to do that.

Then came the smallest of sounds…the soft rush of an exhalation. Her breath was sweet and faintly wine-scented, so close he felt the stirring of it on his own skin. So near to his...her lips parted. Slowly, slowly her eyes closed.

Lord help me, he thought, and lowered his mouth to hers.

He had an impression of warmth and softness, of sweetness and innocence. Of purity. It occurred to him to wonder whether his might even be the first lips to ever have touched hers, and the thought both excited and shamed him. Is that what it's all about? he wondered. Is *that* why I want her so much? Nothing to do with exotic beauty and forbidden fruit, only the thirst of the conqueror for undefiled lands to claim as his own.

His thirst was in danger of blossoming into fullblown lust.

He felt the flutterings of her instinctive resistance. If only he hadn't! If only she'd responded openly, brazenly to his kiss, he might have been able to keep it as he'd intended it to be—blatantly mocking—and end it there. But that tiny faltering, that faint gasp of virginal hesitation... It stirred some primitive masculine response deep within him, so that her hesitation affected him not as a warning, but as a challenge. And an embrace meant only to lighten the mood and diffuse dangerous emotions became instead a seduction.

Instead of releasing her, his fingers stroked sensuous circles over the tightened muscles in her back and waist. Instead of pulling away from her, he gently absorbed her lips' quiverings and delicately soothed them with the warmth of his own mouth. And felt her relax...melt into his embrace...as he'd somehow known she would.

He shifted her slightly, to a more comfortable, more natural position, and felt her body align with his as if it had been custom-made for that purpose, a soft and supple warmth. He lightly sipped her wine-flavored mouth, and only then discovered—too late—that he was famished for the unique taste of her, that he craved her with every fiber of his being.

Tiny lightbursts of warning exploded inside his brain. Reserves of strength summoned from God knew where made it possible for him to tear his mouth from hers—for a moment, no more. He released a sound like the moaning of wind in old trees and buried his face in the graceful curve of her neck. Then…gently, carefully at first, he brushed his lips against the skin there, velvety soft and sweetly scented as rose petals.

The sound she made was breathy and frightened, but he felt the uniquely feminine, seeking arch of her body, and the hot rush of blood through his in automatic masculine response. With a growl of triumph, unthinking he brought his mouth back to hers. Still gently but inexorably now as water finding its own course, his mouth began to follow the shapes and contours of hers…his tongue found its way to the soft inside. She whimpered.

How can this be? Leila thought. *I cannot breathe, my heart is racing so. I feel as if I am drowning…dying…and yet I cannot stop myself—don't want to stop myself—or him. If I am dying, then this must be heaven, because I don't want it to stop…ever.*

Her skin felt hot and prickly all over, from the roots of her hair to the soles of her feet. And yet…she shivered. Her head—her heart—felt light as air, lighter than butterflies and wind-carried chaff, yet her body felt weighted, too heavy to move.

His body was a hard, unyielding weight against her breasts, breasts that had become so sensitive she could feel every ridge and fold of his jacket, the warp and woof of the cloth. Even the rub of her own clothing seemed an intolerable abrasion.

Panting, she tore her mouth free of his and arched her throat, offering that to him instead. And how had she known to do such a thing? Even as she wondered, she felt the press of his lips against the pounding of her pulse, and mounting pressure…and terrifying weakness.

And then the pressure was gone. From a great distance came a raw, anguished sound, and the weight lifted from her breasts. Her throat and lips felt cold, and throbbed with her racing pulse. Swamped with dizziness, afraid she might fall, she clung with desperate fingers to the arms that held her and fearfully opened her eyes. Eyes stared down into hers…eyes that burned with a golden gleam…eyes that burned her soul like fire.

"What—" She meant to whisper, but it was a tiny squeak, like the mew of a kitten.

His voice was so ragged she could hardly understand him. "Princess—I'm sorry. I can't do this. I can't…"

When she felt his arms shift, depriving her of their support, she gasped and caught at his sleeves. His fingers bit into the flesh of her arms as, grim-faced, he held her away from him, then with great care stood her upright and steadied her like a precariously balanced statue. Once more his eyes lashed across her, and she flinched as though from the sting of a whip.

"*Dammit,*" he fiercely muttered, and then, as he turned, added with soft regret, "Another time, maybe…another place."

And he was gone.

Left alone, Leila stood where she was, trembling, hardly daring to move, until the scrape of footsteps on stone had been swallowed up in the *shushing* of waves and the whisper of wind.

Foolish…foolish… The whispers mocked her. *Serves you right. This is what happens to pushy women.*

But…what *had* happened, exactly?

Hugging herself, Leila whirled to face the glittering indigo vastness of sky and sea. She was shivering still, no longer with shock, but a strange, fierce excitement. Cade

Gallagher had kissed her! Kissed her in a way she was quite certain no man should ever kiss a woman who was not his wife.

And that she had allowed it…? Fear and guilt added layers to her excitement, but did not banish it. That she had allowed such a thing to happen was unpardonable.

She knew she should feel frightened, terrified, ashamed. So why was she smiling? Smiling, lightheaded, and absolutely giddy with excitement?

Another time…another place.

That was what he had said. She remembered his exact words. Understanding came; certainty settled around her, comforting as a cashmere shawl.

Back in his own room at last, Cade slipped out of his tux jacket with a grateful sigh. One helluva day, he thought as he tossed the jacket onto the cushions of the surprisingly trendy brown-and-white striped sofa. And thank God it was over. Tomorrow he'd be back in familiar territory, home country. The world of business was where he belonged, where he felt comfortable. It was what he was good at— doing deals, making plans, working out compromises. All this formal socializing, rubbing elbows with royalty—that wasn't his style. Oh, he knew a certain amount of that stuff was unavoidable from time to time, but he was always glad when it was time to roll up his sleeves and get down to the real work, down and dirty sometimes, rough as a bare-knuckle brawl, but that was what he liked about it—the excitement of the game. That, and the satisfaction that came with winning.

Anyway, for sheer stress, all that was a piece of cake compared to what he'd just been through. He'd rather spend three days in cutthroat negotiations than three hours at a formal reception—and in this case, *formal* was putting it mildly. Not that it hadn't been impressive as hell, the palace ballroom lit up like Christmas, the food delicious, the music tolerable, if you went in for that sort of thing. And he'd never seen so many purple sashes and gold medals in one place in all his life, or so many beautiful people—especially the women. Everywhere he looked was a feast for a man's eyes. But there was something about it he couldn't quite put his finger on. Undercurrents.

Undercurrents. Yeah, he thought, that about described it, all right. Underneath all the bright lights and highbrow music, the dazzling smiles and graceful bows, elegant tuxes and designer gowns in rainbow colors swirled together like ribbons in a washing machine…under all that, like a subterranean river, ran a ribbon of tension, a hum of intrigue he could feel in his bones. He wondered whether it was something going on between these Tamiri people and their nearest neighbors, the Montebellans, or if it was just standard operating procedure for royal courts. Not unlike what goes on every day in Washington, D.C., he thought, or for that matter, any state capitol back home.

This thing with Leila Kamal, though…that was another story. *That* particular intrigue was entirely personal, and the tension a steel rod running straight down the back of his neck. It had made for one helluva nerve-wracking evening, trying to avoid eye contact—or any sort of contact whatsoever—with the woman, while being at the same time aware of her with every nerve in his body. Nerve-wracking…intense…but now, thank God, it was over. Finally, he could relax.

With another gusty exhalation, he peeled off his necktie and headed for the bathroom. There, while his fingers dealt with the studs on his shirt, his eyes gazed dispassionately back at him from the ornately framed mirror above the sink.

You were damned lucky, Gallagher.

Oh yeah. He knew just how lucky he'd been. He'd played with fire and somehow managed not to get burned.

That narrow brush with disaster had left him shaken, but he'd managed to put it behind him. All he needed now was a good night's sleep, and tomorrow some mutually advantageous wheeling and dealing with the old sheik, and he'd be himself again.

Stripping off his shirt, he briefly considered another shower. But he was tired, just wanted to hit the sack, so he turned on the tap above the sink instead. He was hunched over the bowl, cupped hands filling up with water to splash over his face, when he heard a light tapping on his chamber door.

What now? One of the servants, probably, they were always bringing him something—towels or fruit or herbal tea—though it seemed pretty late for that. Frowning, he turned off the faucet, grabbed a towel and went to open the door.

When he saw who was standing there, he wondered why he didn't have a heart attack on the spot. At the very least, he was pretty sure he knew now what it might feel like to be speared in the belly with an icicle.

Chapter 4

"**P**rincess—" It gusted from him before he could think. "What're you—why—" And while he was sputtering like that she slipped past him and into his room.

He had a fleeting impression of a light, spicy scent, hair that flowed down her back like an ebony river, a gown made of something pale and floaty—she'd glow in the dark like a candle!

He'd never felt more exposed, or more cognizant of the danger he was in. If anyone happened to walk by...if she so much as raised her voice, cried out, Cade's goose was as good as cooked. Even in this part of the world he doubted they still executed people for such transgressions, but at the very least, any hopes he had of doing a deal with the Tamari people would be out the window, and he might even be out—literally—himself. As in, given the bum's rush. Bounced unceremoniously out the door on his butt. Right now, this minute, in the middle of the night.

Plus, Elena was never going to forgive him—never.

With icy dread crawling down his spine, he gave his face

an absentminded mop with the towel, glanced quickly up and down the corridor, then silently pulled the door closed. He felt as if the door of a trap had just slammed shut behind him.

Leila moved as if through a wall of suffocating heat—holding her breath, feeling her cheeks burn and sweat bloom on her forehead. Knowing instinctively the source of the heat, she kept her face turned away from him—as if that would help!

She reached with her hand to touch the back of the sofa and leaned against it a little, testing it for support, then brushed her fingers over the fabric to hide the fact that she'd done so. She heard the door close behind her and silence fill the room. In it the thump and swish of her pulse sounded loud as the storm surf striking the rocks below the cliffs.

"Princess—" His voice was harsh.

And though she didn't want to, she flinched. Still, as she turned she knew her smile would appear bright and determined. "I thought you were going to call me Leila."

Breath gusted from him, as if he'd been holding it in too long. "For God's sake, what are you doing here?"

But she could not answer. Suddenly she had no moisture in her mouth; she could not seem to move her tongue. Nor her eyes, either, for somehow they had become stuck to the naked masculine chest in front of her, and not even for her life could she tear them away. She did not understand—she had seen men's chests and torsos before...hadn't she? In pictures, at the very least. But if she had, it did not *seem* so. To her this felt like the first time she had ever laid eyes on such a sight...*ever.*

"Look...Leila—" He took a step toward her, face darkened, both hands upraised and fingers tensed, as though he wanted to grasp her with them.

Her breath caught and her heart gave a frightened leap.

Even she could see that it was not a welcoming gesture.
But not a violent one, either. She thought he seemed more
distraught than angry, and her fear was not for her physical
safety. He would not harm her, she was certain of that.

Just as she was certain now that she had made a terrible
mistake in judgment. Somehow, because of the vast difference in their cultures, probably, she had misunderstood
him. She knew that he had not meant what she had thought
he meant. Not at all.

I shouldn't have come.

All of that passed through Leila's mind in the time it took
her to utter a single dismayed gasp. In the next moment,
memory—sensual, visceral, overwhelming—slammed her
with the force of a physical blow. *Hard lips, smooth and
gentle lips…liquid warmth, breath smelling of tobacco, trembling pressure and pounding pulse…*

Her body felt cold, and her legs as if they would not
support her weight. She heard a rushing sound in her ears.
But I had to come…I had to. What else could I do?

She took one step forward…and into a void.

Swearing vehemently, Cade caught her as her knees
buckled. Then, since there didn't seem to be anything else
to do, he scooped her up in his arms. *This is insane. Ludicrous.*

While casting frantically about for a place to deposit his
unconscious burden, he caught a glimpse of himself and
her in the gilt-framed mirror above the tile and marble fireplace—heaving breasts in a filmy gown against the backdrop of his own naked, sweaty chest…her pale throat a taut
and graceful curve…raven hair cascading over his arms
like a waterfall… Damn, he thought with a snort that was
part irony, part disgust and most of all dismay. *I look like
the cover of one of those romance novels women are always
reading.*

He'd about decided to lay his swooning princess on the

sofa when he felt her arms come to twine around his neck. He barely had time to register that fact before her hair began to stir against his skin, an incredible, unimaginable softness.

He shivered involuntarily and felt his nipples harden. As if in response to that, she turned her face toward him and touched him just there in a series of tender and tiny kisses, rather like a kitten, he dimly thought, making tracks across his chest. His heart, already beating hard, gave a lurch.

"Princess..." His voice was faint and airless. "What the hell do you think you're doing?" Her lips were working their way across his collarbone and upward along the side of his neck. His jaw muscles felt so rigid he half expected to hear them creak when he added almost desperately, "Hey—cut that out."

Poised to deposit her on the sofa, he halted, muscles quivering, beset by a new dilemma. If he put her down now, she would almost certainly pull him down with her, which would be nothing short of disastrous. If he went on holding her, with that unnerving weakness creeping through his body, he was afraid he might drop her. To head off that possibility, he brought one knee up under her bottom, braced his foot on the cushions, and tried to shift her to a more secure position in his arms.

Big mistake. Hadn't this happened to him once before?

Yes, and once again as on the terrace, he felt her body mold itself to his as if it had been custom-made for that purpose...an all-over body glove, silky-soft, supple as finest kid. Tiny puffs of her breath brought his sweat-damp skin alive with goose bumps. Her spicy, exotic scent made his head swim. The weakness in his arms oozed into his legs, while in the center of his body his heart was banging like an energetic and enthusiastic bass drummer, sending joyful, giddy impulses and inviting—no, *compelling*—the rest of his body to follow along.

His body's predictable response was, *Oh, yeah. I'm there!* And his heart chimed in with, *Sure would like to…maybe it would be okay…don't you think I could?*

To which the rational part of his brain emphatically replied, *No way, Jose!*

''Princess—'' he began, but the rest was muffled. Leila's lovely and adventuresome mouth had reached its destination at last, and anything else he might have added was swallowed up in its sweet, intoxicating warmth.

For a moment…just a moment, it seemed to Cade he was fighting a losing battle. He thought how easy it would be…what a relief it would be…to just say the hell with it and give in. He thought it would be a little like drowning, to let himself go wherever this might take him, and damn the consequences.

He might have been able to do that—just maybe—if it hadn't been for the strident and insistent clamor of his reason. *Cade, you can't! She's a princess, most likely a virgin! You're a guest in her father's house! You have to stop this. Now!*

He wasn't sure how much longer he might have resisted the voices of sanity inside his head, or if in fact he'd ever have found the strength to end it. What saved him was anger. It came suddenly and unexpectedly, a bright and savage flare of resentment. *Foolish woman—what the hell does she think she's doing? Spoiled brat…she's going to ruin me—ruin everything!*

He let go of her abruptly, and felt her round and firm little bottom come to rest on his drawn-up knee.

''No,'' he said hoarsely as, jerky and shell-shocked, he peeled her arms from around his neck and thrust her from him. The places where she'd touched him felt like fresh abrasions.

Little by little, in ungraceful adjustments, he managed to stand her on her own two feet, and himself as well. And all the while she said not a word, while her eyes gazed up at him, black as ink, glistening dangerously. Her lips, pink and soft and still glazed from *his* mouth, parted slowly. If she speaks, he thought... Or worse, if she cries...

He grasped at his anger like a drowning man reaching for a life preserver and spoke in a ragged and guttural voice. "I said *no*. Do you understand me?" He pulled himself away from her, raked a distraught hand through his hair and fought to get his breathing calmed down. "This isn't going to happen, okay? Not tonight, not ever. I'm sorry—you have to go. Come on—*out*."

Since she didn't appear able or willing to move on her own, he took hold of her arm and gave it a tug. Just a small one. Then he watched in horror as her gown slipped down over one creamy-smooth shoulder. He let go of her arm in a hurry. "Ah, hell—Princess..." He closed his eyes and said it with a groan, almost pleading.

Then, through the pounding of his own pulses he heard a sharp, heartbroken sob...felt the rush and flurry of her passing...and at last, the click of an opening door.

Regret pierced his heart without warning, pierced it like an arrow and sent it plummeting into his belly. Belatedly he was aware of how young, how innocent Leila really was, and how grievously his rejection must have hurt her. He felt as if he'd kicked a puppy, or trampled a lovely blossom into the mud.

Hoping to explain, to soften it for her somehow, he lunged after her as she hurled herself through the doorway, out into the hallway—straight into the arms of her father, the sheik.

Sheik Ahmed Kamal had been feeling quite pleased with himself, and enormously satisfied with the way the weekend's events had unfolded. The wedding ceremony had been as solemn and dignified as should be—in spite of the tendency on the part of young people nowadays to want to adopt certain deplorable Western customs instead of adhering faithfully to traditional ways. The groom's banquet had been enjoyable for all in attendance, sumptuous and generous as was appropriate for a royal couple yet neither excessive nor ostentatious. The exhibition polo matches had been enjoyed by the many guests in attendance, *and* had resulted in gratifying wins for the Tamari team. Tonight's state dinner and reception honoring the king and the crown prince of Montebello had been a grand success.

Yes…and its aftermath even more so. Sheik Ahmed was, in fact, just returning from a most productive private meeting with his Montebellan counterpart, after having personally accompanied the royal contingent to their quarters in the guest palace on the other side of the gardens. He was in an expansive mood; his belly was full of good food and his mind full of plans for Tamir's future, plans that involved economic expansion in a number of areas near and dear to the sheik's heart.

Now, accompanied by his cadre of loyal bodyguards, he was making his way toward his private chambers at the end of a long, empty passageway adorned with mosaics and murals and softly lit by recessed lamps. He was looking forward to discussing the weekend's activities with Alima, his beloved wife, and afterward…a well-deserved rest.

And then—what was this? His youngest daughter, blinded by tears and with garments in disarray—garments, moreover, that would be appropriate only for a woman's chambers, or her husband's—his beloved child running headlong into his arms!

"Daughter, what is the meaning of this?" the sheik thundered, holding her at arm's length while he made hurried and necessary adjustments to her costume. He spared no thought at all for his contingent of bodyguards; being both well-trained and loyal, they had already turned their backs and averted their eyes from the deplorable spectacle.

Besides, if the truth were known, at that moment Sheik Ahmed's thoughts were in too much of a quandary to worry about what his bodyguards might or might not have witnessed. On the one hand, there was a father's understandable wrath at finding one of his offspring in a place and circumstances she had no business being at such an hour. On the other hand...the fact was, the sheik had a secret softness in his heart for his youngest child, and seeing her face so pale and frightened, her eyes overflowing with tears, gazing up into his...

"Leila, explain yourself!" he bellowed, but his anger was more show than substance.

Her lips opened, but she did not speak. He felt her arm tremble in his grasp. About to repeat the command a bit more gently, he hesitated. His focus wavered. A flash of movement on the periphery of his vision caught his gaze and jerked it away from his daughter's frozen face...and beyond. His eyes narrowed.

In the space of an instant his fatherly anger, mostly bombast, bluster and hot air, melted down and solidified into a rage as cold and deadly as any he'd ever known in his life.

Cade had never seen murder looking back at him from a man's eyes before, but he knew beyond any doubt he was seeing it now.

Strangely, faced with his worst nightmare, he felt all fear leave him. His body grew cold and his mind quiet. His eyes never left Sheik Ahmed's face as he waited for what would come.

Rotund and flushed with the effects of good food and good living, the Sheik was still an imposing presence. His snow-white hair and beard and magnificent hawk's beak of a nose gave him an almost biblical majesty, and even though he didn't speak loudly, his voice, welling from the depths of a barrel chest, sounded to Cade like the voice of doom.

"Young man, there was a time, not so long ago, when I could have had you executed on the spot. *Explain yourself.*"

A strangled cry from Leila tugged at Cade's attention, but it was only a flicker, and only for an instant. All of his attention was focused on her father.

Explain himself? Under the circumstances it seemed to him a more than reasonable, even generous demand. Certainly more than he'd expected.

Explain himself. *Well. Your Highness, I was just getting ready for bed, minding my own business, when your daughter, here, came knocking at my door, and the next thing I knew, she was throwing herself into my arms. Did I invite her? No sir, I did not. And…where did she get the idea to come to my chambers, Your Highness? You mean, did I entice her? Lead her on? Well…no sir, I sure didn't… unless you count kissing her earlier this evening until she couldn't stand up….*

Cade sighed inwardly. To explain seemed cowardly to him, and heartless, somehow. His mouth, opened to release the words that were poised on the tip of his tongue, firmly closed.

He looked at Leila, standing so straight and still beside her father. Her face was pale but proud, even with eyes lowered and veiled by tear-clumped lashes. He cleared his throat and determinedly began. "Your Highness, this is not what you think. Your daughter—" He glanced at her again, and saw her eyes go wide and stare straight into his…saw her lips part and her cheeks flood with pink. She reminded him of a doe he'd seen once, caught in a hunter's snare. And again he felt that awful sensation in his midsection, as if his heart had just been speared, and had landed with a thud in the bottom of his belly.

Every rational thought went out of his head. His mind was chaos, a whirlwind of remorse and shame. This was his fault. He'd humiliated this girl—and she *was* a girl. She was a princess and he'd humiliated her. She was almost certainly a virgin, and he'd kissed her frivolously, toyed with her emotions. And now, to make matters even worse, her humiliation was made public, since all at once the hallway around them seemed filled with people—bodyguards, servants, even Leila's mother with *her* servants, come to see what all the commotion was about. The damage he'd done to Leila—and to his own agenda, of course—seemed irreparable. *Unless...*

Just as suddenly as the chaos had come, now calm and certainty descended upon him. There was only one way to fix the mess he'd created. Cade knew precisely what he had to do.

He drew himself up, and with as much dignity as he could muster with his hair standing on end and without benefit of shirt, jacket and tie, looked Leila's father straight in the eye. "Sheik Ahmed, this may seem sudden, but I have fallen in love with your daughter." Ignoring Leila's shocked gasp, he rushed on. "I want to marry her." The gasps had found echoes throughout the gathering; he ignored those, too, as well as the sheik's sudden stiffening. "I respectfully ask your permission—"

"My permission!" Sheik Ahmed's voice shook. His wife laid a cautioning hand on his arm, and he whirled, blindly thrusting Leila toward her.

"Take her," he bellowed. "Take her away—and the rest of you—" he waved his arms, making shooing motions at the crowd. "Leave us!" Without waiting for his orders to be obeyed, he turned back to Cade, black eyes glittering with rage.

"*You.* You would *marry* my *daughter?*" With extreme effort, the sheik seemed to draw himself together and spoke more calmly though with no less anger. ''Mr. Gallagher, I have made you a guest in my house, and you thank me by inflicting this gravest of injuries upon my family.''

Cade frowned. This was not going quite the way he'd expected. ''That was not—''

''*Silence!* And now, to that injury you would add insult? Do you think that I would allow *my* daughter to marry *you*—an infidel, an unbeliever, a man without honor?'' There was a pause, during which Cade could have sworn the sheik grew in height at least a foot before his very eyes. And then, in a magnificent bellow, ''I would sooner see her dishonored!''

Having delivered his exit line, Sheik Ahmed whirled— then spoiled the effect of it somewhat by jerking back to Cade. ''You will leave my house,'' he growled, stabbing the air in his direction with a bejeweled finger. ''Tomorrow—as early as can be arranged.'' Once more he turned, and stalked off down the now-deserted hallway, footsteps ringing on the tile floor.

Protected by an icy shell of calm he knew must be shock, Cade watched until the massive doors at the end of the hallway had closed upon the sheik's broad back. Then he retreated into his own chamber and carefully pulled the door shut after him.

On the whole, he thought as the quivery aftereffects of shock hit him, that had gone pretty well. At least he hadn't been executed on the spot.

Like a gracefully pensive statue, Leila stood in steamy and fragrant warmth and gazed at the familiar back of the woman who knelt beside the bath. Gazed at, but did not really see. Her mind was empty, as bereft of thoughts as her eyes were of tears. She did not dare allow herself to think, not even so much as a single thought; if she did, she feared the anger, humiliation and despair would simply overwhelm her.

Salma Hadi, her mother's most trusted servant and once upon a time Leila's own nanny, hummed nervously as she fussed over the bathwater, adding scent and soap bubbles, swishing the water with her fingers to test the temperature. The tune she hummed was simple and familiar, a children's play song she had sung to Leila long, long ago. Leila found it oddly soothing.

Pushing stiffly to her feet, Salma turned to smile up at her. Holding out her hand, she spoke in Arabic, the language of her youth. "Ah, yes, now it is good. Come, my treasured child, let me help you undress."

Mindlessly, Leila obeyed the familiar voice, lifting her hair to allow access to the fastenings of her gown. She stood, docile and numb, while well-remembered hands gently removed her clothing and twisted her hair into a pile atop her head, securing it there with jeweled clips and combs. Naked, she allowed herself to be taken by the hand and led to the edge of the bath.

"There, my sweet…gently…gently," Salma crooned. "The water will sooth you…take away the pain."

Leila gave her former nanny a puzzled look. *Pain? What pain?* Was Salma getting old? Losing her mind? The pain *she* felt was all inside, deep in her heart, and it would take much more than a hot bubble bath to make it go away.

"Thank you," she murmured as she lowered herself into the fragrant suds, for she had been taught never to take loyal servants for granted. "This does feel good." Closing her eyes, she lay back with a sigh and stretched herself languidly, like a sleepy cat. How good it felt to relax, after such a tumultuous day. How good it would be if she could simply go to sleep right here, and not have to think…

"Princess? Are you—"

There was concern, and something else—embarrassment,

perhaps?—in Salma's voice. Leila opened her eyes. "Yes, Salma, what is it?"

The servant's round face was flushed, and her eyes glistened with kindness. "Princess, I have some oil—it is very soothing. When you have finished—"

"Oil?" Leila frowned. "What kind of oil? What for?"

Salma touched Leila's cheek with gentle fingers. "My little one...it is normal for a woman to have pain, the first time she...is with a man. But after a hot bath...the soothing oil...it goes away quickly—" She stopped, for Leila was shaking her head wildly. She continued in distress, "Princess, it is *all right*—" But Leila went on shaking her head, and brushing aside Salma's anxious fingers, covered her face with her hands.

Her face, her whole body burned with shame; even the bathwater felt cool on her fevered skin. Oh, how she wished she could just...sink to the bottom of the tub and disappear forever.

"Princess—what is it?" Salma's voice had risen with alarm. Lifting her hands heavenward, she uttered a rapid, wailing prayer, which she almost immediately interrupted to ask in a despairing whisper, "Oh, tell me—did he harm you? Are you injured, truly? Tell me—what has he—"

"No, no!" Leila cried, "you don't understand. He did nothing. *Nothing.*"

"*Nothing?*" Salma rocked backward, hushed and wondering. "You mean, you are not—he did not—"

"No," Leila moaned, putting her hands over her eyes once more, "he *would* not. Oh, Salma, it was awful. Just awful..." And all at once she felt herself gathered into loving arms, soapsuds and all, and she was sobbing like a little child on her nanny's shoulder. "Salma," she gulped, "I have been a fool...."

"Yes, my treasure," Salma crooned, rocking her. "Yes...."

* * *

Alima Kamal was worried about her husband. She had never before seen him so angry—his color was quite alarming. Hadn't the doctors warned him about his blood pressure, insisted he must lose some weight? And after such a weekend, so much excitement, too much rich food—and perhaps more of the mild Tamari wine than he was accustomed to—now *this*. What had Leila been thinking of, to do such a thing?

Ah—Leila. That was another worry entirely. She was in Salma's capable hands—that problem could wait until tomorrow.

At the moment Ahmed was in the bathroom, Alima having persuaded him that a warm bath might help him to relax—with the help of a little subtle bribery, naturally, in the form of the promise of a nice massage afterward. She had in mind an old family recipe of Salma's—passed on to her by her maternal grandmother—a mix of fragrant oils and certain herbs that were designed to soothe the mind as well as the body. She had used it on her husband before, with most satisfactory and highly enjoyable results, for her as well. Although, under the circumstances she didn't hold out hope for such a conclusion to *this* evening's activities. Ah, well... Alima sighed.

A discreet tapping at the royal bedchamber's heavy wooden door almost went unnoticed, so engrossed was she in her preparations. When it continued, now a little louder, she glanced at the antique French clock on the mantelpiece. Who would dare disturb the sheik in his chambers at this hour? With a mildly vexed sigh, Alima went to answer it.

"Salma!" Her heart gave a leap of alarm when she saw her oldest and most trusted attendant standing there, almost bouncing on her tiptoes with ill-concealed emotion. "What's wrong? Is Leila all right? Is something—"

"Oh, no, *Sitt,*" Salma interrupted breathlessly, "Princess

Leila is fine. That is why—Oh, *Sitt,* please forgive me for disturbing you, but I must speak with you.''

Casting a hurried glance toward the bathroom where, judging from the sounds coming from within, her husband—perhaps in anticipation of what was to come after?—seemed to be enjoying his bath more than he'd expected, Alima stepped into the hallway and pulled the door closed behind her.

Flat on his belly with his eyes closed, Sheik Ahmed drifted on waves of pleasure. *Ah yes…there…* Alima's strong fingers never failed to find the spot that needed them most.

She wanted something from him, of course. She only resorted to the oils and herbs when she was hoping to cajole him into giving her her way. He knew this, but it did nothing to lessen his pleasure. He trusted his wife implicitly. He knew she would never use the considerable influence she had on him lightly. If she was attempting to manipulate him now, it would only be for something she considered to be of utmost importance. Ah well…she would get to it in her own good time. And meanwhile, as far as Sheik Ahmed was concerned, getting there was the most enjoyable part.

''Ahmed, my beloved…''

''Yes, jewel of my heart? Speak to me.''

They had been speaking Arabic, as they often did on intimate occasions, but Alima switched now to English. ''Ahmed, Salma was here, while you were in the bath. She brought news of Leila—''

''Leila!'' A snort lifted his head and shoulders from the pillows.

Gently but firmly, Alima pushed them down again. ''Hush, my husband—please, hear me.'' After a pause, which she decided to take for acquiescence, she continued in a musing tone, "What she had to say was interesting. I think you will want to hear it."

Ahmed gave a resigned grunt. "Very well...if you must."

Bracing herself for the expected upheaval, Alima bore down with all her strength on one of her husband's most troublesome spots, took a deep breath, and said lightly, "It is possible we have misjudged Elena's friend from Texas." A growl resonated beneath her fingers. She hurried on. "It seems this American may not be entirely without honor, after all. I say this—" she spoke calmly, but her fingers were kneading her husband's tensed muscles as hard and fast as they possibly could "—because of what your daughter has confessed to Salma. In tears." There was that growl again. "Yes, *tears*," she said firmly. "But *not* because this man had *dishonored* her. Quite the opposite. Your daughter was in tears because he had sent her *away*."

Like a small mountain shifted by an earthquake, Sheik Ahmed rolled himself onto his back. Raising himself up on his elbows, glowering fiercely, he bellowed, "*Away?* What do you mean, he sent her *away?* Explain yourself!"

Alima sat with her legs tucked under her, head high and eyes downcast. Her heart was beating rapidly and her hands, clasped tightly together in her lap, were cold. She was desperately afraid, though not of her husband—she could never be afraid of Ahmed! This was another kind of fear entirely—the fear of a mother for her beloved child. Her youngest daughter's future happiness was at stake.

"Yes," she said on a soft exhalation, "I fear it was not the American who behaved badly this evening, but our daughter. And I—" Her voice broke—she had not planned it. "I must say that I am not surprised. I have been afraid something like this might happen. Oh, Ahmed—" She rose and turned quickly from him to hide the tears that had sprung unexpectedly to her eyes. "Leila is so impatient and impulsive—she has always been so."

"Yes." Ahmed actually chuckled.

Whirling back to him, Alima was just in time to see him rearrange his face in its customary glower. "Ahmed, she is a woman. She has the feelings, the needs, the *impulses* of a woman. Every day I have watched her grow more impatient, waiting her turn, waiting for her sisters to choose husbands…"

Yes, and impatient for other things, for other reasons, too, about which Alima knew she could never tell her husband. Ahmed was a good man and a progressive leader in many ways, but he would never understand how bright, intelligent women like his daughters might feel frustrated at being patronized, overlooked, discounted and ignored. Particularly Leila, whom everyone considered silly and shallow, and whom possibly only her mother knew was anything but.

And there was another thing Leila's mother knew. She had noticed the way her youngest child looked at the tall oilman from Texas. Tonight she had seen the soft shine in her eyes, the pink flush in her cheeks….

"Humph," said Ahmed. "I have been more than patient with Nadia, it is true…" He scratched his bearded chin thoughtfully. "Butrus wishes to marry her, and she seems willing enough." He shrugged and gave a regal wave of his hand. "Pah—I see no real value in this tradition of marrying off daughters in order of their birth. So—if you are certain that Leila is eager to marry, and impetuous enough to do something foolish, then the answer is simple enough. I must find her a suitable husband. And now, my beloved, if that is all that is troubling you—" He smiled, and his eyes gleamed wickedly.

Alima hesitated. This was the tricky part. She must be

extremely careful not to give herself away. Breathing a relieved sigh, she bowed her head and said, "Yes, my husband. You are wise, as always. Only—"

Still smiling, he caught her hand and drew her closer to him. "Only? What is it now, my love?"

Bracing her hands firmly on her husband's shoulders, Alima looked gravely into his eyes. "Only, I fear that it may prove difficult to find a man willing to overlook tonight's escapade. Perhaps we should consider—"

"Not the American!" bellowed Ahmed, rearing back in outrage. "A nonbeliever? *Never.*"

"Of course not," said Alima, laughing. "What an idea! No, I was going to say, perhaps we should consider someone older, someone who will give Leila the firm guidance she needs." She paused, then continued demurely, "I hear the Emir of Batar is looking for a fourth wife."

"The Emir of Batar! The man is older than I am," fumed Ahmed, looking horrified. "And I have it on good authority that he treats his wives shamefully. No, no—we must do better for Leila." He gave his wife an absentminded squeeze and turned away from her. "Let me think about it."

"Of course, my husband," murmured Alima, beginning to knead his shoulder muscles. "Perhaps this will help."

After several minutes, Ahmed spoke, slurring his words slightly. "I have ordered the American to leave tomorrow, as early as possible." Alima said nothing, but continued massaging his neck and shoulders. "Perhaps," muttered Ahmed, "that was a bit…hasty. And somewhat unfair, under the circumstances. What do *you* think, dearest one?" He turned to encircle her with his arms. She saw that his eyes were twinkling.

She lowered her lashes so he would not see the gleam in hers. "You know best, my husband."

"I believe I will speak to the man, first thing in the morning."

"Whatever you say, beloved," crooned Alima.

Chapter 5

Cade dropped his toiletry kit into his carry-on bag, added a half-empty pack of cheroots and the zippable daily planner in which he kept his business notes and appointments, then straightened for one last look around. Not that he was afraid he'd overlooked something; rather, his gaze was one of wonderment, reflecting his frame of mind. He was still having a hard time accepting what had happened to him. He tried to remember whether he'd ever suffered such a demoralizing tail-between-the-legs disaster before in his life. He couldn't.

Ah, the car, he thought when he heard the discreet knock on his door. He called, "Be right there," and grabbed up his big suitcase and moved it over beside the door. A little early, he thought, glancing at his watch, but so much the better. He'd have time to grab a bite of breakfast at the airport before his flight. He sure as hell wasn't about to eat anything here at the palace, or for that matter, impose on the Kamal family's hospitality in any way, for one minute longer than absolutely necessary. He'd seen enough of these royals to last him a lifetime. With the exception of Elena, of course. Though he sure wouldn't care to run into her, right now, either. He couldn't even begin to think how he was going to explain this to her.

He zipped up his overnighter, picked it up and placed it beside its bigger twin, then opened the door. The man who stood there, waiting at patient and respectful attention, wasn't wearing the white-and-gold uniform of the household servants, but a western-style suit, dark gray with an immaculate white shirt and blue-and-gray striped tie. He looked familiar—dark, swarthy, probably handsome, in an austere, arrogant sort of way. Undoubtedly Cade had been introduced to the man during the course of the weekend, which meant he was a member of the royal family or somebody high on the bureaucratic totem pole.

Probably a lawyer, Cade thought cynically. For the defense, he wondered, or the prosecution?

"The sheik wishes to speak with you," the man said, in clipped English. "If you will come with me, please."

What now? Maybe he's changed his mind about having me executed, Cade thought sourly as he gave his room one last look and with a fatalistic shrug, pulled the door shut behind him.

His escort didn't say another word as he led the way along the corridor, following virtually the same path by which the sheik had made his dramatic departure the night before. Cade made a conscious effort to relax, and tried not to think about the confrontation to come. Instead he made a point of noticing the arched passageways, the apparently ancient tiles beneath his feet and mosaics on the walls, and the lamps which, set into niches along the walls, added to the medieval look of it all. He half expected to see armored guards with swords and crossed pikestaffs barring entry through the massive carved double doors at the end of the hallway.

Instead, his escort merely knocked twice, paused, then pushed the doors open and gestured for Cade to enter ahead of him. Cade gave the man a nod and a sardonic, "Thank you," which went unacknowledged.

The sheik's office was huge, but was saved from seeming cavernous by the warm opulence of mahogany, leather and Persian carpets. Arched windows along one side of the room looked out on the sea; on the other, Sheik Ahmed waited behind a long mahogany desk. He wore an ordinary business suit this morning, but that didn't make him seem any the less imposing. He still looked positively biblical, Cade thought. Moses in a suit and tie.

The sheik had risen at Cade's approach. Now he nodded at the escort and said, "Thank you, Butrus. You may leave us."

As the man muttered and made his exit, the name came to Cade. *Butrus Dabir. The sheik's most trusted advisor, and according to Elena, one with designs on his daughter, Nadia.*

"Thank you for coming, Mr. Gallagher. Please sit down." The sheik indicated one of several leather chairs in front of the desk, waited until Cade was seated, then returned to his own chair. Like a genial host, Cade thought, except without the smile. In fact, he seemed almost...in anyone else Cade would have sworn he was.... No way around it. The reigning monarch of Tamir gave every indication of being embarrassed.

Sheik Ahmed picked up a pen and put it down. He leaned back in his chair and scowled at the pen with lowered eyebrows. At last, following an introductory rumbling sound, he spoke.

"Mr. Gallagher, I have asked you here so that I may offer you an apology. It seems that, in the heat of the, uh, moment last night, I have made a too-hasty judgment. I believe I accused you of being a man without honor, whereas it seems that you behaved with more honor than most men would have under the same…ahem…the circumstances. I hope that you will forgive my behavior, and that of my daughter.'' And with that, half rising, the sheik leaned across his desk to offer his hand to Cade.

Who was momentarily speechless, with his mouth hanging open like a schoolboy caught red-handed at mischief. Whatever he might have expected, it sure as hell wasn't this. Finally, though, there was only one thing to do, and that was shake the sheik's hand and say thank you. So he did it.

He was settling back in his chair, feeling dazed as a poleaxed steer, when the sheik gave another rumble and continued. ''Regarding your proposal of marriage to my daughter…'' There was a pause while the sheik stared intently at Cade, eyes glittering from beneath lowered eyebrows. Much against his will, Cade's heart began to beat faster. ''Mr. Gallagher, I am fully aware of the circumstances under which it was made, and I—that is to say, your gallant attempt to salvage my daughter's honor is not unappreciated.'' There was another pause. Again the sheik's eyes pinioned Cade with the intent stare of a hawk zeroing in on a cornered gopher.

Cade's mind was racing. What was going on here? The old sheik had an agenda, that was clear enough. What wasn't clear at all was exactly how Cade was supposed to fit into it. Okay, he'd been cleared of dishonoring the princess, apologies had been made, he'd been let off the hook. On the other hand, his banishment hadn't been lifted, not in so many words. He had a very strong feeling that if he said thank you now, shook hands and left this room, he'd be taking that early flight home, no hard feelings, but no business deal, either.

What was it the old fox wanted from him? He'd made his feelings on the marriage issue plain enough. So, what?

His heart was pounding, his mind in chaos. However, only his narrowed eyes betrayed the turmoil he was feeling as he calmly said, "Sir, I assure you—I didn't propose marriage to your daughter merely to save her reputation. My desire to marry Leila was—is—sincere."

God, what had he just said? *Marry Leila?* He felt a bright stab of panic before he remembered that he was safe. Her royal papa was never going to go for it anyway.

At the moment, though, the way the old sheik was staring at him was making him decidedly uneasy. Still intent as a hawk about to pounce, but now—there it was again, that odd little shift of embarrassment.

"Hmm, yes...I see." Sheik Ahmed tapped his fingers on the desktop. "Mr. Gallagher, you must understand that in our culture, such an alliance would be impossible..."

"I understand," Cade murmured, gravely nodding.

"Unless—" the sheik pounced "—you were to convert."

Cade's heart leaped into overdrive. "Convert?"

"To our ways, our culture." The sheik spread his hands and in the white nest of beard his lips curved in a smile. "Then there would be no objection to a marriage between you and my youngest daughter—from me, of course. Naturally, Leila would have to consent to such a match." He actually chuckled.

"Naturally..." Cade breathed. His head was whirling again. What the hell was happening? He gave his head a little shake and tried to smile. "Wow. Convert, huh? That's an...interesting idea. I'll...definitely have to..."

"Of course," Sheik Ahmed said smoothly, "I understand such a decision should not be made lightly. And I would fully understand if you wished to leave us, Mr. Gallagher, after the treatment you have recently been subjected to, from me and, uh...members of my family. However, if you should decide to stay..." another of those strategic pauses, another shrewd glare "…it is my understanding that my son, Hassan, and daughter-in-law, Elena, had scheduled a visit to the oil-producing regions of our country, and a tour of our facilities, before their departure on their…uh…" He frowned, searching for the word.

"Honeymoon?" Cade supplied.

"Yes, honeymoon." The sheik waved a hand and muttered something about "western traditions," then harrumphed and went on. "It is also my understanding that the three of you wished to discuss a possible business arrangement between your own company, Elena's and Tamir."

Cade, who was pretty much in shock at this point, could only nod and mutter, "Yes, sir, I had been looking forward to meeting with you on that subject—"

Sheik Ahmed gave another hand wave and leaned dismissively back in his chair. "I have decided to leave that aspect of my country's business dealings to my son. *And* his new wife, who, as the head of her own company, seems very knowledgeable on the subject. You may consider them my representatives. Any agreement you might enter into with them, especially as a member of the family, if you should chose that course—" the sheik smiled, showing strong white teeth "—would be honored fully by the government of Tamir."

Cade let out a gust of breath. He felt absolutely calm, now, clear through to his insides. The cards were on the table; he was pretty sure he knew both the game and the stakes. He also knew he'd been seriously outmaneuvered.

"I understand," he said as he rose to accept the sheik's proffered hand. "Thank you, Your Highness. You've given me a lot to think about. I'm looking forward to visiting your oil production facilities." He tried a strategic pause of his own, meeting the old sheik's glittery black eyes and locking on as their hands clasped across the mahogany desktop. His smile felt frozen on his face. "I'm sure we can work out something," he drawled, "that'll be to both our advantages."

"He is *what?*" Leila shrieked, slopping hot coffee into her saucer and very nearly her lap.

"He is going to convert," her mother repeated, her face so round and happy she looked like a child's drawing of a beaming sun. Leila felt as though *her* sun had just been covered by a huge black cloudbank.

She was on the terrace with Nadia, having a late breakfast—or perhaps an early lunch—while Nadia, who had already eaten, passed the time in her usual way, with her sketchbook. At their mother's interruption Nadia looked up briefly, then went back to making little pencil sketches of Leila.

While Leila mopped up coffee with her napkin, her mother selected the chair next to her and turned it so that it angled toward Leila before she sat. She took Leila's hand, holding it in both of her warm, soft ones. Tears sprang to Leila's eyes. She had to swallow hard to fight down the lump in her throat.

"Your father has given his permission for the two of you to marry," her mother said in a husky, excited voice. She gazed at Leila with shining eyes. "Oh, my child, I am so happy for you. Mr. Gallagher must love you very much, to honor you so."

Leila was glad she was no longer holding the cup of coffee in her hands; as badly as they were shaking, she would surely have dropped it—or perhaps hurled it into the nearest fountain. Inwardly she was seething with anger, with outrage. Remembering the way he had thrust her away from him, as if she were something vile. Remembering the humiliation. *How dare he!*

Why is he doing this? she thought desperately. What can

he possibly hope to gain? Is he trying to humiliate me even more?

Because she knew, she *absolutely* knew, that whatever Cade Gallagher's motive might be for marrying her, it most definitely was *not* because he loved her.

"Mother," said Leila in a choked voice, "I do not want to marry Mr. Gallagher. I will not." A tear ran down her cheek.

Her mother made a distressed sound and brushed it away. "Oh dear—I thought you would be pleased. But tell me, why not?"

Why not? Because he made me feel like…like I never knew it was possible to feel. Because he opened a door and beckoned to me, showed me a glimpse of paradise, then slammed the door in my face. Because he made me want him…and I cannot stop thinking about him…and I know I will never be able to forget him. How can I forgive him for that?

"He is from America!" Leila cried, brushing furiously at both the tears and her mother's hand. It was the only thing she could think of to say. "From *Texas!*"

Her mother looked startled, but only for a moment. Then she put her arms around Leila and patted her on the back as she crooned, "Yes, of course…I understand. Don't cry, my sweet. Naturally you would not wish to marry someone who would take you so far away from your home…your family. I hadn't thought, but yes—you would have to live in America—in Texas! Your father and I would hardly ever see you. What were we thinking? Hmm. Well. Never mind."

She gave Leila one last little hug and rose. "Don't worry, my sweet, I will explain things to your father." She smiled and leaned down to kiss Leila's cheek. "To be honest, I think he will be glad that you will be staying right here in Tamir."

When her mother had gone, Leila reached for her coffee cup, then pushed it savagely away from her.

Nadia put aside her sketchbook. "Have you suddenly lost your mind?" she asked mildly. Leila said nothing, but stared at her coffee cup with hot, tearless eyes. "Or," said Nadia, "are you merely being contrary?" She gave a sigh of exasperation. "Did I not hear you say, two days ago, how attractive you thought Mr. Gallagher? *And,* were you not talking about how much you wanted to go to America? *Especially* Texas? It seemed like an impossible dream, even I thought so. To have it realized would have taken a miracle. Now, it is as if you had rubbed a magic lamp! All your wishes have been granted. And you would turn them down? Leila—for mercy's sake, *why?*"

"Because I do not love him," Leila said flatly. Her voice was as dry as her eyes. "And he certainly does not love me."

With an exasperated noise, Nadia flung herself away from the table. "Leila, you are such a child."

Leila stared at her, stung. Although it was the sort of thing people were always saying to her, for some reason, this morning, it hurt more than usual. She swallowed, then said softly, "I do not think it is childish to want to be loved. *You* have known love, Nadia. Why should I not have the same?"

For a moment, as she gazed back at Leila, Nadia's face softened. For a moment. Then her eyes darkened with pain and she veiled them with her lashes before she turned away. "You don't know what you are talking about. Love brings only pain. Trust me—you do not ever want to know pain like that."

"I am sorry, Nadia," Leila whispered, belatedly remembering her sister's secret heartbreak.

"Besides," Nadia went on briskly, "we are not talking about love, but about marriage, which is a different thing

entirely. Love is a terrible reason to get married. It is a
recent idea, this notion that one must be in love in order to
marry—don't you know that? And look at what *that* has
done! So much unhappiness. Inevitably, love leads to disappointment, and disappointment to misery and even divorce. No, thank you.''

"So," said Leila grudgingly, "what reason *do* you think
people should marry for, if not love?'' She was by no
means ready to agree with such a cynical point of view,
but there was no arguing with Nadia.

"Why, for practical reasons, of course." Nadia looked
as annoyingly superior as an older sister can. "Marriage
should be entered into as a business agreement—a contract,
mutually advantageous, of course. I, for example," she said
loftily, holding her head high, "have decided to marry Butrus. Why?'' Ignoring Leila's gasp of surprise, she rushed
on, ticking off reasons one by one on her fingers. "One,
Butrus wishes to marry me in order to gain favor with Father, therefore, he knows he must treat me well—very
well—because if I were to be made unhappy, Father would
not be pleased. Two, as Father's advisor, Butrus is away a
great deal of the time. So, I would not only have the status
of a married woman, but at the same time I would be assured a considerable amount of freedom. And three, I wish
to have children. Butrus is handsome and physically well
made. So, we would have beautiful, healthy babies. And,
he has rather nice teeth, I believe.''

"Nadia," Leila said, giggling in spite of herself, "you
sound as though you are buying a horse.''

"It is very much the same thing," Nadia said airily. A
moment later, though, she was serious again as she bent
down to cover Leila's hand with her own and give it an
urgent little squeeze. "Leila—for once in your life, use
your head. *Think.* Cade Gallagher will make beautiful,
healthy babies, too. And, he will take you to America—to

Texas.'' She glanced quickly over her shoulder and lowered her voice. Even so, it quivered with passion. "Away from *here*. Just think, Leila—in America you can do—you can become—anything you want to. *Anything*. Do you understand? The freedom…" She straightened abruptly, biting her lip. "*Think* about it, Leila," she whispered, and snatching up her sketchpad, walked quickly away without looking back.

Leila did not know how long she stayed there, biting her lip and stubbornly frowning at nothing. Bees hummed among the roses, birds came to drink and play in the fountain and a servant came quietly to clear away the remains of the meal. And still she sat…quivering with the burden of unshed tears.

It was the strangest meeting Cade had ever been a part of. Definitely not what he'd expected. Though he'd have had a hard time putting into words just what it was he *had* expected.

One thing, definitely—he'd expected to have at least one more chance to talk with Leila. Alone. But clearly, that wasn't going to happen. Instead they each occupied separate leather chairs facing Sheik Ahmed's long mahogany desk, with several feet of space between them. It might as well have been several miles. Like a cross between a biblical Moses and a junior high school principal facing down a couple of co-conspirators in mischief, Sheik Ahmed presided behind his desk. His wife, Alima, Leila's mother, sat in a comfortable chair near one of the casement windows that overlooked the sea. She wore a serene smile and held in her hands a small, leather-bound book.

As for Leila, she hadn't spoken a word to Cade, or even looked at him. She sat straight-backed in her chair with her head held high, the arch of her throat as pale as the marble columns that graced the palace gardens. There was only a

quivery softness about her mouth to betray any emotion or
vulnerability at all, but to Cade, that was enough. Disliking
the queasy, seasick feeling he got when he saw…when he
remembered…that incredibly ripe, incredibly fragile
mouth, he'd stopped looking at her at all.

With a face as stern as an old-fashioned Texas hang-'em-
high judge, Sheik Ahmed was speaking, "…and that you
have entered into this decision of your own free will, and
with pure mind and sincere heart?"

"Yes—" Cade cleared his throat. "Yes, sir, I have."

The sheik went on talking, something solemn about a
man's heart being the province of God and therefore not to
be questioned by man, but Cade wasn't listening. His mind
was full of the incredible fact that he, Cade Gallagher, an
American businessman living in the twenty-first century,
had just agreed to an arranged marriage. *Arranged*—like in
medieval times! How had such a thing happened to him?

Right now, more than anything, what he felt was dazed,
bewildered, at a loss to explain how a man such as he, a
master at navigating through the most circuitous and complex of business negotiations, could have gotten himself so
completely boxed in. Because the truth was, he just didn't
see any other way out of this. Not unless he was prepared
to take it all back, right here and now, in front of Leila and
both her parents. Say he hadn't meant the proposal of marriage to begin with, that it had been a mistake and he wasn't
prepared to go through with it after all. Say it to her face.

There was no way. He could not do that. No way in hell.

Because if there was anything he'd learned as a kid
growing up in Texas, it was to stand up and take the consequences for his actions like a man.

Consequences.… Elena had said something like that,
hadn't she? They'd had only a few minutes together, while
Hassan was speaking to the foreman at one of the refineries
they'd visited this afternoon about some sort of minor prob-

lem or complaint. Even now, remembering the disappointment in her eyes made Cade squirm. *"Cade, I warned you...."*

"You did," he'd acknowledged, and added, grimly joking, "Don't worry, I take full responsibility for my own stupidity."

But Elena hadn't smiled, and with a sad little shake of her head had murmured, "This isn't what I wanted for you, Cade." Her eyes had gone to where her husband stood with his back to them, deep in conversation with the refinery foreman. "I'd hoped...someday...you'd find someone you could love the way I love Hassan." Her voice had broken then, and Cade had snorted to cover the shaft of pain that unexpectedly pierced his heart.

Why he'd felt such a sense of loss, he didn't know. He'd never expected to experience that kind of love, anyway. The kind of love that lasts a lifetime. From his own personal experience he thought it doubtful love like that even existed.

As for his own feelings about Leila, since they were so confusing to him, most of the time he tried not to dwell on them at all. If he had to define them, he'd have said they pretty much consisted of a mix of anger and remorse. Yeah, she'd behaved like a moonstruck girl, but he was old enough, experienced enough, and he should have known better. He was responsible and it was up to him to make it right. But there was something else in the stew of his emotions that wasn't as easily defined, possibly because it was a whole lot less unfamiliar. The closest he would allow himself to come to defining it was *protectiveness*. With his own carelessness he'd hurt this child-woman immeasurably, and he never wanted to do so again.

Understandable enough. But even that didn't account for the strange ache of *tenderness* that filled his throat sometimes when he looked at her—like now, as she murmured affirmative responses to her father's questions.

Do you agree to this marriage, Leila, and enter into it of your own free will?

Yes, Father....

But still, not once did she look at Cade. And he felt a strange, unfamiliar emptiness inside.

Alima rose then, and came to her daughter's side. She placed the leather-bound book on the shiny desktop. Sheik Ahmed picked it up and handed it to Cade, explaining that it was an English translation of the Quran, which he might wish to study in his own time. Cade nodded, accepted the book and murmured his thanks. The sheik then repeated, in Arabic, the words of the *eshedu,* which Cade would be required to recite later that evening, before the marriage ceremony itself. Cade nodded again. Then Alima touched Leila on the shoulder. Without a word, she rose and followed her mother from the room.

"Now, then," purred the sheik when the women had gone, leaning back and lacing beringed fingers across his ample middle, "let us discuss the *Mahr*... It is our custom that a husband bestow upon his wife a gift. This may be money or jewels, of course—" the sheik waved a hand in a casually dismissive way "—or something of even greater, if less concrete value. That is up to you. You will no doubt wish to give the matter some thought...."

Once again, Cade could only nod. His heart was beating hard, gathering speed like a runner hurtling downhill.

This is real, he thought. *It's actually happening. I'm marrying a princess of Tamir. And a virgin princess, at that.*

Leila gazed at her reflection in the mirror, eyes dark and solemn in her waxy pale face. She saw her mother's hands, graceful and white as lily petals as they plucked and tweaked at the veils that covered her long black hair, veils that soon would be arranged to cover her face as well, until the final moments of the *nikah* ceremony later that morning when her husband would lift them to gaze at last upon the face of his wife.

At least, she thought, there would not be many people present to witness that moment. Only her parents and her sisters, Nadia and Sammi, of course, and Salma, and perhaps a few of the other servants who had known her since she was a baby. She was glad she would not have to face Elena, and especially Hassan. Salma had told her that they had left last evening for their honeymoon trip, right after returning from their tour of the oil refineries with Cade. Most of the guests who had attended Hassan and Elena's wedding had left yesterday, as well, and probably would not even know yet of Leila's humiliation.

Sadly, she thought of the wedding she had always imagined for herself, the most wonderful, beautiful occasion…even more glorious than Hassan's. Instead, it must be only a brief and private, almost secretive affair, with only her closest family attending. Papa would preside over the ceremony, of course. She would not even have a *Walima,* since she and Cade would have to leave for his home in Texas immediately after the *nikah* ceremony, and so how could there be a joyous celebration of its consummation?

Her stomach lurched and she swallowed hard. I wish I had some makeup, she thought. Lipstick, at least. *What will Cade think, when he sees me looking so pale?*

Does he think I am pretty at all?

Will he want to kiss me again, the way he did that night?

Her stomach gave another of those dreadful lurches. Oh, she thought, I do hope I'm not going to throw up.

Another time…another place…

She took a deep breath, and then another. *After tonight I will be his wife. Will he want me then?*

''Are you all right?'' her mother asked, holding her

hands away from the veils and looking concerned. "Do you need to sit down for a moment?"

"I am fine, mother," Leila said, trying a light laugh. "I was just thinking about Sammi and Nadia. Are they *very* angry with me?" Not Nadia, of course—she was the one who had convinced Leila to go through with this. But Leila had not told her mother *that*.

Her mother gave a rather unladylike snort. "Of course they are not *angry* with you." She paused to consider the effect she had just created with the drape of the veils, then threw Leila a quick, bright glance by way of the mirror. "They have been no more happy than you have, you know, with some of our more…restrictive ways. To have one such restriction done away with they see as a victory for themselves as well as for you."

Leila could only stare back at her, openmouthed with surprise. She had never heard her mother speak so freely. It occurred to her then, perhaps for the first time, that her mother was a person in her own right, a woman of intelligence, with her own thoughts, opinions, hopes and dreams. And she suddenly wished with all her heart, now that it was too late, that she could have talked with her about those things.

This time, the lurch was not in her stomach, but in her heart. She made an impulsive movement, a jerky half turn. "Mother—" she began, then paused, because Alima's eyes had darkened with worry…and something else. *Embarrassment?*

Her mother took a small step back and clasped her hands together in front of her ample chest. "Leila…my dear, you are the first of my daughters to marry. I am sorry—I do not know…exactly how…" She closed her eyes for a moment and bent her head over her clasped hands, as if in prayer, then drew a resolute breath. "What is it you would like to know? There must be questions you wish to ask. Please do not be afraid. I will try—"

A strange little bubble rose into Leila's throat—part nervousness, part excitement, a little guilt—but she bit it back before it could erupt in laughter. A wave of unheralded tenderness swept over her; she suddenly felt quite amazingly mature and wise. "Mother," she said gently, "I *know* about sex. Really. You do not have to worry."

"Oh dear." Alima closed her eyes and let out an exasperated breath. "I was afraid of that."

"From *school*." Leila was softly laughing. "It is all right. *Really*." She did not think it necessary to mention to her mother that most of her "education" on the subject of sex had not come from classrooms and textbooks, but from the lurid novels and how-to books smuggled in from time to time by Leila's classmates and examined late at night, by flashlight, under the covers, to the accompaniment of giggles, gasps of amazement and sometimes, outright horror.

Her mother sighed, reached for her and drew her close, in a way she had not done since Leila was a little girl. "Then...you are truly all right? You are not afraid?"

As she fought back tears, Leila briefly considered lying. Then, trembling, she whispered, "Mummy, I am *terrified*."

"Oh, my dear one—"

"He is a stranger to me! *Who is he?* What is he like, this...Cade Gallagher? Mummy, I do not know him at all!"

"Then you will learn," said her mother in an unexpectedly firm voice, putting Leila away from her and making little brushing adjustments to her veils. "And he will learn about you. And, God willing, you will continue doing so all the days of your lives. As your father and I have."

"Mother?" Leila brushed a tear. "Did you know Father well before you married? Did you...love him?"

Alima considered that for a moment, and there was a

faraway look in her dark eyes. Then she smiled. "I knew that he was a good man...." Then she added more firmly, "And I believe Cade Gallagher to be a good man, as well."

She paused as Leila turned from her in frustration. Catching hold of her arm, she gave it a tug and said with exasperation, "Leila, *you went to his room.* Have you forgotten? There must have been a reason. Perhaps you should try to remember what it was about Mr. Gallagher that made you do such an incredibly foolish thing! What made you decide, of all the men in the world, to pursue *him?*"

In the silence that followed, Leila heard her mother's words like an echo inside her head. *What was it about Mr. Gallagher? What was it...what was it?*

Once again she faced her own reflection in the mirror, but now her eyes saw another scene...a sunlit garden, bright with flowers and people and noisy with chatter and the shush of fountains...and a tall man in a pale gray suit and a western cowboy hat with his face lifted to follow the flight of a bird, smiling...eyes alight with wonder, like a child's. And she drew a long, unsteady breath.

Yes. That was it. The moment when I knew. Everything else came after....

For a long moment her own dark eyes gazed back at her. Then, carefully, she lifted the veils and pulled them forward so that they completely covered her face. They would not be lifted again until her husband drew them aside to look for the first time upon the face of his wife.

She turned to her mother and said in a voice without tremors, "I am ready."

It is true, she thought. *It is really happening. I am marrying Cade Gallagher from Texas. I am going to America.*

Chapter 6

"So this is Texas." Leila tried to keep any hint of disappointment out of her voice as she peered through the windows of the big American car at the jumble of tall buildings and looping ribbons of freeways filled with cars—so many cars, all moving slowly along like rivers of multicolored lava.

"It's *Houston*," her husband replied in that drawling way he spoke sometimes.

Glancing over at him, Leila saw that the corner of his mouth had lifted in a smile—a smile nothing at all like the one that had lit his face like sunshine when he turned in the palace garden to watch the flight of the bird. The one she held tightly in her memory as if to a sacred talisman. Nevertheless, she felt encouraged by it. She had seen him smile seldom enough in the twenty or so hours that she had been his wife.

His wife...I am a wife. He is my husband.... How many times had she repeated those words to herself, sitting beside him in airplanes and cars and airport lounges, standing with him in queues, facing him across restaurant tables? And still the words seemed unreal to her…totally without meaning.

Sitting beside him in the airplanes—that had been the worst part. Sitting so close to him, for hours and hours and hours on end! So close, even in the roomy first-class seats, that she could feel the heat of his body…smell his unfamiliar scent…and, if she was not *very* careful, sometimes her arm would brush against the sleeve of his jacket. When that happened, prickles would go through her body as if she had received an electric shock. Once…she must have fallen asleep, because she had awakened to discover that her head had been resting on his shoulder. Mortified, she had quickly made her apology, to which he had grunted a gruff reply. Then, looking uncomfortable and shifting restlessly about, he had offered her a pillow.

She had tried very hard to stay awake after that, and as a result now felt fuzzy-headed and queasy with exhaustion. But, she thought, mentally squaring her shoulders, I will not complain. She was a princess of Tamir, after all, and a married woman, not a child. And even as a child had been much too proud to show weakness or fear.

"It is not quite what I expected," she said lightly, letting her dimples show.

He threw her a glance, a very quick one since he was driving. "In what way?"

"I thought it would be more open—you know, like in the movies. Fewer people, fewer buildings… And," she added, gazing once more out of the windows, "not so many trees." In fact, she had never seen so many trees in all her life, not even in England. In some places they made solid curtains, like tapestries woven of green threads, on both sides of the highway.

Her husband laughed softly, deep down in his chest. She had never heard him make that sound before, and she decided she liked it, very much. It made her feel warm, with quivers of laughter in her own insides.

"Like I said, this is Houston—that's *east* Texas. The kind of wide open spaces you're talking about, that's *west* Texas. Out in the hill country and beyond. I have a place—guess you could call it a ranch—out there." He threw her another of those tight, half-smiling glances. "Which I guess you'll probably see…eventually."

She caught her lip between her teeth to contain her excitement. "Are we going there now?"

He answered her again with laughter—indulgent this time. "Not hardly. It'd take the rest of today and most of tomorrow to drive out there. Texas is a bi-ig place."

"Yes," Leila said with a little shiver of suppressed delight, "I know." She felt her husband's eyes touch her, but did not turn to see what was in his glance.

Instead, looking through the window at the unending wall of trees, she asked, "You live here, then? In Houston?" And her momentary happiness evaporated with the realization that she knew so little about the man she had married—not even where he lived.

"Near there. We've got a ways to go, though, so if you want to, you can just put your head back and sleep."

"Oh, no," she said on a determined exhalation, "I don't want to miss anything."

"Wake up, Princess," said a deep and gentle voice, very near. "We're home."

Home. Leila's eyes opened wide and she jerked herself upright. Her heart was pumping very fast and she felt jangly from waking up too suddenly. She must have been disoriented, too, because the view through the car's windshield seemed oddly familiar to her, like something she had seen in a movie. Not a western movie. Maybe one about the American Civil War.

They were driving slowly down a long, straight avenue with trees on both sides—not a solid wall, but huge trees with great spreading branches that met overhead like a lacy green canopy. Sunlight dappled the grassy drive with splotches of gold, and somewhere in all those branches she could hear birds singing—familiar music, but different songs sung in different voices. Eager to hear them better, she rolled down the car window, then gasped as what felt like a hot, damp towel slapped her face.

Cade looked over at her and drawled, "Might want to keep that window closed," though she was already hurrying to do just that. "You're probably not used to the humidity."

A squirrel scampered across the road in front of them, and Leila gave another gasp, this one of delight. Again Cade glanced at her, but this time he didn't speak.

Now, far down at the end of the shaded avenue, the trees were opening into a pool of sunlight. The driveway made a circle around an expanse of bright green lawn bordered by low-growing shrubs and flowers. On the other side of the lawn, twin pillars made of brick with lanterns on top flanked a shrub-and-flower-bordered walkway. The walkway led to brick steps and a wide brick porch with tall white columns, and tall double doors painted a dark green that almost matched the trees. On either side of the porch and above it as well, large windows with many small panes and white-painted shutters gave the red brick house a sparkly-eyed, welcoming look.

Again, Leila drew breath and said, "Oh…" but this time it was a long, murmuring sigh. She thought it a lovely house—small compared to the royal palace of Tamir, but plenty large enough for one family to live in.

Family. Are we, Cade and I…will we ever be…a family?
She felt a peculiar squeezing sensation around her heart.
Two people—a man and a woman—had come out of the

tall green doors and were waiting for them, standing side by side on the porch between two of the white columns. Neither was tall, but the woman's head barely topped the man's shoulder.

He was thin and bony, with legs that bowed out, then came together again at his western-style boots, as if they had been specially made to fit around the girth of a horse. His white hair was slicked back and looked damp, and he had a thick gray moustache that almost covered his mouth, a stark contrast to skin as brown and wrinkled as the shell of a walnut. He wore blue jeans and in spite of the heat, a long-sleeved blue shirt. One gnarled hand, dangling at his side, held a sweat-stained cowboy hat.

The woman seemed almost as wide as she was tall, with a face as round and smooth as a coin. She had shiny black-currant eyes and skin the exact color of the gingerbread cookie people Leila had learned to love as a schoolgirl in Switzerland and England. Her hair, mostly black with only a few streaks of gray, was cut short and tightly curled all over her head, and she wore a loose cotton dress that was bright with flowers.

"That's Rueben and Betsy Flores," Cade said before Leila could ask, nodding his head toward the couple on the porch. "They take care of the place for me."

"They are your servants?"

He answered her with that sharp bark of laughter. "Well...they work for me. But they're more...friends. Or family."

"Ah," said Leila, nodding with complete understanding. Like Salma, she thought. "And...they live here also? With you?"

Cade shook his head. "They have their own place, down by the creek." He stopped the car in front of the steps and turned off the motor.

Time to face the music, he thought. And inexplicably his

heart was beating hard and fast, as if he was a teenager bringing a girl home to meet his parents. He took a sustaining breath and reached for the doorhandle.

But his bride's hand, small and urgent, clutched at his arm. In a low, choked-sounding voice she said, "Did you tell them? Do they know?" Turning, he saw panic in her eyes.

His throat tightened with that strange protective tenderness. "It's okay, I called them from the airport in New York and filled them in." Except for the part about his new bride being a princess. And, he thought, even without that they're probably still in a state of shock. But impulsively, he put his hand over hers and gave it a squeeze before he reached once more for the doorhandle.

He went around the car and as he opened her door for her, leaned down and said in a low voice, "I should warn you—Rueben's great with horses and dogs, but he's kind of shy with two-legged animals, so he probably won't say much. Betsy'll hug you. They were born in Mexico but now they're American through and through—I doubt they're much up on royal protocol."

"That is quite all right," Leila said coolly. "Since I am an American now, too."

While he was still trying to think of a response to that, she belied it by extending a regal hand and allowing him to help her out of the car. She released him at once, though, and stood for a moment, squinting a little in the hot sunlight, smoothing the skirt and tugging at the jacket of the once-elegant, now badly wrinkled designer suit she'd worn all the way from Tamir. Then, before he could even think to offer her his arm, she slipped past him and started up the walk alone.

And for some reason, instead of hurrying to catch up with her, Cade stood there for a moment and watched the woman who was now his wife…slender and graceful in a travel-worn and rumpled suit the color of new lilacs, her head, with hair coming loose from its elegant twist, held proudly.

American? Well, maybe, he thought with something like awe. But somehow still every inch a princess.

As he watched his bride with dawning wonder, he was surprised by yet another alien emotion—an unexpected surge of pride. It made his eyes sting and his nose twitch, and he had to clear his throat before he went to join her on the porch.

He got there just in time to see her hold out her hand to Rueben and say in her musical, slightly accented voice, "Hello, I am Leila. You must be Rueben. I am very happy to meet you. Cade has told me so much about you."

It was a graceful little lie—he hadn't done any such thing. And he should have, he realized now. Lord knows he'd had plenty of time, all those hours on various planes and vehicles, waiting around in airports; time to tell her more than she probably wanted to know about himself, his home, his life. The truth was, he'd barely spoken to her at all during the trip home—just what was necessary between two strangers sharing the same space, no more. He tried to excuse his behavior now by telling himself it was because they'd both been in a state of shock, that he'd been trying to let her rest...sleep a little, which was hogwash. The reason he hadn't spoken was because he hadn't known what to say to her. He still didn't.

By this time, Leila had turned to Betsy, holding out her hand, face all decked out in dimples. "Hi, you must be—" was as far as she got, though, because just like he'd said she would, Betsy was already hugging the stuffing out of her, cooing to her like one of her little lost puppies.

And no sooner had that thought entered Cade's head than here they came—Betsy's mob of adopted mutts, barking and baying and wiggling and whining, falling over themselves and everybody else trying to be the first to slobber all over the newcomer.

In those first chaotic seconds Cade had his hands full, along with Rueben and Betsy, pushing and scolding and grabbing at collars. So he didn't notice right away that Leila had gone rigid as a post. By the time he did notice, she'd already started backing up, moving stiffly with tiny jerky steps, like a statue trying to walk. She kept backing up until she bumped into Cade's chest, then tried to back up some more, as if, he thought, she was trying to crawl inside his skin.

His first instinct was to wrap her in his arms and help her to do that any way he could. His heart was kicking like a crazy thing against her back and his skin had gone hot and prickly, as if he'd gotten too close to a fire.

Ignoring all that, he took her gently by her upper arms and moved her a couple of inches away from him, then leaned down to mutter gruffly in her ear. "They won't bite. They're just saying hello."

"Are they...yours?" Her voice was trying hard to be normal.

"Nah—they're Betsy's. She picks 'em up here and there. The woman can't resist a stray."

"I am sorry." The tiniest of tremors skated beneath his fingers. "I did not mean to be rude. I am not used to dogs—" she gave a breathless little laugh "—so *many* at one time."

Cade murmured, "Don't worry about it." His tongue felt thick and his thumbs wanted to stroke circles on the tender muscle hiding underneath the fabric of her jacket.

Meanwhile, Betsy and Rueben had managed to corral the dogs, not as many as they'd seemed, now that they were relatively still—only four, in fact. Somehow or other, Betsy managed to exchange her pair of dogs for Leila, and, cooing and fussing, maneuvered her through the pack and into the house. The front door closed firmly behind the two women, leaving Cade, Rueben and the dogs outside on the porch.

For several seconds the two men just stood there, saying nothing at all. Forgotten, the dogs scattered about their business, looking chastened or pleased with themselves, according to their various natures.

Cade cleared his throat and made a half turn. Rueben touched a hand to the top of his head and then, as if surprised to find it bare, resettled his hat into its customary place. He gave one shoulder a hitch. ''Give y'hand with the suitcases?''

''Naw, in a little bit.'' Cade started down the steps, Rueben clumping stiff-legged beside him. Cade glanced over at him. ''Things go okay while I was gone?''

Rueben hitched his shoulder again. ''Sure. No problems.''

At the bottom of the steps, both men turned by unspoken agreement and headed along the side of the house and around back toward the stables. ''Suki have her foal yet?'' Cade asked.

Rueben shook his head. ''Two...maybe three more days.''

''Yeah? How's she doing?''

''Doin' good...real good.''

That was as far as conversation went, until they reached the stables.

Cade went to check on Suki first, naturally. She was his best mare—dapple gray with a black mane and tail, charcoal mask and legs, a real beauty—and this would be her first foal. Not that he was worried. If Rueben said she was doing okay, then she was. But he looked her over anyway, because it made him feel good doing it, and he and Rueben discussed her condition and care the way they always did, which was mostly mutters and grunts with the absolute minimum number of actual words. Then he went out to the paddock to look over the rest of his stock—two mares with spring foals and three more pregnant ones due later in the summer.

He was leaning on the fence railing watching the foals trotting around after their dams, fuzzy little brush tails twitching busily at flies, when Rueben came to join him.

"Doin' real good," he said.

Cade nodded. He'd been wondering why the sight wasn't giving his spirits a boost the way it was supposed to.

"So," said Rueben after a silence, "you got married, huh?"

Cade surprised himself with a hard little nugget of laughter, which he gulped back guiltily. "Yeah…I guess I did."

"Pretty sudden."

He didn't try to stop the laugh this time. "You could say that."

Rueben mulled that over. "Pretty girl," he said after awhile, nodding his head in a thoughtful way.

Cade nodded, too. "Yeah…" and he changed the nod to a wondering little shake "…she is that."

"Seems nice," said Rueben. He stared hard at the toes of his boots, then kicked at the dirt a couple of times, and finally turned to offer Cade his hand. "Congratulations."

They shook, and Rueben gave his shoulder a hitch. "I'm gonna go get those suitcases now." He walked rapidly away in the bowlegged, rump-sprung way older men do when they've spent a good part of their lives sitting on the back of a horse.

Cade thought about going to help him, but for some reason didn't. He stayed where he was, leaning on the fence, watching the foals cavort in the sunshine, smelling the familiar smells of grass and straw and horse manure, feeling the humidity settle around him like a favorite old shirt. This was his world. It was where he belonged. It was good to be home. *Home…*

And then he thought, *What in heaven's name have I done?*

Having suffered through the pain of his parents' divorce at an age when his own adolescent struggles were just getting underway, he'd come to believe with all his heart and soul that if two people got married it ought to be forever. It was why he'd never been tempted to try it himself—he just didn't think he had it in him to make that kind of commitment. And here he was, not only had he gone and committed himself, but to a girl ten years younger, from the other side of the world, with whom he had nothing in common with, and barely knew!

He patted his shirt pocket, looking for the comfort of a cheroot, which Betsy wouldn't let him smoke in the house. Then, remembering they were still packed away in a suitcase, he gazed up into the milky haze and sighed.

It wouldn't have been so bad, he thought, but…well, it was what Rueben had said. Leila was a *very* pretty girl—downright beautiful, actually—but more than that, yes, she was *nice*. Sure, she was a princess, and spoiled and pampered and very, very young. But she had a bright and buoyant spirit. And he'd come to realize, even in the short time he'd known her, that she also had a kind and loving heart. She deserved someone who would love her back, someone who would make her happy. As he was certain he never would.

His chest swelled and tightened, suddenly, with that familiar surge of protective tenderness, and he brought his closed fist down hard on the fence railing. *Dammit,* he thought, *I can't do this to her. I can't.*

At the time, he remembered, it had seemed to him he'd had no choice. Converting…marrying Leila…it had looked like the only reasonable course of action open to him. But

that had been back *there,* in *The Arabian Nights* world of
Tamir. Here, with the green grass of Texas under his boots,
he knew it was impossible. Not so much the conversion—
he'd never had any particular religious beliefs one way or
another, so what difference did it make what label he carried? But marriage, now, that was different. Marriage involved somebody else, not just him. In this case, a nice,
lovely girl. A princess. *And a virgin princess, at that.*

His fist tightened on the fence railing. Somehow or other,
he was going to have to find a way out of this—for both
their sakes. And in the meantime…well, the very least he
could do, Cade figured, was see that the virgin princess
came out of this marriage in the same condition as when
she went in.…

It was late—almost midnight—and Leila was growing
more nervous and apprehensive by the minute. Surely, she
told herself, Cade would come soon. He *must* be tired after
such a long journey. Why did he not come to bed?

This was his bedchamber—bed*room*—she must remember to call it that, now that she was to be an American.
Betsy had told her so. "And yours, now, too," the round,
kind-faced woman had said, and had given Leila's hand a
happy squeeze.

Betsy's husband, Rueben, had brought her suitcases here
along with Cade's, and then Betsy had helped her with the
unpacking until it was time for her to go and prepare the
evening meal. She had even rearranged things in the dresser
drawers and spacious closets to make room for Leila's
things. So few things, really—she had left Tamir in such a
hurry. The rest of her belongings would be packed into
boxes and shipped to her later, though where she would
find room for them all here was a mystery to her.

But would she even need so many things…so many
beautiful clothes, hats, designer shoes…now that she was

married to Cade Gallagher and living in Houston, Texas? She didn't know. There were so many things she didn't know.

It had all happened so fast. She had barely had time to say goodbye to her mother and sisters, to Salma, and Nargis. Thinking about them now, she felt a frightened, hollow feeling, and for one panicky moment was afraid she might begin to cry. She took several deep breaths and blinked hard until the feeling went away. *I must not cry—what would Cade think?*

Perhaps it was just that she was so tired. It seemed a lifetime since she had slept. Cade's bed—big and wide and covered with a puffy comforter in masculine colors, a burgundy, blue-and-green paisley print—looked inviting. But Leila didn't dare to lie down. She didn't dare even sit. In fact, she had taken to pacing, not so much out of nervousness, although she definitely was, but because she was afraid if she stopped moving she would fall asleep. She had refused wine at dinner for the same reason—even the mild vintages at home made her sleepy.

Cade, she had noticed, drank strong black coffee with his meal, and afterward a small glassful of something the same golden brown color as his eyes. Bourbon, he said it was, when she asked. After that he had excused himself and gone into his study—to make some phone calls, he told her.

Betsy had shown her Cade's study, on her tour of the house. To Leila it had seemed the most fascinating of rooms, full of photographs and books and all sorts of personal things that belonged to Cade. There had been a photograph of Cade with his mother and father, taken when Cade was very young, and Leila remembered that Kitty had told her that Cade's mother and father were both dead. She had felt a warm little flash of sadness for the eager-looking golden-haired boy in the picture. There had been a black-

and-white photograph of a bearded man dressed in overalls, standing amongst a forest of tall wooden oil derricks— Cade's grandfather, Betsy had told her, and he had been a ''wildcatter.'' *What was a wildcatter?* Leila had longed to ask that question and so many others, to study the pictures and ask about them...to learn more about the stranger who was her husband.

But there had not been time, then. And after dinner Cade had gone into his study and Leila had dared not intrude.

Instead, she had gone alone to this, the bedroom they would share, to prepare herself for bed. And for her husband.

Butterflies. Oh yes, they were all over inside her, not just in her stomach, but everywhere under her skin. They had caught up with her in the bathroom she and Cade were to share, as she arranged her personal things, her bottles and jars of powders and scents, oils and lotions, her hair brushes, toothpaste and shampoo. There were two sinks, one of which, she assumed, was meant to be hers. The other, barely an arm's length away, was Cade's. And yes, there were *his* personal things, neatly arranged around it.

Daringly, unable to help herself, she picked up a bottle labeled Aftershave Lotion and sniffed it. So this is my husband's scent, she thought. But it was not yet familiar to her. She closed her eyes and tried to imagine him there next to her, brushing his teeth, shaving, patting the spicy lotion onto his smooth, clean skin...and all the while the butterflies frolicked merrily.

She tried to relax away the butterflies in a warm bath scented with jasmine, but although the water made her limbs and muscles feel warm and limp and heavy, the hard fluttery knot in her belly remained. And there was something else—a new, squirmy, quivery feeling between her legs. When she put her hand there and pressed against the quivering, she felt her pulse in the soft places beneath her fingertips, a slow, heavy pace.

She thought, then, about what Salma had told her, that there might be pain the first time she made love with a man. She thought of the bottle of soothing oil her former nanny, with tears in her eyes, had pressed into her hands as she was helping her to pack. A cold little gust of homesickness and dread swept through her, taking away the butterflies and leaving a great hollow void in their place.

I must not be afraid. A woman's first duty as a wife was to please her husband sexually. How could a man—how could Cade—find pleasure in sex if he knew that his wife was afraid? Clearly, there was only one thing to be done. *I must think of some way to not be afraid.*

And no sooner had she thought that, lying there in the water's warm embrace, with the sweet scent of jasmine melting into her pores and seeping into her senses, then here came the memories...vivid, tactile memories... sweeping away all thoughts of Salma and pain and homesickness and fear.

Cade's chest...a landscape of gentle hills and unexpected valleys her lips had explored like a greedy treasure hunter on the trail of lost gold...smooth, warm skin and a musky scent, unfamiliar but intoxicating as wine...the hard little buttons of his nipples...an intriguing texture of hair that tickled when she touched it with her nose....

The throbbing between her legs became heavier. She arched and squirmed sinuously as, under the water, her hands slid over her body, unconsciously following the same paths as the images in her mind. But, oh, what a difference there was between her own curves, and the hard planes and sculpted hollows of the male body she remembered...the body that invaded her thoughts, quickening her pulse and heating her cheeks at the most unexpected and inappropriate times. Cade's body. And now, her husband's.

My husband...will he desire me now? Now that I am his wife? Will he kiss me again the way he did that night on the terrace?

Her heart gave a sickening lurch, as though it were trying to turn upside down inside her chest. Trembling like some-one just risen from a sickbed, Leila climbed out of the bathtub and wrapped herself in a thick, soft towel. She dried herself quickly, ignoring the shivers, then bravely tossed aside the towel and naked, faced her blurred reflec-tion in the steam-fogged mirror. With her lips pursed in a thoughtful pout, she turned this way and that, trying to see herself from all angles. Yes...her breasts were full and yet still firm, with the nipples tightened now into hard, tawny buds...hips also full, but, she thought, not *too* wide...slender waist and firm, flat stomach...thighs well-muscled—probably from horseback riding—and her but-tocks, what she could see of them, round and smooth, and, she hoped, not *too* big.

Almost as an afterthought, with a defiant little flourish, she pulled out the combs and pins that held her hair high atop her head and let it tumble, thick and dark, down her back and over her shoulders. As she watched it her breathing quickened. Her lips parted and a rosy flush spread across her cheeks. The eyes that looked back at her in the mirror seemed to kindle and glow, as if from a fire some-where in their depths.

He kissed me. He desired me then, I know he did.

Confidence welled up in her like a fountain, and her thirsty soul found it more intoxicating, more erotic than wine. *He desired me once, and I will make him desire me again.*

Buoyed on a magic carpet of restored self-confidence and new resolve, Leila brushed her teeth and her hair and rubbed her skin with scented oil until it felt soft and smooth as silk. She put on a modest but alluring gown in a soft, shimmery blue-green—the color of the water in a shallow cove near the palace where she and her sisters liked to swim and sunbathe. Somewhere along the line she noticed that the butterflies had come back, although now it did not seem at all an unpleasant sensation.

I am ready, she thought as she paced nervously, glancing from time to time at the clock on Cade's bedside table. *Ready for my husband...*

It was half past midnight when she heard the creak and scuffle of footsteps outside Cade's bedroom door. Her heart skittered and bolted like the squirrel she had seen that afternoon in the lane as she watched the doorknob slowly turn and the door swish inward, silent and stealthy as a thief in the night, to frame the tall, imposing figure of her husband.

For a moment he hesitated, looking as if he wasn't sure whether he'd got the right room. Then he stepped through the doorway and carefully closed the door behind him. All the while his eyes never left her face, and they reflected the glow of the lamps she'd turned on low beside the bed so that they seemed to catch fire and flare hot as he looked at her.

Her stomach gave a lurch as the magic carpet of confidence she'd been riding on went into a steep crash dive.

Chapter 7

She was every man's dream. And Cade's worst nightmare.

He'd just about driven himself crazy, trying to think what he was going to do about this, his so-called wedding night. How did a man avoid consummating a marriage that never should have happened in the first place, without seeming to reject the woman he'd married and had already thoroughly humiliated once?

In the end, it had seemed to him that the best course of action was also the easiest one: Do nothing at all. If he stalled long enough, he reasoned, Leila was bound to fall asleep, as thoroughly jet-lagged as she must be. Then he could tiptoe in, snag his overnight bag and sneak off to the guest room, and his excuse would be that she needed her rest and he hadn't wanted to disturb her—what a considerate guy he was. Tomorrow morning early he'd be off to work, and after that—well, he had the pretty good excuse of a prior commitment, a weekend hunting trip to the ranch with a client he was trying to woo. No reason he couldn't arrange to fly out a day early, if the client was willing.

On Sunday when he got back, he'd sit Leila down and have a serious talk with her, and they could both try to figure out what they were going to do. By then, he told himself, they'd both be rested up and thinking clearly, and between them they ought to be able to come up with a way out of this farce with a minimum amount of embarrassment for all parties concerned.

It had seemed so reasonable to him, sitting there in his study sipping bourbon and enjoying a cheroot he knew he was going to catch hell for from Betsy tomorrow. He'd dozed a little bit in his chair and woken up stiff and groggy to find that it was well past midnight. Thank God, he'd thought, figuring there was no way in hell Leila would be awake at that hour. It ought to be safe to venture into his own bedroom.

Reeling with the effects of travel fatigue and whiskey, he'd mounted the stairs and made his way down the hallway, conscious of the silence all around him and his heartbeat ticktocking away like an old-fashioned grandfather clock. He was used to the silence of an empty house, but it was odd, he thought, how weighty silence seemed in a house that wasn't as empty as it should be. He was thinking about that, about the usual silence and emptiness of his house at night, when he turned the knob and pushed open his bedroom door.

Then his only thought was: Oh God, what now?

There she was, not only awake but looking like the overture to some erotic dream, a vision in sea-green silk that covered every inch but failed to disguise one centimeter of her curves, her hair cascading down around her shoulders like midnight rain. Every man's dream...his worst nightmare.

He didn't know how long he stood there in the doorway looking at her. Just looking at her, with all sorts of emotions shooting off in every direction inside him so that for a moment his brain function felt more than anything like an explosion in a fireworks factory. *Now what?* What was he supposed to say to her? He couldn't think of a thing.

It came to him gradually, as the shock subsided and his mind began functioning again, that he'd made a serious miscalculation. With all that had happened, he'd forgotten that, from almost the first moment he'd laid eyes on Leila Kamal, he'd wanted her.

He remembered it now. He remembered that the idea had amused him at the time, that he'd laughed at himself for his adolescent foolishness. He wasn't laughing now.

"You're still up," he finally said—as inane an observation as ever there was.

"I waited for you." She said it without a trace of seduction in her voice, facing him bravely with the light from a bedside lamp shimmering in her hair and making deep, dark mysteries of her eyes. She looked so incredibly beautiful...and nothing at all like the buoyant, flirtatious girl he remembered meeting in Tamir. Right now what she looked like more than anything was a virgin waiting to be sacrificed.

"You shouldn't have," he said, but in a gentle tone to temper the abruptness of it. He launched into his prepared justifications as he came into the room, keeping at a wary distance from her like a hiker circling a pit of quicksand. "Look...Leila. You've had a long day—you must be tired. I know I am." He stifled an ostentatious yawn. "I, uh...had a few things I needed to take care of—business things that couldn't wait." He brushed them aside with a diffident wave of his hand. "Things pile up when I'm away. I'm going to be doing a lot of catching up during the next several days...."

"Oh yes," she murmured, "I understand."

For some reason her acquiescence annoyed him, made him feel fraudulent and unworthy. He cleared his throat and ventured a look at her, squinting as if she were a light too bright for his eyes. He continued almost defiantly, "In fact, there's something—this weekend I have a thing I'm supposed to do—I promised a client I'd take him hunting out at the ranch."

A frown appeared between her eyebrows. "The...ranch?"

"Yeah—I told you about it—west Texas?"

"Oh—yes, yes—I remember." She sounded eager, now. "And you will fly there in your airplane?"

His insides writhed with guilt. Furious with himself for it, furious with her for making him feel it, he fought the urge to fidget and cleared his throat instead. "I'll be leaving tomorrow, actually. Straight from work. So I won't be—"

"Tomorrow?" He could hear a different breathiness in her voice now...unmistakable touches of panic.

"Look—I'm sorry. It's been scheduled for a while. It's a client—I couldn't very well cancel at the last minute." Cade chose that moment to escape into his bathroom, too cowardly to risk another look at her. He didn't need to see the shock, dismay and disappointment he knew would be written all over her face...that incredibly expressive face that sometimes seemed to him like watching a video tape on fast forward.

Just inside the bathroom doorway, again he stopped dead.

In only a matter of hours his bathroom had become an alien place. A lush and steamy greenhouse garden, redolent of all sorts of flowery, exotic scents, where jewel-toned bottles sprouted like mushrooms from the marble countertops and a rainbow of fabrics intertwined with the more subtle hues of damp towels bloomed in tropical profusion over every available surface.

Closing his mind to both the chaos and the disturbingly evocative smells, Cade set about gathering up the toiletries

Betsy had unpacked for him, putting them back in their travel case. And while he was doing that he went on glibly talking, telling Leila in a logical, reasonable way how he thought she should spend the time while he was gone, catching up on her rest, settling in, getting to know the place...

But not too well, he reminded himself. No sense in her getting too settled in and comfortable here. This "marriage" was only going to be temporary, after all.

Listening to himself talk like that, without Leila's disturbing presence to distract him and just the sound of his own voice and his reassuringly normal reflection glaring back at him from the mirrors, he could feel his self-assurance coming back. Everything he said sounded reasonable and sane—even logical and wise. And why shouldn't it? He was Cade Gallagher, successful Texas businessman, a self-made man who'd had his first few million under his belt before his thirty-fifth birthday. A man with a far-ranging and well-earned reputation as a deal-maker, a man who knew how to play the game—and win.

Play the game...and win.

It came to him then, a flash of self-awareness like a spotlight trained on a dark corner of his soul, just what had happened to him back there in Tamir. In the first place, he'd gone to Elena's wedding with a business deal in mind. Once there, he'd gotten so caught up in the game and so blinded by the idea of winning, he'd lost his perspective. In order to win the game he'd let himself be coerced into marrying a woman he didn't love, with whom he had nothing whatsoever in common.

But the truth was, he didn't need this "win." He didn't need the old sheik's oil deal. He'd made his millions right here in Texas, and there was plenty more where that came from.

He'd been an ambitious fool and had paid the price, but

all was not lost. He could still get out of this. He could still get his life back.

Just as long as he did not consummate this marriage.

That was it—the key to his deliverance. Because, from what he'd learned of Leila's culture so far, it seemed to him that when it came to marriage, it was all about the *consummation.* Even the *Walima,* the marriage feast, was to celebrate, not the wedding, but the consummation. The way Cade saw it, so long as he didn't make love to his wife, he wasn't even really married.

No problem. So what if she was one of the most beautiful and seductive women he'd ever seen in his life? He was thirty-six years old—a grown man, not a randy teenager. The image that looked back at him in the mirror was confident and mature...eyes world-weary, smile wry, eyebrows set at a sardonic tilt. Yes, he told himself, he had more than enough willpower, he ought to be able to resist one little black-eyed virgin princess.

He picked up his toiletry kit and turned around. And there she was, the virgin princess herself, standing in the bathroom doorway, filling it up so his only escape was going to have to be either through her or over her. Unless she moved out of his way, which she was showing no inclination to do.

As a test of that theory, he took a step toward her. Sure enough, she didn't budge an inch. Instead she watched him with great luminous eyes, and he saw her lips slowly part.

Apprehension shivered through his insides. He took another step...and another. Only a foot or so separated them now. And then she did move, but not away from him. Instead, she lifted one soft, scented hand and laid it alongside his jaw, a touch as cool and light as a flower. His heart began to pound.

''Leila—'' With no spit at all in his mouth, it was all the sound he could manage.

She didn't say a word, just touched one petal-like finger to his lips and shook her head. For a long and terrifying moment she looked deeply into his eyes, and he no longer felt the least bit logical or wise. Then she stretched way up on her tiptoes and kissed him.

His heart and stomach performed impossible acrobatic maneuvers and shimmers of panic danced behind his closed eyelids. His confidence had already evaporated. He snatched at a breath that seared the inside of his chest while every impulse and desire in him pleaded with him to give in…to kiss her back and then some. To carry her to his bed and make love to her for what was left of tonight and let tomorrow and the rest of his future—and hers—take care of themselves.

He might have done it. He wasn't sure what would have happened, in fact, if he'd had both hands free. As it was, while one hand, already tingling with anticipation of the feel of her, hovered indecisively inches from her shoulder, his other hand, filled with the small leather case that held his toiletries, made a lump, a slight but significant barrier between his chest and hers. One she couldn't ignore.

She drew back, one of her hands still resting on his shoulder, and looked down at it. After a long moment, her eyes came back to his. "I do not understand," she said in a husky voice. "These are your personal things. Why do you need them? Where are you taking them? Now… tonight?"

The air seemed to back up in Cade's chest. His tongue felt thick as he tried to explain. "I…uh, I thought I'd, you know, sleep in the guestroom—it's just across the hall…" Why did he feel like an inept thief trying to explain the goodies in his sack, an unprepared schoolboy without his homework?

"But, this is your bedcham—*bedroom.*" She wasn't touching him at all, now, but somehow he knew she was trembling. "Betsy told me. If you do not wish me—" She broke off suddenly, as if she'd been choked, and swallowed hard several times. Then he saw her body stiffen and her chin lift, and his own heart sank. With her face now pale and frozen as a statue, she said in a proud and quiet voice he'd never heard before, "If you do not wish me to sleep here with you in your bedroom, then you must tell me. It is I who should move to the guestroom, not you."

"It's only for tonight," he heard himself say, as his free hand doublecrossed him by lifting to her cheek. He felt himself brushing it with the backs of his fingers, and it was hot and smooth, like the skin of a ripe peach. What the hell was he doing? And why had he ever imagined this would be easy?

"We are both so tired," he gently explained, "and I'm pretty sure if we share a bed tonight, neither of us will get any sleep. There'll be other nights...." Was it a lie? He didn't even know for sure. And if it was, why did it come so easily to him? He wasn't—or never had been—a dishonest man. "We'll have plenty of time. When I get back. Tonight...you just rest, okay?" He ducked his head and touched his lips to her forehead. He'd never felt so confused and ashamed of himself. "Get some sleep," he said huskily, and walked away and left her there.

Leila woke up in a very large bed and for a moment could not think where she was. She felt sweaty and her heart pounded the way it had sometimes done when she was a very little girl, waking from a nightmare she could not remember.

But she was not a little girl, and there was no Salma to stroke her hair and kiss her cheek and tell her everything was all right. And besides, she remembered it all, now. She was in Texas, in America, and the wife of a man named

Cade Gallagher, whom she did not know. And did not understand at all!

In Tamir he had kissed her. She understood that well enough. He had desired her then—surely she had not been wrong about that. And now that she was his wife, he did not seem to want to kiss her at all.

And yet…he had been kind to her. Considerate, yes, and even tender. She stretched languorously, pushing her arms amongst the pillows, then lightly touched the place on her forehead where he had kissed her. The memory of his lips, how warm and smooth they had felt against her skin, made a startling little shiver go through her.

And—she realized it now, though she'd been too humiliated at the time to appreciate the fact—he'd actually proposed marriage to her to save her from public disgrace! A foolish thing to do, but in a way very sweet.…

Sweet? She remembered now—that was what Elena's friend Kitty had said about Cade. That he was sweet, like a… what was it? *A marshmallow?* Leila actually giggled; it had seemed then, and still did seem a very unlikely way to describe a man.

Maybe—the thought came suddenly—it was not such a good thing for a man to be *too* sweet. At least, not *all* the time.

But her outlook was brighter as she threw back the covers. She felt much more like her usual buoyant self. It was as Cade had said, that they both had been very tired yesterday, from all the traveling and the emotional stress of what had come before. Her husband had been right, and wise, to postpone consummating their marriage until they had both had a chance to rest and—how had he put it?— yes, *settle in.*

Little shivers rippled through her as she dressed for the day in cool gray slacks and a simple white blouse. *It is true—it has really happened. I am in America—in Texas!*

A married woman! Over and over she said those words to herself, adding to those another, perhaps incongruous thought, *I am free!*

She realized that for most women marriage might mean the opposite of freedom, but for her it seemed to promise endless possibilities. Yes, she was a wife, and she would work hard to be a good one. *But she was in America.* Here she could do anything—go to college, become a doctor, or a teacher—perhaps even a lawyer, or the head of her own company, like Elena. No longer would people laugh indulgently at her and treat her like a child. She was Mrs. Cade Gallagher, and she was in America. *She was free.*

She told herself these things, but in a state of fearful wonderment, not quite able to believe they were true—like a caged bird who hasn't yet realized that the door has been left open, or a child too young to grasp the fact that the wonderful new toys in the gaily wrapped packages are hers to keep. This is my house, she thought as she walked slowly down the curving staircase, trailing her fingers on the polished wood banister. *This is our home…mine and Cade's.* The thought produced more of those happy shivers, and she was biting her lip and smiling as she went into the kitchen, like a child with a secret.

Betsy was standing at the sink, stemming strawberries and singing along with the music from a radio turned down low. When Leila said ''Good morning!'' she turned with a little cry and a smile of welcome that made her cheeks look round as pomegranates. ''You're awake! I bet you're hungry. Sit down, sit down—I'll make you some lunch.''

''Lunch!'' Leila looked for a clock. ''What time is it?''

Betsy leaned sideways to peer at a digital clock on the back of a gleaming white stove. ''Almost two.''

''Two! In the afternoon? But—I have never slept so late!''

''Jet lag,'' said Betsy, waving a hand. ''Take you a couple days to adjust. Here—have some strawberries. They're pretty good right now—don't even need sugar. I thought I'd leave a bowl in the fridge for you—they'll be good for your breakfast tomorrow, too." She pushed a blue bowl heaped high with the berries over in front of Leila and put a fork beside it.

Leila picked up a berry with her fingers and closed her eyes as she bit into it, wondering how Betsy could have guessed that strawberries were one of her favorite foods.

"I guess Cade told you he's not going to be home tonight—got a business trip this weekend." Betsy sounded wary.

"Yes, I know." Leila picked up another berry. "This afternoon I think I would like to see the outside—the horses."

"You sure?" Betsy seemed relieved as she cocked an eyebrow. "It gets hot out there, middle of the afternoon."

"That is good, I like the heat," said Leila, showing her dimples. "It will make me feel as if I am at home."

Betsy gave her a doubtful, sideways look as she opened the refrigerator. "If you say so, hon."

Leila ate a delicious meal of strawberries and a chicken salad made with strips of roasted sweet red peppers and pecans, sitting in a breakfast room with a wall of windows that looked out on a swimming pool surrounded by lawns and flower gardens. Beyond that she could not see, because of course there were more trees, making walls of green all around the garden. She also drank a very delicious iced beverage made with tea and lemon and a great deal of sugar. *If I am not careful I will get fat, here in America,* she thought.

When she had finished her lunch, Leila opened a door in the breakfast room and stepped out onto a flagstone patio. Once again she gasped involuntarily when she felt the slap of hot, wet air, and heard Betsy call out from the kitchen, "I told you."

I keep forgetting about the humidity, Leila thought as she forced herself to breathe the thick, soupy air. But it was only a small thing, and she would get used to it.

She lingered at the pool, pausing to trail her fingers in the clear, tepid water and sniff some roses that had no scent. Then she set off briskly, following a flagstone pathway that led along the side of the house and through a wrought-iron gate. Just past the gate she came to the corner of the house, and there the walls of greenery ended. Interrupted by only a few very large trees and bisected by a curving gravel lane, the grassy ground swept away to the stables, which were made of wood, painted white with green trim. Beyond the stables were fields and paddocks of emerald green, ringed by white-painted fences, and in the paddocks she could see horses—mares with foals!—and Rueben, leaning on the fence, watching them.

Her heart quickened with excitement and she no longer noticed the heat and humidity. As she hurried along the gravel lane she was thinking, *These are Cade's horses— my husband's horses.* And, with a sense of awe, *Mine, too.*

As she came nearer to the paddock where the man stood vigil, she could see that it held only a mare with a mottled gray body, darker face and legs, and jet-black mane and tail.

"She is very beautiful," she said as she joined Rueben at the fence, keeping a respectful distance between them. She did not ask what was obvious, even to her, but after a moment said, "She will have her foal very soon, I think."

Rueben glanced briefly at her, as if she had surprised him, then looked back at the mare and nodded. "Maybe today…maybe tonight. Maybe tomorrow."

Leila didn't say anything, but her insides had those joyful shivers again. The birth of a foal—she had never seen such a thing. It must be the most wonderful thing that could happen, she thought. She wondered…she hoped…if she was very careful not to get in the way, if Rueben might let her watch.

But that would be later. Right now there was something else she wanted to ask him, and after a long and oddly comfortable silence, she did. "The horses that are here— are there any that may be ridden?"

He gave her that look of surprise. "You like to ride?"

"Oh, yes," Leila breathed, "very much."

Rueben lifted up a shoulder. "Okay, sure—we got a couple that're real gentle…" Leila didn't tell him that "gentle" was the last thing she wanted. "Not right now, though," said Rueben. "Too hot. Maybe this evening. Tomorrow morning."

"Thank you," said Leila. "I would like that very much. And…where can I ride? Only here, in the pastures…?"

"The pastures, sure." Rueben gave his shoulder another hitch. "There's a trail, too. Goes down along the creek."

Leila nodded, but didn't say anything. She was looking at the neat green paddocks with their white rail fences, and remembering her dream about riding across endless plains with the wind in her face and her hair blowing free. So, here I am in America, in Texas, she thought. But…where are the vistas?

"You want to ride, tell me," said Rueben. "I fix you up."

"Thank you," said Leila softly. She turned away from the paddocks and walked slowly back to the house.

She woke in the darkness and was strangely wide awake and rested. Jet lag, she thought, stretching her body in the great wide bed she had yet to share with her husband. *My days and nights are turned around.*

Knowing it would be useless to try to sleep any longer,

she threw back the covers and got out of bed. Without turning on the light she made her way to the window and stood with her arms around herself, looking out on the shadowy, dark landscape.

"This is Texas...America."

She said the words deliberately as she had been saying them over and over to herself all day, but they failed to give her those joyous and optimistic shivers. Around her the house was empty and still, and there was a hollow feeling of loneliness inside her. She missed Tamir, and the palace that was always so full of people—her family, the servants. She remembered that she had sometimes had to steal away to secret corners of the gardens to find moments to herself. Now, as the silence of the house pressed in around her, she would have given almost anything for the sounds of laughter...people's voices.

But...there—surely that was a light! She peered into the thick gray darkness, trying to see through the deeper blackness of trees, remembering that earlier she had seen glimpses of the stables through the leaves and branches. Excitement gave a kick beneath her ribs. Rueben had told her the mare, Suki, would have her foal soon. *Maybe today...maybe tonight...*

Without stopping to think whether or not she should, Leila turned from the window and was already pulling her nightgown over her head. She dressed quickly in the same slacks and blouse she'd worn that day, slipped bare feet into her shoes and ran down the stairs. At the back entrance she remembered just in time to turn off the security alarm before opening the door.

This time she was ready for the warm, wet slap of humidity. What she hadn't expected was the noise. Inside the well-insulated and air-conditioned house she hadn't realized how loud the night was, in this place of so many trees and lush vegetation, so many ponds and fields and streams.

All around her the night was filled with sounds—busy sounds, ratcheting, chirping, hooting, clicking, screeching sounds.

After the first surprise, Leila decided she liked the racket. *And here I thought that I was alone.* She almost felt like singing along with the night creatures herself as she found her way along the flagstone path. To be out alone in the night gave her shivery feelings of excitement, anticipation and a delicious sense of adventure.

She unlatched the gate and slipped silently through. And her nice little shivers exploded all through her muscles like slivers of steel. Her scalp bloomed with prickles and her heart rocketed into her throat. All of a sudden the night was full of large warm bodies, wiggling, snuffling shifting bodies, pressing in on her from all sides. As her back slammed against the gate she sucked in air and whispered, "Oh—good dogs...nice...dogs..."

Something warm and wet slapped the back of her hand—then the other hand as well. She moved her fingers and felt them burrow through silky-soft fur. She could hear coming from the squirming, waggling shapes little whines and whimpers and panting sounds that sounded like laughter. Friendly sounds.

Taking a deep breath and summoning her courage, she pushed away from the gate and took several tentative steps. The dogs moved with her, arranging themselves in front and in back and on both sides of her, keeping just out of range of her feet as she walked. Just like my father's bodyguards, she thought, as the last vestiges of her fear slipped away.

The dogs followed her to the stable door, but made no move to go inside with her. Clearly, they knew this was not allowed.

Although the lights were on in the stable, no one was inside. Finding her way through a stall filled with sweet, clean straw, Leila found herself in the paddock where she had seen the mare, Suki, that afternoon. There, in a corner of the paddock just to the left outside the doorway in which she stood, by the light leaking through the stall's half doors, she could see the mare's pale shape lying on the darker grass. Rueben was there, too, crouched on one knee with his fingers braced on the ground, like a runner at the start of a race.

Leila ventured toward them as silently as she knew how. Rueben glanced at her as she crouched down beside him, but without much surprise—almost, it seemed to her, as if he had expected her to come.

"She's not doin' so good," he said in a low voice.

"What is the matter?" Leila breathlessly whispered back.

"Got halfway and quit. Happens sometimes. I think she'll be okay, though—just have to give her a little help."

"Help?"

"Yeah...gonna pull a little bit. She should start pushing on her own then."

"Should she not be inside, in the stable?" Leila's heart was beating very hard.

Rueben lifted one shoulder in his familiar shrug. "She's where she wants to be. Horses are meant to have their babies in the open. It's their nature. If the weather's bad, I bring her inside. When it's nice like this, I let her choose." He pushed himself up from his crouch. Leila did the same.

"What can I do to help?" she whispered.

He nodded toward the mare, who had her head up and was quietly watching them. "You can keep her calm, if you want. Just pet her...talk to her. Rub her under her jaw, like this..."

Leila nodded and began to move cautiously toward the mare's head, crooning to her softly in Arabic, the language her nanny had used to soothe her when she was a baby.

Her heart hammered and her lungs ached as she felt the slick, warm horsehide beneath her fingers, and smelled the familiar salty horse-smell. The mare gave a little whicker of uncertainty as Leila began to stroke her sweat-damp neck, but didn't try to rise. "Beautiful, noble lady…" Leila murmured. "You must be strong…you must have the courage of a lioness."

The mare grunted. Leila felt the surge of powerful muscles, and then a groan that seemed to come from deep inside the mare's belly.

"That's it—she's pushin' good now," said Rueben after a moment, panting a little. "Okay…okay—that's good. Let her go—she'll do it herself now, I think."

Leila pushed herself away from the mare's surging body and scrambled around to join Rueben just in time to see the foal's body slither onto the grass like a puddle of spilled ink.

"Nice filly," said Rueben. "Nice big girl."

"Is she all right?" Leila asked fearfully. The foal had not moved. Leila's heart was knocking painfully; she felt as if she could not breathe. "Is she…dead? She is not breathing."

"She'll be okay." Rueben pulled his white T-shirt off over his head. "Here—wipe her head a little bit," he said as he tossed it to her.

Then she was on her knees in the wet grass, trying not to shake as she wiped frantically at the film of mucus that covered the foal's mouth and nose. Sweat trickled down her sides, dripped from her nose and ran stinging into her eyes. She kept making desperate little whimpering noises, but didn't realize then that she was crying. Not until the foal suddenly jerked her head up and shook it hard, her long ears making a slapping sound against her neck.

"She'll be fine now," said Rueben, as Leila collapsed

backward onto the seat of her pants with a loud, quivering sob.

But she was laughing, too. Laughing and sobbing as she gathered the newborn foal's head into her arms and pressed her cheek to its soaking wet hide.

Chapter 8

Betsy and Rueben were in the kitchen when Leila came down to breakfast the morning after the birth of the foal. She'd heard their voices and didn't mean to listen in, but then she'd heard her own name and naturally that made her hesitate.

"I wish you could have seen her, Bets. That black hair of hers—you couldn't tell which was her and which was the filly."

Rueben's chuckle was lost in a loud metallic clang. "I wish *he* could have seen her, that's what *I* wish. He should have been here." Betsy's voice sounded angry. "Ooh, sometimes that man… Brings home a new bride and then goes off and leaves her!"

"He said it was business." She couldn't see it, but Leila knew Rueben had lifted a shoulder in his special little shrug.

"Huh. He couldn't cancel it? Just once? What kind of thing is that to do? Go off and leave his bride all alone… And such a nice girl, too. Really sweet, you know?"

Leila had gone into the kitchen, then, and her cheeks were hot and her heart beating fast.

Now it was Sunday afternoon, and Leila was lying on a chaise longue beside the pool, remembering that conversation from two mornings ago, and the moment that followed when she had walked into that room that was flooded with sunlight and the warm smells of coffee and bacon and toast.

Rueben had been at the sink preparing a large plastic bottle with a long red rubber nipple on it for the new foal, because, he said, the mare's milk wasn't comin' in so good yet, and maybe Leila would like to help him feed the baby in a little while. Betsy's eyes had lit with welcome and her smile had been warm.

Leila remembered the strange little lump of yearning that had come into her throat just then, the sting of lonely tears that she had blinked hastily away. Because she understood that she had interrupted a moment of special intimacy between these two long-married people—she knew because she had encountered such moments between her own parents, many times before. There was such *ease* between them. She could hear it in their voices—trust and understanding, respect and friendship. It was, she thought, just what a marriage should be like. It was what she wanted *her* marriage to be like.

But…what of her marriage? Would she and Cade ever know that kind of ease? Right now such a thing seemed impossible.

Hopelessness settled over her, more oppressive than the midday heat. She'd managed to keep it at bay the past two days, spending most of her time in the stables with Rueben, working with the new foal. Oh, and she'd been riding, too, and was getting more and more comfortable with Western-style saddles. At night she watched old movies on television until she fell asleep on the sofa.

But now, lying on her stomach beside the swimming pool with the sun like a hot anvil between her shoulders and her forehead resting on her hands, she could not stop the tears from seeping between her eyelids. She had never, even as a child in those first wretched months of boarding school, been so lonely.

Because today was Sunday, Rueben and Betsy had the day off. Rueben had come early to feed the horses and then had gone off to his home on the other side of the pasture, taking the dogs with him. Betsy had left fruit salad and cinnamon rolls for Leila's breakfast, and deviled eggs and sliced ham and tomatoes stuffed with tuna salad and sliced strawberries to eat with ice cream for later. She would be cooking at home today, she had told Leila, because her kids were coming over. According to Betsy, she was going to have a "houseful." *You should come on down,* she had said to Leila. *You should come and join us.*

But Leila had not wanted to intrude on their day off, on their family's time together.

Now she thought that she had been very foolish to say no. Proud and foolish. Because of course she would not have been intruding at all. If there was one thing she had learned in these past few days, it was that Rueben and Betsy Flores had hearts as big as the wide-open spaces Leila had come to Texas expecting to find. They would welcome her with open arms, she was sure of it. And if she was feeling lonely and sorry for herself right now, then she had only herself to blame.

She could hear them down there now, on the other side of the pasture. If she stilled her own breath she could hear distant music—sometimes Mexican music and sometimes American country and western music. She could hear shouts and laughter.

Finally she could stand it no longer. She rolled over and sat up. A particularly loud burst of laughter at that moment settled her resolve; she would *not* play this role she despised—the pitiful abandoned bride. She was Princess Leila of Tamir. She had been invited to a party, and she would go.

She was in America, now. She could do whatever she pleased.

She rose and dressed quickly, putting on a brightly colored wraparound skirt and a loose-fitting T-shirt over her modest one-piece bathing suit. She had braided her hair for swimming, one long braid that hung straight down her back. It would do fine as it was, although she did dip her hands in the pool and smooth back the loose wisps of hair around her face. Then she slipped into her sandals and set out.

She walked briskly, following the well-trodden path she had seen Rueben use, past the stable, along the paddock fences, then through a gate and straight across the pasture. Almost at once she could feel her spirits lift; it was not Leila's nature to be gloomy for long. And it was not so humid today. There had been a little rain in the night, and this morning some leftover mist and fog, but that had blown away in a light cool breeze and now the sky was a bright blue patterned with a few billowy clouds. The pasture was spotted with little yellow flowers, and white butterflies fluttered dizzily among them as if they had been sipping fermented honey. Once a bird flashed by in front of her, a stunning streak of blue that made her gasp in wonderment.

The pasture sloped gently downhill. Soon, in the little valley just beyond the lower fence, Leila could see trees, and the pale gray roof of a long, low house made of red bricks. Near the house, in the shady spaces between the trees, she saw a volleyball net, a metal stove for cooking outdoors and long tables laden with food. And people. People seemed to be everywhere, gathered around the stove and the tables or sitting in chairs under the trees. Some

held babies, or watched indulgently while small children
played on the grass near their feet. Older children darted
here and there among the adults, and a few were hitting a
ball back and forth across the net.

All four dogs bounded out to greet Leila as she came
through the gate from the pasture. Then someone else noticed her and called out, "Ma—you got company!"

A door to a screened porch opened and Betsy came out,
wiping her hands on a huge apron. When she saw Leila
she threw her hands up in the air and gave a squeal of
welcome. "Oh, good—you changed your mind. I'm glad
you came. Come here—come and meet my kids. Hey,
everyone, look who's here—it's Cade's new wife! Everybody—this is Leila."

There were squeals of amazement and surprise: "*What?*
Cade got *married?* When did that happen? I don't believe
it!"

Shouts of welcome: "Hey, Leila—you're just in time,
food's almost ready. Hey, Leila, come on down! Hi, Leila,
hope you like chili..."

Betsy began to point to people left and right and call out
names. A few of the children she got wrong, which made
her clap a hand to her forehead while everyone laughed
and teased her about losing her memory. Leila's head was
spinning. How many children did Rueben and Betsy have?
She had lost track of who was married to who, and she
knew she would never remember anyone's name, but it did
not seem to matter. She knew nobody really expected that
she would.

A brown, stocky boy of about ten, wearing only a pair
of blue jeans that had been cut off above the knee, came
running up just then, yelling, "Gramma—Gramma—can
we go swimming?" He was flushed and sweaty from playing volleyball and wore an expression of extreme pain on
his face as he pleaded, "*Please?*"

Betsy gave him a stern look, which it was clear no one believed. She called across the yard to where Rueben and several younger men were gathered around the metal cook stove. "Hey, guys—how soon is dinner gonna be ready?"

Somebody lifted the lid of the stove, peered into it then yelled back, "'Bout half an hour…maybe little bit more."

Betsy put a heavy hand on the boy's head and glared at him. "Okay, but just a quick one, you hear me? If your momma says okay…"

The boy was already dashing off across the grass, yelling at the top of his lungs, "Mom—Gramma says it's okay! Hey, you guys, did you hear that? We can go swimming!"

"Where do they swim?" Leila had not seen a pool. Perhaps she should invite the children to swim in Cade's—in *her* pool.

But Betsy waved a hand toward a thick, dark bank of trees. "Oh, there's a place down at the creek where they like to go. Been there a long time."

"That's where I learned to swim," said one of Betsy's daughters, and another chimed in, "Yeah, I think we all did."

Leila gazed at them with a combination of fascination and doubt. She and her sisters had enjoyed swimming in the sea, in a secluded cove near the palace, but she could not imagine how one would swim in a murky creek, among all those trees. "May I…see this place?" she asked, both hesitant and eager.

"Oh, *sure!* Yeah, go on—it's nice!" several voices immediately responded, and Betsy added, with another wave of her hand, "Go right on down—the kids'll show you. Just follow all the hollering."

Leila hesitated only a moment more, her lower lip caught between her teeth and her breath quickening. Then she set off after the disappearing children, and after the first few steps broke into a light, skipping run.

Following shrieks and shouts of glee, she made her way along a well-worn pathway across the lawn and into the trees, and soon came to a place where the creek widened into a small pond, where large rocks and very old trees fought each other for space along the mossy banks and sunlight sparkled on the dark surface of the water. Leila caught her breath and laughter bubbled up in her throat as she watched children of all shapes and sizes hurl themselves into the water from the rocks and low-hanging branches, arms waving, legs pumping, smooth brown bodies gleaming in the sun. Entranced and envious, she crouched down on one of the rocks with her skirt over her knees and her arms wrapped around them and watched the children surface, slick and agile as otters, blowing and wiping water from their faces, laughing and splashing one another.

"Look," one of them cried suddenly, pointing at Leila, "it's that lady."

Several of the children drifted toward Leila's rock to gather in a half circle around her, curious and friendly as a school of dolphins.

"Hey, are you gonna swim with us?"

"You can come in—it's deep enough. See?" To demonstrate, several of the children sank beneath the surface, like dolphins sounding, to rise again seconds later blowing water and wiping grins with their small brown hands.

"Come and swim with us, lady. It's not too cold—a little bit, but it's fu-u-n!" And again they subsided, amidst waves and splashes and shrieks of laughter.

Oh, Leila thought, if only I could!

And then she thought: Why can't I? There were no men around, only children, and besides, she was in America now. Such things were permitted here.

Almost as quickly as the thought formed in her head, she was slipping off her sandals and pulling her T-shirt over her head, and her teeth were clamped on her lower lip to hold back laughter. The wraparound skirt was still settling into a multicolored puddle on the rock as she jumped. She felt for only an instant the rush of soft air, and then the water's cool and delicious embrace. Her lungs contracted; her feet met the sandy bottom of the pond. She pushed herself upward and exploded from the surface with a gust of breath and a cry of delight. Several of the children paddled around her, blending their giggles and squeals with hers and looking as pleased as if Leila were a protégé of whom they were especially proud.

"See?" they cried. "We told you—it's fun, huh? And look what I can do—can you do this? Watch me—I can do a backward somersault, can you?"

And for a short and wonderful time, Leila became one of them, those anonymous, exuberant children. Never in her life had she felt so free, not even when she herself had been a child such as they. For a short and wonderful time she did not think at all about the stranger she had married who did not seem to desire her, or the home and family she had left behind.

It seemed as if Cade had been hit with just one surprise after another. Ever since, returning from his hunting trip several hours earlier than expected, he'd walked into his house and found it empty. That had been the first surprise. The second had come when he'd realized how much he minded.

It wasn't that he wasn't used to coming home to an empty house; most days, by the time he got home from work, Rueben and Betsy would be long gone and his dinner left for him, wrapped and microwave-ready in the refrigerator. And he *sure* didn't plan on getting used to having a little wife waiting for him, either. The wife was a temporary circumstance; he'd already made that decision, it was just a matter of finding the right time and place to finalize everything with Leila.

So why today did his house seem to ring with silence? What was this strange heaviness he felt in his chest as he wandered from room to room, calling the name of someone he hadn't even known ten days ago? Could it possibly be…disappointment? Had he actually been looking forward to seeing her again?

Ridiculous. The denial came so quickly it bordered on panic. Hell, he told himself in disgust, I'm responsible for the girl. If she's run off, or been kidnapped… *Ridiculous.*

Nevertheless, it was with as much relief as exasperation that he discovered the towel-draped chaise longue beside the pool and the backyard gate open. That, together with the salsa music he could hear pumping up from the Flores' place gave him the obvious answer. Rueben and Betsy were having one of their family barbecues, and Betsy, being the mother hen she was, would have insisted on inviting Leila. Mystery solved.

Less easy to explain—if Cade had bothered to try—was the fact that he didn't even take time to shower and shave and change out of his ranch clothes before setting out for the Flores' place. Before going to find his wife.

Nobody noticed when he came through the pasture gate; everyone in the Flores' yard was gathered around the food tables, loading up their plates with hot dogs and hamburgers, spare ribs and chicken, potato salad, cole slaw and, of course, Rueben's special five-alarm Tex-Mex chili.

Cade had been to enough of Rueben and Betsy's gatherings to know that for the next ten or fifteen minutes or so, nobody was going to be paying attention to anything but food, so instead of announcing himself right away he paused and leaned a shoulder against the trunk of a pin oak tree.

He was feeling just a tad wistful, as he always did when

he saw their family together like this and thought about how lucky Rueben and Betsy were. They'd known each other forever, just about, had grown up together and knew each other so well. Theirs was a great marriage. A great family. The kind of marriage, the kind of family Cade would have chosen for himself, if he'd had any say in the matter. The kind he'd never had, and finally accepted he probably never would have.

Definitely not with Leila.

He straightened abruptly and lightened the heaviness inside him with a breath while his eyes searched for her in the crowd.

She wasn't easy to find. Naturally, with that black hair of hers she'd blend right in with this Flores bunch as if she belonged there. When he finally did spot her, in the thickest part of the crowd around the food table, it was because he'd heard somebody call out her name.

"Hey Leila—you ever eat chili?"

"Chilly?" Her voice was unmistakable and instantly recognizable to him—another surprise—and musical as a flute. "I do not think so. This means cold, no?"

There was laughter, and someone yelled, "I don't *think* so!"

Then there was a clamor of voices explaining, urging Leila to try some chili…some warning her not to. Cade had moved unconsciously closer, alert as a bird dog on point as he tried to see what was happening in the center of the knot of people gathered around the chili pot. He was a little apprehensive, too—Rueben's chili was notorious. After eating a bowlful Cade didn't stop sweating for hours. And he was used to the stuff.

An expectant silence had fallen around the food table. Cade found that his heart was beating faster. He really did wish he could have seen Leila's face when she tasted that chili.

And then the knot of people seemed to loosen and shift, as if everyone had decided to give her a little more breathing room. And suddenly he *could* see her face—perfect oval, breathtakingly lovely, smooth and fresh as a child's—as she lifted a spoonful of the rich, red-brown chili to her mouth. Cade's heart gave a kick, then seemed to stick at the bottom of his throat, thumping away to beat the band while Leila chewed and the suspense grew. Cade held his breath along with everyone else while a tiny frown etched itself between her eyebrows. Then she tilted her head, and her lilting, slightly husky voice carried even to where he stood.

"It is very good...." she said, still with that uncertain little frown, and now she was turning her head, as if she were looking for something, there on the table "...but I think I would like—yes, *there*—what are those little yellow peppers called? Jalapeños—yes. I think I would like some more jalapeños in mine, please."

There were shouts of amazement and laughter from everyone, and smatterings of applause which Leila acknowledged with a winsome display of dimples. Cade let out the breath he'd been holding. He was smiling in spite of himself. The suspense had broken, so why was his heart still beating so hard and so fast? And why this growling in his stomach when he wasn't hungry?

"Hey, Cade—hey, Ma, look who's here! Come on over, Cade, grab yourself a plate."

His cover blown, he grinned, shrugged and pushed away from the tree trunk. But while the grin, shrug and a little deprecating wave of his hand were for the assembled crowd, his gaze stayed where it had been, on Leila. So he knew exactly the moment her body stiffened and the dimpled smile froze on her face, when the liveliness drained out of her so that she seemed to become a flat black-and-white photograph of herself.

So, he thought dismally, she isn't exactly happy to see me. Did that surprise him? Why would he expect her to be? But his heartbeat now was a slow, dirge-like pulse, and his breath tasted bitter in his throat.

The knot of Flores' family loosened and Leila came toward him, carrying her plastic plate in both hands, carefully, like a child. And it seemed to Cade that she carried herself the same way. *With constraint.* Yes, that was the word he was thinking of—as if she held her natural exuberance under a tight rein. But a moment ago with the Flores bunch she'd been lighthearted and free as a bird, so it was pretty obvious she felt that constraint only because of *him.*

He felt heavy, suddenly. And his heart hurt, as if the heaviness was right there, pressing in all around it.

"I did not expect you until later." Her voice sounded breathless, although her face remained pale and calm.

He shrugged that aside. "Hunting was lousy and the power went out at the ranch, so we decided to leave early." He nodded his head toward her. "Looks like you've been having fun."

It had just occurred to him that she was wet, under the loose oversized T-shirt she was wearing. Her hair hung in a thick, sodden braid down her back, except for tiny spikes and tendrils around her face and neck that had begun to dry. The T-shirt clung to the dark wetness of the bathing suit, outlining her breasts in bold relief, and it came to him with a small sense of shock that until that moment he'd had no idea what her body was actually shaped like. That one glimpse made him feel the way he did when he was good and hungry and smelled Betsy's bread baking in the oven.

"I have been, yes." Leila said, responding to something he barely remembered saying, and she was nodding earnestly, obviously completely unaware of the direction his

gaze—and his thoughts—had been taking. "Betsy and Rueben have such a nice family, have they not? They have
been very kind to me, all of them. Even though," she
added, showing him a brief glimpse of dimples, "I do not
think I will remember any of their names."

"I see you've been swimming," Cade said bluntly.

Her eyes flicked downward toward her own chest, then
jumped quickly back to his. Her lips parted in dismay. Letting go of her plate with one hand, she plucked the shirt
away from herself as color blossomed slowly in her cheeks,
going almost imperceptibly from delicate to sublime, like
a sunrise.

"Yes—with the children. In the creek. Was this all
right?"

"What? Sure, it's all right."

"You do not mind?" Again her voice sounded breathless.

"Why should I mind?" His voice sounded angry, though
he wasn't. And damned if his heart wasn't beating too fast
again. As if they were having an argument. Which they
weren't, not as far as he was concerned. He wasn't so sure
about her.

"I am very glad you do not." Her head was high and
her eyes seemed to flare and blaze like coals, with something that looked like defiance—though he couldn't think
what she might be in defiance of. *He'd* never told her she
couldn't go swimming—or anything else, for that matter.
And he had no intention of ever doing so. He was her
husband, dammit, not her father, even if she was ten years
younger than he was.

"Because I liked being with the children," Leila went
on. "Very much. I like children. I would like—" She broke
off and looked away, and her throat moved with a swallow.
He knew she'd meant to say more, but had no idea what it
might be.

I want to have children. A lot of children—like Betsy and Rueben. I want to have your children, Cade Gallagher.

A little shudder quivered through Leila as she realized that she had almost said such a thing out loud. Perhaps, she thought, it is wrong for a wife to be too proud with her husband. But she was not only a wife, she was a princess, and she could not—she would not say such a thing to a man, husband or not, who did not seem to want to make babies with her at all.

"Have you been to this place where the children swim?" she asked after a moment, watching him from under her lashes. "Did you swim there also, when you were a child?"

"What?" Cade was staring at her with that fierce, rather puzzled frown. "Oh—no. I only bought this place about six years ago. Rueben and Betsy came with it—Rueben had worked for the previous owner forever. Most of their kids grew up in this house. But no, I never swam there when I was a kid."

In spite of the photograph she had seen in his study, Leila could not imagine Cade as a little boy, with knobby arms and legs and a lean brown body, golden hair dark and slick as a seal's, leaping and splashing and squealing with pleasure, like Betsy's grandchildren. Not this man, with a face so rugged and shoulders so broad, in his cowboy hat and blue jeans, and whiskers beginning to show on his chin. What was it Samira had called him? Oh yes. *Imposing.* It would be hard, she had said, not to be intimidated by such a man.

But Leila Kamal would *not* be intimidated, not by *any* man.

"You do not have to be a child to enjoy this swimming place," she said with a lift of her chin. "I am not a child."

He did not answer. For a long moment he just looked at her, and she realized suddenly that her mouth and throat felt dry. She saw Cade's throat move as if he had swallowed, and then she wanted to swallow, too. She felt hot in spite of the wet bathing suit she wore under her clothes, a peculiar heat that filled all her insides in ways that even Rueben's famous Texas chili had not.

"Hey, Cade, come on, man—better get yourself a plate, before it's all gone."

Leila jerked as if she'd been roused from a daydream. Rueben was coming toward them across the grass, carrying a long fork with two prongs and leather strips hanging from the handle. He looked younger today, she thought, less shy than he usually did.

Cade put out his hand and shook the older man's. "Ah, thanks, Rueben, but I better take a raincheck."

Rueben looked at him as though Cade had gone insane. "What, are you kidding me? We got plenty—steaks, chili…come on, you gotta eat something."

Cade was laughing, but also shaking his head. "No, really—I had a sandwich at the airport. I just came to collect my…wife." Leila glanced at him curiously. His smile seemed as though it had been carved from wood.

Rueben nodded toward Leila. "Hey—she tell you already?"

"No…tell me what?" Then Cade caught a breath and snapped his fingers. "Suki had her foal."

"Yup," said Rueben. "Nice little filly. Think she's gonna look just like her mama."

"How is she? Everything go okay?" This was man-talk, and Leila saw that Cade had already turned toward Rueben, automatically excluding her.

Leila was used to that kind of treatment. But before she could even begin to feel her usual frustration and resentment, Rueben had begun to back away. "Hey, let *her* tell you about it," he said. "She was there." Then he glanced over at Leila and, to her complete amazement, *winked.* "Lucky she was, too. Suki couldn't of done it without her.

"Well—hey, I gotta get back to my burgers—see you in the morning, boss." And he hurried off to join his family, agile in spite of his funny disjointed walk.

Leila looked at Cade, who was frowning at her as if she were a strange creature, perhaps in a zoo. He cleared his throat. "What the hell did he mean by that?"

Leila smiled, showing her dimples. "Oh, I think he was making a joke." But pleasure was flooding through her, warming her insides the way a hot drink does when the weather is cold. "I helped a little—but only a *very* little. I only spoke to her—in Arabic. I think she liked that—"

"Who, the foal?"

"No, Suki—the mare. And I petted her while Rueben pulled on her feet—"

"Suki's?"

Leila gave a little crow of laughter. "The *foal's*. Then, after she was born, I had to wipe her nose and mouth so she could breathe. And later I fed her with a bottle because her mother did not have milk for her right away. But she is fine now. And—oh, Cade—she is so beautiful. You must see her. May we go to see her now?" And she checked in surprise, because they were standing in front of the pasture gate and she had not even realized that they had been walking.

Just then someone noticed them leaving. Many voices called out goodbyes, and Leila waved and answered with thank-yous and promises to come back and visit again some time. Cade waved absently as he opened the gate and held it for her.

"Maybe you'd better tell me about it," he said gruffly as they started up the gentle slope, walking together, side by side. His feelings were mixed, and very confusing.

He kept glancing at her as she talked, stimulated in unexplainable ways by that little burr of roughness in her voice, entranced by the way her dimples came and went, like a

baby playing peek-a-boo. His heartbeat had quickened
again, and he knew it was not from the exertion of the
climb. He told himself he was glad to see the color back
in her cheeks and the bounce in her step. He told himself
he was happy to see the dimples again, and hear the musical
peal of her laughter. But there was a place inside him...a
kernel of disappointment...a leaden little cloud that
wouldn't let him forget. *It's not me. It's not me. It's Suki
and the foal that's made her happy, not me.*

Happy? What about that? *Was* she happy? Whether it
was Rueben and Betsy's clan, or Suki and her foal that had
made her so or not, right now it sure as hell seemed as
though she was. Uncertainty filled Cade's belly. His resolve
to undo this crazy marriage, based as it was on the justifi-
cation that Leila wasn't and could never be happy with him,
trembled....

She stopped in the stable long enough to fill a can with
grain for Suki. Cade stood in the doorway of the stall and
watched her cross the grassy paddock, graceful as a nymph
in her long wraparound skirt and sandals, T-shirt knotted
at one hip, dark braid swaying as she walked. She approached the dappled gray mare confidently, murmuring in
a musical language he assumed must be Arabic. How exotic
she is, he thought. And yet...somehow she wasn't. That
sunny paddock, beautiful gray mare and beautiful woman,
spindle-legged black foal butting at her back... Cade had
never considered himself a connoisseur of art, but he
thought if someone were to paint this scene, it would look
incredibly beautiful...and exactly right.

"She thinks I am her mother," Leila said to Cade as he
joined her, laughing as the foal again butted impatiently at
her hip. "Because I fed her with a bottle. No, no, little one,
you must drink from your own mama now." And she bent
down to encircle the foal's neck with her arms and press
her face to the fuzzy black hide.

The hollow feeling in Cade's belly pushed into his chest, and he struggled to haul in a breath for which he had no room. "I've been thinking," he said, and because it was a lie—the idea had only that moment come to him—his voice was scratchy and filled with gravel. Still cradling the foal, she looked up at him, waiting with bright and expectant eyes. "I haven't given you your bride gift—what do they call it?—the *mahr?*"

She nodded, frowning a little. "The *mahr,* yes."

Cade tipped his head toward the foal. Nerves jumped in his belly. "She's yours, if you want her. For your bride gift."

He was unprepared when Leila sucked in air in a cry that sounded more like grief than joy. Unprepared, too, for the tears that suddenly glistened in her eyes. She looked so stricken, in fact, that he tried to apologize. "I know it isn't jewelry, or money—"

"I have no need for jewelry or money! Oh, Cade—she is so beautiful—this is the most wonderful bride gift—more wonderful than I ever dreamed of." She buried her tear-wet face in the foal's coat, then as quickly was smiling up at Cade again. "I will name her—*may* I name her?"

"She's yours," Cade said gruffly. "You can do anything you like."

"Then I will name her Sari," she said with a fierce, impassioned joy. "In Arabic it means, 'most noble.'" She turned to face him squarely then, smiling with a radiance that took his breath away. "Thank you, Cade. Thank you for my bride gift." And she stepped forward, put her hands on his unshaven jaws, and kissed him.

Chapter 9

Her lips were warm and soft, but with an enticing little bite to them that he recognized, even in that moment of shock, as Rueben's chili. But there was something else, too, a salty coolness he knew could only be tears. It was that as much as anything, he thought later, when he was capable of it again, that reminder of her vulnerability, the fragile state of her emotions he'd violated once before, that made him stiffen when she touched him. That made him hold himself rigid while his insides quivered with unanticipated longing, his arm muscles tensing until they ached with the control it took to keep from wrapping them around her.

"You're welcome," he said as he took her by the arms and held her where she was, a few critical inches away from him. Any closer, he knew, and he'd never be able to resist her. If he let her body touch him he was finished. "I'm glad you like her."

His thoughts were as bleak as his words were gentle, and as uncompromising as his touch. *It's gratitude, nothing more. It's the gift—it's the horse she loves, not me.*

* * *

I don't understand him, this man I have married, thought Leila. He seemed so kind…yes, even sweet—Kitty had been right about that. But at the same time, so distant it seemed impossible that she would ever know or understand him.

What if I can't? What if I never do?

The thought filled her with the cold emptiness of panic. She could not endure such *aloneness* for long. And what must she do then, go running back to Tamir, to her mother and father, like a little child with a bumped knee? To even think of such a thing made her cheeks burn and her heart quicken. *No—I cannot. I will not go back.*

No, she was not ready to give up. Not yet.

Tonight, she had decided, she would try again to seduce her husband. Except…no, she did not think *seduce* was exactly the correct word. She had looked it up in her English dictionary, and it seemed to mean that she would be trying to make Cade do something bad. What could be bad about a man making love to his wife? No—she did not like this word, seduce. Not at all.

So, what *would* she call it, this business of trying to make her own husband desire her? And more important, how could she accomplish it? She had not had any success at being pushy, so it was clearly time to try something else. But what? Leila was not accustomed to having to work to get her way. All her life she had been the baby of the Kamal family, the palace darling. All that had been required in order to wrap her family and servants around her little finger was to flash her dimples, be her winsome and charming self.

Be herself? Was it possible? Could her own winsomeness and charm be enough to win over such a man as Cade? Leila didn't know, but since nothing else seemed to be working, it was definitely worth a try.

Yes, she thought, watching herself in the bathroom mirror as her small white teeth pressed into her lower lip and her dimples magically appeared. *Tonight…* Tonight, she would make herself so appealing, not even Cade would be able to resist her.

Cade was accustomed to fixing his own Sunday evening meal. He'd eat it alone in the kitchen, sometimes standing at the counter, or, if he'd remembered to pick up a Sunday paper, at the table in the breakfast room with the sports and business sections spread out in front of him. Tonight was no different, except that he had company.

Leila had come in while he was filling his plate from the array of covered containers and foil-wrapped packages Betsy had left for him, looking scrubbed and delectable in a belted robe the soft pink of wild roses. He'd tensed automatically when she first appeared, armoring himself against her appeal and gearing up to do battle with the unwanted desire for her that was beginning to gnaw at him like a hunger in his belly.

But she hadn't made any attempt to touch him again, or even get close to him, leaning instead against the counter and nibbling strawberries while she chattered on about the day she'd had. He thought he should have found her presence annoying. He wished he did. With all his heart he wished he didn't enjoy the sound of her voice so much. He wished his mouth wouldn't water at the sight of those soft lips of hers lush with strawberries.

She followed him into the breakfast room and sat down across the table from him, so he never did get to his newspaper. Instead, while he ate he listened to Leila telling him all about swimming with the children at Rueben and Betsy's, and how much she'd enjoyed meeting all the Flores family. She asked him all sorts of questions, and seemed so interested he told her everything he knew about Rueben and Betsy—how they'd grown up together in the same small village in Mexico, had married as teenagers and come to the United States not long after that, like so many others, to find work. How they'd been lucky enough to both find jobs with the same estate, Betsy as cook and housekeeper, Rueben as caretaker and horse wrangler. How they'd raised eight kids in the house down by the creek, and sent every one of them to college—they'd all graduated, too, except Tony, the youngest, who was still at Texas A&M studying veterinary medicine.

While he was telling her all this, he couldn't help but notice how the glow in her eyes had grown misty, and that her smile seemed wistful, even sad. It had a bad effect on him, that smile. It made him ashamed of himself. It made him think about his behavior toward her—especially the way he'd treated her since he'd married her and brought her here, to this place so far from her home and family. God, how lonely, how homesick she must be. No wonder she'd enjoyed Rueben and Betsy's bunch so much. And she'd never once complained. He—Cade—was a jerk, a selfish, thoughtless SOB, thinking only about how he was going to get out of this marriage mess, and nothing at all about what *she* must be going through.

Being thoroughly ashamed of himself didn't exactly put him in a frame of mind to be sociable, so as soon as he'd finished eating, he excused himself rather abruptly and shut himself up in his study to brood. It didn't take him long to discover that being exclusively in his own company wasn't doing much to improve his mood, and that it probably wasn't going to get any better until he'd figured out a way to make it up to Leila.

Meaning to step out into the backyard for a cheroot, he found himself climbing the stairs instead. He halted in front of the closed door to the bedroom that wasn't his anymore and raised his hand, only to discover that it still held the unlit cigar. He tucked it in his shirt pocket, then knocked.

So was his heart, knocking so loudly he barely heard Leila's musical, "Come in."

She was sitting on the bed—his bed—half-sideways to him with one leg drawn up, giving him enticing glimpses of smooth legs that were either naturally tawny or lightly tanned. There was the promise of other intriguing secrets in the deep vee of her robe, but they were screened from his view by her upraised arms, from which the sleeves of her robe had slipped down to reveal still more of that silky, cream-with-a-dash-of coffee skin. Which was more of her skin than he'd ever seen before at one time, come to think of it. His memory chose that moment to replay the thought that had struck him down at Rueben's, the incredible fact that he'd never actually seen his wife's body.

What was more incredible was the realization that, of all the women's bodies he'd seen in his life, in all stages of sexy and alluring undress, he'd never been so turned on as he was by those tiny, half-imagined glimpses of golden-tan skin.

With all that going on in his mind, it took him a minute or two to realize that what she was doing was braiding her hair. A tortoise-shell brush lay on the bed beside her and a length of pink ribbon was draped across her lap. She looked flustered, as if he'd caught her in a private act. She murmured something he couldn't hear and struggled to bring the braid over her shoulder so she could finish the task, and he murmured something back that was meant to tell her she didn't need to rush on his account. She watched him come toward her with apprehensive eyes. He wondered if she could hear his heart thumping.

She pulled her eyes away from him. Holding the braid with one hand, she picked up the length of ribbon with the other.

"You need some help with that?" His tongue felt thick; his voice sounded furry. Her eyes jerked back to him as he sat on the bed beside her and reached out a hand to take the ribbon.

For a moment she seemed mesmerized, gazing at him without comprehension. Then she gave herself a shake and murmured, "Oh, yes—thank you…" Her eyes dropped behind the veil of her lashes as she watched his big-boned hands tie the delicate piece of ribbon around the glossy rope of her hair. Her lips parted. She seemed to be holding her breath. He knew *he* was.

He tried to clear his throat. "Just out of curiosity, how were you going to manage this before I happened along?"

She gave him a sideways, upward look through her lashes. "Like this—" Her dimples winked at him as she demonstrated, with lips tucked between her teeth, how she would have held the braid in her mouth while she tied the ribbon around it.

He finished the task and held it up for her inspection. "Okay—how's that?"

"That is very nice, thank you."

For some reason he didn't relinquish the braid right away, but held it for a moment, staring at it and measuring the warm, damp weight of it in his hand. He had a sudden powerful urge to yank off the ribbon he'd just finished tying, unravel and bury his face in the soft, fragrant mass of her hair. *Your hair is beautiful.* He wanted to say that to her, but he didn't.

Instead, as he felt the smooth rope slide through his fingers, he cleared his throat and said, "I've been thinking…"

With a single graceful motion the braid disappeared over her shoulder. "Yes?" Her eyes waited, expectant, vulnerable.

He knew he should be more careful with her. He knew he ought to move away, at least. But he seemed to be drowning in those midnight eyes. For one panicky moment he couldn't remember what it was he'd wanted to say to her.

"I've been thinking," he said firmly, and struggling against the spell of those eyes was like swimming up out of a whirlpool. "It's been almost a week since we left Tamir. I thought you might be feeling...you know, a little homesick." She straightened almost guiltily and gave her head a little shake, ready to deny it, but he checked her with a gesture. "Hey, it's natural you'd be missing your family. What I thought, is, maybe you'd like to give them a call."

She tried to catch back the cry with her fingertips, but it was too quick for her. Above her hand, her eyes were suddenly bright with tears.

"I should have thought of it before this," Cade said gruffly. "I guess I was just so busy...business...catching up..." He felt thoroughly ashamed of himself. "Anyway, if you like, we can make the call right now. It would be..." he frowned at his watch "...early in the morning in Tamir."

"I would like that...very much." She'd turned a shoulder to him and was trying to wipe away a tear without him noticing. Then she jerked back to him, eyes wide and stricken again. "But I do not know the number. Is that not terrible? I do not even know my own telephone number!"

"I doubt you've had reason to call it," Cade said dryly.

"Not since school, that is true. That was so long ago."

"It doesn't matter. I just happen to have it, right here."

He reached into the pocket of his shirt for the slip of paper he'd written the number down on and found his forgotten cheroot there instead. Distracted, he handed the cigar to Leila while he retrieved the paper and reached with the other hand for the cordless phone on the bedside table. He dialed the number, and while he waited for the overseas connection he looked over at Leila and saw that she was still holding his cigar. Sort of rolling it between her fingers in an exploratory way, holding it to her nose and sniffing it.

Just as he was about to take it off her hands he heard the phone ringing on the other end, and immediately after that a voice saying, "Royal palace, family residence, may I help you?"

A few minutes later Leila was laughing and sobbing joyfully into the phone and didn't even notice when Cade walked out of the room. He had a knot the size of a fist in his belly, and just about the last thing on his mind was that damned cigar.

He went straight down to his study and poured himself a double shot of bourbon. He couldn't have felt worse if he'd been torturing kittens. *What kind of man am I?* he wondered as he gazed morosely into the amber depths of his whiskey glass. *What kind of selfish idiot was I, to have convinced myself I could marry a girl from a completely alien culture, haul her thousands of miles away from her home and family and expect her to be happy?* The look of sheer joy on her face when he'd handed her the phone, her radiant, tear-wet eyes, haunted him.

I have to make it right, he thought. *Somehow.*

Half a bottle of bourbon later, she was still haunting him, but in a vastly different way. As the level of liquid in the bottle dropped, so, it seemed, did the focus of his thoughts. The image he couldn't get out of his mind now wasn't her eyes, or even her dimpled smile. It was those taunting glimpses of creamy skin vanishing into the shadowed slashes of her robe, one at her breasts, the other her thighs. And he kept coming back to the fact that she was his wife, and he'd never seen either of those parts of her, not to mention others even less accessible.

She's my wife, dammit. And I want her.

Oh yeah, he kept coming back to that, too, like a little kid nagging in a toy store.

A few more sips of bourbon and he was starting to rationalize pretty effectively, with much the same sort of creative thinking he recalled employing as a teenager. Then he'd been under the influence of hormones, not whiskey, but the effect was the same. He began to convince himself that she *wanted* him to make love to her. After all, back there in Tamir she'd asked *him* to kiss her, hadn't she? And she'd come to *his* room, hadn't she? Hell yes, she had. She wanted him, he wanted her, they were married—so why *shouldn't* they have each other?

It began to seem ridiculous to him that he'd been married nearly a week and hadn't yet made love to his wife. He couldn't even recall his reason for not doing so—something about her being a virgin?—but whatever it was he was sure it couldn't have been very important. Not nearly as important as how full and hot and hard he was right now, and how much he wanted her.

But then, high on hormones, the teenage boy he'd been hadn't given much thought to tomorrow, either.

That's it, he thought, enough of this bull. She ought to be about talked out by now, homesick or not. He knocked back the last of the whiskey, plunked down the glass and marched out of his study and up the stairs. He almost barged right into his bedroom without knocking, but at the last minute thought better of it and tapped softly with one knuckle. When he got no answer, he opened the door part way and poked his head through the crack, calling her name. Then he stopped. He let out his breath in a long slow hiss, like something deflating.

His princess bride was lying on his bed, curled on her side with one hand under her cheek, the other cradling the telephone against her breasts. She was sound asleep. And those elusive legs of hers, slightly bent at both hip and knee, had escaped the confines of the robe through the front overlap and were finally displayed for him in all their glory. It was a sight to make a man's mouth water and his belly howl.

He tiptoed over to the bed and stood looking down at her...this lovely, exotic creature he'd married. The hormone-and-whiskey high was ebbing, and he felt a strange, indefinable sadness, an ache of longing he neither liked nor understood. It scared the hell out of him, as a matter of fact. What did it mean? Was he *falling* for this girl? God help him if he was, because things were complicated enough the way they were.

He was easing the phone out of her grasp when he made another unsettling discovery. Pillowing her cheek, her hand was still curled around his forgotten cheroot. What did *that* mean? His heart skittered and bounded like a startled rabbit. He flicked the comforter over those delectable legs, turned off the lamp and went out and closed the door behind him, feeling shaky and weak in the knees.

He woke the next morning with a severe headache and a sense of having escaped unthinkable disaster. No question about it, he was going to have to get this marriage thing solved right quick. Before he got himself in so deep he couldn't get out, at least not without permanent damage to his heart.

Meanwhile, he was swearing off bourbon.

When Leila woke up Monday morning, Cade had already gone—to his offices in Houston, Betsy told her. And after that, she said, he was going to fly up to Dallas to meet with some people about a refinery he was going to rebuild and modernize for them out in a place called Odessa. There was a lot of planning to do—probably take several days, she said, so Cade would be staying in Dallas most of the week. Betsy's face looked stern as she told Leila this, as if she were angry.

Later, she heard Betsy talking to Rueben in the kitchen. "...makes me so mad. Why is he acting like this? What did he marry her for, if he's just going to leave her alone all the time? Why doesn't he sleep—" And she broke off quickly as Leila came into the room.

I don't know why either, Leila wanted to say. Although, unlike Betsy, she did know why Cade had married her. He had married her because she had disgraced herself, and he felt sorry for her. And because he did not want to displease her father, the sheik.

And now she was trapped, every bit as trapped as she had been in Tamir, only worse. There, at least, she had been surrounded by people who loved her, even if they did treat her like a child most of the time. Here, she had only a husband who did not love her at all, and Rueben and Betsy, who were kind.

"Just give him some time," Betsy told her with a sigh, as if she were talking about one of her own children who was misbehaving. "He's real busy right now, but he'll come around. You just have to give him time."

Yes, Leila thought, *but I do not know how long I will be able to stand this loneliness.*

She kept busy during the day, working with the foal, Sari, reading books beside the pool and swimming. Once, two of Betsy's grandchildren knocked at the back door and said, "Can Leila come out and play with us?" And so she enjoyed a wonderful afternoon swimming with them in the creek.

But the thing she liked the most, besides working with Sari, was following Betsy around the house, asking questions about Cade. She especially liked the photograph albums Betsy gave her, and spent hours poring over them staring at the grainy black-and-white or faded color photographs of Cade when he was a boy, and the people who had made him who he was.

One album was older than the others, made of black paper pages between stiff leather covers. It had been Cade's mother's, Betsy told her, and the pictures were of her father, who had been the "wildcatter." There were many pictures in the album like the one Leila had seen framed in Cade's study, of grimy men with blackened faces standing beside wooden derricks or oil well pumps that reminded Leila of giant insects. Betsy explained that a wildcatter was someone who searched for oil, and that Cade's grandfather had found a lot of it, back in the nineteen-twenties, and had become very rich.

"Ah," said Leila, nodding. But she was puzzled, too. For some reason it had not seemed that Cade had always been rich.

But then Betsy explained that Cade's father had been a gambler and an alcoholic, and had lost almost all of his wife's money before she divorced him, when Cade was twelve. And then had died a short time later.

Leila's eyes had filled with tears when Betsy told her of Cade's mother's death only a few years after that, in a tragic accident. There was something about the pretty blond woman with the kind eyes and gentle smile that reminded her of her own mother. Even now, Leila could not imagine her world without her mother in it, and to think that Cade had been no more than fifteen... The photographs of Cade at that time showed a solemn-faced boy with broad shoulders that looked as if they carried a great weight, and now she understood why.

Earlier, though, there were pictures of a younger, much more carefree Cade with his mother and a handsome dark-haired, hawk-nosed man, and a little girl who looked familiar. Leila looked closer, then gave a cry. "But this is Elena!"

Yes, Betsy told her, and the man was Elena's father, Yusuf Rahman. Betsy's mouth tightened when she said that name.

"Then...Cade's mother and Elena's father were lovers?" In the photographs they seemed close, like a family, Leila thought.

But Betsy shook her head and said, "You'd have to ask Cade about that."

She had gone on about her dusting, and her whole body quivered with indignation and disapproval—though it was not, Leila understood, of *her*. She already knew, from things Elena had told her, that Yusuf Rahman had been an evil man, that he had even killed his own wife, Elena's mother, and would have killed Elena, too, if Hassan had not shot him first. She had not known how close that evil had come to touching Cade's life as well.

She had gone on to study the photograph albums alone after that, and if she felt disappointed it was because she wished she *could* ask Cade, as Betsy had suggested—about many things. She liked listening to Betsy talk about Cade's background and family, but she wished she could have talked of those things with her husband instead.

Someday he will talk to me. I must believe that. And maybe then I will understand why he does not want to love me.

Cade returned on Friday, just as Rueben and Betsy were about to leave for the weekend. They were all in the kitchen when he came in. Betsy was showing Leila the food she had prepared for their weekend meals, and Rueben was sitting at the small kitchen table drinking a glass of sweetened iced tea. Cade nodded at Rueben, who nodded back.

"Huh," said Betsy as she closed the refrigerator door with a loud smack, "what're *you* doing home so early?"

Even Leila recognized the sarcasm, and not for the first time she thought how different Rueben and Betsy's position in this house was from that of the servants back home in Tamir.

Cade pulled out a chair and sat down at the table. He looks very tired, Leila thought, watching him draw a hand over his eyes and rub them briefly. Her heartbeat stumbled as those deeply shadowed eyes slid past her...but when he spoke his words and half smile were for Betsy. "Got any more of that tea?"

Betsy gave him a look, but did not say anything as she took a glass from the cupboard and poured tea from the pitcher in the refrigerator. Then she handed the glass to Leila. Leila took it, not comprehending; *she* had not asked for tea. Betsy jerked her head toward Cade and made a motion with her hand that he could not see.

Then she understood. Of course—she was to serve her husband. What a lot I have to learn about being a wife, she thought. When it came to food and drink, Leila was accustomed to *being* served, not the other way around.

Her heart hammered and her hands shook as she placed the glass of iced tea on the table in front of her husband. His eyes flashed briefly at her from their shadows as he mumbled, "Thanks." Leila nodded and retreated until she felt the cold edge of the tile counter at her back. She slumped against it because her knees felt weak and she was grateful for the support, but she remembered her pride and straightened just in time. *A daughter of Sheik Ahmed Kamal does not slump.*

Betsy asked again why Cade had come home so early, and what his plans were for the coming weekend. He took a long drink of iced tea before he answered. "I thought I'd fly out to the ranch...do some repairs. That was more than a little bit embarrassing last week, having the power go out, with a client."

Leila felt strange, as if she were standing all alone on a great empty stage, and thousands of people were looking

at her. She heard herself say in a loud, clear voice, "I
would like to go with you." The strangeness dissolved and
she saw that there were only two people looking at her—
Cade with silent shock, and Betsy with a little smile of
approval. Rueben, with his back to her, drank tea with a
noisy clanking of ice cubes.

Leila stepped forward, and her stomach quivered with
butterflies. "I would like to see this ranch that I have heard
about," she said, and there was no quiver at all in her voice.
"I would like to see more of Texas."

Cade was opening his mouth to speak, and she knew that
he was going to say that she could not go. She did not
know what she would do if he told her that. I will not be
left alone again, she thought, trembling now with anger.
Anger and a new determination. *I will not be abandoned
again.*

"That's a good idea," said Betsy. Cade shut his mouth
on whatever it was he had planned to say and glared at the
short, brown woman. She glared back at him. Her arms
were folded on her great soft bosom, and her round face
looked as though it had been carved from wood. "You
should take your wife—show her the ranch. Have a nice
weekend together—just the two of you."

The silence in the kitchen was profound. It seemed to
Leila that they must all hear each other's hearts beating.
Then Rueben gave his shoulder a hitch and said, "Yeah,
you should take her."

Cade flashed him a look of pure shock. Leila held her
breath while seconds ticked by. She knew that this was
important—maybe the most important moment of her life,
a crossroads. If he refuses me, she thought with cold resolve... If he leaves me again...

His eyes came back to her. She felt them as a strange
kind of heat, a melting fire that spread through her chest.
"It's pretty primitive out there," he said. "Not very com-

fortable. Are you sure you want to go?'' And she knew
that she had won.

She gave a happy sigh. "*Very* sure.''

The twin-engine Cessna 310 arrowed upward through the
East Texas haze and leveled off above the outer limits of
Houston's suburbs. This early in the morning there were
no thunderheads to reckon with, so Cade set a course
straight across the checkerboard of farmland and small
towns toward the hill country west of San Antonio. Flying
time to the ranch was anywhere from an hour and a half
to two hours, depending on wind conditions.

He looked over at his passenger. She hadn't said much
since he'd buckled her into her seat, just kept looking out
the window with her face pressed right up against the glass.
Reminded him of a little kid staring through the walls of
an aquarium, oblivious to everything except what was going on in the alien world on the other side.

Not completely oblivious. As if she sensed his look, she
glanced over at him. "America is so...*big*,'' she said, her
voice breathless and wondering. She sat back in her seat
with a happy-sounding sigh. "It is just as I imagined. And
all of this—'' she turned once again to the window, as if
she couldn't help herself ''—is still Texas? It must go on
forever!''

"Not quite,'' said Cade dryly, "but just about.''

She was silent, gazing down on the crazy-quilt landscape. Then she said, "I understand why you felt 'cooped
up' in Tamir.''

Cooped up. He felt a strange little shiver go through
him—not déjà vu, exactly, just an instant of total sensory
recall. Hearing those words, for a moment he was back
there in Tamir with Leila, the night of the state reception.
She was flirting with him on the terrace overlooking the
sea, and he was feeling again that unnerving and mystifying

sense of accord with a woman as exotic and alien to him
as anyone he'd ever met. Thinking about it, and about everything that had happened to him since, he wondered now
if it had all begun with that moment. He sure as hell hadn't
felt like himself since.

"Yeah," he said in a gravelly voice, "Pretty hard to feel
cooped up out here."

"You would think so…" Her voice was wistful and soft,
and he wondered how words so gentle could cause such a
fierce and painful wound, right in the vicinity of his heart.

There was no more talking after that. Leila gazed out the
window and Cade was left alone with his remorseful
thoughts. And some that were wistful, too. He kept thinking
about those days and nights in Tamir, remembering the
gardens, the scent of flowers and the music of fountains, a
princess's enchanting smile. And it seemed to him that
there had been a magical innocence about that time, remembered, like a fairy tale from his childhood, with a sense
of regret, an awareness of having had something precious
that was now lost. Something he wished he could find
again, and had no idea how.

Time went quickly, and in no time at all the Cessna was
circling over dun-colored hills dotted with gray-green live
oaks and darker splotches of juniper. There was the pale
ribbon of road—smoother-looking from up here than the
corduroy it was—and the landing strip with its wind sock
hanging limp at this time of morning. Cade pointed them
out to Leila—the maintenance shed next to the runway,
then the slate-gray roof of the farmhouse, and on the other
side of the house, shielded from the landing strip by a grove
of live oaks, the barn and corrals. She didn't reply, just
gazed down at everything in silent awe.

And suddenly, in his mind he could hear Betsy saying,

"...show her the ranch. Have a nice weekend...just the two of you."

Just the two of us. The whole weekend.

The knot in his stomach felt a lot like fear.

Chapter 10

"Well—this is it." Cade dropped the key into his pocket and pushed open the door, then reached around it to a light switch. "Okay—at least we have power." He looked sideways at Leila and made a motion with his head. "Sorry about the mess. I wasn't expecting to bring company this trip, or I'd have had Mrs. MacGruder—that's my next-door neighbor—she takes care of things here for me—feeds the horses, things like that. I'd have had her come in and clean."

"I can clean," Leila said, stepping over the threshold. She heard Cade make a disbelieving sound as he picked up the thermal cooler containing food that Betsy had sent with them and followed her into the living room. She tore her gaze from the room to give him a look. "Do you think I cannot? Because I am not required to clean does not mean I do not know how."

"Oh yeah?" Cade lifted a skeptical eyebrow at her as he passed. "So tell me—where did you learn how to clean house?"

"Well...not *house*, exactly." Her smile was brief and distracted; there was so much to see. "In boarding school, we were required to clean our own rooms and make our beds, so I do know how to sweep and dust. Frankly, it is not that difficult."

Cade grunted. Through an open double doorway she saw him put the cooler on a table in what could only be the kitchen. "Well, I told you it was primitive."

"I do not think it is primitive at all." Leila had visited some of the poorest parts of Tamir with her mother and sisters. She knew what primitive was. She clasped her hands together to contain her excitement. "I think it is...perfect."

In fact, she had fallen in love with the house at her first glimpse of it. It was made of yellowish-brown stones, with a wooden veranda that ran straight across the front and a roof made of dark gray composition shingles, which Cade told her had replaced the original wooden ones. And the room she was standing in seemed so familiar to her she was sure she must have seen one just like it—perhaps more than one—in western movies. At one end there was a large fireplace made of the same stone as the outside of the house, with a sofa and several comfortable-looking chairs gathered in front of it. The floors were made of wood, covered with rugs made of cloth that had been tightly braided and then coiled. There was a set of antlers, perhaps from a deer, above the fireplace, and, oddly, the actual skin of a cow thrown over one of the chairs, like an afghan.

She let out her breath in a happy gust. She thought it was just what a house on a ranch in Texas *should* be.

She went into the kitchen where Cade was taking things out of the cooler and putting them into the refrigerator. He looked around at her, or rather, at the overnight bag that was hanging from her shoulder. "I'll show you where to put your things, and then we can have some breakfast."

Leila nodded. Once more she was too busy looking to reply. The kitchen had white-painted cupboards and blue linoleum on the floor, and a yellow plastic cover on the table that was covered with tiny blue and white flowers. Directly opposite the wide door from the living room, another door with a window in the top opened onto what appeared to be a screened-in porch. Just to one side of the door, a window above the sink looked out on dusty-looking trees, and beyond that, the barn and corrals she had seen from the airplane. Her heart quickened when she saw movement in the corrals. *Horses.*

"Bedrooms are in here." Cade was waiting for her in another doorway that opened off the kitchen to the right. He moved aside to let her pass, and she found herself in a small hallway with an open doorway—including the one in which she stood—in each of its four walls. Through one she could see a bathroom, with a deep iron tub with feet shaped like claws. The other two were bedrooms.

"Take your pick," he said, waving her toward them. "I think they're both about the same."

Leila peeked into both rooms, then walked through the doorway closest to her and placed her bag on the bed. She noticed that it was a much smaller bed than the one in Cade's room in Houston, but she did not linger and look as she had in the other parts of the house. There was nothing personal here, nothing to tell her which room Cade used when he visited the ranch. She felt a strangeness in being there with him so close behind her, and yet, so very far away. With so much unsaid between them there was awkwardness in the silence.

But, she thought, that is why I am here, because these things must be spoken of—they *will* be spoken of. *But not now. This is not the right time.*

Leaving her bag on the bed, she fixed a smile on her face and turned. "You said we could have breakfast? That is good, because I am hungry.'' She had eaten some toast with her one cup of coffee before leaving that morning, but it seemed a long time ago. ''What must I do to help?'' She felt strange little showers of shivers inside and rubbed her arms, though she wasn't cold.

''You want to *help?*'' Cade looked at her, again with that *so* superior half smile that so clearly said he didn't see how she could. Leila was beginning to be very annoyed by that smile.

Back in the kitchen, he opened a drawer and took out a metal tool, which he placed on the countertop. Then he opened a cupboard and took out a large brown can. ''If you want to help, why don't you open that while I get the coffeemaker going.''

Leila picked up the tool, which was unlike anything she had seen before. It had two legs that opened when she pulled them, like a pair of scissors. Obviously, she was meant to use the tool to open the brown can, which contained coffee, she could see that. *I will not ask him. I will not.*

My God, thought Cade, she doesn't even know how to use a can opener. He wondered if she'd ever seen one before.

''It's...a can opener,'' he said gruffly, moving closer to her.

She glanced up at him—a patient look, as if he had said something stupid. ''Yes, I know. It is just that I have never seen one...like it...before.'' There was a smudge of color in each cheek, and he wondered if it was pride, or embarrassment.

''It's, uh...pretty much just your classic can opener.'' He edged closer still. ''They're kind of a basic necessity around here, since about the only things we can leave in the house are canned goods. Power's unreliable, so we can't leave anything in the freezer. And then there are the mice…''

''Mice?'' She was gazing at him, not with the maidenly horror he'd expected, but with a bright and childlike delight. ''Oh, do we have mice? I would very much like to see one.'' She tilted her head and dimpled thoughtfully. ''I do not think I have ever seen a real mouse before.''

Why am I not surprised? Cade thought. Aloud he muttered, ''They're a damned nuisance.''

''Perhaps you should keep a cat.''

''Who'd take care of it when there's nobody here?''

''Perhaps…your neighbor, what was it? Mrs. Mac-Gruder? Since they must come to tend the horses anyway?'' Her eyes were wide and ingenuous. He wondered how he'd come to be close enough to her to see himself reflected in their depths.

''What, once a day? Nah—animals need attention. You can't just leave them on their own all the time.''

''Oh yes,'' she said softly, ''that is true.'' And she looked at him just long enough before she said it that he felt a mean little stab of guilt.

''Here, why don't you let me do that?'' he said roughly, reaching for the can opener.

She held it out of his reach. ''No. I would like you to show me how to do it.'' And she added as a breathless afterthought, ''Please.''

Cade was awash with feelings he didn't know what to do with. Part of it was anger, or something close, and part was the kind of thing he imagined he might be feeling if he were trapped on a rocky shoal with the tide rising fast. And part of it, if he was honest with himself, was just plain old sexual excitement. It was her body heat, her woman's scent, partly familiar, partly exotic. He should never have let himself get so close to her. He was having trouble keeping his breathing quiet so she wouldn't hear how fast it was. He hoped she couldn't hear his heart hammering.

"Okay, here's what you do—here, let me show you." He reached again for the can opener.

And again she pulled it away, out of his reach. "No—I want to do it. Just please show me how."

What could he do? Gingerly as a rattlesnake wrangler, he reached across her and covered her hands with his. "First you have to open these up..." God, he could hardly breathe. "Then, you chomp down on the edge of the can— like this, see? That little hiss means you broke the seal. Then, you turn this..."

He felt like he was going to pass out, honest to God— just like the way he felt when he hadn't eaten in way too long. Only he didn't think he'd ever known hunger quite like this, couldn't remember ever wanting a woman the way he wanted this one. No, not wanting, *needing*. Like, if he couldn't have her right now, this minute, he might keel over right there on the floor.

It occurred to him that her hands weren't moving.

"I think we are finished," she whispered, and she was looking at him, not the can.

Oh, yeah, Cade thought, we're finished, all right. All his high-minded resolve? Dead...cooked. This was going to happen, and there wasn't a thing he could do to stop it.

It had come down to a matter of seconds...heartbeats. He could feel her heat and her scent seeping through his shirt and into his skin. His nerve-endings were learning the shape of her breast. She looked up at him and he stared down at her parted lips, and his throat was parched, thirsty almost to the point of madness for the taste of her.

The taste of her. He remembered it now. Oh yeah, it all came rushing back to him. And he knew in that moment that he'd never stopped thirsting for the taste of her.

He made a sound...whispered something, maybe her

name. His head dropped lower, closing that taunting distance between himself and the thing he craved....

A loud banging noise made him jerk upright with adrenaline squirting through his system like ice cold fire. The door—dammit. Someone was knocking on the back porch door.

A moment later, before the shock of that had begun to subside, there came a lighter tapping at the kitchen door. It opened, and a short, bandy-legged man with a completely bald head and cheeks as red as Santa Claus stuck his head in. His neighbor, of course. Deb MacGruder.

"Hey, how you folks doin'? Heard you come flyin' in."

It was impossible to stay irritated at ol' Deb, who had to be one of the nicest people ever put on this earth, and Cade didn't even try. Hoping he didn't look or sound as jangled as he felt, he invited the man in, introduced him to Leila and relieved him of the plastic grocery bags he'd brought with him.

"Edna sent you over some fresh eggs and a jug a'milk— figured you could use some." Cade noticed then that ol' Deb was sort of fidgeting and looking sideways at Leila and blushing like a tongue-tied teenager, and when he glanced over at her, he understood why. She had her dimples turned on, full wattage, and was looking about as lovely and charming as it was possible for a woman to look. Deb rubbed a hand over his sunburned scalp and coughed. "I, uh...put up some of the mares in the corral, just in case the two of you were wantin' to do some ridin' while you're here." He sounded as if he thought the possibility remote, under the circumstances.

But Cade heard a gasp from somewhere behind him, and Leila's voice, breathless and excited. "Oh, yes, thank you!"

And he realized that he ought to be feeling grateful. He'd been given a reprieve. All was not lost, after all.

Sure, he thought, what he had to do was keep his wife out riding all day until they were both so worn out and saddle sore they wouldn't be thinking about doing anything tonight except sleeping.

And tomorrow, well...that was another day. He'd cross that bridge when he came to it.

"Hey, what do you think you're doing? Come back here!"

Leila's answer to that was a peal of laughter. Crouching low over her mount's neck, she urged the mare to full gallop. Sure-footed like all of her breed, the roan mare's hooves seemed to fly over the hard ground. Dark shapes of the trees Cade had called junipers flashed by on either side of her, and their spicy scent rose into the muggy air.

At the top of the gentle rise Leila had a brief and exhilarating glimpse of forever, and then her heart lurched into her throat as the mare plunged over the top of the hill and skidded down...down into a sandy valley. With a squeal of sheer exuberance she urged the mare on across the sand and up the slope on the other side. And there she finally halted, with the wind whipping her hair and the view before her stretching all the way to the base of billowing black clouds. Laughing and out of breath, she waited for Cade to catch up.

"What the hell were you doing?" she heard him bellow as his horse's chestnut head with a white blaze appeared atop the rise. A moment later she saw Cade's face, and it was dark and stormy as the thunderclouds that filled the sky above their heads. "What're you trying to do, get yourself killed?"

Somehow, though, Leila knew the light in his eyes was not anger, and she tossed back her hair and smiled as she called back, "Killed? No, no—I am *living!*"

"Huh!" Muttering soothing things to his mount and patting her sweat-soaked neck, he brought her beside Leila's. "Living?"

"Oh, yes—do you not know? I am living a dream. *My* dream." She threw her arms wide and lifted her face to the sky. "I have dreamed of this—riding like the wind…land that goes on forever."

"Yeah, well, the land may go on forever, but my piece of it doesn't. You see that down there?" He jerked his head toward the limitless horizon, and he was throwing his leg over the saddle in a dismount that Leila was sure only a man with long legs and the body of a cowboy could accomplish gracefully. "That's where my property ends. If you'd decided to keep on going to the next hill over there, you *and* the mare would've run right smack into a barbed wire fence."

Leila was quite sure nothing of the sort would have happened, and that either she would have seen the fence in time to stop, or the mare would have. And then, most likely, they would have jumped over it.

But a wife must not argue with her husband. "Please, do not be angry with me, Cade. If you only knew—"

"I'm not angry with you," he muttered as he ducked under the chestnut mare's neck and came into the space between the two horses. "Here—your stirrups are too short. Put your leg up."

"Oh, but I like them this way. I am learning to ride Western style—Rueben has been teaching me—but I am not very good at it. He said I should get used to it a little at a time."

Cade gave his head a shake. "Looks like you were doing okay to me." He tipped back the brim of his hat and squinted up at her. "Where did you learn to ride like that?"

She felt a warm little rush of pride, felt it spread right into her cheeks. "My brother has horses—I told you that, remember? At the polo match. Arabians, like yours. I used to ride a lot when I was younger, before—'' She did not say, *Before I became a woman, and no longer had the freedom of a child.* ''Before I got too busy with other things.''

''Huh.'' He made a thoughtful sound and grudgingly added, ''Well. Doesn't look like you've forgotten how.'' He looked at her for a long, silent moment, one hand on her saddlehorn, his arm resting on her horse's neck. He jerked his head and said, ''Come on—get down for a bit. We'll give the horses a breather.''

''A...breather?''

''A rest. Then I think we'd better be heading back. I don't like the looks of that sky.''

Leila nodded and began to dismount. Then she stopped. She could not possibly manage the kind of graceful one-step dismount that Cade had used. Her stirrups were too short and her legs were, too. To dismount as she usually did, she would have to hold on to the saddle and lay her stomach across it while she freed her foot from the stirrup, then slide to the ground. But if she did that now, with Cade standing where he was, her backside would be only inches from his face. She was wearing jodhpurs, the only riding clothes she owned, and although they were not tight they did fit closely. If she was bending over, as she must, they could hardly help but outline her figure very clearly. The thought made her cheeks burn and her heartbeat quicken, but...not at all unpleasantly.

''Here—I'll give you a hand.'' He held out his arms to her, ready to help her dismount. His face had no expression at all. Even his eyes told her nothing; they were hidden in the shadow of his hat brim.

With pounding heart she considered her two choices. And then, with a sense of giving up a tiger in favor of a lion, she put her hands on his shoulders. She felt his hands, strong on her waist. Her throat closed and her breathing stopped.

Cade thought, what am I doing? He knew he should be more cautious around her, but something inside him was clearly enjoying this flirtation with disaster. He was like a child playing with matches, one old enough to understand the danger and arrogantly sure of his ability to avoid it.

Ah, but what a waist she had…slender and supple in his hands. Not so delicate and tiny he imagined his hands could span it, but firm and strong, with muscles that tightened under his palms as he lifted her down from the saddle.

He sensed a stiffening in her, too, that was more than the physical tensing of muscles, and to his profound regret, he thought he knew what it was. Not fear, exactly—he could see that she desperately wanted to feel at ease with him. It was as if she dared not allow herself to be. What she reminded him of—and his heart ached to realize it— was something he'd seen in Betsy's adopted strays, the guarded hopefulness of a once-friendly dog only lately grown used to unkindness.

Guarded. Yes. He understood, now, that where once she had been open to him, innocently eager and certain of her welcome as a well-loved child, now she was fortified against him. Against his rejection of her, at least. Pride had taken the place of innocence—she would not allow him to hurt her again.

The thought made him feel dismal and defeated, the more so because of the intensity with which he wanted her, right then, at that very moment. He remembered that night on the terrace overlooking the Mediterranean, his awareness that she was "forbidden fruit," and his wondering if she might have been the more desirable to him because of that. And if that was true, then what did it say about his character? Was he, Cade Gallagher, who prided himself on his honesty, on his sense of honor and responsibility, after all no more than a spoiled, contrary kid, wanting what he couldn't have?

A sound interrupted his dismal reflections—the soft rumbling of a cleared throat. Then it seemed that the thunder picked it up and carried it off into a darkening sky like a rolling echo, while Cade gazed down into the flushed face and luminous eyes of the woman he'd married, and felt that same rumbling in the back of his chest...the bottom of his belly.

A dust devil danced across the crest of the hill and swirled beneath the horses' feet. While the animals sidestepped nervously, it sprang like a teasing sprite into the sky, and Leila's laughter rose after it as, taking no chances, she held on to her hat with both hands. The hat reminded Cade of the one he'd retrieved for her from the polo field, and he could see from the way she suddenly went still and the way her eyes clung to his that she was remembering that day, too.

The dust devil had gone on its way, but the wind still tugged at him, nudging him as though it was trying to get his attention. It came to him in a fierce little gust of exultation: *She's not forbidden fruit. She's my wife. My wife!*

The thought crossed his mind that, as reprieves went, that one sure hadn't amounted to much.

He watched himself insert a wondering, wary finger under the cord that was supposed to keep her hat from blowing off, and slowly...slowly pull it out from under her chin. Questions sprang into her eyes, but she held them back with strong white teeth pressing into the softness of her lower lip. Moving as slowly as he did, she lowered her hands and let him take the hat. But he could see she had no idea what he meant to do. She couldn't hear the blood rushing through his body, like the sound of wind inside his head, or the merciless pounding of his heart.

Her eyes never left his face as he looped the string of

her hat over the horn of her saddle, then slowly took off his own hat and hung it right over hers. His breath felt heavy, and seemed to stick in his throat. Nerves jumped and quivered in his belly. And still she didn't know.

He put his hands on the sides of her head and smoothed back her sweat-damp hair with his thumbs. Tiny wrinkles appeared in her flawless forehead, like ripples in satin. He gazed at them, fascinated, while his thumbs stroked gentle furrows above her ears. And *now* she knew.

A faint sound…a tiny movement drew his gaze, and he saw that her lips had opened. He knew the question that must be poised there—he'd heard it once before. *Do you want to kiss me?* He also knew that she would never ask him that question again.

Remembering the sweetness of that time, the innocence, pain stabbed at him, ruthless and brutal. *What have I done to her?* With a guttural little cry, he lowered his mouth to hers.

The first shock that came to him then was how familiar she seemed. As if, during all the time since he'd last kissed her, his unconscious mind had gone right on learning the shapes, tastes and textures of her. He wondered now if he'd dreamed of her, those nights in the guest room or in the hotel room in Dallas, when he'd woken up with the sheets in a tangle and his body in a sweaty fever, aching with unfulfilled desire.

How unbelievably good her mouth tasted to him—his very favorite food when his belly was empty…cool pure water when he was dying of thirst. Like a starving man, he tried to remind himself to go slowly, to not be greedy, lest he overwhelm himself and her. And so he separated his mouth from hers and pulled back a little…but only a little, and only long enough to savor the misty puffs of her exhalations, so soft and sweet he thought it must be like a flower breathing. He thought of that, and of their own volition, just before they touched hers again, his lips formed themselves into a smile.

So caught up was he in his own sensations, he didn't notice right away that she was trembling. When that awareness did penetrate the blissful fog he was in, he felt a bright stab of pain. Like a shaft of sunlight, it melted away the insulating blanket of reason he'd kept wrapped around his emotions, and he felt the burn of desire...unsuppressed, unshielded, inescapable.

He had no defenses for it. He wanted her. Wanted her under him, her thighs making a cradle for him, and her breasts pillows for his chest. He ached to be inside her, to feel her soft, enfolding warmth around him. He wanted...he *needed* her, more than he needed his next breath.

A shudder rocked him from head to toe and a groan rumbled deep inside his chest as he let go of her head and wrapped his arms around her, enfolding her and bringing her body against him with all the restraint he could muster. It cost him dearly, that restraint; he could feel himself tremble. But oh, how good it felt to hold her, that marvelous body he'd never seen, so strong and supple he could feel every line and curve even through the clothes she wore. Avidly, he skimmed her body with his hands like a blind man exploring a new and wondrous gift. Eyes closed, he immersed himself in the sensual banquet of her body...the warmth and textures of her...the taste and smell, even the whimpering, whispering sounds—

No—that wasn't Leila. The horses. Close on both sides of them, they were tossing their heads and sidestepping, whickering nervously. An instant later there was a deafening *boom.* Cade jerked as if he'd been shot.

For one moment, Leila wondered if *she* had been shot. For this was just what she had always imagined it would feel like to suffer calamitous injury—a cold emptiness and no pain at all, only a trembling that would not stop.

"Are you okay?" Cade was holding her by the arms, looking down at her with dark, smoky eyes.

"Yes, of course." And she could not imagine how her voice could sound so okay when she was anything but. It was the night on the terrace all over again; she could not imagine how she would stand alone if he let go of her. Deciding she did not want to find out, she reached behind her with a surreptitious hand and grasped a stirrup for support.

"That lightning was close. We'd best get off of this hilltop before the next one comes." His voice sounded as if he needed to cough.

Leila nodded. Without another word she turned her back to him and reached up to grasp the saddlehorn as he bent down to make a stirrup for her with his hands. A moment later she was sitting in the saddle, calmly adjusting her hatstring under her chin as thunder rumbled and growled in the vast roiling sky above her head. *That is how I feel,* she thought, gazing up at it. *So much darkness and tension and tumult.*

She was glad to follow Cade down the slope into the sandy wash, then quickly up the other side…glad to break into a gallop when the first raindrops came. She had known thunderstorms, of course, but to actually be outside in one was very different from watching from the calm and safety of the royal palace, or Cade's solid brick house near Houston. Suddenly those endless vistas she'd longed for, that vast sky that had seemed to promise freedom and limitless possibilities, now was filled with violence and danger, forces powerful beyond imagining. It was awe-inspiring, yes, but frightening, too. And Leila was glad. Glad that her mind was all taken up with awe and fear and coping with powerful forces of nature, and that, for the moment, at least, there was no room left for thoughts of Cade, and what had just happened to her.

The first little shower passed quickly, hard pelting drops that stung like pebbles. But the storm seemed to be following them—chasing them, Leila thought. Spiteful Nature, bellowing and grumbling at two thoughtless trespassers and hurling handfuls of stinging raindrops at their backs. The day seemed to grow darker, until it seemed as though day had become evening. She could see the lightning flashes now, not just hear the thunder that came after, and she was glad when they reached the live oaks that told her they were coming close to the ranch.

They had been moving at an easy gallop, a gait Cade had told her was called a lope, riding single file, following a well-worn path through the trees because the sandy ground there was all but covered with clumps of low-growing cactus. As she followed along behind Cade, for some reason—perhaps because they were nearly home and shelter was not far off—Leila's thoughts began to creep back to the terrifying thing that had happened to her, there on the hilltop. Her thoughts were still full of awe and fear and powerful forces of nature, but now those things had a name, a face—*Cade's*.

She stared at his back as they loped along through the twisty, gray-green trees, thinking how strong and powerful he looked, with his broad shoulders and long, lean body, admiring the way he sat so tall and straight, with his butt firm in the saddle, the American—the *Western*—way. Like a cowboy. And her heart began to pound almost with the same rhythm as the horses' hooves. What is happening to me? she wondered. Something had happened to her when he kissed her, something awesome and frightening. Something wonderful. She had trembled with it.

And then, like a lightning bolt, it struck her. *It happened to him, too. I know it did. Because I felt him tremble, too.*

Seized by a tremendous exhilaration, she urged her mount forward until she had caught up with Cade. There was barely enough room on the path for two horses to go abreast, but she nudged her roan mare right up beside the chestnut, until her leg brushed Cade's. She looked over at him, not smiling, her gaze intent and searching. He looked back at her....

There was almost no warning at all. Just a sizzling sound. An instant later a flash and a tremendous *Cr-ack*.

Leila's mount tensed, then lunged forward in full stampede. It took Leila only a few seconds to bring the terrified animal back under control, and as she was walking the mare in calming circles, crooning to her in Arabic and patting her sweat-slick neck, Cade's chestnut mare came galloping past her, eyes wild, white-ringed with panic.

Without Cade.

Chapter 11

Leila stared after the riderless mare, refusing to accept the evidence of her own eyes. Then her heart grew cold and she wheeled the panting roan sharply on the narrow path and raced back the way she had come. As she rode she called Cade's name and whispered prayers under her breath. *Oh please, God, most merciful God, please let him be all right...*

She found him without any trouble at all. Cade was only a short distance from the path, lying on his back on the ground with the upper part of his body raised and his weight on his elbows. Once she was assured—both by his position and the glare of helpless fury on his face—that her prayers had been answered, Leila's next impulse was to laugh. As she had laughed when her brother Rashid had been thrown from his pony once while they were racing on the cliffs overlooking the sea. Oh, how she had laughed to see the regal and arrogant Rashid flat on his backside in the grass! But crown prince or not, Rashid was only her brother. Cade was her husband! She should not laugh at her husband!

Horrified—and helpless to stop it—Leila clapped a hand over her mouth as she reined the roan mare to a halt. She was snuffling with mirth as she hurled herself from the saddle.

"Cade—what has happened? Are you all right?"

"Not…really." His voice sounded airless and strained, and she realized that he was trying to hide a grimace of pain.

She started to go to him, feeling even more terrible for laughing when he must be hurt after all. But he threw up a warning hand with an urgent gasp. "No—don't come any closer. There's cactus everywhere." His lips drew back over tightly clenched teeth. "I think I must have landed in a patch of it."

This time her hand flew to her mouth in time to muffle her horrified cry. "Oh, Cade—what must I do? How can I help you?" She was bending over him, having disregarded his warning and picked her way through the cactus to his side.

He shifted in an experimental way and then grunted. "Not…much you can do to help. Unless you think you could throw me over your shoulder and carry me home." He flicked her a glance and a crooked, embarrassed smile.

Cade Gallagher—*embarrassed?* Only this morning such a thing would have seemed impossible to her, but now…oh yes, she could see it very clearly. Her so very imposing, intimidating, commanding husband was embarrassed. Quite humiliated, in fact.

Realizing that, she felt a surge of feeling so alien to her that it was a minute or two before she understood what it was. *Power.* For the first time in her life, Leila felt…powerful.

"No, I do not think I would be able to carry you," she said as a strange, protective tenderness began to layer itself with the newfound strength inside of her. "But perhaps the horse—"

He snorted disgustedly. "Don't think I'm going to be sitting on a horse—or anything else—not until I get these damn spines out of my backside, anyway."

Leila smiled, gently sympathetic. "I was not suggesting that you should sit. But I think, if you were to lay yourself on your stomach across the saddle—"

"Hell no!" He reminded Leila very much of an unhappy child. "I'm not about to be carried home like a sack of oats—no way."

She lowered her eyes. "I am sorry. I was only trying—"

"Look—" He touched her cheek, and she felt a stirring of pleasure, understanding then that he was only gruff with her because he was so frustrated. "I told you—there's nothing you can do, okay?" But he made a liar of himself by adding, "Just...give me a hand up."

"Forgive me, but I must ask," said Leila, when he was more or less on his feet again and working himself carefully inch by inch upright. "If you cannot ride, how *do* you propose to get back to the ranch?" Before he could answer, she touched her fingertips to her lips and exclaimed, "Oh! And your poor horse, will she be all right? Should I not go and look for her?"

He gave her a sideways, reproachful look. "My 'poor horse?' Hell, she's long back at the barn by now. *Bibi.*" He snorted, then muttered, "Never did like that horse."

"What happened to her? I heard such a loud noise—"

"Lightning struck a tree," said Cade, and his voice was tight with pain as he cautiously eased his weight from one foot to the other. "Pretty close by, too. Didn't you feel it?" As if to underline the question, thunder grumbled and rolled across the grove of trees, and leaves rustled in the rising wind.

"Well, yes, but then I was too busy trying to control my

Kamilah, here—yes, and you are my 'perfect one,' yes, you are…'' Leila crooned, as the roan mare, perhaps recognizing her name, began to nibble at her hair. The mare had been waiting on the path—like cow ponies, all of Cade's horses were trained to "ground tie," or stand still when their reins were dropped to the ground—and she was growing impatient for Leila's return. "Kamilah was also very frightened—weren't you, my sweet? She tried to run away." Leila took great care not to mention the fact that *she* had not landed in the cactus.

Nevertheless, Cade gave her a dark look and grunted like a bad-tempered camel. "At least yours took off in a straight line. Mine went sideways. Next thing I knew, my butt was bouncing through the cactus." He paused as if listening to the words he had just spoken, then grinned crookedly at her, in a way that made her heart feel fluttery and soft. "This is probably going to seem funny as hell to me someday, but right now it hurts too damn much to laugh."

Leila didn't feel like laughing, either. She realized that what she wanted more than anything in the world was to put her arms around him—or at least touch his face…stroke and soothe him. But she sensed that would be the last thing he would want from her now. Still, she could not resist asking, in a voice husky with concern, "Are you…in very much pain?"

Then, of course, being a man, he must try to be heroic and act as though he was not. "Oh, hell—I'll live. I guess I've been in worse shape." He paused in the middle of hobbling back to the path to tilt his head sideways. "Been awhile, though."

Leila gave a small gasp. "Do you mean that this has happened to you before?"

"No, no—" his laugh was dark rather than humorous "—I was thinking of the last time my dad tanned my backside with his belt. I guess I must have been twelve."

"You do not mean—he *beat* you?" Her tender heart was appalled. "But...that is terrible!"

He paused to look down at her. Her heart jumped nervously, then began to beat with a quick and painful rhythm. "Hey, what can I say?" he said softly. "He was a drunk. I guess I never told you that, huh."

No, Leila thought, precarious and wondering. *Betsy did, but you didn't. And little else about yourself, either.* And she held her breath and prayed that he would not stop now.

He lifted his head to gaze beyond her. "Actually, he was a pretty decent guy when he wasn't drinking. Of course, he was drunk most of the time. Although to be honest, on that particular occasion—from his point of view, anyway—I probably deserved the licking."

"What did you do?" Her voice was hushed; she did not believe he could have done anything that would deserve a beating.

He gave a bark of laughter and his eyes came back to her. "Took my bike apart. Brand new—just got it for my birthday. Don't know what it cost, but it had to be expensive. I'd been begging for one for months, knowing my parents couldn't afford it." He shook his head; his eyes seemed to glow with remembering. "I couldn't believe it when I went out that morning and there it was." He paused, but Leila did not interrupt.

After a moment he drew a breath that seemed to hurt him, but inside, not where the cactus spines were. And when he tried to smile again, there was only the slightest flicker at the corners of his mouth. "Anyway, when my dad came home that evening, I had that bike in a million pieces. Had 'em all spread out on a blanket on the floor of the garage. I thought he was going to kill me. Darn near did. Then he rolled all those pieces into the blanket and threw 'em in the back of his truck and drove off. Last I

ever saw of my bike.'' He drew the pain-filled breath again.
''That hurt worse than the licking.''

''But, why?'' Leila dared to whisper. ''Why did you do
such a thing to this bike you wanted so much?''

He shrugged. ''I just wanted to see how everything
worked, find out how it all fit together. I was going to put
it all back. It's just the way I am—the way I've always
been.'' He frowned, looking past her again. ''My mom understood that, but for some reason Dad…'' After a moment
he brought his eyes back to her, and the pain in them almost
made her cry out in instinctive response. Because, as before, she knew this pain was not caused by the cactus
spines, but by memories carried deep in his heart. ''Anyway, my folks split up a couple months after that. For years
I thought it was because of me. Silly, huh?'' He gave his
head a rueful scratch.

Then, in what even to Leila seemed an obvious attempt
to escape these ''unmanly'' emotions, he gruffly muttered,
''Where the hell's my hat?''

No, she thought, I do not think you are silly at all. I
think you are a very strong and imposing man with a little
boy inside you. A little boy who has been very much hurt.
And I love that you have told me these things, even here
in the middle of a cactus patch. I wish that you would not
feel embarrassed that you have told me. And I wish that
you would not stop.

But all she said out loud was, ''There it is. Wait—I will
get it.'' And she ran to scoop up his cowboy hat from the
path. ''Now it is my turn to rescue *your* hat,'' she said in
a bumpy voice as she held it out to him, and as she did,
touched his eyes with hers. And with that look, with all
that was in her eyes, she was offering her compassionate
woman's heart to the hurt little boy she had seen in his.
Offering her newfound strength to him as she might have
given her hand to a child.

The look lasted for uncounted seconds, in a silence that seemed to shimmer with electricity, to rumble with tension like distant thunder.

Leila spoke at last, in a choked whisper. "We do not seem to have very good luck with hats, you and I."

And at that moment the rain came, rain such as Leila had never seen before. It fell with a great rushing sound, hard and heavy, straight down on their heads, as if someone had turned on a giant faucet in the sky. In seconds they were both drenched and gasping, and Leila's hat, which, unlike Cade's, was not meant to withstand all kinds of weather, had begun to wilt like a paper boat in a fountain.

"*You* sure don't," Cade shouted, and reached out to tip the sodden wreck of her hat backward and off of her head. "Look, why don't you go on—you know the way back to the ranch from here, don't you? Take the mare and go. I'll meet you back—"

"Are you *crazy?*" Leila shouted back through the curtain of rain, not even thinking that perhaps it was not the sort of thing a woman should say to her husband. "Do you think I would go away and leave you?"

"What, do you think I'm helpless?" Cade sputtered, looking very much like a stubborn donkey. "Go on—get in out of this!"

"Of course I do not think you are helpless. And I do not dissolve in water. This is only a little rain. So, we will walk home. It cannot be far."

Cade glared at her. The rain was already beginning to slacken at little, so he did not *really* have to shout at her the way he did. "Do you know that for a princess, you are awfully damn stubborn?"

"Yes," she said, flashing her dimples, "I suppose that I am." And she was surprised, because it was the first time all day that she had even remembered that she was a princess.

* * *

"Damn," Cade said gloomily, "I should have known." He flicked the light switch up and down again, with the same result. The power was out again. Naturally.

"It is not so *very* dark," Leila said as she slipped past him. "We can see quite well. It will not be night for several hours. By that time perhaps the electricity will be back on."

Cade made an ambiguous sound as he closed the door behind him. Then he stood for a moment and regarded her warily in the dim, shadowy light. He wasn't quite sure what to make of this new Leila, couldn't even decide in exactly what ways she *was* new. Her cheerfulness in the face of all the various discomforts and inconveniences he'd put her through was unexpected, maybe, except when he stopped to realize that he never really had heard her complain. Ever. Then there was the way she'd stood by him, out there in the cactus and the rain, when she could have been nice and cozy in a dry house. And he hadn't forgotten what had happened between them up there on the hilltop. God, no. But this "newness" didn't have anything to do with those things.

No...if he had to put a name to it, he'd probably call it self-confidence, though that commodity wasn't exactly new to her, either. She'd sure had no lack of it when he'd first met her. But this...whatever it was...was nothing like the unabashed cheekiness that had made her seem so young— and which he'd found so alluring-in the fairy-tale atmosphere of Tamir. He couldn't quite put his finger on why, but he knew this was different. And that his awareness of it, and her, was a vibrating knot of energy in the core of his body, like a miniature dynamo pumping out electrical impulses along all his nerves, keeping his senses charged to full capacity and tuned to her precise wavelength.

Those humming nerves made him cranky and snappish. "Yeah, well, it's gonna be tough to see to pull out these damn cactus spines,'' he growled, hunching his shoulders and heading for the kitchen like a man walking on eggs.

She pivoted as he passed her, then followed him. ''How are you going to do that?''

''What, pull out the spines?'' He was rummaging in the drawer where he kept the flashlights and other essentials, and didn't look at her. Though he could have gauged his distance from her as accurately as if he'd been equipped with his own personal GPS. ''Only thing I know of that'll do the job is a pair of needlenose pliers. Like these right here.'' Having located his in the drawer, he brandished them at her.

''No, I mean, how are *you* going to do it?'' She was regarding him calmly, all shades of black and gray in the murky light. ''The cactus is in your back, is it not?'' He glared at her, unable to think of a thing to say. She came toward him, and his skin shivered with goose bumps. ''I think that you will need help to pull out these spines.'' And she had taken the pliers from his hand before he could stop her.

When she would have taken the flashlight as well, though, he jerked it away from her like an obstinate child. ''No,'' he croaked. ''No way. I'll manage. I'll...I'll use a mirror.''

''And who will hold the flashlight?'' He was sure he could hear laughter in her voice. ''Will you grow a third hand?'' Cade made a growling sound in his throat and headed for the bathroom. In his wake he heard a patient little sigh. ''Cade, please do not be stubborn. You know that you cannot possibly do this by yourself. You must let me help you.''

She stood in the bathroom doorway and watched him struggle with it, watched him strain to find a reason why she must be wrong. She did not know why it was such a struggle for him. That was why she sighed.

Daringly, she said, "Is it so difficult for you, to let a woman tend you? Perhaps I do not understand. Is this not allowed in America—in Texas? Is it not—what is the word I have heard—*macho?*" She dimpled shamelessly at him; whether or not he could see them in the dimness, he would hear them in her voice.

He must have, because the sound he made was only a half-hearted snort. He did not growl at her as fiercely as before.

But then pain hissed between his teeth. He had unbuttoned his shirt and pulled it open, and was trying to shrug it away from his shoulders and back. The flashlight in his hand was an encumbrance to him now, and she thought it a minor victory that he did not object when she took it from him.

She switched the light on and trained it on his back.

"How bad is it?" He was straining to see over his shoulder.

She hastily turned off the light. "Not so terrible as I expected." She imagined the lie balanced on her tongue like a soap bubble. "I will have them out in no time. But first, we must have some antiseptic, I think. There is something here, surely? A medicine kit?"

Cade braced on the sink and glared at his hands, anchoring himself in the familiar shape of them, dark against the white porcelain as he felt his world, his life spin out of his reach. He felt an odd sense of fatalism, like an off balance skier heading down a treacherous slope. One way or another he was bound to get to the bottom.

"Yeah, in the plane," he muttered. "Somewhere around here, too, probably, but I'm damned if I know where."

"Never mind, I think I have seen something…" Her voice, somehow both breathless and tranquil, had retreated back into the kitchen. "Yes—here it is. This will do, I think…"

Curious to see what it was she'd found, afraid he already knew, he met her in the hallway. Sure enough. There was just enough light for him to see the bottle in her hands.

"Hey," he said, in a voice ragged with outrage, "that's good bourbon."

"Yes—it is alcohol, is it not?" He watched as she unscrewed the cap and took a sniff. His jaws cramped and his mouth began to water. "Mmm, and it smells good, too. Much nicer than the medicine kind. Come—" she waved the bottle imperiously "—it will be better, I think, if you lie down."

Cade meekly followed her into the bedroom she'd chosen—the one with her things in it. His heart was thumping and the energy dynamo inside him was whining away at fever pitch. And this rushing noise in his head—was that the sound of his life—events, fate—racing by, just beyond his reach?

She stood beside the bed and watched him come to her, the bottle of bourbon in one hand, the flashlight and needle-nose pliers in the other and her eyes full of mysteries. She drew a breath and when she spoke her voice was breathless still, but no longer the slightest bit tranquil. "First," she said—and he *knew* he could hear a tremor in it— "it will be necessary for you to remove your trousers."

And he felt a shivering, quivering, wholly unexpected desire to laugh when she abruptly turned her back and closed her eyes. He thought it was so like her. His virgin princess...

Oh, Leila thought, I really wish my voice had not trembled. She felt shaky all over, and she really could not allow that. It was not fear that made her tremble—she still felt that heady and wonderful sense of power, a kind of strength she somehow knew must be uniquely female. No—she shivered now with *excitement*. Something new...something she had never felt before. She shivered and shivered and could not seem to stop.

"I think," Cade said in a muffled voice, "that's about the best I can do. Hurts too much to bend over..."

She opened her eyes and turned, and her heart felt as though it had lodged in her throat. He was lying facedown across the bed, looking all gangly and ungraceful with his feet hanging over the edge. His trousers were bunched around the tops of his boots. Except for that, and a strip of white cloth across his buttocks, he was naked.

She placed the bottle of bourbon, the pliers and flashlight on the bed and gulped a breath of air. "Well," she said brightly, "I told you you would need my help."

She snatched another breath. Then she firmly grasped one booted foot and pulled. She felt his muscles tighten and pull against hers, and in another moment the boot slipped off and dropped onto the floor with a thump. Light-headed with that triumph, she went to the other foot and quickly did the same. Then she took hold of both legs of his blue jeans at the same time and pulled them off, then dropped them on top of the boots. By that time her legs were trembling so badly, it was a relief to sit down on the bed.

Except that when she did, she heard the gasp of Cade's indrawn breath. "What?" she whispered, afraid that she had hurt him. *Already!* She had not even begun to pull out the cactus!

"You're all wet," he mumbled. "You'll catch cold."

Yes, she was. Strange, but she had not thought about her wet clothes at all. Leila was quite certain she would not catch cold—she was never ill—but clearly she could not proceed with this delicate business dressed as she was.

There was only one thing to be done. One by one she pulled off her riding boots and dropped them on the floor beside Cade's. Then she stood up. "I will only be a mo-

Kathleen Creighton 197

ment,'' she whispered, and sternly added, when he raised himself on his elbows to try and see what she was doing, ''No—you must lie still. And...close your eyes.''

Then, as quickly as she could manage with nerveless, shaking fingers, she peeled off her blouse and jodhpurs and let them fall to the floor along with the rest of the wet clothing.

Her flesh cringed with goose bumps as she sat once more on the bed, taking care this time not to let her clammy skin touch Cade's. Her breasts felt hard as marble, and hurt where they brushed the inside of her bra. She drew yet another deep breath—why could she not seem to get enough air?

''I am ready,'' she whispered. Cade's only reply was a mutter she could not understand.

She picked up the flashlight and switched it on—caught her lower lip between her teeth and exhaled carefully through her nose. She had seen men's naked bodies before in pictures, of course, and in Rome and Paris, and in the British Museum there had been statues. But there was a great difference, she was discovering, between flat paintings and cold bronze or stone, and a warm, vital male body. What astonished her most was an almost overwhelming desire to *touch*. That little valley low on his back, just above the waistband of his underwear, dark with a furring of golden brown hair. The longing to bury her nose and mouth in that valley, to feel the softness of his hair on her face...it was so intense it made her head swim. Even as a small child Leila had liked to explore with her nose and mouth, lips and tongue, smelling and tasting as well as touching.

And she would—she silently promised herself that. But first there was the impediment of the cactus spines to deal with....

They did not look like much, really, just a scattering of prickles not very different in color from his skin, and a few drops of blood. Some of the prickles had already come away with his clothing. There were a few on his shoulders and elbows and thighs, more on his lower back, and quite a few more, she was certain, imbedded in the white cotton that covered his backside. Her hand shook as she picked up the pliers. She set them back down on the bed and picked up the bottle of bourbon instead.

"Well?" Cade's voice sounded muffled. "What's the holdup? Let's get this over with."

"Be still," she said. Her voice sounded cracked and strange. Balancing the flashlight across her lap, she unscrewed the top of the bottle. The flashlight teetered as she pulled up one leg and turned herself toward him. Carefully, she poured a tiny amount of the liquid in the bottle into that golden nest of hair.

His muscles contracted and his spine arched. He muttered something she could not hear.

"What?" Breathless, she held the bottle poised... motionless.

"I said, 'That's a helluva waste of good bourbon.'"

"Do you think so?" Leila tilted her head and regarded the bottle thoughtfully. Then she sniffed it again. It did smell good. Perhaps... She lifted the bottle to her lips and took a very large swallow.

What the hell—? Cade pushed himself up on one elbow to stare at Leila, who all of a sudden had begun to gasp and choke and wheeze as if she were dying. It took him about half a second to figure out that it wasn't lighter fluid she'd swallowed, but only a pretty good slug of his bourbon. He snaked out a hand and rescued both the bottle and the flashlight while he waited for her to get her breath back.

"But—it tastes *terrible*," she croaked when she could speak again, glaring at him accusingly, as if it were somehow Cade's fault. "How can you drink this?"

"It grows on you," he said, and automatically, because

of his father, added, "Too much, if you let it." But his mind wasn't on bourbon, or the words coming out of his mouth.

Because he'd just realized what he was looking at, pinioned in the yellow circlet of the flashlight beam. Something that up to now he'd only dreamed about. Leila...wearing bikini panties and a lacy white bra and absolutely nothing else. It was a sight to fill a man's dreams...an athlete's thighs, smooth and sleek...womanly flare of hips... The waist he'd held in his hands up there on the hilltop seemed even more slender than he'd imagined, contrasted with the lush femininity above and below. And her breasts... It was all he could do to keep himself from reaching out, pulling those bra straps down over her shoulders.

Then, for an instant he wondered if she'd somehow guessed his thoughts, when she pressed a hand to her chest and her skin seemed to darken to a dusky rose. But he realized that she was stroking, not hiding, and making an odd little pleasure-sound, like a large cat purring.

"Mmm...oh," she murmured. "Yes, I see what you mean. It feels very nice, now. Nice and warm...all over inside me." She gave herself a shake and added with delightful primness, "Well—it is a pity that something that smells so nice and feels so good must taste so awful. But, perhaps it is just as well, since I do not believe it is very good for you." She plucked the bottle and the flashlight from his hands. "Now you must lie down and let me finish," she said, and gave him a severe look that had the opposite effect on him than she probably intended.

He obeyed her with a groan, somehow managing to quell the impulse he'd just had, which was to just say the hell with the cactus, and roll her under him and kiss her breathless.

He never knew how he got through the next hour, quite

possibly the most intense pleasure and the most exquisite agony he could ever have imagined. And the cactus spines had very little to do with it.

Lying there on his belly with his mind full of the last image he'd had of her—lush, curving flesh and taunting strips of lacy white—first he'd feel a tiny *zzt* of pain, then the sweet burn of the bourbon, and then the far sweeter warmth of her mouth…gentle heat and drawing pressure…and sometimes, when she forgot to hold it back out of the way, the cool silky kiss of her hair. Between times, she sang to him in a sweet, soft voice, in a language he didn't know. And when she had cleared an area of spines large enough, she would pour more bourbon into her hands and rub him all over with it…stroking, massaging…kneading the sting and the ache away. That was the pleasure.

The agony was elsewhere. In his groin, of course, but in his belly, too, and the muscles of his arms and legs, his neck and jaws. Desire had taken over his body; it was a white-hot starburst in his brain. He was being consumed by desire. Sooner or later, he knew, he would have to do something about it, and when he did, he was desperately afraid he wouldn't be able to control the monster that was eating him alive.

And he knew the worst was yet to come. She'd worked her way down his back to the elastic waistband of his shorts. She'd plucked the last of the spines from the backs of his arms and legs. When he felt her fingers slip under that elastic he knew he'd endured all he could. He made a sound somewhere between a sob and a groan and tried to turn.

"No, no," she said softly, "you must let me finish." Gently but firmly she pushed him down. Even more gently she lifted his shorts away from his pricked backside, drew them over his legs and tossed them away.

And he found there was more he *could* endure, after all.

But just barely. He'd never felt so vulnerable. The cool air stirring over exposed skin, like a touch that never quite came, the cold wet tickle of alcohol between his legs and down his sides, and then—with all his strength he braced for it—*her mouth.* Yes, even there, laving, sucking…soothing away the sting. He could hear her quick, shallow breathing above the labored pounding of his own heart—for some reason, she'd stopped singing.

He knew when she'd pulled the last of the spines. He heard her take in a breath and let it out in a soft and oddly replete little sigh. He felt her weight shift as she set the bottle of bourbon on the nightstand. Then shift again. He felt the cushiony weight of her breasts as she bent over him. Relief and alarm slammed into him and his heart skidded and lurched out of rhythm. *No.*

Had he spoken? What did it matter? His body shuddered and shivered with adrenaline as he caught her around her waist. In an instant he'd pinned her, flat on her back, to the mattress.

The flashlight rolled away somewhere, but it spilled enough light across the bed that he could see her face staring up at him…the dark enigma of her eyes, utterly without fear, just tiny lines of puzzlement between them.

Her breasts heaved beneath his arm as she whispered, "You do not wish me to continue?"

"No." This time he knew he'd spoken, but it was in a voice he didn't recognize. "And it's not a matter of wishing. I can't let you."

"Why? I do not understand. Do you not like it?"

Looking up and away from her, he gave a soft, croaking laugh. Then he brought his eyes back to her, and was caught off guard by a treacherous, shimmering fog of overwhelming tenderness. Like that strange, protective tenderness he'd felt for her before, only this was much, much worse. He couldn't speak, but had to look away again, and take deep breaths and laugh a little the way men do when they dare not humiliate themselves with symptoms of emotion.

When he was able to look at her again, he lifted a hand to touch her face. Softly, with wondering fingers he traced the ink-black line of her eyebrow, the clean, pure sweep of her cheek and jaw.

"Don't you know?" He shrugged one shoulder and said it with aching simplicity. "You're a virgin."

Chapter 12

She didn't say anything for several seconds, while her heartbeat fluttered against the barricade of his arm like a captive bird struggling to free itself. Then she made a sound, a perplexed and impatient little sigh.

"In my culture," she whispered, and her frown deepened as she searched his face, "a man would consider a woman's virginity a treasure…a gift. I think that for you this is not true. I think…for you it is only a burden."

"Not so much a burden…" He considered, his voice gravelly and soft. "More like…a responsibility."

"But…why?" She gave a hopeless little sigh and said again, "I do not understand."

And again Cade had to gaze into the shadows beyond the light while he gathered his courage. She couldn't know, could she, how hard it was for him to talk about such intimate things? "I'm too full…too hard…right now. Too…aroused." He took a breath, but the words wouldn't come, and finally he whispered it brokenly, "I don't think I could stand it if I hurt you."

"Oh," she cried, "is that all?" Her eager innocence

nearly shattered him. Her fingers closed around his wrist. She turned her lips into his palm like a bird snuggling into its nest, and he could feel them form a smile against his skin. She closed her eyes, and something glimmered like tiny diamonds in her lashes. She whispered, "I thought...it was because you did not want me."

He was too precarious; he dared not laugh. With a soft groan he lowered his forehead until it touched hers. "Not want you? No, no, it's that I want you too much."

Her fingers left his wrist and wove themselves into his hair. Her face tilted and her lips touched searchingly here and there on his face...his chin, the edges of his jaws, the corners of his mouth. Between touches, in breathless little puffs he heard words. "But I am...your wife. How...is it possible...to want...your wife...too much?"

Your wife. He replayed the words in his head and his heart shuddered as if from a violent collision. In a sense it was—a collision between heart and head...between reason and emotion. If you do this, his head reminded him, it can't be undone.

To which his heart responded, *I don't care!*

In slow, sighing surrender he brought his mouth into alignment with hers...barely touching...brushing her breath with his. He felt her go motionless with wonder. Her lips opened in a blissful, waiting smile. She moved her head slowly back and forth, caressing his lips with hers, mercilessly teasing nerve-endings already honed to needle points. He felt the caress in his temples and breastbone, in the soles of his feet and the backs of his knees, in the pit of his stomach...and with a deep, burning ache in his groin.

If I kiss her now, he thought—he absolutely knew—I won't be able to stop.

"It is all right," she murmured, as if she'd heard his thought, her words tickling his lips. "I have been told it is normal for there to be pain the first time. I do not mind."

With a quick, violent motion he caught her wrist and

held it pressed against the bedspread while he drew back to look at her. Her breasts rose and fell in uneven rhythm, brushing against his arm. He frowned down at them and muttered groggily, "Who told you that?" Whoever it had been, in his heart he was vowing there and then to make that person a liar.

"Salma. When I was very small she was my nanny. Now she is my very dear friend. And she gave me something to help soothe the pain…a special recipe of herbs and oils. She said it is from her grandmother."

Herbs and oils? He was beginning to get *The Arabian Nights* feeling again. That sense of unreality grew more encompassing as he listened to the muffled thump of his heart…heard his own voice as if through layers of wool. Carefully, trying not to smile, he said, "And you…brought this magic stuff with you?"

"Yes, of course—I have it right here, in my bag." And lithe as an otter she twisted under him, rolling onto her stomach as she stretched an arm to reach for her overnighter.

He barely knew when she opened it and began to rummage through its contents. Raised on one elbow, he gazed at her body…the pale, curving shape of it against the darker bedspread…and paler still the narrow stripe across her back…the triangle that barely succeeded in covering the rounded mounds of her bottom. He was thinking about himself in just that position, the treatment she'd put him through…his terrifying vulnerability, the exquisite sensations…his overwhelming arousal.

She gave a soft "Hah!" of triumph and held up a bottle, graceful in shape and iridescent in color. But before she could roll back to him, he growled, "Not so fast," and with a hand on the small of her back, pinned her there on her belly. In a moment he was kneeling astride her thighs, bending over to whisper in her ear, "Now it's my turn…."

Though the pain of desire, the pressure of his arousal as

merciless as before, now his mind, at least, was clear. He felt in control again, of himself and of circumstances. Confidence surged like a drug through his veins. He felt light-headed with his power over her, and at the same time he quivered inside with tenderness.

Oh, so gently, because he knew from firsthand experience how helpless and vulnerable she must be feeling, he drew the silken skein of her hair away from her face and neck, pausing to trace, with a delicacy he'd never known he possessed, the outline of her ear. He heard her exhale as he brushed her cheek with the backs of his fingers, and felt the tickle of her lashes as she closed her eyes.

He straightened, then, and deftly unhooked the fastening of her bra, and with his fingers fanned outward like a moth's wings drew his thumbs downward along her spine, acquainting her with his touch. Her skin felt hot and smooth, as if she had a fever.

He eased the bottle from her curled fingers and opened it, then held the bottle to his nose. The fragrance was exotic...mysterious...intoxicating...all the things he associated with *her.* It filled his head with images...impressions...memories...of sun-drenched gardens heavy with the scent of roses, of laughing fountains and brightly colored birds, and of a black-haired princess with a winsome, dimpled smile.

Setting aside the cap, he poured a small pool of oil into the valley between her shoulderblades. He began to spread it over her body, working like a master sculptor, kneading and molding, sometimes with his fingers, sometimes with his whole hands, utterly engrossed in the artistry of her body, the utter perfection of her muscles, the way they arranged themselves so beautifully over her bones. The clever symmetry of her spine...

She wasn't as relaxed as she seemed. She stirred when he eased himself backward, fingers reaching under the lacy top of her underpants.

"Fair's fair," he whispered as very slowly he peeled them over the rise of her bottom, and forgot to breathe as he watched with a schoolboy's fascination this final unveiling of her nakedness. He moved to her side at last in order to shuck her panties the rest of the way off, and felt her spine contract when he leaned over to kiss, like one bestowing a benediction, the matched set of indentations just where the firm resilience of muscle began.

With upmost care, and marshaling all the self-control he had left, he poured oil into the gentle valley at her waist. Then began to spread it downward...down her sides, over the smooth mounds of her buttocks to the backs of her thighs. He poured more oil and with it slipped his fingers into the cleft between her buttocks, gauging minutely her response to this first invasion of her body's most private places.

Her breathing grew quick and distressed. She stirred again, and it was instinct, perhaps, that made her move her legs a little apart. He lay beside her, then, stretching his body all along hers and raising himself on one elbow so he could murmur assurances to her as he caressed her. She tried to turn her face toward him, searching...seeking...but he pressed his face against the side of hers to keep her still and kissed her ear, and then her neck. She gasped and squirmed closer to him, but didn't try again to turn.

And then he soothed her with kisses and wordless sounds while he slipped his oiled fingers between her thighs and penetrated for the first time her virgin softness.

She was tight...so tight...breathing in little pants and whimpers, but not, he knew, with pain. Gently, he withdrew, then penetrated once again, then again, easing farther into her body each time. The oil and her own moisture made it easy. Her skin was hot where it lay along his, her hair damp with sweat and musky with her own unique, exotic scent. His heart pounded wildly, giddily, as he brought his open mouth to her nape and immersed himself in the heat and smell of her…as he pushed deeper, and yet deeper into her body. And when he had penetrated her as far as he could in that way, he heard her give a sharp little cry—more surprised than frightened—and felt her flesh contract and pulse around his finger. He held her so gently, housing her safely in his hand, soaking himself in her heat, and his own body was shot through with ripples and shudders—of pleasure, and other emotions even more bewildering.

Presently, when her body had quieted, she turned her face again—not toward him, this time, but downward, as if she wanted to hide from him. With her arms drawn in under her she spoke in a muffled voice to the bedspread. "Cade, I am sorry. I did not mean for that to happen…I do not know why—I could not help it. Such a thing has never happened to me before."

Please, oh please, he thought, just let me do this right.

With careful gravity, he said, "No, probably not. What you felt, Princess, was an orgasm." He paused. Then, letting a smile leak into his voice, he added, "A small one."

She lifted her head to stare at him, half her face veiled behind the midnight fall of her hair. "Really? Is this true? I did not know it would feel like that. I have read about this in books, but—"

"Books?" It was such a relief to laugh. "Where in the world did you get hold of a sex book?" There were obviously unplumbed depths to this princess of his.

"In boarding school, one of the girls had one. I think she was French. We used to look at it at night under the blankets with a flashlight." She looked down, catching her lip and dimpling at remembered mischief. Then she brought her eyes back to him and in that feeble light he caught the tiny movements of her swallow, the quivering of her mouth. "But it is impossible to know from reading a book how something will *feel*."

He lifted his hand, slipped it under her hair and gently

cupped her cheek. "I don't know, either, how it feels for you," he said softly. "I only know how it feels for me."

She tipped her head, resting it in the cradle of his hand as her eyes clung to his face. "It must feel very, very good for you, then."

"Oh, yeah…" The words vibrated under his sternum like a tiger's purr.

Her lips quivered again, this time with a smile that flickered out before it could reach her dimples, then vanished when she turned her lips into his palm. "I want you to have this feeling," she said huskily as her eyes drifted closed.

"Oh, I will, don't worry about that." Again, the laughter felt good to him.

"And…you must not be afraid of hurting me."

For a moment he was silent, struggling with emotions new to him and words he didn't know how to say. He'd been enjoying the interlude; it was new to him, this quiet intimacy wrapped in a cocoon of almost-darkness, with his mind at least temporarily at peace and his body like a pressure cooker on slow simmer. He'd been in no hurry to have it end, using those moments to marshal his strength and shore up his sagging self-control. Because he knew, as she didn't, that she was nowhere near ready for him, not if he was going to have a prayer of keeping the promise he made to her then, in a fierce and determined growl, "I'm not going to hurt you, Princess."

She gave a patient, acquiescing sigh. He allowed her to turn onto her back then, and his eyes to feast on the banquet of feminine beauty he'd only seen, before tonight, camouflaged in the modestly elegant clothes she always wore. Camouflaged now by the darkness, allowing him veiled hints of creamy mounds and dusky hollows, of purple-rose areolas and an ink-black triangle, kitten-soft above the juncture of her thighs. Hungry for more, he was reaching for

the flashlight when she spoke, raising herself up on her
elbows.

"I would like to see you," she said.

And he kissed her instead, and murmured against her
mouth, "You will...but not now."

"But why?"

So he kissed her again, and more and more deeply until,
overwhelmed, she sank back onto the bedspread and
reached hungrily for him, already panting and gasping and
arching her body toward him as she drove her fingers into
his hair. He drew back, then, and stared down into her
dazed, midnight eyes. "You have to trust me," he said.

Trust me... What choice did she have?

She was lost in a world she could not have imagined, a
world of senses and sensations, some so exquisite and
lovely she wanted to reach for them, hold them in her hands
like a child grasping at soap bubbles. Some so overwhelming she was in awe of them, frightened by their power, like
one standing on the edge of a waterfall. She was lost, and
yes, she was frightened, too. But there was a delicious,
shivery excitement to her fear. Because there was Cade.

Yes...she trusted him. There it was...as simple and glorious and mystifying as that. She trusted him with all her
heart and soul. Her body was no longer hers to command—
she was his, now, completely, only clay in the potter's
hands.

A potter? No. Though she had no scale by which to judge
such things, to her it seemed he must be an artist...a master.
His hands...his mouth...they commanded and consumed
her...controlled and demanded, molded, manipulated and
presumed. But never, never did they cause her pain. Only
the most exquisite joy and unimagined pleasure. Twice
more she felt the strange and wonderful sensations as her
body first seemed to grow hot and huge and intense as the
sun, then come suddenly apart into a cascade of a thousand
pulsing infant stars, once when he had drawn apart her

thighs with his hands and kissed her…kissed her the way he kissed her mouth, deeply, with his tongue…just *there,* where she was already so hot and swollen and sensitive to the slightest touch. The feeling then…it was so intense she cried out and arched and trembled in his hands, not knowing whether she struggled away from, or toward the terrifying sensations, only certain she could stand no more than this—more than this, and she would surely die.

Then…and now it seemed too quickly…he was holding her tightly and she was rocketing over a precipice and falling, falling, breath forced from her lungs in pants and cries, and her body throbbing inside and burning, tingling all over, in every part of her, and she understood finally what Cade had meant when he had said, "A small one."

She trusted him. Completely. And when at last he drew her legs wide apart and knelt so carefully between them…when he had taken Salma's bottle of soothing oil and poured some in his hand, then stroked it gently between her legs and deep, deep inside her…when he leaned over, bracing himself on his hands, and looked a question and a promise deep into her eyes…she gazed back at him from under half-closed lids that had somehow grown too heavy to lift…and smiled.

She trusted him. But she gasped when she felt him fit himself to her softness; she couldn't seem to help it. She gasped again when she felt the first intense, steadily building pressure. And instantly he was there, taking her face between his hands and stroking her cheeks, her eyelids, her temples with his thumbs. Taking over her consciousness, whispering urgently into her mouth, *"Stay with me…relax, sweetheart…don't tense up on me now…"*

She nodded, let her breath out and opened herself to him.

By slow and careful degrees she let him come into her body, and she accepted the mounting pressure with something akin to triumph. *Was* this pain? She did not know, and anyway, if it had been she would not have let *him*

know. She simply did not care, for this was her husband...from this moment he would forever be a part of her.
She could never have imagined such a fierce and all-
consuming joy.

Oh, but now, as the pressure in her body was increasing
almost beyond her ability to endure it, so was another kind
of pressure altogether. She could feel it coming, feel it filling her throat, making her chest jump and quiver...making
her breath whimper and her eyes sting. She tried to stop it,
but it came anyway, like that other tumult her body could
not control.

"I am sorry," she gasped, and her chest was heaving,
her voice high and broken with panic. "I do not mean to
cry—I do not want—it does not mean—please do not think
you are hurting me. I do not know why—I cannot seem to
stop it—"

She had trusted him in all else, she should have trusted
him to understand this, as well.

For he only whispered, "Shh...it's okay," and she could
hear a smile in his voice as he kissed her and stroked her
puddled eyelids. "It's just emotions...go ahead and cry if
you want to."

Then, strangely, she began to laugh instead. But it was
a different kind of laughter than any she had ever
known...laughter mixed with tears, gentle, wondering
laughter. Miraculously, he seemed to understand that, too,
kissing her tears, then her lips, again and again, mixing his
laughter with hers.

"You do not have to stop," she murmured, awed and
sated by the feel of him inside her.

"Yeah, actually, I do," he said with an odd, breathless
little chuckle. He lowered his head to touch a tiny kiss to
the end of her nose. "That would be...about as far as I can
go—in more ways than one." He kissed her again, her
mouth this time. She could feel tension vibrating in his
arms, could hear it in his voice, as if his jaws were

clenched. "I'm afraid...I've had about all I can take. It just feels...too good inside you, sweetheart. I think...you're going to have to let me have that feeling, now..."

Before she could even really understand or prepare, she felt him gather himself...felt him pull back and his muscles bunch and harden...felt him surge into her with a force that drove the breath from her lungs. Dazed and a little frightened, she was simply caught up and swept away by the strength and power of his maleness...and for the first time understood the extent of his control, the depth of his restraint, the price of his gentleness.

This was Cade—*her husband*—imposing and magnificent and powerful.

Yes, but vulnerable, too. Along with her understanding of her husband's maleness, for the first time she understood her own femininity as well. Understood that this man she had married might be bigger and harder and physically stronger than she was, but that *she* was powerful, too. Because, all his wonderful strength and vitality he must pour finally into *her. She* had the power to make this strong man tremble...to make *him* vulnerable.

That realization came to her in a great wave of that strange protective tenderness she'd felt for him, out there in the rain. Only now she knew what it was.

But...this can only be love, she thought in wonderment. *Yes, it must be. It is true. I love him.*

Another wave of emotion swept over her, this one cold and terrible, full of longing, and it made her hold on to him with a kind of fierce desperation as his big body surged and emptied into hers.

Cade, I love you! Her heart cried it, but she could not say it out loud. She loved him. She knew it, now. And that made it all the more terrible that he did not love her.

The evening had long since eased into night and the flashlight had burned itself out hours ago. Leila's breathing was soft and even in a darkness thick as wool when Cade slipped out of bed and made his way—with a confidence born of regular practice—to the bathroom. With the door closed he felt for the matches on top of the toilet tank and lit the candle he'd left there…oh, hours ago, now…stuck in a coffee mug with its own melted wax. How Leila had loved that.

He closed his eyes and gripped the edges of the sink with both hands as images swamped him…memories so recent, so sharp and clear he could actually see her now, right there, lowering herself into the bathtub, wincing a little when her soft feminine parts touched the barely warm bubbles. He'd felt such anguish, and had thought of bruised fruit and crushed flower petals, but then she had looked up at him and smiled that irresistible dimpled smile of hers, and a moment later he'd slipped into the tub behind her and what was meant to be the aftermath of something incredible had become instead the beginning of something even more.

Even now, exhausted and drained beyond all endurance, just remembering the feel of her soap-slippery bottom fitting itself between his legs, and himself sliding between hers…yes, somehow, both at the same time…her body arching and his hands filling with the sweet, hot weight of her breasts…even now, remembering that, his groin ached and his head swam with desire. How could it not?

He lifted his head and stared at himself in the medicine cabinet mirror. The candlelight made his face gaunt, his eyes shadowed and bleak. What the hell was the matter with him? A bridegroom after a night like this—he should be considering himself the luckiest, the happiest man in the world. Either that, or, considering his circumstances, he ought to be kicking himself all the way to kingdom come and back. In actual fact, he wasn't feeling either one of those things. Truth was, he didn't have any idea what he was feeling.

So, he'd made love to his wife. He'd consummated his marriage, even knowing what it would mean to both of them—so much for his willpower. And it had been about the most mind-blowing, intense pleasure of his life. And, except for the fact that it pretty much committed him to this marriage whether he wanted it or not, what had it changed? The woman sleeping in there in his bed was still, in almost all the ways that counted, a stranger to him. The woman he'd committed to share the rest of his life with came from a culture so different from his, she might as well have been from another planet. The woman he'd held in his arms, immersed himself so totally in he couldn't have told where he left off and she began...the woman into whom—God help him—he'd poured his genes...was still Leila Kamal, princess of Tamir. Wasn't she?

So why did his arms feel empty now without her? Why did his body still ache with wanting her? And most mystifying of all, what was this terrible ache of tenderness he felt for her in his heart?

Having no answers for himself, he went into the bedroom where he'd stowed his overnighter, took out a clean pair of shorts and put them on. Then he went out onto the porch and sat on the steps and watched the dawn come.

At least he knew what he was feeling, now. Blitzed, shell-shocked, bewildered. And scared half to death.

Leila woke up with a delicious stiffness in every muscle and joint, the kind that felt so *good* when she stretched, long and luxuriously, like a great, lazy cat. There was also a mysterious swollen ache between her legs that registered her pulse in little pleasure taps, tiny echoes of what had happened there not so long ago. Under the blankets, she hugged her nakedness against a shiver of...what? Fear? Happiness? Perhaps, Leila thought, what I am is fearfully happy.

She was not surprised to find herself alone in the bed

she had shared with Cade, but she was disappointed. When, she wondered, would she finally know what it was like to wake up in the morning beside her husband?

But she would never say anything of the kind to Cade. She must not presume too much. After all, just because he was her husband, just because he had *made* love to her, did not mean he *loved* her. She was not so naïve as to think those two were the same. And just then she was far too vulnerable to want to know the truth about how Cade felt about her.

Last night he had seemed so tender. She had even allowed herself to believe he *must* love her, in his own way, perhaps in some buried part of him. But this morning, he was gone from her bed, and no…she would not allow herself to presume. Never again. The risk was far too great. She would guard herself, as she had been doing ever since that terrible moment in Cade's bedchamber in the palace, when she had realized how disastrously she had misunderstood him.

Her body was now and would always be Cade's. So was her heart. But that was *her* secret, and for now she must bury it in the innermost keep of her soul.

She rose and dressed quickly in slacks and a long-sleeved blouse—and she really must, she told herself, buy some blue jeans, which seemed to be all people in Texas ever wore. After a brief stop in the bathroom, she went looking for her husband. He wasn't in the house, and for the tiniest moment she felt twinges of unreasoning panic—ridiculous, of course, did she think he would leave her here? But then through the living room window she caught a glimpse of him, on the front porch. Before going to join him, she paused and with her forehead pressed against the door, said a prayer. *Please, God, let my face be serene. Please…let it not show him how hard my heart is beating.*

He was leaning against a post and looking out over the railing, smoking one of his thin, brown cigars and holding a heavy crockery mug with symbols on it that Cade had told her were brands for cattle. Though he did not look much like a cowboy this morning, wearing blue jeans, yes, but with a white short-sleeved polo shirt and sunglasses. He looked fresh and clean as rain, lean and relaxed...and utterly unapproachable.

He turned when she came onto the porch. His face was composed as he lifted his mug to her and said, "Good morning."

"Good morning," she said back to him. She wished she could see his eyes. She wished he would smile at her, just once with that lifting, unfettered joy she'd seen that morning in the palace courtyard. *Just once.* Then I would know, she thought.

"Want some coffee? There's still plenty..."

She glanced over her shoulder toward the house, then shrugged and said, "Yes, thank you. I will get some in a minute." She hesitated, then asked, "Have you been up long?" Making it light, casual, not presuming too much.

He took a sip of coffee, then the cheroot. "Awhile," he said, blowing away the smoke. Then, softly, "How 'bout you? Sleep well?"

Her heart gave a bump, and to keep it from her voice, she took a deep breath. "Yes, I did, thank you. Very well." We are like two strangers, she thought bleakly. How she wished she could go to him and slip her arms around his waist with the perfect faith that should be natural between husband and wife, lay her face against his chest and tell him joyfully and without reservation what was in her heart, that this morning was beautiful beyond words because he was in it.

Instead, she walked to the railing a little distance from him, and, leaning on her hands, looked out upon a morning that was fast becoming less beautiful. "It smells fresh, after the rain," she said, filling her lungs with air that felt heavy and smells that were alien. "Will it be a nice day, do you think?"

"Hard to say." Cade shifted restlessly and tossed away his cheroot. "This is thunderstorm weather. You never know where they'll pop up."

"Will we ride again today?"

Cade threw her a look of surprise. After last night, how could she even suggest such a thing? Either she wasn't thinking clearly, or he'd done a better job of taking care of her than he'd thought. He smiled crookedly. Memories made his voice husky. "I don't think so. My backside's still a little bit sore. Besides—" he drank coffee and tossed away the dregs "—I think we'd better tidy up the place and then head on back."

"So soon?" She looked at him and then quickly away, but not before he saw the look of disappointment that flashed across that all-revealing face of hers.

"I think we better. If we wait till this afternoon we're liable to run into thunderstorms, and I don't know about you, but I wouldn't care to fly through something like what we had yesterday." His voice was rough with gravel, and he kept his face turned away from her so she wouldn't see the tension in it. Even with sunglasses on he didn't trust his own eyes.

And hell, why was it he couldn't just tell her how he felt, which was that he'd love nothing better than to stay here indefinitely with her in this old broken-down ranch house, live like a couple of bohemians, stay naked most of the time and make love whenever either of them felt like it? He didn't know why, except that even thinking about saying such a thing to her made him feel too vulnerable. He wasn't ready, yet, to hang his heart out in the open like that. Maybe he never would be.

"Besides," he said, more abruptly than he meant to, "I have a whole hell of a lot of work to do to get ready for the week. Got a schedule coming up that won't quit." He lifted his coffee mug, saw it was empty and grimaced at it instead. Dammit, he'd done it on purpose, too, that was the hell of it. Scheduled himself to the brink of oblivion just to give himself an excuse not to go home to his wife. Well, *hell.* How was he supposed to know things were going to change on him so fast, and that he'd be *wanting* to spend time with her? "I doubt I'm gonna be home much," he said bitterly, "at least for the rest of the week."

"Of course...I understand," she murmured. "Then...I will go and get ready. Let me know when you would like to leave." And she turned and walked into the house, tall, elegant and regal. Even with her hair a tumbled reminder of a night of passion and unrestrained sex, she was every inch a princess.

As Cade watched her walk away from him he tried to think of her that way, naked and moist, panting in his arms. But though he could call the memories to his mind, he couldn't quite seem to make them touch his senses, not in the gut-wrenching, groin-tightening way they had come to him first thing this morning. Already, it seemed, his mind was protecting him, drawing an insulating veil around the night just passed.

In a little while, if he was lucky, maybe last night would begin to seem like those days and nights in Tamir...like something that had happened to someone else, long ago, in a fairy tale.

Chapter 13

On Friday, Cade phoned to say that he would be home early, perhaps even in time to have dinner with his wife.

When Leila heard this she felt first a great surge of joy. That was followed almost immediately by an equally powerful wave of anger. She had been experiencing this same roller coaster of emotions all week long, while her husband had been hundreds of miles away in a place called Odessa. She was, in fact, a cauldron of emotions, bewildering emotions. Loneliness and longing, frustration and fury were only the few she could name.

Over and over she thought, How could he do this to me? How can he be so cruel? To have opened the doors of Paradise to her, to have shown her such happiness, all that her heart had ever desired—and in the next moment to have snatched it away from her, slammed the door shut and trapped her once more in her lonely cage.

Yes…that was what it felt like. She was locked up in a cage. *No! A coop,* she thought, remembering what Cade had told her that night on the terrace. For the truth was she felt more ''cooped up'' here in Texas, with all its wide open spaces, than she ever had in the royal palace in Tamir.

Tamir. When she thought of the palace, with its clean white lines, with its gardens and courtyards and clifftop terraces overlooking the sea, and of her sisters, her mother, Salma and Nargis…and Papa, with his great comforting girth and snowy white beard, and eyes that always held a sparkle of affection for her…she was almost overcome with homesickness. And that was followed inevitably by anger.

I will not take this treatment much longer, she told herself, fortifying her faltering reserves of self-confidence with something she had always had in great abundance. *Pride.* After all, she reminded herself, I am a princess!

But then she remembered the feeling of power that had come to her there on the ranch, in the cactus patch and in Cade's arms. And an even more exhilarating, ennobling thought came to her: *I am a woman. I deserve better. I deserve to be loved.*

And she would tell Cade that, she had decided. This evening, after they had shared the dinner Betsy had prepared.

But for some reason, to Leila's dismay, Betsy decided on this particular Friday that she must leave work early. She had things to do, she and Rueben, and they must make a trip into town. Leila was not to worry, dinner was all prepared, all she would need to do was heat it up in the microwave. Betsy showed Leila the platter of beef kabobs—cubes of marinated beef skewered on sticks with chunks of onion and peppers and tomatoes, already grilled and arranged on a bed of fluffy rice that had been seasoned with broth and sweet red peppers. It was one of Cade's favorite dishes, Betsy said, guaranteed to put him in a good mood for the evening. And she had given Leila a wink. Then she had caught her up in a hug and had whispered, ''Don't give up on him, honey. You just need to be patient.''

Patient? Well, it was true that patience had never been one of Leila's greatest virtues. And as the time approached for Cade to arrive, she became more and more impatient and nervous. She paced in the kitchen, looking again and again at the digital clock on the stove. Was it time yet? Should she take out the food now? She had never prepared and served a meal for her husband before. Many times she went over the checklist in her mind—she had already arranged the dishes and silverware on the table in the dining room, just the way Betsy had taught her, and had even cut some roses from the bushes in the yard and arranged them in a crystal vase. There was iced tea chilling in a glass pitcher in the refrigerator, and Cade's favorite bourbon on a silver tray on the sideboard.

Everything was ready. But where was Cade?

He had told Betsy he would be home early, in time for dinner—but what did that mean? Six o'clock? Seven? And now it seemed to Leila that it was growing dark very rapidly. What if something had happened to him? An automobile accident, perhaps, driving home on those freeways with so many cars.

She paced and paced, growing more and more nervous. Finally, she could stand it no longer. She would at least get out the food. Put it in the microwave oven, so it would be ready at a moment's notice, the minute he came home…

Thunder rumbled in the deepening dusk outside as she opened the refrigerator and oh, so carefully slid the heavy, plastic-wrapped platter toward her. She picked it up in both hands and turned to bump the door closed with her hip.

From out of nowhere, it seemed, came a great boom of thunder. With all her concentration on the platter in her hands and her nerves honed to knife-points, Leila reacted to the sound as if she had been shot. She gave a startled cry and the platter dropped from her hands.

Her heart seemed to stop. Her world went silent. Encased in a bubble of shock, she stared down at the swath of rice and juices, chunks of meat and brightly colored vegetables scattered across the tile floor amidst sparkling icicle shards of glass.

No! her mind shrieked, refusing to believe what was before her own eyes. Refusing to believe such a disaster could have happened, and that *she* was responsible. *No!* This could not be her fault. She had never done such a thing before in her life.

This would not have happened if she had not been so nervous, so worried and upset. About Cade. *Cade! Yes!* This was all *his* fault.

With a howl of unprincesslike fury, Leila hurled herself across the kitchen, snatched open the door and plunged outside into the rain that had just that moment begun to fall.

Cade couldn't remember when he'd ever been so glad to be home. He couldn't believe, either, how much he was looking forward to seeing his wife. The nice buzz of anticipation he'd been nursing all day had intensified during the time he'd spent sitting in rain—and accident-snarled traffic on Houston's outbound freeways until now it was a throbbing weight in his belly and a smoldering fire in his groin.

He hadn't been able to get her out of his mind all week. Images, bits and pieces of the day and night they'd spent at the ranch, kept invading his conscious and unconscious thoughts, making a joke of his concentration during the day and total chaos of his nights.

The truth was, he'd done quite a lot of thinking about Leila and his marriage during those lonely nights in a barren motel room out there in the vast Texas midlands. And the conclusion he'd come to was that, since it looked like he was stuck in this marriage for the duration, he'd better find a way to make it work. He'd come back to Houston full of new vows and determination—to spend more time with his wife, for one thing. He thought—he hoped—if they did things together, if he got to know her better, maybe he'd find they had something in common after all. Maybe he'd even learn how to talk to her.

One thing for certain: he was tired of fighting his desire for her. Literally. Worn out. It was sapping his strength, physically, mentally and emotionally, and if he didn't do something about it, sooner or later it was going to start affecting his ability to run a business. Not to mention what it was doing to his disposition.

By the time Cade got home rain was coming down in buckets, so he parked his car right beside the back gate, the better to make a run for it. Conveniently for him, the gate was wide open. Surprising, too, since it was a poolyard gate and therefore supposed to be self-closing. The way it looked, the gate must have been thrown back with some pretty good force, so that the latch had caught on the fence, holding it open. Which was unusual, but not unheard of, and probably explainable because of the rain—somebody running for cover in a big hurry. He didn't begin to feel alarmed until he saw that the kitchen door was wide open, too.

Calling Leila's name, he went into the kitchen. His heart was already beginning to pound. He was so intent on looking for her that he almost stepped in the mess on the floor before he saw it. "What the hell—?" he muttered. Quickly skirting the disaster, he stuck his head into the hallway, calling more urgently now. And he was halfway up the stairs when the significance of the open door and thrown-back gate finally penetrated the alarm-clamor in his brain. Then he knew exactly where he'd find her.

Leila was in the center aisle of the stable. She was brushing the foal, Sari, while Suki, her mother, watched with anxiously pricked ears from a nearby stall. Leila was singing in Arabic as she usually did when she worked with horses, not in her usual soothing croon but in short, breathless whimpers that were not soothing to anyone. Least of all Leila.

When she heard the scrape of footsteps on concrete, she did not want to look. She wanted to go on calmly brushing Sari as though she had not a care in the world, but how could she, when every beat of her heart felt like a blow that rocked her whole body, when her hands could not hold the brush steady, but instead jerked and shook as if she had a violent chill.

Then, of course, she *must* turn to look. And she did not even think how melodramatic it looked—Cade, drenched and wild-eyed with his hair all on end, framed in the stable entrance while lightning flickered and flashed behind him like a scene from a horror movie. She was utterly lost in the storm of her own emotions. And what a bewildering mix of emotions! Relief, and longing...overwhelming love and unreasoning fury.

"Leila?" He came rapidly toward her, and his voice was hoarse with concern. "Hey, are you okay? What are you doing out here?"

"Your dinner is ruined." It seemed to Leila that her voice came from somewhere outside her own head. Half-forgotten in her nerveless hand, the brush traced an erratic zigzag across the foal's mottled charcoal back. "There was thunder...I dropped it on the floor."

"Yeah, I saw." He touched her arm gently, a tentative turning pressure. "Hey, look—it's okay. It doesn't mat—"

She whirled on him like a dervish. *"Where...were... you?"* Her fists thumped against his chest, her eyes spurted fire and tears together. "You said...you would be home early. And I waited and waited...and then it got dark..." The pressure of pent-up emotions had finally blown, and she could not have stopped herself if she'd tried. "And I thought...I did not know where you were!" She wasn't aware, nor did she care what she looked or sounded like, or whether she was acting like the classic shrewish wife.

"And I thought...I thought...that you were..."

"I'm sorry—the traffic was...the rain...there were accidents." Cade mumbled, dazed. His brain was reeling. All he could think was that this felt a lot to him like the moment out there in the live oak grove when his horse had abruptly gone one way and he another. His emotions and desires were all of a sudden galloping off in unexpected directions, beyond his ability to control.

After a brief struggle he gave up trying. He got his arms around Leila's quaking body and caught her hard against him. Wrapped his hand in the humid tangle of her hair to hold her still, and kissed her.

What came next was a conflagration. It exploded upon them so unexpectedly and burned so voraciously it gave him no time to think at all.

When he first kissed her, Leila gasped in surprised outrage, then struggled against him—for all of two seconds—and the next thing he knew they were panting and whimpering and tearing off each other's clothes. He dimly remembered backing her into an empty stall...the deep cushioning straw coming up to meet him and his body already half-entwined with hers.

With almost a week's worth of pent-up desire clawing at his insides and fogging his brain, it didn't even occur to Cade that he might have pushed into her too abruptly, or too soon. Nor to Leila, either, not then. She gave a sharp cry, but it was of passion, not pain, and her body arched against him, not away. Her body was hot...so hot, feverish in his arms, and she wrapped herself around him like that all-over glove he remembered. And it felt good...so *good* to be inside her...as if, after a long and perilous journey, he'd finally found his way home.

A fierce, exultant joy invaded him as she met his thrusts with tiny passion-cries...when she gasped out his name as he released the flood of his passion into her. When she writhed and clung to him as he kept thrusting, until only moments later he felt her come apart...her body go light, limp and pulsing in his arms.

Exhilarated, happier than he could ever remember being in his life, quaking with it, wanting to share his shaky, wondering laughter with Leila's, Cade slipped sideways enough so he could touch her face. His joy turned to despair. Laughter hardened inside him and became instead a throbbing lump in his belly.

She was crying. Not the half sobbing, half laughing overflow of emotions that had bewildered and dismayed her so when he'd made love to her the first time—*that* he'd understood. This was different. This was *misery*. Grief-stricken, heartbroken despair.

"Sweetheart, what is it?" His voice was rasping and raw. "Did I hurt you? I'm sorry—"

She shook her head wildly, and because there was no one else from whom to seek comfort, turned her face to his chest.

But what could he say to comfort her, when he didn't begin to understand the reason for her tears? So he said nothing at all, while his mind battered helplessly against the bars of his ignorance. Until, with a glimmering of hope, he thought of something that might, just possibly, make her feel better.

"Hey," he murmured to her still-quaking silence, gazing down through a fog of mystified tenderness at the damp tendrils of hair draped across her ear. "I didn't have a chance to tell you. Guess who called today?" After only the briefest of pauses he gave her the answer. "Elena. And Hassan. They're back from their honeymoon. Just got back a couple days ago."

She pulled away from him just enough so she could look at him. "Really?" She sniffed. One long hand came, furtive and embarrassed, to wipe at her tears. "They are here? In Texas?"

Cade nodded. "Yep. They're going to be at Elena's ranch this weekend. How'd you like to pay 'em a visit?" His throat ached as he smiled.

She gave a little gasp and sat up, both her tears and her nakedness forgotten. "A visit? Elena has a ranch? I did not know. Is it very far? Will we fly?"

"A little one…and not far at all, just outside of Evangeline. An hour's drive from here. How's tomorrow sound?"

"Tomorrow? Oh, yes—oh, Cade…" She kissed him, and her face, still wet with tears and alight with happiness, was like the sun coming out after a rainstorm.

Cade's heart was in dark despair. Just as when she'd kissed him after he'd given her the foal for her bride gift, his thoughts now were bleak. *It's gratitude. She's only happy because I've given her something she wants. And it's not me.*

Elena came out to greet them, waving from the wide front porch of a house that, although it was made of white painted wood rather than brownish stone, reminded Leila of Cade's ranch house where she had been so briefly and blissfully happy. Reminded her of it so much, she had to swallow hard and blink away tears.

Cade had barely parked the SUV before Leila was out of the car and running up the graveled path. She met Elena on the steps. "Oh, I am so glad to see you," she breathed impulsively as she returned the other woman's hug. And now she *did* lose control of a few tears. Elena seemed very like a sister to her now, which made her miss her own sisters all the more.

She drew back, though, when she saw Hassan's tall form, standing just behind Elena. She did not know how to greet this relaxed and smiling man who seemed so different from her so-arrogant older brother, who had always lorded it over her and tried to intimidate her with his piercing black eyes. "Hello, Hassan," she said formally, and was even more bemused when he stepped forward and caught her up in a hug as warm as his wife's had been, and laughed and called her "Little sister." In *Arabic*. Hassan almost *never* spoke in Arabic!

Then Elena was hooking an arm around hers and saying in a happy rush, in her Texas way, "We're just so glad you guys came—we're barely unpacked ourselves, but we just decided to say the heck with it and come out here for a few days. We'll have some lunch in a little bit, but right now, I just can't wait to show you around."

"But...shouldn't we—" Leila looked toward the men, who had shaken hands and now were deep in conversation and drifting off across the porch in the direction of what looked like stables.

Elena waved them away with a smile. "Ah, let 'em go— they'll just want to talk horses and oil. What I'm dying to hear about is *you* guys. I still can't believe it—talk about sudden! I wish Hassan and I could have stayed for the wedding. So...tell me all about it. How was the wedding? Did you have a honeymoon?" She paused to consider her own question. "Probably not, if I know Cade. Well—we're going to have to do something about that."

"Cade has been very busy with his work," Leila said carefully, and Elena gave her a piercing look that made her glad she had decided to wear sunglasses to hide the tear-shadows around her eyes.

Leila summoned a smile as she tried to divert Elena's attention. "It seems as though you and Hassan are very happy."

Elena closed her eyes and smiled in a way that made Leila's heart ache with envy. "Oh, yeah. I can't tell you. Actually, if you want to know the truth, it's even kind of surprised me." She threw Leila a bemused look. "Not that I had any doubts that we loved each other—finally—but I thought it was going to be a lot harder to make it work."

"Work?" Frowning behind the sunglasses, Leila paused to look at her.

Elena gave a rueful laugh. "Oh, yeah—marriage takes work, don't ever kid yourself about that." Her laughter grew light again. "Especially when you have two people as different and bullheaded as Hassan and I are."

"At least...you know your husband loves you." Leila hardly knew she had spoken it out loud. They had been walking as they talked, past the stables and up a gentle slope covered with grass and the same little yellow flowers that grew in Cade's pasture. Now, standing on a hilltop overlooking still more hills that rolled away to banks of trees and a huge hazy sky beyond, she thought of her dreamed-of spaces and was almost overwhelmed with misery. She hardly even knew Elena had put her arm around her shoulders until she spoke.

"Oh, honey, of course Cade loves you!"

"No," said Leila with a proud lift of her chin, "he does not."

"Look," said Elena flatly, "I know him. He wouldn't have married you if he didn't love you."

Leila firmly shook her head. "He only married me to save me from disgrace."

Elena gave a hoot of laughter, which she quickly stifled when she saw the tears leaking out from under the edges of Leila's sunglasses. She gave her another hug and said with an exasperated sigh, "Okay, hon, tell me why you think that husband of yours doesn't love you."

"He does not act as though he does." Leila's voice was choked and angry. "And he certainly has not ever *said* so." She was startled and a little hurt when Elena made a very rude noise in reply.

The older woman shook back her short, dark hair and looked up at the sky for a moment as if in hopes of divine guidance. Then she put her arm around Leila's shoulders again. "Let me tell you something about your husband," she said quietly, as she began to walk with her back down the hill. "Cade Gallagher is just about the sweetest, most good-hearted man alive, and the best friend a woman could ever have. But the truth is, when it comes to emotional issues, he's pretty closed up. That's why he's never gotten married, I think—he never could find a woman he trusted enough to open himself up to. He wasn't always that way, I don't think. I think it happened when his mother died— he told you about that, I guess? It was a car accident—a hit-and-run driver ran her car off the road into the river, and she drowned."

Leila tried in vain to stifle a horrified cry, and Elena glanced at her in sympathy. "Yeah, I know…terrible, isn't it? They never did find the one who did it.…" Her voice trailed off, and Leila saw a grim and bleak look settle briefly over her features. Then she went on, in a voice that was harder and more clipped than before.

"It happened about a year after his mom got involved with my father. He'd have been…fifteen, I think—I know I was only about eight when I first met him. But I remember he had this wonderful, absolutely spectacular smile—it would light up his eyes, I swear, brighter than the lone star of Texas."

And Leila caught her breath and looked intently at her. *Yes,* she thought, her heart quicking. *I have seen it too, that smile! Just once…*

"Anyway, after his mom died," Elena continued softly, "I never saw that smile again." Her lips curved, but not with a smile. "And I don't think it helped that a few years later he found out my father, the man who'd adopted him after his mom died and treated him like his own son, had actually cheated him out of his inheritance."

Leila gave another horrified gasp. "Oh, yeah, it's true," said Elena. "I only found out myself recently—Cade told me just before I married Hassan." She took a breath. "It was a shock, believe me. His mom had left a will naming

Yusuf Rahman as Cade's guardian, as well as trustee of her estate, which at that time was what was left of her daddy's oil company after Cade's dad had pissed away most of it. When Cade turned twenty-one, he found out my father had worked it so there wasn't anything left of his mother's holdings at all. Everything had been absorbed into Rahman Oil.''

She stopped walking to look back at Leila, who was standing still with her fingers pressed against her mouth. ''So you can see,'' she said gently, ''why the man might be a *little* bit slow to trust anybody with his heart, even after all this time.''

''But,'' Leila whispered through trembling lips, ''what can I do? I do not know how to make him open himself up to me.'' The task seemed too hard, the obstacles enormous...insurmountable. She felt overwhelmed, defeated before she had even begun.

''For starters, have you tried telling him how you feel about *him?*'' Elena's voice was dry, as if she already knew the answer.

''Of course not,'' said Leila, drawing herself up stiffly. ''And I will not—not until I know for certain that he has the same feelings for me.'' She was a princess. She had her pride!

Elena made an exasperated sound. ''You Kamals! You're all alike—the most bullheaded, proud bunch of people I ever met.'' They walked on down the hill in silence. Until...

''I think...I have an idea.''

Leila looked at Elena in hope, and was surprised to find that she was smiling...smiling and gazing down the hill toward the stables, where Cade and Hassan could be seen leaning against the corral fence, still deep in conversation. She turned back to Leila, and her eyes were once again serene. ''Hon, what you need to do is take a little trip.

How'd you feel about a nice visit to Tamir? You know—
go home and see your folks?"

"Leave…Cade?" Leila's heart gave a leap, and she felt
a cold wash of panic. "But—I don't understand. How—"

"Hey," said Elena with a placid shrug, "it worked for
me."

"You mean, *you* left—"

She shook her head, and her smile was a little crooked,
now. "Uh-uh. Hassan left *me*. I'd refused to marry him—
I guess I was afraid I didn't love him enough…*then*. So
off he went, back to Tamir. It took me…oh, maybe a day
to figure out I'd made the biggest mistake of my life. So I
went after him. The rest," she added with a sound like a
cat's purr, "is history."

"But," Leila mumbled, "what if I go to Tamir, and
Cade does not come for me?" Her heart was hammering.
If Cade did *not* come for her, she knew she could not possibly come back here, not to live as she had been living for
these past weeks. And yet, the thought of never seeing Cade
again…never feeling his arms around her…frightened her
so she could scarcely breathe.

"Oh, he'll come," said Elena. "Trust me."

"But…I cannot possibly ask him—"

"Hey—don't worry about it. You just leave this to me."

Cade leaned against the corral fence and watched them
come toward him…two women, one he'd known nearly all
his life, as familiar as the grass around him, the other as
alien and exotic as an orchid blooming in the desert. Both
beautiful, but for one he felt nothing but the deep, abiding
affection of a brother for his sister, while the other made
his pulses thunder like a buffalo stampede. Why did it have
to be the wrong one? He felt betrayed, somehow. Doublecrossed by his own heart.

"Hey, guys," Elena called out when they were near
enough. And Cade watched with a pang of envy as she

came with the ease of certainty to kiss her husband, while his own wife hesitated and hung back, unsure what she should do. "Catching up on the latest gossip?" Elena teased, an arm around her husband's waist.

Cade squinted at her and shook his head, while Hassan said loftily, "Men do not gossip."

"Right." Elena laughed. "No, I mean, from Tamir. Hey, what did you guys think about Nadia?"

"Nadia?" Leila was alert and tense. "What about my sister? I spoke to her only last week. Is she all right?"

"She's getting married," said Elena. "Can you believe it? The fourth wedding in the Kamal family this year." She nudged Hassan. "I guess that just leaves Samira, huh?" Then she looked with concern at Leila, who had her fingertips pressed to her mouth and a stricken look on her face. "What, aren't you happy about it?"

Leila cleared her throat and said faintly, "Then...she will marry Butrus after all?" Elena nodded, and Hassan said gruffly, "With our father's blessing."

"But," said Leila, "she does not love him. She told me so." Her cheeks were pink, and Cade could see that, at her sides, her hands were clenched into fists. "She cannot do this—she must not. Oh, if only I could talk to her!" Her voice was tight with distress.

"Why don't you?" Elena asked, as if it were the simplest thing in the world.

"I have. But on the phone it is not—"

"No, I mean, go to Tamir." Elena looked at Cade.

A great stillness seemed to fold itself around him. Leila seemed not to be breathing. He looked at her and she averted her face quickly, but not quickly enough. Even with her sunglasses she couldn't hide the light of hope, a flash of joy so keen and pure, he was sure he'd felt it pierce his heart.

"Sure, why not?" Elena went on, enthusiastic...oblivious. "Go for a visit. It's not like you can't afford to send her, Cade. Leila *should* be with her sister at a time like this.''

Cade cleared his throat. His heart lay in his stomach like a dead weight—and how well he remembered *that* feeling. ''What about it?'' he asked Leila, keeping his voice carefully neutral. ''Would you like to go to Tamir? Visit your folks?''

She lifted her head and looked at him a long, suspenseful time, while he stared at his own reflection in her glasses and wished with all his heart that he could see her eyes. Except for the briefest tremble in her mouth, then a tightening, her face was utterly still. For the first time in his memory, he couldn't read her emotions there.

Then she drew a lifting breath and smiled. ''Yes—oh, yes,'' she said softly. ''I would like it very much.''

''Well, there you go,'' said Elena with a shrug. And she and Hassan exchanged a secret look.

''Well, okay,'' Cade said, squinting as he met the radiance of his wife's smile, ''I guess you're going to Tamir. How soon do you want to leave?''

''Is…tomorrow too soon?'' Oddly she sounded as if she was one good breath away from bursting into tears.

''Tomorrow it is.'' And on a hot and sunny May day in Texas, Cade felt cold clear through.

That evening, Cade went into the bedroom where Leila was packing her suitcases. ''All set,'' he said on an exhalation. ''Plane leaves here at two. You're gonna have a little bit of a stopover in Atlanta, but not too bad. You're nonstop to Athens…arrive there Monday morning, local time. Then it's just a short hop from there to Tamir.''

''Thank you.'' Her voice sounded muffled as she watched her hands…watched them methodically smoothing filmy cloth. Her hair had fallen over her shoulder, hiding her face from him. He resisted the urge to pull it out of the way.

''Need any help?''

''Thank you, but no. I am nearly finished.'' She straightened and tossed her hair back over her shoulder, though she still didn't look at him. A frown pleated her forehead. ''I do not think I will need to take much with me...so many of my clothes are still in Tamir.''

Maybe he should have found reassurance in that. Instead, he felt a sudden surge of anger that was mysteriously mixed with grief. Childishly, he wanted to shout at her. *What kind of a woman are you? How can you go away and leave me like this?* Selfishly, he wanted to plead with her. *Please don't go. Forget your sister—I need you!*

What he couldn't understand was *why*. It had been his idea to send her back to Tamir from the first. So why this gnawing fear that, once she was there with her own family, she wasn't ever going to come back to Texas?

She was trying to fold over the top of the suitcase to zip it closed. ''Here—let me get that,'' he said roughly, needing some activity, an outlet for his emotions. And reaching heedlessly across her, brushed her breast with his arm.

He went absolutely, deathly still. Except for the lifting of each breath, so did she. Then, slowly, slowly, he turned toward her. She turned, too, and tipped back her head to look at him. It went on so long, that look, and in such tension and stillness...it reminded him of something.

Then it came to him—that evening on the terrace. And the memory was so vivid, so immediate, it seemed to him he could hear the pounding of the surf on the rocks below the cliff...until he realized it was only the beating of his own heart. He remembered the way she'd looked at him so intently, and what she'd said to him next....

''Do you want to kiss me?''

He didn't know he'd said it aloud until he saw the flash of recognition in her eyes, and heard her say in a small, tentative voice, in a much more delightful French accent than his had ever been, ''Kees you? Oh, *oui, Monsieur...*''

He didn't even realize, then, the significance of that moment, that mutual, instant understanding, the acknowledgment of a history of shared intimacy, the first of countless moments like it that would form a bond to last a lifetime. He only knew that he was terrified. My God, he thought as he slowly lowered his mouth to hers, I can't let her go! *I love her.*

How can I leave him? Leila thought as she opened herself to her husband's embrace. *I love him so...* If only, she thought, he would ask me to stay...tell me not to go. Then I would know he loves me...

But he didn't say anything at all, though his kiss was so deep and poignant it made her ache in every part of her being, and it would have been easy to believe he meant it as love. Leila was not so naïve.

No, Elena was right. She must go to Tamir. If her husband loved her, he would come for her and bring her home. *And if he does not?* Her heart trembled, then plummeted inside her, and she clung to him in desperate, unreasoning fear. *He must come for me. He must.*

But how to ensure that, and yet preserve her pride? Trying without words to let him know the love and longing that was inside her, she gave him her body with a kind of desperate tenderness, worshipped his with such unreserved devotion...and hoped that he would somehow hear and know what was in her heart.

Dazed by the intensity of her lovemaking, shaken by the intensity of his feelings for her, Cade buried his face in the fragrant fall of his wife's hair. *For the last time?* He held her closer and shuddered with fear.

On Monday afternoon, Cade called Elena from his office in Houston. "Well," he said, "I hope you're satisfied."

She responded with a little trill of laughter. "What in the world are you talking about?"

"Leila's gone," he said morosely. "She called a little

while ago to tell me she made it home okay. Sounded happy to be back with her folks.'' He paused, took a deep breath and tried to make it sound as if he didn't care. ''I don't think she wants to come back…anytime soon.'' He added the last part only to keep from sounding too melo-dramatic.

''Well, don't say I didn't warn you, Cade.'' She made an exasperated sound. And after a pause, ''What do you intend to do about it?''

He snorted right back at her. ''What *can* I do? I sure as hell can't seem to make her happy here.''

''Oh, for—that is just *so* like a man!'' There was a pause, and then, bluntly, ''Cade, do you love her?'' And before he could answer, ''Don't you know, it doesn't take any more than that to make a woman happy? If she loves you…''

''Well,'' said Cade with gravel in his throat, ''that's the question, isn't it?''

There was another, longer pause, while he swallowed hard a couple of times. Then Elena's voice came softly. ''You can't stay closed off from your emotions forever, Cade.''

He righted his chair with an angry thump. ''What the hell do you mean by *that?*''

''Come on—you've been shut down ever since your mom died—and…what my father did to you.''

''That's ridiculous. I have emotions.''

''I'll bet you do. But you sure don't like to show 'em.''

''How does that make me different from almost any other man you know?''

''It doesn't,'' she admitted, ''but most men trust *some-body* enough to let their feelings show. I know Hassan trusts me. Do you think because of what happened with your mom and my father, that you're afraid—''

''Cut the crap, Elena. That's just psychobabble bull—''

''Cade, can I ask you something?'' Her voice was different, now. Hesitant…almost fearful. He waited, half-resentful, saying nothing, and after a moment she came out with it. "Do you think…has it ever crossed your mind, since all this has come out about my father…Rahman… about him killing my mother, and…all that…that he might have been the one responsible for your mom's accident?"

He couldn't answer, just stared at the Houston haze through his office window. His pulse tapped nervously at his belt buckle.

"It must have occurred to you, Cade. You were supposed to be in that car, too, remember? If you hadn't talked your mom into dropping you at your friend David's house on the way home…"

"What do you want me to say," he said harshly. "What's the point? The man's dead. Can't very well kill him twice."

"No," said Elena quietly, "but you can sure as hell kill your marriage if you don't find a way to come to terms with this. You have to find a way to trust, Cade. Trust yourself to love. Trust somebody to love you and not let you down."

"Psychobabble crap," Cade muttered.

"Maybe it is." He heard tears in her voice. "Maybe I just want everybody to be as happy as I am." And damned if she didn't hang up on him.

That evening, Cade was in the stable checking out a new foal with Rueben when Betsy came down with the bottle she'd prepared. She handed it to her husband, then stood back, planted her hands on her hips and glared at Cade.

"Okay," she said, "when are you leaving?"

"What?" He had his arms full of a balky colt just then, and couldn't look at her. "Leaving for where?"

"Tamir—whatever the name of that place is. When are you gonna go get Leila and bring her back?"

Cade snorted. After his conversation with Elena, he was feeling about as cooperative as that foal. "I guess she'll come back when she's ready."

"Uh-uh," said Betsy, "you got to go get her." She glared at him and folded her arms across the shelf of her bosom. "How else is she gonna know you want her to come back? You ever tell her?" She gave a snort of monumental exasperation. "I bet you never even told her you love her, did you?"

He let go of the foal, who was finally beginning to get the idea there was something good for him in that rubber nipple. "She never told *me* that."

Betsy threw up her arms. "She's a *woman.* You expect her to tell you *first?*" Cade didn't say anything. He looked over at the foal, who was nursing greedily, now. "I packed your suitcase already," Betsy said.

Cade looked at Rueben, who lifted one shoulder in a shrug. "I think you better go get your wife," was all he said.

Alima was having breakfast with Leila on the east terrace, though she had eaten only a few bits of fruit and some tea. It was difficult to swallow when her throat was aching so...when her mother's heart was breaking for her youngest child.

"I do not understand why she will not listen," Leila was saying stormily. "Nadia thinks she knows so much, because she is older, but she does *not.* She does not know what it is like to be in a marriage without love. She does not know what she is doing!"

"But," Alima gently reminded her, "that must be Nadia's decision, must it not? Your sister must make her own choice." She paused, then placed her hand over Leila's, which was restlessly tearing an orange peel into tiny pieces. "My dearest one, why does it trouble you so much? What is really bothering you? Are you...so very unhappy in America?"

Leila's hands jerked, then went still. Then, all in a rush, she raised them to cover her face...and a sob. "Oh, Mummy, I do not know what I should do. I believe Cade is a good man—I do. And I want to be a good wife to him. But I have been so lonely—and I do not understand him at all." Her voice dropped to a whisper. "I do not even know whether or not he loves me."

"Leila," her mother began, fighting anger against the man who had made her precious one so unhappy, "you must not give up on your marriage...." A movement caught her eye, drew it across the tiled terrace to where a tall figure stood framed in the arched portal that led to the gardens. A little breeze blew in through the portal, bringing with it the scent of roses.

Alima took in a breath of it...and smiled. "My daughter," she said softly, without taking her eyes from that tall figure, "if you truly love your husband, you must never give up on him. Tell me the truth...*do* you love this man, Cade Gallagher?"

Cade stopped breathing while he waited for her answer. It seemed an age...an eternity before Leila slowly drew her hands away from her face, revealing its radiance...and desolation.

"Oh, yes...I do. I love him. I did not believe it was possible to love someone so much. So much... sometimes...it hurts...inside." She placed her fist over her heart, and he felt himself moving toward her, though he had no sense of his feet touching the ground. "And then I am so frightened...and I do not know how I will survive it if I am never to see him—"

Leila felt a hand touch her shoulder, a hand that shook.

"Why would you think you'd never see me again?" said a voice—a voice as ragged and torn as the bits of orange peel on the table in front of her.

She stared at the bits of orange, not moving...not breathing. Her mother smiled at her, lifted her eyes and murmured an Arabic blessing, then rose from her chair and quietly left her.

I am a princess...I am a princess... Shaking like a blossom in the rain and clinging to the shards of her pride, Leila drew herself together. "What," she demanded breathlessly, lifting her head but without turning around, "are you doing here?"

Cade's heart gave an odd little quiver...of laughter, of tenderness and pride. Well, hell, she's a princess, he reminded himself. He tightened his hand on her shoulder, and felt his voice grow deeper and even more gruff. "Thought you might have forgotten where you live. Or that there's a lonesome little filly who needs you. Thought I'd better come and bring you home."

"Why?" she asked, hurling her question at him in defiance, like an obstinate child.

Bravely, Leila lifted her chin still higher and looked into his face. *Did he hear me?* she wondered, quaking inside. *Oh, he must have heard me say I love him.* She had never felt so vulnerable, not even lying naked in his arms. *Oh, please, let him say it to me now. If he does not, I do not know what—*

"What do you mean, *why?*" Fear made Cade's voice harsh. He'd never felt more vulnerable in his life, not even when his mother died. How could he expose himself so? He hadn't the courage....

She's a woman. You expect her to tell you first? And all at once he felt himself relax. His heart grew warm...and light filled all his insides.

"Why do you think?" Cade's voice had lost its roughness. It was tender...tender as a caress. "Because...I love you, Princess." She caught her breath, but he wasn't finished. "I love you!" he said. And again: "I *love* you!"

Then she saw it. At last, the smile she had carried so long in her memory...the smile she had longed for...the smile that lit his face and eyes with purest joy.

And she knew that it was true.

Epilogue

Sheik Ahmed Kamal sat at the head table in the Great Courtyard of the Royal Palace of Tamir and beamed upon the assembly that had gathered to celebrate the *Walima* of his youngest daughter and her husband, Cade Gallagher. Sated with good food and good wine, he felt humble, and richly blessed.

Had any monarch ever had more reason to sing the praises of Allah? First his sons and now a daughter well and happily wed, and soon there would be yet another wedding, this one as satisfactory as he would have wished. His oldest daughter was to marry his closest advisor—what could be more desirable?

Relations with his neighbors the Montebellans were on solid footing at last, and with the addition of oil-rich Texans to the family, Tamir's economic future had never been brighter. And next spring, if things went as he hoped, perhaps there would be more grandchildren to keep Alima happy…and, he must be honest, himself, as well.

Yes…life is indeed good, thought the old sheik.

* * * * *

Royal Spy
VALERIE PARV

To the authors and editors at Silhouette who
helped me bring the worlds in this book to life,
and to Melissa B who inspired me to
live in them.

ROMANCING THE CROWN

The royal heir to the kingdom of Montebello is safe. But a traitor lurks in the heart of the neighbouring kingdom of Tamir, waiting to destroy the countries' new alliance!

Meet the major players in this royal mystery…

Princess Nadia Kamal: The eldest Tamiri princess hides her passions behind a veil of gentility. But when a handsome stranger uncovers her secrets, there's nowhere left to hide…

Duke Gage Weston of Penwyck: Playing an everyday average man is second nature to this sought-after spy. But royalty is in his blood – as is a certain standoffish princess!

Dear Reader,

It seems to me that when you're a member of a royal family, life can be complicated. Duty must come before personal choice. Business before pleasure. Finding ways to be together privately can be almost impossible. You only have to look at the royal families of the world to see that a crown and a fortune can't guarantee happiness. This is the double-edged sword I set out to explore in *Royal Spy*. In the process I found myself examining the drive we all have to choose our destinies. Like Princess Nadia, we want to rule our own lives, although, like her and Gage Weston, we don't mind surrendering provided it's to the rule of love.

Long may love reign in your life.

All the best,

Valerie

Chapter 1

Gage Weston could think of worse ways to spend an afternoon than watching a princess get undressed. Sights like that were rare, even in his profession, but made putting his life on the line to spy for his country even more worthwhile. What other job in the world could offer such a bonus, where he wouldn't be considered some kind of Peeping Tom? Fortunately he only peeped by invitation or in the line of duty, as he was doing now.

He was determined to find out what the princess was up to. Certainly not legitimate royal business, or she would have left her father's palace dressed for her task, instead of waiting until she was out of sight to furtively exchange clothes with her maid.

Princess Nadia Kamal was the eldest daughter of Sheik Ahmed Kamal, ruler of Tamir, who was famous for his old-fashioned morality. Nadia was equally well known for pushing the boundaries of convention, but Gage would bet her father knew nothing about this little caper.

Not that Gage planned to tell him. He wasn't working for the sheik, but for his opposite number, King Marcus of Montebello. Marcus needed to know who in Sheik Ahmed's circle had ties with the terrorist group known as the Brothers of Darkness, to prevent the Brothers from derailing the fledgling peace process between Tamir and Montebello.

Gage had a more personal reason for spying on the princess. The traitor was also involved in the murder of his best friend, Conrad Drake. This ranked as a higher priority with Gage than even the king's mission.

With luck, he could trap the traitor and Conrad's murderer while on the one assignment.

He tightened his grip on the binoculars, a sense of loss sweeping over him as he thought of Conrad, who should have been at his side at this moment.

They'd been like brothers. Conrad hadn't been a member of royalty, as Gage was, but then Gage rarely used his ducal title, so the issue had never come between them. They had grown up together, studied economics and law at university, flown side by side in the Royal Penwyck Air Force and eventually become partners.

With Conrad's cool temperament moderating Gage's hot-headedness, they had conquered the stock market almost as a game, amassing a fortune that continued to snowball.

Just as well their finances were sound, because they had discovered their talent for undercover work when the head of a company they had invested in was kidnapped and held for ransom. Gage had known the man well, and had made it his business to track down the kidnappers, free their client and bring the perpetrators to justice.

Word had spread until Weston Drake Enterprises became the cover for a wide range of intelligence operations on behalf of major corporations and world leaders.

Now Conrad was gone, gunned down while feeding information back to Gage from the United States, where Conrad had been covertly investigating the Brothers of Darkness, searching for clues to help Gage identify King Marcus's traitor.

Gage sighed. Conrad hadn't completed the mission. Anger gripped Gage as he thought of his friend's life ending on a back road in Texas where a bullet had been put through his head. The only clue to his assailant had been the word that Conrad had scrawled in the dust as he lay dying beside his car, the engine still running when he was found: DOT.

Road rage, the American police concluded, not knowing that Conrad was any more than the tourist he posed as. They thought he'd tried to scratch out a message to his fiancée, Dorothy Gillespie in Penwyck, but Gage knew better. He'd introduced the couple, and Conrad had never called Dorothy anything but Doro. She hated the nickname Dot. The letters had to mean something else.

As boys, they'd made up their own code using initial letters, challenging each other to decode the message. Gage invariably won, and Conrad used to say it was because he had the more devious mind.

It worked in his favor now. After hours of sifting through alternatives, Gage had linked the *O* to Octopus, the symbol used by the younger, more reckless members of the Brothers of Darkness. The *T* was more of a challenge—until he settled on Tamir, the country the Brothers stood to gain the most from destabilizing.

The *D* had kept him up for many sleepless nights. Finally Gage went with his gut feeling that it stood for Butrus Dabir, attorney and key adviser to Tamir's ruler. Conrad had told him he was suspicious of Dabir, whose associates included underworld figures reputed to be involved with the Brothers. That was good enough for Gage.

Dabir. Octopus. Tamir. Three words that could be clues to Conrad's killer. Gage was determined to find the person responsible.

Could he be looking at her now?

He trained the high-powered glasses on the princess again. She was the most beautiful sight he'd had in the crosshairs for some time. Her short, raven-colored hair was feathered around her face, making her look a lot different from the other women in her family. With her tall athletic figure, from a distance she might have been taken for an American. Close up, her exotic features and high cheekbones belonged to a heroine of an *Arabian Nights* tale.

It wasn't hard to picture her reclining on a bank of embroidered cushions, veiled and clad in brightly colored silks. It would be a pity to veil such a tempting mouth. No veil, then, but keep the cushions and the silks. The same untamed imagination insisted he paint himself into the scene, resting on more cushions while she popped succulent dates into his mouth. His heart picked up speed at the notion.

When did you become so fanciful, Weston? he asked himself on a swell of annoyance. Her behavior was downright suspicious. He couldn't afford to be distracted by her looks, nor by the dazzling smile he saw her exchange with her maid. The reminder didn't stop him from imagining how he would feel if she smiled at him like that.

Princess Nadia was talking to the maid, both of them shielded from any eyes but Gage's by a thick screen of bushes, but she didn't stop moving, swiftly shedding her culottes and white silk shirt until she was clad only in a lacy camisole and panties that left her legs bare.

They had to be the longest legs in the sheikdom, Gage thought. Movements like hers, so graceful and unconsciously seductive, while she was clad in so little, should be outlawed in Tamir. Come to think of it, they probably were.

Pleasure shafted through him, as inappropriate as it was unexpected. Instead of seeming furtive, as befitted a potential traitor, her movements and ready smile made her look young and carefree, as if she had shed her cares with her clothes.

He frowned as the maid slid out of the traditional Tamir long dress called a *galabiya,* which she'd worn to accompany the princess from the palace. The maid took the culottes and shirt and put them on, while the princess pulled the *galabiya* over her head and settled the folds around her slender body. The two women were of a similar size, so everything fit. And the movements were so slick that Gage guessed this was a regular routine.

Within minutes, the maid was the image of her mistress, except for the long hair she tucked away under a wide-brimmed straw hat. The princess draped the maid's floaty silk scarf over her cropped tresses and shoulders. Both women popped dark glasses over their eyes. Voilà. Instant transformation.

From his research, Gage knew that the maid's name was Tahani. She was a cousin of Nadia's personal attendant, Nargis. Hearing that Tahani had artistic talent, the princess had agreed to teach her to paint in exchange for her services. At least that was the official story. Seeing them together now, Gage suspected that the maid's resemblance to the princess had a lot to do with Nadia wanting Tahani at her side.

Gage panned the glasses in a wide arc. Where the devil was the princess's bodyguard while all this was taking place? Or was the man in league with his mistress? Seconds later he had his answer. On the other side of the bushes, the bodyguard was unloading a heap of equipment from the back of the princess's car. As Gage watched, the man carried the load back to the two women. They kept their faces averted, pretending to talk, so the man didn't notice anything amiss.

The equipment turned out to be painting gear, Gage saw as the man set up an easel, stool and other artist's paraphernalia. Immediately the maid, in the princess's clothes, settled herself on the stool and began to sketch. The princess gave a low bow to her supposed mistress, then hurried away.

Nicely done, Gage thought with a twinge of professional jealousy. As far as the bodyguard knew, he was still keeping an eye on the princess while her maid was sent off on some errand. Gage decided to find out what the errand was.

She had aroused more than his curiosity, he admitted, not convinced that his interest was as professional as he wished.

He gave himself a few seconds to see in which direction her car was headed, then retrieved his rental car from where he'd secreted it in a grove of trees after following the group from the palace.

Being careful to stay out of sight of the painting pair, he found a track he could use to cut through an olive grove and come out slightly ahead of the princess on the only main road in the area—the one she had to take, unless she was

heading back to the palace. Gage would stake his inheritance
that she wasn't going home.

He was right. By the time she drove carefully around the
bend behind him—taking no chances on breaking any laws
that got her noticed, he assumed—he was in position. His
car was half off the road, the front wheels in a ditch, and his
forehead resting against the steering wheel. He'd used the
trick a half dozen times in his covert career, and it never
failed to get a result. Who could resist a lone motorist in
trouble?

Not the princess. He slitted one eye in time to see her pull
up ahead of him and get out. When she reached his open
window, he gave a convincing groan and lifted his head. She
touched a hand to his forehead. "Don't move, you could be
seriously injured."

Her hand against his skin felt blissfully cool, her touch
feather-light. He was tempted to do as she commanded and
stay where he was, hoping she'd go right on caressing his
fevered brow. But if he did, she'd probably insist on calling
an ambulance, ending his chance of speaking to her alone.
Given the usually restricted life led by the princess of Tamir,
he might not get another chance to decide for himself
whether she was traitor material or not. The opportunity was
too good to waste.

He opened his eyes, finding that she was every bit as
lovely close up as she had appeared in his field glasses.
Something twisted inside him. She was more than lovely. She
was breathtaking. His hand itched to remove the dark glasses
so he could get a good look at her eyes. Black as the pits of
Hades, he told himself. Black as the night, with the light of
a thousand stars in them, his errant mind insisted.

He resisted the image. Black nights could hide deadly secrets, like the identity of his friend's killer. However tempting the idea, for Conrad's sake and for King Marcus, Gage
couldn't afford to let himself fall under Nadia's spell.

Still, poetic images insisted on forming in his mind as he
looked at the princess. Not the princess—her maid, he reminded himself. He wasn't supposed to know that they'd

traded places. He made himself rub his eyes as if dazed. "I ran the blasted car off the road. I was too tired to be driving."

He saw her assess the car, one of the more expensive Branxton sports models, and guessed she was theorizing about him and how he came to be here. "You're not from Tamir," she said.

"England," he supplied, quoting from his cover story. He saw her forehead crinkle above the glasses. He added, "I'm here to head up a British trade mission to your country, although I won't present my credentials to Sheik Ahmed Kamal until tomorrow."

His home country of Penwyck retained enough historic ties with the English monarchy that his own Hugh Grant-like accent was utterly convincing. It wouldn't have mattered. Gage could do several American accents, broad Australian or Italian equally well. But he felt comfortable reverting to his native accent and was pleased to see by her expression that she had accepted his cover completely. Mentally he thanked his godfather, the British ambassador to Tamir, who had agreed to let Gage use the embassy as the base for his fictional trade mission.

"Welcome to Tamir, Mr...."

"Gage Weston. Please, call me Gage." He offered her his hand through the car window and saw her smile at the foolishness of the gesture, given the circumstances.

"Tahani Kadil. I work for the Kamal family," she said. "We should save the rest of the formalities for later. Right now you need an ambulance."

"Really, I'm perfectly all right," he assured her. "If you could just help me out so I can get some air..."

She levered the door open with difficulty, since she was pulling uphill. Strong, as well as lovely, he thought, struggling against the admiration that threatened to cloud his judgment. A wonderful jasmine scent filled his nostrils as she leaned across him to undo his seat belt, her full breasts brushing across his chest. He wasn't entirely acting as he worked to catch his breath.

Nadia slid an arm around Gage and helped him out, becoming aware of the strength in him and the fast beating of his heart, which she blamed on his accident. Her own was beating a touch too fast, she noticed, not wanting to think that the stranger was the cause.

He wasn't handsome enough to turn her head, even had she been susceptible. His features were a touch too well defined, his jaw too thrusting, his lips too full and sensuous. Too arrogant and self-assured to be her type, although she accepted that the collective effect stamped him as a man to be reckoned with.

She felt the heat from his body steaming through her, pushing up her internal temperature. The air seemed to crackle with warmth and energy, and she sensed it had little to do with the balmy summer day. At least, she hadn't noticed the charged atmosphere until she touched Gage.

What had she unleashed by stopping to assist him?

Nothing she couldn't handle, she told herself firmly. After her one tragic experience of love, she had vowed never to be swept off her feet again. So it mattered little if Gage was or wasn't handsome, could or couldn't cause her heart to race, did or didn't force visions into her mind of being held in strong arms, kissed with a tenderness that brought tears to her eyes, loved as only a real man could love.

Stop this, she commanded herself before her imagination could run away with her completely. Gage was a diplomat. Her father's court was awash with his kind. They were charming, sometimes flirtatious, but ultimately out to achieve their country's aims by whatever means they had.

She had been courted before by men wanting to gain her father's ear. Probably would be again. Her resistance should be well developed by now, she thought as she assisted Gage to the side of the car before releasing him.

So why did he make her feel as though she had no resistance at all?

Gage rested his back against the car, making a show of recovering slowly. "Lucky for me that you stopped by. I was looking for the road to the British Embassy and must have taken a wrong turning."

"You certainly did. You're headed in the opposite direction." Her smile was the epitome of innocence and beauty. Maybe beauty, but not innocence, he thought, hardening his heart. Innocent people didn't parade around in disguise, using false names.

"Perhaps you'd be good enough to point me in the right direction," he said.

She looked shocked. "You can't mean to get behind the wheel again, can you? You could have a concussion. Even if your car is drivable, which I doubt."

He glanced at it and nodded agreement. The Branxton was perfectly drivable, but he had no intention of telling her that. He wanted her to do exactly what she did next. "I'll take you to Marhaba. I'm meeting someone there who can check you over. Marhaba is a large town, so once we know you're all right, you can have your car towed there for repairs and hire another car to take you to the embassy."

Meeting someone? A contact with whom she shared state secrets? A lover? Gage was surprised at the intensity of his resistance to the idea. It was the most logical one, next to her being a traitor, but he found he didn't like to think of her being either. Hardly a professional assessment, he knew, but he couldn't seem to avoid it.

He had the feeling that Princess Nadia was the most dangerous woman he had ever met. With a nature that screamed seduction without any effort on her part, and looks to distract any man, she could start a war—or finish one—and not even know she'd done it, he thought. Tamir's answer to Helen of Troy.

Minutes later he was settled in the passenger seat of her car. They were riding in half-a-million dollars' worth of customized Bentley, he calculated, appreciating the elegance of the leather seats and burred-walnut paneling. As he got in, he'd noticed a bar and television in the back seat, where presumably the princess usually traveled.

If he'd been the bodyguard, he'd have had a few qualms about letting the maid take off in such a valuable car, Gage mused. Tamir had no prohibitions against women driving, but a princess would normally have a chauffeur. He wondered how Nadia came to be so competent behind the wheel.

"What do you do at the palace?" he asked

She kept her attention on the road while she spoke to him. "Have you heard of Princess Nadia?"

"Sheik Ahmed's eldest daughter," he supplied, knowing she'd expect a diplomat to have been briefed on such details.

"Tahani Kadil is her personal maid," Nadia went on.

She was careful not to compound the lie, he noticed. A late rush of conscience, or a wish to stick to the truth as much as she could? He found himself hoping the latter was true. He pushed the thought aside, annoyed. Much more of this and he'd be writing her an alibi himself, rather than facing facts. Her actions today had shot her to the top of his list of suspects.

Since starting this investigation four months ago, Gage had come to agree with Conrad that the most likely traitor in the Kamal circle was the sheik's closest adviser and attorney, Butrus Dabir.

Was it coincidence that Nadia was engaged to marry Dabir? And how much of an accomplice did it make her?

Gage didn't believe in coincidence, so either Nadia was a traitor or Dabir was, and he was using her in some way, or planned to. The more Gage learned about the people Dabir did business with, the more he accepted Conrad's dying suggestion, carved in the dust, that Dabir had ties with the Brothers of Darkness. All Gage needed was evidence.

Nadia could be in league with her fiancé. Until he had some answers, Gage couldn't afford to let himself get sidetracked by her, although he recognized how easily that could happen.

He hadn't been sidetracked by a beautiful woman in a long time. Five years, his statistics-loving mind supplied. Five years since he'd fallen hook, line and sinker for the daughter of a man he'd been investigating on suspicion of selling government secrets to his country's enemies. The man had been caught with enough evidence to put him away for life, but Gage had found nothing to implicate the daughter, Jenice.

Gage had believed her story that her father had blackmailed her into helping him, threatening to kill her if she betrayed him.

She had seemed so frightened, so impossibly lovely and fragile, that all of Gage's protective instincts had been aroused. He had taken Jenice home with him to Penwyck, introduced her to his family and his uncle Morgan, the king. They had taken the lovely, fey creature into their hearts, and the king had promised to grant her asylum. Gage had been there every step of the way, helping her adjust to life in his country, knowing he was falling in love with her but unable to stop himself.

What was the saying about a fool for love? Conrad had accused Gage of behaving like a giddy teenager, instead of an experienced intelligence specialist who should have known better. He should have listened to his friend.

Jenice had promised to marry him as soon as he came home from his latest assignment. He still didn't know what would have happened if he hadn't returned a week early to find her in the arms of the man who had hired Gage to put her father away. Under relentless interrogation, the pair admitted that they had set her father up so they could get their hands on his considerable assets, at which point they planned to run away together.

In floods of tears, Jenice had sworn that she loved Gage, that none of this had been meant to happen. He presumed she meant the nights she'd spent in his bed, vowing her undying love, and wondered whether she had intended to tell him the truth before or after they were married.

He hadn't waited to find out. Ignoring her pleas, he'd escorted them back to their own country, leaving them to the mercy of the local authorities. Then he'd returned to Penwyck and gone on a bender that lasted a week, or so Conrad told him afterward.

When the headache had cleared, Gage had promised himself that never again would he fall for a woman's wiles. If he married, it would be to a Penwyck woman whose pedigree he knew as far back as his own. Love wouldn't enter into the bargain. He would provide for her to the best of his ability, and in return, she would give him the children he wanted.

Belatedly he became aware that Nadia was speaking to him. "What is your area of interest, Gage? Aerospace products? Electronics? Chemicals?"

He masked his surprise. A Tamir princess with an interest in trade? "The invisible economy," he said, testing her.

She nodded. "Stockbroking, banking, insurance, worth over a hundred billion pounds to your country last year."

This time he couldn't hide his astonishment. "You're remarkably well informed for…"

"A woman?" she queried, sounding defensive.

"I was going to say for someone who must lead a relatively sheltered life at the palace," he said, impressed in spite of himself. Brains, as well as beauty. Even more reason to watch himself.

Her hands tightened on the wheel. "In Tamir, education is for all."

But not equal opportunity for women, especially royal women, he knew from his research. Obviously it was a sore point with the princess. Sore enough to make her turn to the Brothers of Darkness to fulfill her need for greater challenge? Or perhaps to get even with her father for holding her back? Gage knew he couldn't discount either possibility.

"Will you get into trouble for picking me up?" he asked, thinking of the restrictions he knew applied to women in her country. Tamir was more liberal than most of its neighbors, but being born male was still a definite advantage.

She shrugged. "It wouldn't be the first time."

"You make a habit of collecting stray motorists?"

"Hardly. And this was an emergency."

"Hardly," he echoed her tone. "I could have waited until a male driver came along."

He saw her hands tense on the wheel. "He couldn't have done any more."

So he had hit a nerve. Good. Gage decided to press the point, hoping to learn more. "He could have helped me push my car back onto the road."

Her dark gaze flickered over him, then back to the road. "Male chauvinism? I thought you British believed in equality."

"You know the saying about some being more equal than others?"

"Only too well."

He winced at her bitter tone. "I didn't say I believe it."

"What do you believe in, Gage?"

Her question caught him unprepared. "The usual virtues."

"Money, power and status?"

He found he didn't like being thought so shallow, even by a possible traitor. "They have their uses. But I wouldn't call them virtues. I was speaking of the right to live your own life your way, provided you don't harm anyone else."

"Your wife is a lucky woman," she observed dryly.

Fishing? he wondered, at the same time feeling foolishly flattered by her interest. "I'm not married. What about you?" he asked, although he already knew the answer.

She gave a quick shake of her head. "Not yet."

Her tone said *Not ever.* Interesting, given what he knew about her and Butrus Dabir. "But you have plans?" he persisted.

"I'm engaged to be married, yes."

He wondered what her resigned sigh said about her relationship. "Your fiancé won't object to me driving with you?"

"He's away a lot of the time."

What Dabir didn't know wouldn't hurt him, Gage read into her comment. He tensed. He might have his suspicions about the man, but he was entitled to the truth from his fiancée. Having suffered at the hands of a scheming woman himself, Gage didn't wish the experience on anyone else.

The princess didn't look like a scheming woman, he thought. With the breeze from the open window tugging strands of raven hair out from under her scarf and bringing a flush of peach to her cheeks, she looked beautiful, exotic, kissable.

He subdued the notion. He couldn't afford to feel anything

for her when the lifestyle she obviously resisted might have driven her to extremes. Even to being in league with Conrad's killers? The sooner he found out for sure, the better.

"We've arrived," she said.

He looked around with interest. Expecting a village, he was surprised to find them approaching the shell of an old fort set on a hill overlooking a large modern town. Marhaba, he assumed. The big faceless fort, with its whitewashed walls, would have looked at home against a backdrop of reed and mud-brick huts a century ago. Thick stands of greenery surrounded the approach to the fort.

The princess drove the car into a walled courtyard, and he saw that the outward appearance of the building was deceptive. Inside, apart from the cobblestones and whitewash, the building had been completely modernized.

The other thing he noticed was the throng of children who rushed to the car. They ranged in age from about four to eleven or twelve. All of them seemed to want to be close to Nadia.

"Who are all these children?" he asked as they got out.

She was immediately surrounded. Over the heads of the youngsters vying for her attention, she smiled. "They're orphans from Marhaba's poorest families, waiting to be adopted or placed in foster homes." She hugged each child in turn.

"Who's this?" Gage pointed to the toddler peeping at him from behind her skirt.

"Samir. I call him Sammy. He doesn't care for strangers."

"You going to say hello, Sammy?"

The boy buried his face in Nadia's skirt. Gage squatted at child level. "Hey, I don't bite." He reached behind Sammy's ear and pulled out a coin. It was the oldest trick in the book, one Gage had taught himself when he was only a few years older than Sammy. The toddler's eyes went round as saucers.

"More."

This time Gage made the coin disappear. Sammy shook his head and felt his hair, obviously mystified. Gage reached behind the child's other ear and plucked out the coin, then placed it in the small hand. The other children watched in fascination.

Sammy giggled and held out the coin to give it back. Gage closed the toddler's fingers around it. "You keep it. Every kid needs a magic coin."

About as much as they needed parents, he thought. How had Sammy lost his? Gage was surprised by how much he wanted to know. He also wanted to know what Nadia was doing here. Not playing Lady Bountiful, or she'd have arrived as a princess. The children's welcome suggested she was a regular—and popular—visitor. What in blazes was she up to?

Sammy held out his arms and Nadia picked him up. "What do you say to Mr. Weston?"

"'Tank you." The little boy tugged at Nadia's concealing scarf, almost dislodging it. "Candy for Sammy?"

She tucked the scarf back into place. "Later, sweetheart, after you eat all your lunch." She glanced at Gage. "You're welcome to join us."

"You've done enough for me already," he said. "I can walk to the town from here, so I'll be on my way." In the town he might be able to find out more about this place and Nadia's role in it. If it was a front for the Brothers of Darkness, it was amazingly convincing.

Like the princess herself. Seeing her with Sammy in her arms, Gage had trouble believing she was anything but what she seemed, a caring compassionate friend to these children. Maybe dodging her royal role was the only way she could get to see them.

And maybe it wasn't.

Over Sammy's objections, she set the child down. The toddler grabbed a handful of her skirt and hung on, making Gage smile in spite of himself.

"You're not going anywhere until Warren has checked you over," Nadia insisted. "If you collapse on the way to town, I'll never forgive myself."

He was more likely to die of curiosity than anything else,

but she believed he had injured himself running his car off
the road, so he murmured a reluctant assent.

She untangled Sammy from her skirt and sent him off to
play with the others, the coin clutched tightly in his fingers.
Then she led Gage through a double set of carved wooden
doors that looked as old as the fort.

Beyond them was a spacious room set up as an infirmary.
A tall, thin, red-haired man with an abundance of freckles
was putting a dressing on a little girl's grazed knee. From
the state of the room, the girl was the last of a long line of
patients. Gage felt a stab of guilt, wondering if Nadia would
have been helping out here if she hadn't been delayed by his
staged accident.

The little girl smiled when she saw Nadia. "Hello, Addie."

The doctor looked up. "Hi there, running late today?"

"I picked up a passenger on the way," she said.

Addie? How many names did this woman go by? Gage
gathered that Warren was a doctor, but how did he—and this
place—fit into Nadia's secret life?

The doctor washed his hands, then lifted the child off the
examination table. "There you go, Drina. Next time try walking across the courtyard, instead of tearing across at ninety
miles an hour."

The little girl giggled. "Thank you, Dr. Warren."

The doctor shepherded the child out and closed the door,
then held out his hand to Gage. "Welcome. I'm Warren
Walsh. I gather you're a friend of Addie's?"

Gage shook the man's hand. "Gage Weston. I had a little
accident on the way, and...Addie was kind enough to give
me a lift."

"Gage ran his car into a ditch and knocked himself out on
the steering wheel," she supplied helpfully. "I thought you
should take a look at him before we let him wander off."

"Quite right. Sit yourself on the table."

Gage hesitated. "I'm perfectly fine now."

Warren frowned. "A period of unconsciousness, however
brief, is always cause for concern."

Nadia gave Gage a little push. "You should be at least as brave as Drina."

Gage found he didn't care for the way she lumped him in with her young charge. He moved stiffly to the table, perched on the edge and submitted to the doctor's checkup, trying not to grit his teeth too obviously.

"You're in pretty good shape," the doctor said after giving him a cursory going-over. "Are you an athlete?"

"A diplomat," he amended.

"With the British Trade Delegation," Nadia added.

Gage knew he had to get out of here before the doctor stumbled across any of the battle scars he carried. Considering his line of work, he hadn't done too badly, but the number of scars would arouse any doctor's curiosity.

He slid off the table. "See, I told you I was fine."

"I'm inclined to agree," the doctor said. "You're in the best shape of any diplomat I've ever met."

"I work out a lot," Gage explained, deciding it was time for a change of subject. "What do you call this place?"

"The Marhaba Children's Shelter," Nadia explained. "The children live here until homes can be found for them."

"Which sometimes takes longer than we like," Warren contributed. "These children are the poorest of the poor. Better-off families are sometimes reluctant to adopt them."

Nadia nodded. "Although they are the most delightful children you could ever wish to meet."

Like Sammy, Gage thought. The little fellow couldn't be more than four, but he had bright eyes and a radiant smile. He was obviously attached to Nadia, or Addie or whatever name she went by here.

"How did you get involved with this place?" he asked Nadia.

Warren laughed. "She doesn't have enough to do back home."

Nadia shot Gage a quick look. "Don't worry, Warren knows who I am, but once I drive through the gates, I'm simply Addie, the children's friend. I come as often as I can to help out."

That explained two of the multiple identities, Gage thought. Did Warren know her as Tahani, the maid, or Nadia, the princess? Since he wasn't supposed to know about her royal identity, he couldn't very well ask. He pulled out his wallet. "In return for your help today, I'm happy to make a contribution."

"We don't need your money," Nadia said. "The children are provided with everything they require. What they don't have are loving homes."

Gage felt a ripple of something he couldn't pin down. Nadia couldn't possibly know that he wanted children of his own. "In my job, I'm hardly in a position to give a child a home," he said.

"Then we'll settle for your money, Gage," Warren said cheerfully. "The infirmary could use some new equipment."

Nadia frowned at him. "You should have told me."

The doctor rested a hand on her arm. "You do enough as it is. Risk enough as it is."

Gage's professional instincts went on alert. Now what did the doctor mean by that? Was the place a front for something underhand, after all? Gage peeled off some notes, hoping he wasn't making a donation to the Brothers of Darkness. He handed them to the doctor, who nodded his thanks.

"Now that I know I'll live, I'll be on my way," Gage said. "Thank you, both of you, for your help."

The doctor tucked the money into his shirt pocket. "You're welcome."

Nadia smiled. "Try not to fall asleep at the wheel next time."

"Good advice. Maybe I'll see you at the palace sometime."

A shadow fell over her lovely features. He couldn't see her eyes behind the dark glasses, and he found himself wishing he could. He had a feeling her eyes were her most beautiful feature. Time to get out of here, he told himself. The lady was trouble.

"I don't usually have much to do with the diplomatic corps," she said. "Sheik Ahmed will no doubt receive you in the reception hall. My place is usually in the family apartments.''

No wonder she wasn't worried that he'd spot her and recognize that the princess and ''Tahani'' were one and the same. She was counting on him being kept out of her way. He'd have to do something about that. A bit of research should turn up the ways and means. He gathered that no one except her maid knew about her extracurricular activities, so he'd have an edge when they met again.

He was determined they *would* meet again. In fact, he was looking forward to it. He still didn't know whether she had any connection with Conrad's death or with the Brothers of Darkness, but she was definitely up to something. Unmasking her was going to be a pleasure.

Chapter 2

"Aren't you concerned that your British diplomat will blow the whistle on you at the palace?" the doctor asked as soon as the infirmary door closed behind Gage.

Nadia frowned. "He thinks I'm Tahani, the ladies' maid. As long as I stay out of his way when he presents his credentials at court, there's no reason for him to think I'm Princess Nadia."

The doctor tidied away his instruments. "I still don't understand why you don't simply tell your father what you're doing here. Sheik Ahmed should approve of you doing charity work with orphans."

Nadia began to help him restore order in the infirmary. "I don't want my father's approval. I want this work to be my own, independent of my royal status. If my father found out, he'd expect me to come here as Princess Nadia, with the full entourage. As plain old Addie, I can relax and be myself, get my hands dirty without someone rushing to take over and let the children rush up to me without a minder going into guard-dog mode."

The doctor's expression softened. "You could never be described as plain or old. And I can understand your guards wanting to protect you."

His tone made Nadia look at him in astonishment. "You aren't getting soft on me, are you, Warren?"

"Me, soft? You know me better than that."

His quick denial sounded unconvincing, and for the first time Nadia asked herself if she was doing the right thing working so closely with Warren when she had no interest in him romantically. She had thought he felt the same, but now she began to wonder.

"Don't worry, I'm not terminally lovesick yet," he assured her, as if reading her mind. "As long as you know I'm here for you anytime."

"I know," she agreed, her conscience troubled. Warren was a good man. After qualifying as a doctor, he had left his native Australia to work in parts of the world where his skill could make a difference. He had come to Tamir on holiday and fallen in love with the island kingdom, he had told her when they were introduced at an art gallery two years ago.

Hiking around the hills, he had stumbled upon a group of children living by themselves in the ruined fort and had contacted the princess to see what could be done for them. With her help and money from her private allowance, they had made the fort into a comfortable facility that now housed more than a dozen children at a time until homes were found for them. Warren had recruited a team of women from Marhaba to take care of the children on a roster system.

"You should be proud of what you've done here," Warren said.

"Not as much as you should be."

"I don't have to deal with the same restrictions that you do."

Of course not, he was a man. She didn't want Warren to know, but he was the main reason she couldn't tell her father what she did here. The sheik would be furious if he knew his eldest daughter was working side by side with a man, not to mention an unmarried one. He would probably forbid her to set foot in the orphanage again.

She gave a deep sigh. "I wish I could do more. By now I should be running my own show, not living at the palace like a dutiful daughter, having to sneak around in my maid's clothes to have the freedom to pursue my own interests. If I was a man, I'd be a minister in my father's cabinet by now."

Warren squeezed her shoulder. "The government's loss is the children's gain."

"I suppose so. When I was twenty-five and approached my father about a real job, he said my time would come. I never dreamed I'd still be waiting around a decade later."

"You haven't exactly been waiting around," Warren pointed out. "Between the sculptures you created for the royal palaces and your paintings, you have a body of work any artist would envy."

"Try telling my father that." She had tried many times, but the sheik seemed unable or unwilling to understand the importance of her art in her life. He tolerated her activities as a hobby, even allowing her to exhibit her work to raise money for charity, but plainly didn't regard her the way she saw herself, as a serious artist.

"Your father probably thought you'd be married by now, and the question would have resolved itself," Warren said.

With a savage gesture, she shook out a clean sheet for the examination table. "He tried hard enough, until I told him if he paraded one more minor royal in front of me like cattle at a livestock sale, I was going to throw a tantrum right in the middle of the Grand Ballroom. I wouldn't marry a princeling if he was the last man on earth."

Warren laughed. "Why ever not?"

"The only reason any of them want to marry me is because of who I am."

With the ease of long practice, Warren returned instruments to their respective trays. "You underestimate yourself, Addie. You're one of the most beautiful women in the kingdom, also one of the most intelligent."

''That's my problem. Most of the marriage prospects my father has dredged up don't want intelligence. They want compliance. Can you imagine me, compliant?''

Warren masked his smile. ''It is rather difficult.''

She felt her temper reach boiling point. ''I'd sooner marry that...that British diplomat who can't even keep his car on a perfectly straight road.''

''Gage Weston? He hardly seems your type.''

''Precisely my point. He'd be the sort of man I could manage, instead of having him manage me.''

Warren closed the instrument cabinet. ''Are you sure about that? When I was checking him over, he didn't strike me as the manageable type.''

Nadia had to concede that Gage hadn't seemed especially compliant to her, either. His accident had been foolish, but then, he had admitted to being exhausted. He hadn't told her where he'd flown in from before Tamir, so he could easily have been suffering from jet lag.

As the doctor had observed, Gage Weston was in superb physical condition. Helping him out of the car had made her aware of how lean and muscular he was, a rarity among diplomats, who spent much of their time behind a desk or socializing after dark. She had a feeling that socializing wasn't what Gage preferred doing after dark. What he might prefer, she didn't want to think about.

He had compassion, too, also rare in her experience. Most men wouldn't have bothered trying to win Sammy's trust, but Gage had taken the trouble. And on the way to Marhaba, he had said he believed in equality between men and women. Accepting her help proved he wasn't just paying lip service to the belief.

Altogether a formidable man.

Why was she letting him disturb her so? If she saw him again, it would be from a distance, at some royal function with hundreds of other members of the diplomatic community. She didn't even have to talk to him if she didn't want to.

The thought was oddly bothersome.

"If you're so against marriage, why did you agree to your father's wish that you marry Butrus Dabir?" the doctor asked. "Surely he couldn't force you?"

She wasn't fooled by his casual tone. Now that she knew Warren was attracted to her, she resolved to be careful not to hurt his feelings. "I'm not in love with him, if that's what you're asking. And he doesn't love me. We respect one another, and his position as my father's closest adviser makes him a suitable match."

"It sounds a bit coldhearted."

"Royal marriages are frequently arranged for reasons other than love. If I must marry, I'd rather it be to a man like Butrus, who doesn't dress up his reasons for proposing."

The doctor looked surprised. "He actually told you he doesn't love you?"

"Not in so many words, but I've known him for many years. He's more interested in money and power than in love. Marrying me guarantees him both. Don't worry," she assured the doctor, who looked more and more unhappy, "as a married woman, I also gain independence from my father."

"Surely any husband could have freed you from your father."

She nodded. "Unlike Butrus, most men aren't traveling much of the time. While he's away, I'll have the freedom to do as I please."

She straightened. "I'd better round up the children for their lunch. I have to return to the palace early today. Father wants to see me about something."

"Tahani will be disappointed. I gather she likes taking your place and dabbling in art while you're here."

Nadia frowned. "Sometimes I wish I could be in two places at once. Then I could spend more time painting, as well as looking after the children."

"Beats me how you get so much done as it is. I saw your new show at the Alcamira Gallery and the work is wonderful."

Nadia bit her lip. She was her own toughest critic and knew Warren's praise wasn't empty flattery. She *did* have talent. She only wished she could have attended one of the world's fine art schools, instead of studying subjects her father considered more appropriate. Like her siblings, she had been sent abroad, carefully chaperoned, to complete her education. In between her approved courses, she had studied art as best she could by visiting galleries, talking to the artists and convincing her father that attending hobby classes was a harmless indulgence.

Some hobby, she thought and grimaced. "I work twice as hard when I do get time to paint."

"As long as you don't burn yourself out."

"I won't." Her patience would give out before her energy.

"While I was at the gallery, I was tempted to buy one of your watercolors of the hills near here. They're wonderful," Warren said.

"I'll arrange for you to have one as a gift," Nadia said, glad that there was something she could do for Warren, since she couldn't give him what he plainly wanted.

His face flushed. "I'll treasure it, both for artistic excellence and because you painted it."

"You always know how to cheer me up." She wished she could do the same for him, but knew she could never feel more for the doctor than friendship.

"I'll live, you know," he said quietly.

She stared at him. Had he been reading her mind? "I'm glad, because you're very special to me," she said. "You're the first man I've met with whom I can simply be myself."

Gage Weston had also treated her like a normal person, came the unexpected thought. But he'd believed she was Tahani Kadil, the maid. He was bound to behave differently if he knew she was Princess Nadia. All the same, she found herself wishing she could meet him again, if only to see his reaction when he found out who she was.

Nadia should have remembered the saying about being careful what you wish for. She had barely returned to her apartments in the royal palace and changed into a gold-embroidered *galabiya,* when she received a summons from her father.

Anxiety rippled through her. Had he somehow discovered where she'd been? She lifted her head. If he had, she would deal with it. She was a woman, not a child to be dragged over the carpet for some misdemeanor.

In this rebellious frame of mind, she stalked past the guard holding open the massive door for her and into her father's study. Actually, "study" was a misnomer. The room was larger than the living rooms in most ordinary households. The sheik's long mahogany desk stood at the far end of a vast, hand-woven carpet that depicted aspects of Tamir's history.

Automatically Nadia's glance went to the chair next to the sheik's desk, where her mother frequently sat, silently supportive as she worked at her embroidery. Alima would never be so indiscreet as to disagree with her husband overtly, but her gentle smile was always encouraging, and she held strong opinions of her own that she shared with the sheik in private. Today the padded chair by the tall arched window was empty and Nadia was on her own.

She tried to moderate her stride to a more womanly walk as she crossed to his desk, then abandoned the attempt when the Sheik didn't look up.

"You wanted to see me, Father?" she said to gain his attention.

He signed a document with a flourish, added the royal seal and handed the paper to a hovering attendant with a few words of instruction. Naturally her father would finish whatever state business was on hand before attending to her. Ahmed had been on the throne of Tamir since he was twenty, and he put his country ahead of everything, even family concerns.

He looked every inch a ruler, she thought with a contrary feeling of pride. Well into his sixties, his once-dark hair and beard now almost white, he still lived up to his nickname, the Lion of Tamir. Just sometimes, she wished he could be more father than monarch.

Without waiting for an invitation, she seated herself in one of the leather armchairs opposite the desk. Sheik Ahmed looked up at last, a frown etching his forehead.

She knew exactly why he was frowning. "Father, I like my hair this way. I think it suits me."

"That is a matter of opinion, my daughter."

"And yours is very clear on the subject."

"Nadia," the Sheik said on a heavy sigh, "why does our slightest interaction have to involve confrontation?"

Why couldn't she be more compliant like Samira and Leila? she read between the lines. "I am as I am," she said with a typically Tamir shrug.

Ahmed's hawklike features softened. "And your mother and I cherish you as you are."

She heard the "but," although he didn't say it. She also saw the deepening lines around his eyes, and the shadows under them. When he had spoken of giving up the throne in favor of Nadia's brother, Rashid, Nadia had thought unlikely that the sheik would actually step down. Now she started to wonder if Rashid had interests of his own he wanted to pursue. That she might not be the only member of the family chafing at the restrictions of her position was food for thought.

"Are you well, Father?" she asked.

"Worried about me, Nadia?"

"Of course. I love you."

He looked pleased. "I know you do, in spite of our differences. And I love you, my daughter."

She felt a momentary pang at the thought that he wouldn't always be there for her and had to blink away the moisture that sprang to her eyes. "I don't suppose you summoned me with an exciting project you want me to undertake," she said in an effort to lighten the moment.

He massaged his eyes. "One day I might surprise you."

She knew better than to take him seriously. "Is something wrong?"

"Relations with our neighbors in Montebello aren't as smooth as I wish they could be, but as you would say, what else is new?"

"I thought King Marcus's attitude toward Tamir had improved greatly since Hassan saved the life of the king's son and restored him to his home." On that occasion, her brother had been a true hero, she thought.

The sheik nodded. "My sons possess great qualities of leadership. Having Rashid married to Marcus's daughter has also improved relations between our two countries, so there is hope yet." He smiled, some of his usual vigor infusing his strong features. "I actually want to discuss a more personal matter with you—Butrus has petitioned me to nominate your wedding date."

"He asked you, instead of me?"

"Butrus knows the value of following protocol."

He would, she thought in annoyance. As an attorney, Butrus did most things by the book.

She thought of her conversation with Warren, reminding herself that Butrus was handsome, worldly and intelligent. She subdued the voice insisting that love should come into the bargain somewhere. Once had been enough for that.

His name was Gordon Perry. He was British, and five years younger than Nadia. Gordon had been an art teacher on sabbatical in Tamir with a backpack filled with sketchbooks and pencils. Nadia remembered their meeting vividly. Six years ago she had decided to go to the seashore to sketch. Unbeknownst to her, Gordon had the same plan.

With her bodyguard watching, she couldn't talk openly to a strange man, so they had started to exchange furtive notes. Like a couple of schoolchildren in class, she thought, feeling her mouth curve into a smile of nostalgia. She had no doubt that the enforced silence had added to his allure. A wealth of meaning could be contained in a look, she had found.

Their friendship grew, starting with written notes about

each other's work and blossoming into more personal matters. Lulled by the apparent innocence of the meetings, the bodyguard relaxed his vigilance enough that they could talk briefly. She still treasured the encouragement Gordon had given her, and the advice he had offered about her work.

After several supposedly chance meetings outdoors, they had arranged to meet at her studio, in the guise of Gordon giving her and her sisters art lessons. With her father's approval, she had engaged Gordon to redesign the studio so they could spend more time together.

No one had suspected that she was in love with the handsome art teacher until her father had surprised her by paying a rare visit to her studio and found them kissing. Gordon had been dismissed from the palace and she had endured long lectures about honor and duty. Instead of stemming her father's fury, telling him she wanted to marry Gordon had fired the sheik's wrath to new heights.

She had been agonizing over how she could contact Gordon when she saw on the television news that he had drowned while swimming off a notoriously dangerous stretch of the coastline. She would never know whether the ending of their affair had affected his judgment, but it had certainly affected hers. His body had been flown home to his family in England for burial, leaving her no ritual way to assuage her grief.

Instead, she had painted his portrait with all the love searing her soul. Then she had burned the painting as a symbol of the futility of someone in her position wanting to marry for love.

The acceptance hadn't been enough to make her look kindly on any of the men her father paraded before her over the next few years. Her feelings for Gordon had been too precious, too raw. But time and her father's persistence had finally worn her down.

When the sheik had suggested that Butrus would make a suitable husband for her, she was beyond caring. The man she loved was gone forever. She might as well marry Butrus

and make her father happy. Butrus's involvement in state
business meant she would be free of his supervision a lot of
the time.

"Have you decided on a wedding date?" she asked her
father, wrenching her thoughts back to the present.

"Three months from now should give you time to make
the final preparations. Your mother already has her plans in
hand, I understand."

The sheik sounded uninterested, as most men were when
wedding plans were mentioned, she had noticed. Not unlike
herself, she thought. She submitted to discussions and dress
fittings to please her mother, but wanted only to get the formalities over with.

She knew her attitude bewildered her sister, Samira, who
was far more enthusiastic than Nadia. Samira should marry
Butrus, Nadia thought, knowing it wasn't possible. There was
already a man in Samira's life. Her eyes sparkled whenever
Nadia brought up the question, but so far Samira was remarkably closemouthed about the details.

"There is something else," Sheik Ahmed went on, recap-
turing her attention.

"Yes, Father?"

"England has sent a new emissary to lead their trade delegation to Tamir. He presents his credentials to me tomorrow.
Following the formal proceedings, I have arranged a gathering to welcome the delegation. Since many of the delegates
will be accompanied by their wives, I should like you to act
as hostess on this occasion. Butrus will be there."

A huge lump rose in her throat. "The emissary's name?"

"Gage Weston. He is the godson of the British ambassador, and his credentials are of the highest. Have you heard
of him?"

She had done far worse, but she couldn't very well say so
to her father. She struggled to find her voice. "Wouldn't
Mother be a more suitable hostess?"

The sheik looked irritated with her for stating the obvious.

"Naturally, but Alima has decided to spend another few days in Montebello with Rashid and Julia and our grandson."

Nadia thought fast. She couldn't simply attend the party as Princess Nadia and expect the Englishman not to react. When he did, Butrus would want to know how they'd met, and her cover would be blown.

No longer would she be able go out as Tahani without anyone being the wiser. Nadia should have known the scheme couldn't go on indefinitely, but she was surprised at how keenly she felt the prospective loss.

How would the orphans feel when she was no longer their benefactor? Little Sammy already had to deal with losing his real parents in the fire that had also destroyed his family's farm. He clung to Nadia—his Addie—as to a lifeline. How could she let him think she had abandoned him? Her heart constricted at the thought of being cut off from him and all the other children. Visiting them in her official capacity would be a poor substitute, she knew.

"Samira would make a better hostess. You know I'm likely to say or do something to offend someone," she said on a note of desperation.

Ahmed gave her a knowing look. "Perhaps you should consider this additional practice. As Butrus's wife, you will be his hostess, so you may as well accustom yourself to the role."

"Very well, Father," she said on a note of resignation, and got up to leave.

Her father's voice stayed her a moment longer. "You may be cheered to hear that Gage Weston asked the British ambassador to request an introduction. Evidently Mr. Weston purchased one of your paintings and wishes to meet the artist in person."

Alarm coiled through her. "Surely you don't approve of such a request."

The sheik smiled. "Your reticence is commendable, but your talent is God-given and entitled to be celebrated."

What a time for her father to decide to be conciliatory,

Nadia thought in frustration. Her dislike for Gage Weston grew. "Butrus may object to my having a male admirer," she said.

"An admirer of your work," the sheik corrected. "Butrus wisely knows the difference." He added, "You tell me you wish to be useful, yet when I seek to involve you in state affairs, you're still unhappy."

"Making small talk and ensuring everyone's glass remains full hardly qualifies as state affairs," she said bitterly. "Any competent servant can do that."

"But a servant cannot smooth the way between nations with a smile. Or listen to what is and is not being said, and share his or her thoughts with me afterward."

She was forced to smile. "You make hostessing sound like undercover work."

He nodded. "Diplomacy involves more than overt negotiation. The social route may be indirect, but it is often the oil that lubricates relations between countries."

She knew he was trying to make her feel better about her role and gave a wan smile. Her father couldn't know that her reluctance wasn't to acting as his hostess, at least not this time, but to the prospect of facing Gage Weston again.

His image sprang to her mind much more vividly than she expected. He was taller than she was by a head, with green eyes that looked as if they could see all the way to her soul. Warren had said that Gage was in superb physical condition. Thinking of the muscles rippling under her touch and the energy that had enveloped her as she'd helped him out of the car, she could hardly argue. But what was he like as a man? Could she prevail on him to keep her secret? What would he expect in return?

She wasn't melodramatic enough to think she had saved his life. The accident had been a minor one, and her assistance inconsiderable. But as a diplomat he would want her family's favor. Surely that alone would be enough to buy his silence?

At the same time, she couldn't subdue her fear that Gage Weston was not a man to be bought so easily.

Chapter 3

Samira Kamal bounced into her sister's bedroom and stopped short. "Nadia, what on earth are you wearing that for?"

"Father wants me to act as hostess at tonight's party. I decided to look the part," Nadia told her sister with a calmness she was far from feeling. The prospect of confronting Gage Weston again weighed on her mind and had influenced her choice of dress for the occasion.

Samira looked nonplussed. "But isn't national dress a bit over the top, especially for you?"

Nadia's hands stilled on the veil she was adjusting. "What do you mean, especially for me?"

Samira hesitated. "You must admit you're the most adventurous member of the family, even a bit reckless at times."

Nadia pulled in a steadying breath. "In what way?"

Samira looked flustered. "Going out on your own for hours at a time on those painting expeditions. Father may believe you're indulging in your hobby, but I'm sure there's more to it. I've been dying to ask, do you have a lover?''

Nadia almost laughed. Trust her younger sister to suspect such a thing. "No, I don't have a lover. I'm an engaged woman. I was going to ask you the same thing."

She had turned the question on Samira as much to deflect her sister's attention as learn if it was true. Now she was intrigued to see color flood Samira's cheeks. "What if I do?"

"You…you do?"

Samira wrung her hands. "You wretch, Nadia. You didn't know, did you."

"I do now. Is he anyone I know?"

Samira shook her head, her lovely black hair flowing around her shoulders in shimmering waves—the way their father would like to see her older sister's, Nadia thought ruefully. No such luck. Hair like Samira's took lots of work to keep looking so fabulous, and Nadia hated wasting time on such pursuits.

"He isn't from Tamir," Samira confessed. "That's why I've been keeping my feelings to myself."

"You think father may not approve?"

"I know he won't. He wants me to marry a Tamir man of noble birth."

"Like Butrus Dabir," Nadia said.

"Butrus is a good catch. Handsome, personable. Maybe a little cold at times, but he's a man. They're all the same."

Not Gage Weston. The thought sprang to Nadia's mind with disturbing certainty. She had seen his reaction to meeting little Sammy. Butrus would have kept his distance, afraid of catching something. But Gage had stepped forward without hesitation and set out to win the little boy's trust. Sammy had responded just as warmly. No, Gage couldn't be described as cold.

"You've gone away from me," Samira said. "Tell me what's really going on with you."

In fairness Nadia couldn't involve her sister in her affairs and risk getting her into trouble with their father. "Nothing's going on," she replied. "What's wrong with wearing national dress if I feel like it?"

"Nothing, if you don't mind looking like an escapee from a harem. Aren't you the one who says we're living in a new millennium and should modernize accordingly?"

Nadia turned to the mirror, inspecting her outfit critically. White trousers ballooned around her legs, the fullness caught at each ankle by gold embroidery. Her narrow waist was cinched with a gold circlet. Above it she wore a gossamer-thin blouse of pale-green silk, threaded with gold, the billowing sleeves captured at the wrists by more embroidery. Beneath the translucent blouse, she wore a modest shift of midnight blue. The costume had been passed down to her by her grandmother, and Samira was right; it was rarely worn outside tourist venues or on the most ceremonial occasions and could hardly be called modern.

"Tradition has its place," she murmured, turning to check the back. She frowned. "I don't really look as if I belong in a harem, do I?"

"Actually, no," Samira said. "You look amazing. I wish I were as tall as you and could wear anything I wanted to—although you still haven't told me what you're up to."

"What makes you think I'm up to anything?"

"I know you too well. The last time father conscripted you to act as his hostess, you wore a low-cut, western evening gown to annoy him. That's it, isn't it? You're hoping to deter him from imposing on you again."

Relieved that her sister had arrived at a satisfactory explanation for her choice of dress, Nadia nodded. She had really chosen the costume for the diaphanous veil, the only way she could think to hide her features when she met Gage Weston. Her choice, fueled by desperation, was bound to cause comment, as it had done with Samira. Few women in Tamir wore the veil nowadays. Those who did usually let it hang to one side of the face rather than fastening it across their features as Nadia intended to do.

She slipped the veil into place across the lower half of her face, amazed at how mysterious and feminine she suddenly looked. Her eyes, highlighted with kohl, seemed huge and intriguing. She looked downright seductive, she thought in amazement.

She had never thought of herself as especially feminine, and she didn't approve of using womanly wiles to get her own way. She preferred the direct approach, much to her father's horror. But dressed like this, veiled and perfumed with her favorite jasmine scent, she not only looked as if she could seduce a man, she *felt* as if she could.

Tempted to tear the veil from her face before she got any more crazy ideas, she kept her hands at her sides. This wasn't for her, but for the children at the orphanage. The thought of them waiting in vain for her to return lent her the strength to move toward the door. "I'd better go. Duty calls."

"Have fun," Samira said to her sister's departing back.

Fun? thought Nadia derisively. She would rather be boiled in oil. Making polite conversation with the wives of the trade delegates was hardly her idea of a stimulating evening. Her father would be shocked if she followed her inclinations and conversed with the men, because they would be talking about the really interesting matters, like international trade and diplomacy.

She wondered what Sheik Ahmed would think if he knew how keenly she followed her country's affairs, resulting in her being as well-informed as any of his advisers. He would probably remind her that she would have little need of such interests once she was married, when children and domesticity would be sufficient to occupy her mind.

Children she didn't mind. Obviously, or she wouldn't be so anxious to help the orphans. There were times when she could hardly bear to be around the younger ones because her longing for a child was so overwhelming. The rest of the package was what alarmed her. Being restricted to domestic concerns terrified her. Why couldn't she marry, have children *and* be involved in world affairs?

She knew she was focusing on these matters to avoid her

real worry—Gage Weston's reaction when they were introduced. Perhaps he would be like the men of her own country, greeting her politely while glancing around for someone more interesting to talk to.

Somehow she knew he wouldn't be.

First she had to deal with her father's reaction. In deference to his guests, Sheik Ahmed was dressed in an impeccably tailored business suit, the only mark of his rank, his flowing headdress fastened by a coiled gold *'iqal.* The other Tamir men wore similar attire, but minus the *'iqal,* which was worn only by men of royal blood.

Nadia breathed a sigh of relief when she noticed a couple of other women guests wearing traditional dress, although they hadn't veiled their faces.

Butrus Dabir, who regarded himself as a man of the world, had dispensed with the headdress. In a western-style business suit, she had to concede that he looked impressive, more like a sheik himself than an attorney. Of course, he would be a sheik once they were married. Her father would confer titles and land on Butrus, as befitted the ruler's son-in-law. Not that he was penniless now. Coming from a noble family, Butrus was wealthy in his own right. Married to a princess, he would be one of the most powerful men in Tamir.

As she made her entrance, she saw an expression of thunder settle on the sheik's features. He said a few curt words to Butrus, who immediately came and took her arm. "What do you think you're doing?"

"Acting as hostess at my father's request," she said smoothly, struggling to keep the tremor out of her voice. "I thought you'd appreciate my effort."

"If I knew this get-up was a genuine attempt at womanly modesty, I might."

"How do you know it isn't?"

His eyes narrowed with suspicion. "You're telling me that your status as my bride-to-be has persuaded you to moderate your wilfulness?"

She nodded, casting her gaze down, glad that Butrus

couldn't see the twitch of her mouth behind her veil. "Father told me yesterday that you have set our wedding date. Preparing myself seemed like a good idea."

Butrus looked pleased. "Very well. I shall accept your gesture in good faith and look forward to seeing more of this new Nadia." He leaned closer. "I should tell you that I find the veil extremely provocative."

A shudder rippled through her. In the mirror she had seen for herself the effect the veil created. Butrus's reaction confirmed it. She could only hope that Gage Weston wasn't similarly intrigued. That was the last thing she needed.

She hadn't been able to stop herself from scanning the assembly for signs of him. Tamir was a country of tall imposing men, but Gage was even more prepossessing. A man among men, he might be described as. She quickly recognized the British ambassador, Sir Brian Theodore, and his beautiful wife, Lady Lillian. Nadia's father had said that Sir Brian was Gage's godfather, but he wasn't with them.

Butrus introduced her to the wife of a trade delegate and returned to the sheik's side. Nadia concentrated on conversing politely, containing herself with an effort her father would have found commendable, if unusual.

Without removing her veil, she couldn't eat or drink anything, and her throat began to burn as the others around her enjoyed refreshments. She distracted herself by listening to the music being played by the palace quartet from a low dais at one end of the courtyard.

Explaining the significance of her costume to the curious western women for the umpteenth time was starting to become tiresome—when she spotted him.

Gage stood at the top of the sandstone steps leading to the courtyard where the reception was being held, his green eyes taking in everything.

Amazing how twenty-four hours could distort a memory, she thought, feeling her limbs go weak. She had convinced herself that he couldn't possibly be as compelling as she had first imagined.

He was more!

The authority in his pose took her breath away. He was only a leader of a trade delegation, not even an ambassador, yet he carried himself as if he was accustomed to giving orders, not taking them.

She ducked her head, feeling conspicuous. Wearing the costume had been a mad idea from the start, but changing was hardly an option now.

She could swear she felt a burning sensation as his gaze settled on her. Tilting her head slightly to monitor him through her lashes, she felt her gaze collide with his and almost gasped in shock. He knew, she thought, seeing his expression change swiftly from cool indifference to a searing and blatantly sensuous assessment.

Somehow, she couldn't imagine how, he already knew who she was under the veil, and his challenging look was a gauntlet thrown down. He probably thought because he knew her secret, he could stare at her as he wished, without fear of retribution from her father or fiancé.

Guilty conscience was leading her to imagine his predatory focus on her, she told herself. As a foreigner, he was probably curious about her attire, that was all. But she hadn't imagined what she saw in his gaze. She had only to remember how Gordon used to look at her to be sure that a man only looked at a woman that way when he desired her.

Defiance surged through her. If she kept her head, whatever advantage Gage thought he had over her would be useless. Her word as a princess was worth more than his as a minor foreign diplomat.

Over the head of the woman chattering to her about how much hotter it was in Tamir then back home in wherever, Nadia saw Gage break his stride in her direction and veer to the sheik's side. She waited for her father to greet him politely, then dismiss him in favor of more important guests, but to her dismay, the sheik seemed to welcome Gage's company. Merciful stars, he wasn't reporting her to her father, was he?

Her heart pumped as the sheik turned his head in her direction. He was smiling. Surely he wouldn't smile if Gage had just told him that his daughter made a habit of eluding her bodyguard to behave in ways the sheik would regard as unbefitting a princess.

Her breath caught as the sheik moved toward her, Gage at his side. Her mind raced. She would deny everything. No, she wouldn't. She would confess to her father before Gage could betray her. Then she would hold her head high and face whatever music her unconventional behavior had invited.

The sea of dignitaries parted for the sheik and his companion. By the time they reached her, Nadia's veil fluttered with the effort of controlling her breathing. "Father, I need to tell you…"

The sheik gestured her to silence. "In time, my daughter. I wish to present the emissary from England, Mr. Gage Weston. Mr. Weston, Her Highness Princess Nadia Kamal."

Gage executed a skillful bow that managed to mock her at the same time. "Your Highness."

Her dry throat made her voice husky. "Welcome to Tamir, Mr. Weston."

"Mr. Weston has expressed an interest in our customs, in particular the dress you have chosen to wear in his honor," the sheik continued.

Hardly in his honor. He *was* the driving force behind the choice, but not for the reason her father evidently believed. "I'm glad Mr. Weston appreciates it," she said through clenched teeth.

"Oh, he does, my dear, as do I."

Her father sounded amused, she thought in confusion. For once, she was glad to keep her gaze properly downcast to avoid having to meet Gage's blatant appraisal. She was utterly convinced that he had recognized her. Her glimpse of his determined expression as he approached was enough to warn her that he intended to use his knowledge, although to what end, she didn't want to think.

Her palms grew moist as she waited for Gage to betray her to her father, but he only stood rock still beside the sheik as if he had all the time in the world. She decided two could play this game, and willed herself to silence and stillness, although every nerve in her body tingled with awareness.

"I informed Mr. Weston that your costume is traditionally worn for the performance of the Water Dance," the sheik went on.

"Yes, Father." Volunteer nothing, she instructed herself. Never had she found being silent more difficult.

"Then you *do* intend to perform the dance for us, daughter?"

Startled, she lifted her head to find the sheik pinning her with a hard glare that belied the amusement in his expression. Gage Weston merely looked interested, as befitted a visitor of his status. But in *his* eyes, she saw a sensual challenge that shook her to the core.

Gage was waiting for her to refuse and get herself into deeper trouble with her father, she thought, again disturbed by the almost telepathic communication between them.

Her father had suggested the dance to punish her for making an exhibition of herself. Knowing how much she would hate being forced to perform for the assembled businessmen and their wives, the sheik had chosen a devastating way to exact his penance.

Her father probably expected her to slink away in disgrace and apologize later for her behavior. She saw a similar expectation in Gage's expression. Was that why he hadn't unmasked her? Was he waiting to see the sheik bring her to heel so he could have the last laugh?

Over her dead body.

If her father wanted her to dance, then dance she would, she thought defiantly. Not humbly or reluctantly, but with style. Let Gage see that she wasn't afraid of him or any man. She felt his gaze following her as she mounted the dais and heard her father announce the entertainment to his guests.

* * *

Gage watched the princess in reluctant admiration. Arriving with Sir Brian and Lady Lillian, he had waited outside the courtyard, ostensibly to renew an old acquaintance, but really so he could observe the later arrivals. He had slipped into the shadow of a statue when Nadia walked in. Her choice of national costume had startled him, too. She looked like a butterfly among a collection of moths.

He had seen her fiancé lecturing her and hadn't been fooled by her downcast eyes, although Dabir evidently had been. Why had she risked his anger and her father's wrath by dressing so outlandishly? Of course, the veil. She didn't know Gage had seen her exchange clothes with her maid and had no doubt thought to prevent him from recognizing her. Even if he hadn't already known her secret, his first breath of her distinctive jasmine perfume would have given her away.

He didn't need intelligence skills to work out that ordering her to dance was the sheik's way of teaching her a lesson, and Gage's conscience was troubled. Outwardly Nadia seemed comfortable at the center of attention. But he'd noticed the lines around her eyes. Gage didn't like witnessing her distress and wished there was something he could do about it. Telling himself that she had started this with her deception didn't help. He had no option but to watch her dance.

The story was a simple creation myth such as existed in many cultures. In Tamir's version, the original humans were Ishara, the giver of water, and Ranif, the giver of light and life. Nadia danced a wonderful Ishara, managing to conjure up the invisible Ranif with her poetic gestures and lissome movements.

In the myth, Ranif readily released his gifts over the land, bringing light and life, but couldn't persuade Ishara to offer her gift of water. So he decided to leave, forcing her to admit her love for him. Her tears of sorrow released water into the land as the precious gift it remained to this day. Ranif returned and married Ishara.

Gage knew that countless films had distorted the concept of veil dancing. The Mata Hari idea of peeling back layers of veils to tantalize onlookers was as much a myth as the Ishara story. Using a veil in such a way would amount to a striptease, unacceptable in Tamir culture. So Nadia's dancing had none of the seductive mockery of the western version. Yet seductive she was, in subtle ways that were many times more effective. Gage had never felt so aroused by a dancer in his life.

Was it the lure of the unattainable? Veiled and moving so fluidly, she projected a mystique that spoke to his soul, making him want to rip away the covering and possess her utterly.

Looking around at the attentive audience, Gage was astonished to feel anger snarling through him. He didn't like Nadia's being the cynosure of all eyes. Suddenly he understood why the men of some cultures insisted on women being veiled. Keeping Nadia to himself, her beauty for his eyes alone, had a powerful appeal.

The dance ended and he shook off the thought. She was engaged to Butrus Dabir, Gage's number-one suspect, for goodness' sake. She could well be in league with Dabir, or herself be the traitor Gage sought. Letting her get to him was playing with fire.

Letting a woman like Nadia get to him at any time was playing with fire.

She acknowledged the rapturous applause gracefully enough, but her eyes shone with moisture as she came down off the stage. She kept her head down and almost ran into Gage in her haste to escape.

He parked himself in her way. "You were wonderful, Your Highness. Or should I say, Addie."

Anger and humiliation swirled in her expressive eyes. "Are you pleased you've had your revenge, Mr. Weston?"

Gage would never have put her through such an ordeal, and he didn't like being lumped in with the man who had. "The dance was your father's idea, not mine," he protested.

"When did you first recognize me?"

Telling her he'd seen her change clothes with her maid would blow his cover, so he said, "Since you found me on the side of the road."

"So this was for nothing."

"I wouldn't call it nothing. Your dance was magnificent."

She tore the veil off her face, letting the gossamer fabric hang down one side. "There's nothing magnificent about being looked upon as an amusement, a plaything. My father would never humiliate one of his sons this way."

Gage started to wonder if he was on the right track. Nadia was such a bewildering mixture of innocence and worldliness that he found it increasingly hard to believe she could be a traitor to her family and her country. A worry, yes, but a traitor?

You're getting soft, Weston, he told himself. The best spies were invariably the last people anyone suspected. The thought made him remember that he had a job to do. "I want to see you again," he said in an undertone.

The panic in her expressive eyes was quickly masked by resolve. "If you think you can blackmail me with what you know…"

"This isn't blackmail," he said quickly. "I only want to visit the orphanage again. I know someone who may be able to help the children find homes. Will you take me with you when next you visit?"

Her long lashes fluttered acceptance of her lack of choice. "Very well. I'll be going again on Thursday morning. You can meet me there."

Gage saw Dabir making his way to them through the throng, a frown on his face. So the attorney didn't like another man chatting to his fiancée. Gage could understand that. "I'll be there," he said quickly, and she nodded.

She moved to intercept Dabir. Gage lifted a glass of chilled juice off the tray of a passing waiter, but didn't drink. His thoughts were too busy. He did know someone who could help the orphans—his sister, Alexandra, who was married to a British duke. But Gage's main reason for revisiting the orphanage was to investigate whether it could be a front for the Brothers of Darkness. He hoped not, but in his business, it didn't pay to discount any possibility until he had checked it out thoroughly.

The princess didn't have to be with him for that, so why take the risk of arranging a meeting? Instinct, he told himself, and almost laughed aloud. Hormones, more likely. Although she hadn't danced to seduce, she had aroused him in a way no woman had done for a long time. The need to see her again was like a fire in his blood. He caught her watching him over her fiancé's shoulder and lifted his glass in a silent tribute to their next encounter.

Chapter 4

Long accustomed to the ritual, Nadia stood impassively as her sleeping robe was lifted from her body and she was helped into her morning bath. As the silken waters closed around her, she wondered how it would feel to bathe herself and wash her own hair.

She knew better than to suggest such a thing to her personal attendants. Not only would they be scandalized that a royal princess should wish to do such menial tasks for herself, but they would also fear for their futures. If she denied them the honor of serving her, what else would they do?

As she knew from bitter experience, meaningful work was at a premium for females in her society. Mostly they were expected to occupy themselves with their husbands and children. If the Almighty didn't grant them such blessings, they had two choices—inflict themselves upon their relatives or go into the service of some more fortunate woman.

Nadia sighed. She was that woman, so why didn't she feel fortunate? Because but for an accident of royal birth, she would have been one of society's misfits, she knew. Unmarried for all this time and preoccupied with her art, she was hardly an example of the ideal Tamiri woman.

She moved her limbs restlessly in the delicately scented bath, which was as big as a child's pool. Closing her eyes, she tilted her head back as her hair was lathered with sweetly perfumed lotion. The massaging action soothed her in spite of the faint guilt she always felt at being so pampered.

With only her thoughts to occupy her, she took an inventory of her attendants. Nargis was the one doing her hair. Although no older than Nadia, she regarded herself as Nadia's second mother, always ready with advice whether Nadia wanted to hear it or not. Nargis had the advantage, depending on how one looked at it, of knowing almost everything that went on around the palace and being almost unable to resist sharing her knowledge. While Nadia didn't like to encourage gossip, she knew there were times when Nargis's information had its uses.

On both sides, the princess's hands had been captured for attention by Thea and Ramana. They were twins, raven-haired and also close to Nadia in age. The only reason they hadn't married was their insistence on staying together. Should a man show interest in one of them, he invariably learned that a permanent house guest—the other twin—came as part of the package. Not surprisingly most men found the prospect daunting.

Then there was dear Tahani, Nadia's partner in crime, who was at this moment restoring order to Nadia's bedchamber. Tahani could well have her own family by now, Nadia thought with a twinge of remorse, but her loyalty to the princess was too strong. Somehow Nadia would have to persuade Tahani to think of her own future. She should have done so already, she knew, but without Tahani's willing assistance, how was she to escape the confines of her royal life?

Nargis, Thea and Ramana were devoted to her, but she suspected they would balk at disobeying the sheik so flagrantly. Only Tahani shared Nadia's adventurous spirit. In a more equal society, she would have been a success in some creative field, Nadia knew. They often made a game of imagining their lives differently. In the game, Tahani was an interior decorator, or a set designer for the movies. Nadia imagined herself as a great painter, her works hung in the world's most respected galleries and sold to discerning buyers, not only out of charity, but because they spoke to the buyer's soul.

Buyers like Gage Weston, she thought dreamily. She would see him again this morning when she kept their appointment at the orphanage.

The thought of the meeting made her eyes flutter open, letting a trace of shampoo trickle into them, stinging horribly. With a cry of alarm, Nargis dipped a fresh towel in clean water and dabbed at Nadia's eyes until she could see again.

"My princess, my carelessness has harmed you. How can I make amends?"

The effusiveness of the apology only made Nadia feel worse about her errant thoughts. "It wasn't your fault, Nargis, so you can stop acting as if you're about to be beaten." The servant knew as well as Nadia that such a thing had no part in Tamir culture. "We both know I should have kept my eyes closed."

The remorse fled from the attendant's expression. "I'm more interested in what shocking thought made them fly open."

Nadia pretended innocence. "Why should my thoughts be shocking?"

Nargis had served Nadia's family for a long time and knew her as well as anyone. "They invariably are. Let me guess, you were thinking of a man."

Was she so transparent? "If I was, why would that be shocking?"

"As long as the man was Butrus Dabir, it wouldn't be. Were you thinking of your husband-to-be?"

In the privacy of the boudoir, Nadia felt no need to dissemble. "No," she said on a heavy out-rush of breath. She decided to change the subject. "Did you know Butrus has petitioned my father to set our wedding date?"

Nargis held out a huge velour towel, a sign for Nadia to step out of the bath and be swathed in the folds. As she did so, her attendant said, "Palace gossip speaks of a wedding day, not that I pay any attention to gossip."

Nadia kept a straight face. "Of course not."

"You are blessed to have such a distinguished man as Butrus Dabir, my princess."

Nadia nodded, wishing she felt more blessed. "You're right of course."

She was aware of Nargis's giving her an assessing look as Ramana tucked the towel around Nadia like a sarong. Thea wound another around her hair, then she was steered to a chair so Ramana could massage perfumed lotion into her arms and legs, making her skin silky smooth. Not that anyone would get to appreciate the results, Nadia thought with an inward sigh. Not for her, the freedom to wear skirts that showed off her long legs, or a bikini on the beach to allow the sun to kiss her body.

As a result, her skin was milky and unblemished. At least she didn't have to worry about turning into a dried-up prune in her older years, she consoled herself, trying to think positively. Nor did she ever have to deal with unwanted male attention. Her way of life had some benefits.

"You're thinking of him again," Nargis said with bothersome insight.

Nadia swung her head up, almost dislodging the towel swathing her hair. "Who?"

"This man who isn't Butrus, who makes your cheeks glow and your eyes shine."

"He doesn't. I mean, you're imagining things, Nargis. Get on with your work and stop being so fanciful."

"Humph. I doubt I'm the one being fanciful."

Nadia knew she had earned the other woman's disdain. Complaining about the strictures of royal life, but pulling rank when it suited her was hardly fair. It didn't help that

Nargis was right. Nadia was preoccupied with thoughts of a man.

Gage Weston.

His name sent a shiver through her. She hadn't seen him since the sheik's reception three days before, but he had appeared in her thoughts more often than she wanted. She told herself it was because he had insisted on today's meeting, but knew there was more to her preoccupation.

The prospect of seeing him again made her feel more elated than she had any business being.

She remembered the expression she had seen on his face when her father insisted she perform the Water Dance for his guests. Gage had understood that her father intended to punish her, and the sympathy she had glimpsed had almost been her undoing.

During the dance she had seen a look of black anger descend on Gage's features, and at first thought he was as annoyed with her as her father was, until gradually she realized that Gage's anger was on her account. He hadn't liked the way the other guests were looking at her, she had noticed, unwillingly gratified. In fact, he had looked as if he wanted to slug someone, possibly her father, for putting her through the ordeal.

Nargis had said she was being fanciful, and no doubt she was. But she couldn't shake the belief that Gage had been on her side. In desperation, she had looked to Butrus for some sign of leniency, finding none. Throughout the dance her fiancé had glowered at her from under lowered brows, as if to say he hoped she was learning her lesson. He and her father were a pair, she thought, both making their disapproval painfully evident.

The other male guests had watched her with enough interest to make her squirm inwardly, unaccustomed as she was to disporting herself for the eyes of men. Like all Tamiri women, her training in dance had been to develop graceful movements, not to entertain others.

Only in Gage's face had she seen concern for her as an

individual. Inspired, she had danced to the limit of her skill. As she interpreted the romantic legend, she had felt herself transported beyond the disapproval of her father and fiancé, even beyond the cupidity of their male guests, until she felt as if she danced for Gage's eyes alone.

Afterward when he complimented her on her dancing, she had seen nothing but compassion and—dare she think it?—admiration in his eyes. Until he spoiled everything by insisting on another meeting. With her secret in his keeping, he must have known she couldn't refuse. Why hadn't he betrayed her to her father? Was he hoping to use what he knew for his own benefit? In Nadia's experience, it was what most men would do. She found herself hoping he wasn't like most men.

Ramana held out a silky robe and Nadia slipped out of the towel and into the robe, belting the sash around her slender waist. In her bedroom, Tahani had set out her mistress's clothing for the day. Nadia surveyed the choices. A long skirt in tones of sea-green and blue threaded with gold, a matching silk shirt, a wide blue sash and silk-covered pumps in the same iridescent blue. Nadia suspected that Tahani herself coveted the outfit. Since the maid would be the one wearing it for most of the day, why not?

"Excellent choices for a day of painting," she told Tahani as the maid helped her to dress. She regarded Tahani's own outfit with approval. "I'm glad you're wearing the blue *galabiya.*"

Tahani's dark eyes sparkled. "It is one of your favorites, Your Highness."

"Blue has always been my favorite color." It also lent a sparkle to her dark eyes, she knew, wondering at the same time why she cared what she looked like when she was only going to visit the orphanage. The children certainly didn't care what she wore.

Annoyed with herself, she shifted impatiently as Tahani fluffed her hair into a becoming halo around her head. Her father might not approve of the style, but Nadia appreciated

the sense of freedom it gave her. Considering how little freedom she did have in her life, she savored what she had.

At long last, Tahani stood back to admire her handiwork.
"You look breathtaking, my princess. Were I Butrus Dabir,
I would walk over hot coals to win the heart of such beauty."

What would Gage Weston do to win the heart of the
woman he loved? Nadia found herself thinking. She made a
dismissive gesture. "Butrus has no need to make sacrifices
on my account. He has already won my hand."

If Tahani noticed that Nadia didn't include her heart, she
refrained from commenting. Instead, she said, "Perhaps."

Nadia felt a prickle of unease. As well as having an artistic
eye, Tahani was known for her prescience. Since joining Nadia's service a few years before, Tahani had made many predictions, and Nadia hated to think how many of them had
proved accurate.

"There's no 'perhaps' about it. I'm to marry Butrus and
that's that."

Again her maid gave a maddening half smile. "Perhaps."

Unsettled, Nadia brushed a nonexistent speck off her
blouse. "You drive me crazy when you do that."

Returning brushes and cosmetics to their places, Tahani
paused, looking genuinely puzzled. "Do what, Your Highness?"

"Hint at a future only you can see."

Tahani capped a tube of eye shadow and replaced it on
Nadia's dresser. "You must know by now that I can't see
the future, Your Highness. Sometimes an insight just comes,
like a whisper in my ear."

Nadia kept her hands at her sides, although she wanted to
twist them together. "Does your whisper tell you any more
than 'perhaps' where Butrus and I are concerned?"

Tahani gave an apologetic shake of her head. "When you
stated so emphatically that you were to marry him, the word
popped into my head. I don't even know what it means.
Probably no more than a woman's foolishness."

Nadia tried to ignore the sudden hope welling inside her

like the flickering of a candle flame. No amount of soothsaying was going to show her a way out of marrying Butrus, nor was she looking for one. She would meet Gage today as agreed, but make it clear to him that it must be for the last time. Then she would do her duty.

Astonished at the regret accompanying this thought, she said, "We all have our moments of foolishness. Gather my painting materials and have Mahir bring the car around. It's time we were on our way."

Tahani brought her palms together at breast height and bowed over them before hurrying away to do Nadia's bidding.

Nadia sat for a few moments, barely aware of her reflection in the mirror in front of her. What was going on here? She had believed herself resigned to marrying Butrus. Yet one word from Tahani, suggesting that a different fate might lie in store for her, had set Nadia's hopes soaring.

She quashed them with a determined shake of her head. Nothing was going to change, so she might as well accept it. She would be Butrus's wife and that was that.

Still, she was aware of the hope flickering persistently inside her like a flame that refused to be extinguished as she made her way out to the courtyard where her driver, Mahir, would be waiting with Tahani and the car.

The courtyard was deserted.

She schooled herself to patience. Something was probably amiss with the car, and they were changing to another. She gave a start when a hand dropped on to her shoulder. "I told Tahani to tell Mahir you won't need him until later today."

She swung around to find Butrus looming over her, and she felt her heart beating ridiculously fast. "Butrus. I didn't expect to see you this morning."

"I rearranged my schedule so we could talk."

She glanced around the courtyard as if doing so would conjure up her car. "Now?"

Butrus frowned. "From your maid, I understood you were

only going out painting. What difference can it make if you go in the afternoon, instead?''

She let her hands flutter at her sides. ''The morning light is better.''

He frowned. ''The light is the light. I have appointments this afternoon.''

His message was clear. He wanted her attention now, and her own plans would just have to wait. Thinking of Gage waiting for her, she debated whether to argue, but knew she would only arouse Butrus's suspicion. ''You're right, I can paint this afternoon,'' she conceded. She would have to send a message to Gage, telling him she had been detained.

Butrus let his hand trail down her arm. ''You'll have little time for hobbies after we're married, little one.''

She drew herself straighter. They were almost of a height and his use of the endearment rankled almost as much as his dismissal of her work. ''My art is hardly a hobby.''

He smiled indulgently. ''Your passion, then. As your husband I shall provide more womanly outlets for your passion, so you'll have no need of art.'' The gleam in his gaze told her what kind of outlet he had in mind.

She would always need her art. It was as natural to her as breathing, but she could see that Butrus would never agree. Her heart ached. How could she commit her life to a man who refused to understand the simplest thing about her? ''Surely there's room in life for more than one kind of passion?'' she asked.

He took her hand, leading her back inside to where servants had set out tea and exquisite pastries for them.

After they were served and the servants withdrew to a discreet distance, Butrus said, ''Your experience of the world of men has necessarily been limited. But I promise, when you are awakened to the passion that can exist between a man and a woman, you will desire no other.''

His conceit almost made her laugh out loud. She might have been raised in the cloistered environment of the royal palace, but she had known true love. She doubted that Butrus could transport her to more-earthly delights than she had known with Gordon while they were together.

"I'm not a child," she insisted, stirring against the bank of cushions at her back. "My education was quite thorough."

He chuckled softly. "I don't doubt it, but theory and experience are very different things, my princess, as you will discover in time."

She restrained a heavy sigh. He was determined to regard her as a hothouse flower, virginal and innocent of the ways of the world. "I'm sure I will, with you to guide me."

Her reply gratified him, she saw as his expression softened. Butrus was right. Theory and experience were very different. From her mother and attendants, Nadia had learned what to say and do to please a man. She hadn't expected the words to stick in her throat like insufficiently cooked meat.

How did her mother endure such a proscribed existence? Why couldn't she say what she meant and have her opinions respected? Nadia despised the idea of getting her own way through flattery and manipulation, however effective.

She set her cup down, shaking the empty cup to signal to the servant rushing to refill it that she had had enough. Facing Butrus, she said. "There's something you need to know about me."

Leaning closer, he silenced her with a finger pressed to her lips. "I know all that I need to know, little one. You are beautiful, innocent, a little headstrong perhaps, but marriage and motherhood will soon tame your wilder instincts."

She reared away from his touch. "I'm not a horse in need of taming."

He frowned as if unaware he'd said anything wrong. "Gentling, then. I will be gentle with you, Nadia, even as you submit to my dominion."

She had to struggle not to raise her voice. "Taming, dominion, can you hear yourself? I understand marriage to be a partnership."

"It is a partnership," he agreed somberly, then ruined the

effect by adding, "In every partnership, there can be only one leader."

"You, I suppose," she said.

Butrus looked pleased. "See? We are close to an understanding already."

This understanding was keeping her from her meeting with Gage, she thought, striving to conceal her restlessness. She stood up. "I'm glad we had this talk. Now I really must go."

Snagging her wrist, he pulled her down beside him, his fingers tracing a line along her arm before he pulled away with obvious reluctance. "I can see I've upset you by talking of the passion within marriage. Forgive me, Nadia. Your beauty fills my mind with little else, but I am a man and men's needs are different. Let me make amends by speaking, instead, of our wedding date."

She felt color flood her cheeks and was guiltily glad Butrus blamed it on embarrassment at his choice of subject matter. "Father told me you'd petitioned him to set the date," she said, hoping to end this quickly.

He nodded. "Three months will seem like an eternity."

She wished she could say, "For me, too," but couldn't bring herself to lie. She settled for, "I'm sure my father knows what's best."

"No doubt. He has offered us the royal yacht for our honeymoon cruise."

Her heart sank at the prospect of being confined to the yacht, playing the part of the dutiful wife. "Can you spare the time from your business?" she asked.

"I thought of combining the two. A few meetings aboard ship won't get in the way of our truly getting to know one another," he promised.

"Sounds wonderful," she said weakly, aware that the heirloom clock on the wall was ticking away the minutes. Gage must be wondering where she was. Butrus hadn't given her the chance to send a message.

"Then it's settled. Now all we need to discuss are a few formalities. As his wedding gift to us, your father intends to build a private apartment for us within the palace grounds, so your family can provide company for you when I have to go away.''

She almost groaned out loud. Living within the palace was the last thing she wanted. ''I understood we would live at your estate at Zabara.''

''You flatter me, but my home is hardly suitable for a princess and her consort. As his son-in-law, I'll be more useful to your father if I am nearby.''

And more privy to the workings of the court, she thought. ''You've thought of everything,'' she said, knowing the irony would be lost on Butrus.

''I'm pleased you agree,'' he said, unwittingly proving her point. He held out his hand to help her to her feet. ''I wish we could spend more of the morning together, but I'm afraid I have business I must attend to.''

''Of course.'' She kept her expression bland, but inwardly, she despaired. More than an hour had passed. By now Gage would know she wasn't coming, and it was too late to get a message to him. She shivered, wondering what he would do now.

Chapter 5

Gage had half expected the princess to stand him up, but still, he felt disappointed. Not because he wanted to see her again, he assured himself, but because he needed answers.

In his line of work it was prudent to suspect everyone's motives, even women as beautiful and apparently innocent as Nadia Kamal. Especially women as beautiful as Nadia.

When he'd decided he'd waited long enough, he set about investigating the orphanage on his own. Probably better that way. He could look where he wasn't supposed to, go where she wouldn't have taken him.

It was late morning by the time he'd investigated the buildings and immediate surroundings, careful not to be seen by the children or their caregivers. The noise level of the children playing in the courtyard provided a welcome cover for his movements.

When the doctor, Warren, emerged from his dispensary, Gage ducked under a stairwell that was cloaked in shadow. Waiting there, he was startled to feel a tug at his sleeve. He looked down to find Sammy crouching farther back in the same space.

"Sammy hiding, too," the child whispered solemnly, his large dark eyes luminous.

Steadying his unsettled nerves, Gage smiled. "I won't tell on you, if you won't tell on me."

Sammy nodded and patted his ear. Gage took a minute to work out what he wanted, then remembered. Keeping a wary eye on the doctor talking to some of the other children in the courtyard, he pulled a coin out of his pocket, showed it to Sammy, then made it disappear, only to reappear magically behind the little boy's ear.

The child's giggles caught the doctor's attention. He squinted toward the shadows. "Sammy, are you under there?"

Gage gave the boy a gentle push and whispered, "Sorry, son, you've been found. Off you go."

Sammy tried to tug his new friend out with him, but Gage shook his head. "They haven't found me yet." With any luck they wouldn't. He was relieved when the little boy trotted out into the sunlight and soon became absorbed in a new game.

Deliveries of what looked like groceries and other supplies were made, but as far as Gage could tell, nothing untoward took place. Of course, nighttime might tell a different story, and he resolved to return under cover of darkness to test that theory.

Until then, he felt safe taking the orphanage at face value.

He wasn't so confident about the princess's involvement. The orphanage itself might be clean, but could still be a drop for information or a meeting place for the Brothers of Darkness. With only his own finely honed suspicion that Butrus Dabir was involved with the Brothers, speculation was all Gage had for the moment. As Dabir's fiancée, Nadia could well be part of the organization, too, which meant there was probably a connection with the orphanage somewhere along the line.

Gage decided it was time to pay the lady a visit. He waited until the children were shepherded inside out of the sun, then made his way safely back to where he had hidden his car.

Getting into the palace without an invitation was more of a challenge than infiltrating the orphanage. He was used to slipping in and out of places uninvited, but most of them didn't have watchful guards at every entrance and hordes of twittering females between Gage and his target.

It took him an hour of careful reconnaissance before he found a way in. A private stretch of beach had been reserved for use by the women of the royal family and their attendants. The pristine sands held a number of bathing pavilions, where the women could change or rest out of the hot sun. Substantial grilles at both ends deterred strangers from wandering onto the sand. The beach was, at present, unguarded, although Gage presumed that a guard would be posted when the beach was in use.

When he tested the grilles, he found them strongly embedded into rock; they wouldn't give at all. From their appearance, they had been in place for a long while, allowing time for the tides to alter their pattern. At low tide, he was able to slip around one of the grilles, soaking only his shoes and the cuffs of his pants.

Sticking to the rocky areas to avoid leaving footprints, he crossed the beach swiftly, clambering up a cliff path that led, as he had hoped, straight to the women's quarters. Locating the princess among the rabbit warren of rooms was almost as big a challenge as avoiding the twittering hordes. Twice he was nearly caught.

Slipping into a side room to avoid yet another pair of chattering females, he got his break when a familiar voice said from behind him, "What on earth are you doing here?"

His heart pounded with shock, awareness following a split second later. He turned and sketched a mocking salaam. "Princess Nadia. I'm merely keeping our appointment."

"How did you get in? You shouldn't be here."

He grinned. "As I recall, neither should you."

She blushed. "I was prevented from keeping our appointment by my fiancé."

"Did he know you were supposed to be meeting me?"

She looked startled. "Of course not. And I wasn't meeting you, as you put it. I was merely going to guide you around the orphanage."

"I managed to guide myself," he said, not enlightening her as to his method or reasons.

"The children—were they all right?"

"Judging by the noise level, having a great time," he said.

She subsided against her cushioned banquet with a look of relief. "I'm glad."

He paused long enough to lock the door, then moved closer to her. In one hand she held a sketchbook and in the other a stick of charcoal. Her fingertips were smudged, he noticed. He looked over her shoulder. She had captured one of the little orphans in a cheeky pose that was so lifelike, Gage half expected the drawing to speak. "You have a lot of talent."

"I believe you already own one of my paintings, Mr. Weston."

"I told you to call me Gage. And yes, I do. A study of a sea eagle on a clifftop somewhere near here. You captured the bird in the split second before takeoff, so you can practically see the muscles bunching under the feathers. Impressive stuff."

Nadia felt color seep into her cheeks. The sea-eagle series was among her favorites. She was inordinately pleased to hear that one of the pictures was in the hands of someone who appreciated it, not for the pedigree of the artist, but for its own sake. "I'm glad you like it," she said.

Irritation darkened his eyes. "'Like' is too tame a word for what the painting makes me feel. There's a sense of freedom about to be regained, as if the artist knows a thing or two about breaking free from limitations."

She looked away. "All worthwhile art contains an element of the personal, Gage."

He studied the sketch of the child. "You really care about the orphans, don't you."

"Why do you think I go to such lengths to spend time with them?"

"In your position, writing a substantial check would be easier."

She tightened her grip on the charcoal. "You think it's that simple?"

His gesture encompassed the opulence of the room around them, and by implication, the palace beyond. "Why not? You're obviously not poor."

"My father isn't poor."

She saw a shadow flit across Gage's strong features and wondered at the reason for it. Did he doubt that she had access to her family's fortune only through her father? If so, he was no different from the other men she'd known, who were more interested in her position than in the woman who occupied it. Gordon had been the single exception and had assured her he would love her if she had only the clothes she stood up in, as long as they could be together.

"I have limited resources of my own," she went on coldly, chilled by the doubt she'd glimpsed in Gage's expression, and more hurt than she wanted him to see. "I do what I can with what I have, but there is always more that needs to be done."

"Why not ask the sheik for help?"

"You must know why I can't."

"Because your father would question how you know so much about the orphanage, and the nature of your involvement would come out," Gage said, supplying his own answer.

She set the drawing materials to one side and folded her hands in her lap, pretending a composure she was far from feeling. "He would forbid me to go to the orphanage unescorted. As for working side by side with a single man, even a doctor..." She let her shoulders lift and fall.

"'Get thee to a nunnery,'" Gage quoted. "I assume being

found talking with me in your apartment won't win you any prizes?"

"I can always scream for help and tell the guards you forced your way in here," she pointed out. "It isn't too far from the truth."

"But you won't," he guessed with maddening assurance. "Because then I'd have to blow the whistle on your extra-curricular activities."

She kept her expression carefully impassive, although her heart was racing and her palms felt clammy. "Why haven't you done so already?"

He massaged his chin between thumb and finger. "I honestly don't know."

She felt the first stirring of expectancy. "Then you didn't come here to blackmail me with what you know?"

"I came here because you intrigue me," he said flatly, not sounding particularly pleased about the admission.

As an engaged woman, she shouldn't have been pleased, either, but a totally inappropriate frisson of satisfaction rippled through her. Gordon had been the last man in her life to admit to being intrigued by her, moments before he took her in his arms and kissed her for the first, although not the last, time.

How would it feel to be taken in this man's arms and feel his mouth claiming hers? The shocking thought rocketed through Nadia's mind before she could arrest it. "If I'm supposed to be flattered..." she began, disturbed by how much she was.

"Don't be," Gage said, dispelling any hint of pleasure. "I don't believe in flattery. If I pay a compliment, it's because it's earned, not to gain favor."

"Then you are an unusual man," she observed. "In my experience, compliments are common currency between men and women."

"A currency soon devalued if used to excess."

"And you are not given to excess?"

Why had she asked such a stupid question, she wondered

as soon as she saw his gaze flash in response to her comment. What was it about Gage Weston that made her want to provoke him so? It wasn't as if she liked him or had any wish to know him better.

She would do better to pretend agreement, as her mother had taught her to do, giving him no excuse to continue the discussion. She still didn't know why he was here, and he seemed in no hurry to enlighten her.

"I prefer my own kinds of excess," he said.

She stood up, feeling the urge to meet him eye to eye. His greater height made that impossible, but at least she could face him directly. The energy radiating from him almost made her step back, but she held her ground. "This is not an appropriate conversation for us to be having."

He slanted an amused look at her. "For a princess and a commoner, or a man and a woman?"

She became vividly aware of the lock she had heard him turn when he came in. They were alone in the room, unlikely to be disturbed for some time, as her attendants were getting ready for the noonday meal. Nadia licked her lips, finding them annoyingly dry. "Either will do."

They became drier still as his gaze fastened on her mouth. He wanted to kiss her, she knew. To her horror, she actually felt herself lean toward him, as if to meet him halfway. The unusual fragrance he wore reached out to her. Not something from Tamir, and probably not English, either. Something tantalizingly wild, and alarmingly erotic.

She almost moaned as his hands slid up her arms, coming to rest on her shoulders. His touch felt like fire through the silk of her blouse. Her lashes began to flutter closed, but she held them open with an effort of will.

"No," she managed to force out.

He gave a sigh that was part regret, part promise, and released her with obvious reluctance. Moving stiffly, he crossed the room and began to pick up a collection of brass trinkets, one after the other. She could swear he hardly looked at them before setting them down.

"Why did you come?" she asked belatedly, wondering if he had just given her the answer.

He kept his back to her. "When you didn't keep our appointment, I wanted to be sure you were all right."

She recognized the lie as soon as he uttered it, but suspected she wouldn't learn the truth unless he wanted her to. Who was he? What was he? She couldn't accept that he was merely a minor diplomat. No minor diplomat of her acquaintance made himself so much at home in royal surroundings or dealt so familiarly with a member of the royal family.

Not for Gage, the deference accorded to his betters, she thought. He was definitely more than he seemed, but how much more?

"Now that you've satisfied yourself, you should leave," she said shortly.

He swung around. "If I had satisfied myself, you wouldn't want me to leave."

She pretended ignorance, fighting the riot of unwelcome sensations tearing through her. "I have no idea what you mean."

His dark eyebrows canted upward, his gaze reading her like a book. "Oh, no? I wasn't the only one wondering what it would be like if we kissed."

"Wondering is not the same as finding out," she said shakily.

He shot her a look of unmistakable regret. "Unfortunately it isn't. And you're a princess and engaged to be married, so we'll have to go on wondering."

Fine with her, until he added softly, "For the moment."

She lifted her head, fixing him with a regal glare that refused to acknowledge how shaken she was by his words and the promise underlying them. "You presume a great deal for someone I could have thrown into jail at the snap of a finger."

He stalked to the door and unlocked it. "The ball's in your court, Princess."

"You'd like me to call someone, so you could throw me to the wolves."

He crossed his arms over his chest, a smile curving his mouth. "As I said, your call, Princess."

She wasn't going to turn him in, and it galled her that he knew it. "How did you get past the guards, anyway?"

"The grille fencing off the beach doesn't reach all the way down at low tide."

Her gaze went to the telltale dampness around his ankles. "How do you plan to get out? You won't be able to use the same route now that the tide is in."

"I was hoping you'd help me."

"What can I possibly do? I can't be seen with you."

"Unless you were to come across me wandering lost in the palace grounds and help me to find my way."

He composed his features into such an expression of foppishness that she was forced to smile. "It might work, although you could have trouble explaining your wet footwear."

He looked down, then back at her. "I stumbled into one of the ornamental ponds on the palace grounds."

How easily the lies sprang to his lips, she thought with a twinge of unease. She would do well to bear that in mind if he complimented her again. Not that such a thing was likely. By trespassing on royal property, he had evened the score between them. If he betrayed her, she could equally betray him, having him removed from Tamir and almost certainly ending his diplomatic career. If he realized that, he didn't seem troubled by the possibility, she noted.

She went to the window and looked out. At this hour, many of the palace staff were indoors avoiding the heat of the day. Her attendants would be looking for her soon to escort her to her noonday meal. "If we're going, we'd better hurry while the grounds are quiet," she urged.

Tension coiled through her as she led the way along a maze of corridors to an open pavilion with a lily-covered pond at its center. She skirted around it, the heels of her shoes clicking on the ancient tiles.

"This walkway leads to the public rooms," she explained, her voice husky with anxiety. Until they were clear of the women's apartments, she had no way of explaining his presence that wouldn't cause a scandal.

When they emerged, unchallenged, in the area of the palace reserved for offices and meeting places, she began to breathe a little easier. At least here Gage's story of becoming lost would seem plausible, if not likely. Visitors were usually escorted while within the palace, but it wasn't unheard of for someone to take a wrong turn and lose sight of his guide.

She saw Gage looking around with interest. "I think I know where I am now. Isn't that the pavilion where the reception was held the other night?"

She wished he hadn't reminded her. "These rooms are often used to receive visitors," she said, her tone reflecting her acute discomfort.

He caught her elbow and pulled her into the shadow of a pillar. "There's no need to feel anything but pride about the way you danced that night."

She shrank away from him, daunted as much by her response to his nearness, as by his words. "You don't understand anything about our culture, do you."

"I understand that you were a vision of grace and beauty up on that stage."

"I was a laughingstock," she said bitterly.

His grip tightened. "You were admired by everyone who saw you. You are only a laughingstock if you decide to be. Addie wouldn't allow anyone to touch the core of who she is, no matter what happened to her."

Her eyes blurred and she blinked hard. "Addie lives in a different world from mine."

"I think if you look closely, you'll find they're not so different. There's a way out of any box, provided you want it badly enough."

How she wished he was right, but he wasn't allowing for

her country's traditions, forged over thousands of years. No amount of wishing could change things that easily, as she well knew. "There's no time for this," she said.

He stepped out into the sunlight, towing her with him. "Think about what I've said."

Suddenly he let her arm drop and came to a kind of attention. She understood why when Butrus emerged from behind a pillar. How long had he been standing there, and how much had he heard?

Her fiancé's smile revealed nothing, but his tone was equable as he said, "Nadia. Mr. Weston. Is there something I can do for you?"

"I lost my bearings on the way out. Her Highness was kind enough to give me directions," Gage said smoothly.

Butrus's eyes narrowed. "Were there no guards you could ask to escort you?"

"None he could find," Nadia slipped in. "I'm so glad you're here, Butrus, because Mr. Weston was just telling me how much he admires your work."

Her mother's lessons had their uses, she thought, as she saw Butrus's hard expression soften slightly.

"How is it that you know of my work when you are new to Tamir?" he asked Gage.

"Before joining the diplomatic corps, I studied economics, then took a second degree in law," Gage explained. "At university, your redrafting of the constitution of Tamir was regarded as exemplary in the field."

Butrus looked pleased. "Constitutional law is an interest of yours, then?"

Gage nodded. "One of many."

"Perhaps you'd be interested in seeing how I conceived some of the elements of the document," Butrus suggested. "The new preamble is still to be written, so I am assembling some business associates at my estate in a few days' time to arrive at a suitable draft. You would be welcome as an observer. Much of my work on the new constitution was done at the estate, and I have retained my notes there. If you would like to join the party, I'll be happy to discuss them with you."

Gage inclined his head. "Are you sure I won't be intruding between you and your fiancée?"

Belatedly Butrus seemed to remember her existence. "Her Highness will accompany the party, naturally, but we do not put the same store on spending time alone as you British do. In our culture, it is regarded as unseemly."

"I shall be chaperoned by my attendants," Nadia explained. "My role is to provide cultural enlightenment and diverting small talk." She let her tone convey how unappealing she found the prospect.

Butrus didn't seem to notice, but Gage flashed her a wry look. "Then I accept with thanks. Naturally I shall have to approach our ambassador for his approval."

Butrus gave a knowing smile. "Since Ambassador Theodore is your godfather, I am sure he will be delighted. The ambassador was invited to participate in our deliberations but had to decline, due to pressure of other commitments. He will be gratified that you are able to attend in his stead."

The tightening muscles around Gage's eyes told Nadia that he wasn't sure he liked Butrus's being so well-informed. Didn't he realize that this was Tamir? Information was a kind of currency, and the best-informed people were invariably the most successful. Butrus made it his business to be well-informed.

She felt excitement quiver through her. The house party, which had seemed dull in the extreme, held far more promise now that Gage was going to be there. She resisted asking herself why. Her duty was to Butrus, and she would give him no cause to find fault with her behavior. But she saw no reason she couldn't enjoy Gage's presence, like a touch of spice in an otherwise bland dish.

Gage's gaze remained on Nadia as he added, "I shall look forward to the occasion."

"I shall escort Mr. Weston from here, Nadia," Butrus said.

He didn't add, "Run along," but his tone conveyed the dismissal equally well.

Concealing her annoyance, she nodded agreement. "As you wish, Butrus. We'll meet again at my fiancé's estate, Mr. Weston."

As Gage returned her salaam with a practiced one of his own, not by a flicker of an eyelash did she let him see how eagerly she found herself anticipating the experience.

Chapter 6

So much for anticipation, she thought a week later as she fed bread to the swans craning their graceful necks toward her on the ornamental lake at Butrus's estate.

Their party had arrived at Zabara two days ago, and the only people she had spoken to were Butrus, his servants, her sisters on the telephone and the women who would have attended her at the royal palace, anyway.

She might as well have remained at home. Then at least she could go to her studio to paint or sculpt. Her hands ached with the need for something to occupy them, and her brain felt as if it was turning into humus.

Her sketching materials lay on a table in the shelter of a filigreed-metal pavilion. Seated on cushioned banquets in the comfortable structure, she had made several sketches of the swans this morning, but they weren't nearly enough to satisfy her. She yearned for the tactile excitement of fresh clay under her fingers, a piece of marble to chisel or a blank canvas driving her to cover it with paint.

She also missed her visit to the orphanage. Were the children missing her as much as she missed them? On her last visit, she had explained to them that she wouldn't see them for a week because she had to go away. She had almost changed her mind when she saw little Sammy bite his lower lip to stop himself from crying.

He had become used to people disappearing from his life and probably thought she was going to do the same. She had assured the child she would be back, but he had looked at her with tragically round eyes, as if she was already lost to him. She made up her mind to buy the children special presents to take with her when she returned.

Frustration continued to gnaw at her. She had asked her fiancé if she might sit in on the discussions about constitutional law with Gage and the other businessmen, but Butrus had assumed that her reason for asking was because she wanted to watch him at work. It had never occurred to him that she might have something to contribute.

"I appreciate your wish to support me, little one, but I don't want you to be bored," he had said. "The estate is at your disposal. Go where you will within the boundaries and enjoy yourself."

Always the qualification "within the boundaries," she thought, crumpling a piece of bread savagely. She wished she could swallow her anger as easily as the swan swallowed the bread she threw to it. At least her father permitted her mother to join him in his office and be a party, however passive, to the affairs of state. It seemed Butrus didn't intend to allow Nadia even that much involvement in his activities.

A masculine voice behind her startled her. "I know swans can be savage when they have young to protect, but the look on your face makes you seem far more fierce than these beautiful birds."

She swung around to find Gage leaning against a tree, watching her. For some reason, she was troubled that he had seen the anger she went to such lengths to conceal from her fiancé. She gathered her royal dignity around her like a cloak. "You shouldn't be speaking with me. Tahani has only gone inside to fetch a cool drink for me. She'll be back at any moment."

"And you'll be the one getting into trouble for talking to a man alone," he guessed. "How do you stand it?"

She threw more bread to the swans, pretending ignorance. "Stand what?"

"Being kept at arm's length from anything remotely important and treated as if you don't have a brain in your head."

The keenness of his observation rankled. Bad enough to be excluded from the discussions, without Gage being so aware of it. His opinion shouldn't matter, but it did. "What makes you think I have brains?" she asked, lacing her tone with irony.

He came to her so quickly and silently that he was behind her before she knew it. His hands on her shoulders were rough as he spun her around. "The woman who painted the eagle hanging on the wall of my study back home isn't stupid. To represent nature so accurately, she needs to have studied anatomy, aviculture, botany, and have a sharp eye for observation, before we even get to artistic ability."

No one except her attendants touched a member of the royal family, much less as roughly as Gage had. Nadia knew she should be shocked, but instead, she felt a disturbing thread of excitement wend its way through her.

He was so close that she felt the curl of his breath against her cheeks. The sun glinting off his features chiseled them to almost sculptural sharpness. The fine lines radiating from eyes and mouth suggested a life far removed from diplomatic ease and comfort. Not an indoor man. A man of action, she concluded, the impression at odds with the little she knew about him. Perhaps he had been a soldier before becoming a diplomat.

The compulsion to touch his face to see if he was as hard as he looked was almost irresistible. His green gaze flashed a challenge at her, as if he sensed what she barely restrained herself from doing.

Only years of royal practice kept her hands at her sides and the reaction from reaching her face. Afraid that her gaze might betray her, she lowered her lashes. "Take your hands off me," she said in a commanding tone that any Tamiri would have obeyed without question.

As troubled by her response as by his touch, she wasn't surprised when he made no move to release her.

"When you admit I'm right about you," he insisted.

She opened her eyes, almost closing them again as his masculine aura slammed into her anew. "You're a man. It goes without saying," she said, striving to sound matter-of-fact. She suspected she failed miserably.

He continued to study her with unsettling intensity. "Not in my country."

"You are not in England now," she pointed out, struggling to keep her breathing even. She was torn between wishing that Tahani would return and interrupt them, and desperately hoping she wouldn't.

"I'm not…" he began. She saw him visibly check himself before saying, "I'm not talking about any particular country, but about basic human rights. You're a grown woman." His voice softened, and now it sounded like a caress. "You're a beautiful intelligent woman, and you have a right to your opinions."

What had he been about to say before he so obviously stopped himself? That he wasn't from England originally? She had worked that out for herself. He was right about the artist in her having well-developed powers of observation. They functioned even when she didn't want them to. Now they told her that his cultured English accent overlaid another, more musical accent, the language of his birth, perhaps. She found herself speculating on where that might be.

He thought her beautiful and intelligent, a traitorous inner voice said. The men of her own country appreciated beauty, but rarely endorsed her gender with intelligence. She had to fight the glow of pleasure that enveloped her at Gage's words. "You're not from Tamir," she said tiredly. "When you've been here a little longer, you'll see that our way is different, but not necessarily wrong."

He seemed to have forgotten that his hands still rested on her shoulders. The bite of his fingers had eased to a comfortable weight, his palms sliding down to her upper arms in the suggestion of an embrace. She knew she should move away or insist that he move away. She did neither, finding the touch far more enjoyable than was wise.

"Stopping people from reaching their full potential is always wrong," he persisted. His voice sounded husky, as if the closeness was affecting him, too, finally.

She felt her eyes start to swim as she stated the obvious. "My potential lies with my husband and the children we shall have. The only one stopping me from achieving that potential is me."

"Why?"

The question caught her off guard. With Tahani she had often discussed the paths their lives might have taken had things been different. But never with a man, not even Butrus. He had never been interested enough to ask, she thought with a touch of bitterness.

"Perhaps I was waiting for change," she whispered, recognizing the truth in her heart. Gordon had represented change, and he was gone. Now she had finally accepted that waiting was getting her nowhere.

"Change doesn't come to you. You make it happen."

Gage would make change happen, she thought, hearing his voice ring with conviction. He seemed like a man who took life by the scruff of the neck and shook it until it did his bidding.

The belief struck her as being at odds with his role as a minor official in the British Embassy. "Considering who you are, you're hardly in a position to talk," she challenged.

His hold on her arms tightened and his eyes narrowed. "What do you mean?"

She sensed his attention sharpening and wondered what she had said to provoke the change. "You speak like a man of action, yet you occupy yourself with trade and diplomacy," she explained.

He let his hands drop. She felt a rush of disappointment, as if she had wanted the touch to turn into something more. Such a thought was so morally wrong that she shuddered inwardly.

"You're right of course." But he sounded amused rather than angered by her accusation. She waited for him to justify his choice of career in light of his provocative talk, but instead, he gestured toward the ornamental lake. Tired of waiting for more largesse from her, the swans had glided gracefully away, heading for the reed beds on the far side of the lake. "This fantasy setting tends to make one idealistic."

She should be pleased that the conversation had shifted to safer ground, but she felt regretful that the verbal sparring was at an end. It had made a refreshing change from her usual experience. She told herself she didn't rue the loss of Gage's touch, almost making herself believe it. "The estate is remarkable, isn't it?" she observed.

His gaze took in the acres of manicured gardens, leading down to a private, white-sand beach, overlooked by a turreted mansion furnished with antiques and priceless works of art. "Your fiancé must come from a wealthy family."

In Gage's expression she saw mirrored her own curiosity about how Butrus had amassed the fortune this place must cost him to maintain. His family, though wellborn, were not as wealthy as the estate implied. Loyalty to Butrus made her say, "Reasonably so. He has also done well in my father's service."

"Your father is obviously a generous man and will be even more generous, no doubt, once Butrus becomes his son-in-law."

Anger coursed through her, as much at herself for letting this insolent man touch her as at his outrageous comments. That he might be echoing her own deepest concerns, she didn't like to think. "That's hardly any of your concern, Mr. Weston."

A smile curved the corners of his generous mouth, taunting her. "So it's Mr. Weston again, is it? Am I to be punished for speaking the truth?"

"Your kind of truth."

"Surely there can be only one truth."

She dragged in a steadying breath. "Are you a man of honor, Mr. Weston?"

Something indefinable flickered across his features, making her suspect that she had touched on a truth he didn't wish her to know. She would give a lot to know what it was.

"Most men like to think of themselves as honorable," he said.

She recognized his evasion and wondered again what he was keeping from her, but decided she would gain nothing by taking the direct approach. Better to watch and wait, see what he revealed in time. Another feminine skill her mother had imparted. "If you are truly a man of honor, you will keep a respectful distance from me in future, instead of trying to make me think less of the man I am to marry," she said.

Gage crossed his arms over his broad chest. "Is that an order, Your Highness?"

She inclined her head with regal grace. "You may consider it so."

"Then I must refuse."

Her head came up and she made no attempt to conceal her shock this time. No one refused to obey a royal command. "I can have you thrown in jail or deported from Tamir for such insolence."

He gave a careless shrug. "It's hardly insolent to tell you what you already suspect."

She turned away, wishing she had more bread to attract the swans, anything to occupy her hands and whirling thoughts. But she had nothing, so she pretended interest in inspecting a rare orchid just coming into bloom beside the lake. Cupping her hands around the bloom, she said, "You presume a great deal."

He placed his hand under hers so that they shared the orchid. "Bad habit of mine, I'm afraid." He didn't sound in the least regretful. "How well do you know Butrus Dabir?"

As Gage's palm grazed the backs of her hands, she suppressed a shiver of reaction. Such a light touch, but it resonated through her like the most passionate embrace. Taking her hands away would be far too revealing, so she stayed where she was, the sound of the blood pounding in her ears making it hard to concentrate.

"I've known Butrus most of my life. He is my father's closest adviser and a respected emissary for Tamir abroad."

"But how well do you really know him?"

Absently Gage's fingers twined with hers, making the orchid shiver against Nadia's palm. The sensation was unbelievably erotic, and she almost closed her hand around the delicate flower in shocked response, stopping herself barely in time.

"I'm not sure what you're implying, Gage."

She hadn't meant to use his first name but it slipped out, and she saw the gleam of gratification in his eyes. "This estate and everything in it didn't come from nowhere. Have you considered that your fiancé may be involved in something more than royal affairs?"

She had considered it, dismissing the possibility as far-fetched. No one in her father's service would be involved in anything underhand, and certainly not criminal. She had accepted Butrus's refusal to involve her in his business matters as male chauvinism. She resented Gage for attempting to make her think there could be a more sinister reason.

She shook her head, forcibly driving away the suspicion. "I don't know what advantage you hope to gain by undermining my faith in Butrus, but it isn't going to work. I command you to refrain from making such heinous remarks about him. Is that understood?"

He took his time removing his hands, letting them slide under hers slowly, provocatively, until she felt dizzy with the need for more of his touch. She wanted to find out what it would be like to be held in his arms completely, kissed by him, drowning in the desire that tantalized her at so slight a contact.

What was she thinking? Hadn't she just lectured him on showing respect for Butrus? What was she doing, if not dishonoring the man she was to marry by her very thoughts?

"I understand completely, Your Highness," Gage said softly. "From now on, if I speak of Butrus at all to you, I shall only speak in the most glowing terms."

She tried to feel mollified but was too shaken by Gage's effect on her. "Thank you," she said, hearing her voice come out infuriatingly husky.

Unexpectedly he caught her hands and lifted them to his lips, kissing her fingertips. "You're welcome, Princess."

Pleasure coiled through her, hot, sharp and totally inappropriate. She pulled her hands away as if burned. "It would be best if you rejoined the other men." Best for whom, she wasn't sure and was glad he didn't ask.

He gave the mocking salaam she had begun to expect from him. "Your wish is my command, Princess. I shall see you at dinner."

Anxiety gripped her as she watched him walk away. She had forgotten that she was to dine with the other guests and their wives that evening. She recoiled from the prospect. How could she sit at Butrus's right hand and act as if nothing had happened between her and Gage this afternoon?

Nothing *had* happened. A few looks, a casual touch or two, hardly amounted to disloyalty to Butrus, did they? Only if she accepted that they had meant more to her than they should have done. They hadn't, had they?

She was probably reading more into the encounter with Gage than was warranted because of the novelty of being touched by a man, she told herself.

She had allowed Gordon to touch her, and look where that had led. Afterward she had promised never to leave herself open to such heartache again. Agreeing to marry Butrus was a way of keeping that promise.

She told herself she was happy for her world to remain a

sheltered one where her attendants and female doctors were
the only people permitted to touch her. Even Butrus had done
little more than take her hand in greeting or when they parted.
By custom, he would do no more until they were man and
wife.

Gage wasn't of their culture. To him, kissing Nadia's fingertips was probably no more than a gallant gesture, forgotten moments later. She wished she could forget it as swiftly.

She had lifted her hand to her mouth in imitation of his
touch before she became aware of the movement and let her
hand drop to her side. A rustling along the path brought her
head up, expectancy coursing through her, try as she might
to subdue it. Had Gage forgotten something and returned?

But it was only Tahani, bearing a tray. "I'm sorry to take
so long, my princess. The foolish kitchen maid dropped the
first pitcher of lemonade and I had to wait while she prepared
another."

Lemonade was the furthest thing from Nadia's mind right
now. She felt as if champagne was the only drink capable of
matching the tumult inside her, and she had never craved
such a drink in her life. What was it about Gage Weston that
put such thoughts in her head?

"I don't mind," she said, wondering exactly to what she
was referring. "I'm no longer thirsty, anyway. But I'll drink
a little of the lemonade," she added, seeing Tahani look distressed.

The attendant placed the tray on a wrought-iron table in
the shade of the pavilion and poured a drink for Nadia, who
insisted Tahani have some, too. When they were seated out
of the sun, Tahani said, "I saw Gage Weston coming from
this direction, Princess. I hope he didn't intrude on your privacy."

If she only knew. "No, no. I was busy feeding the swans.
They are lovely creatures, aren't they?"

As she'd hoped, the comment diverted Tahani from
thoughts of Gage, and they began to discuss the many birds
inhabiting the grounds of the estate. Despite Tahani being

her closest confidante, Nadia was glad that the maid didn't know that talk about the swans and the hummingbirds only occupied part of the princess's mind.

Another part insisted on replaying a scene where she held an orchid in her hands, and Gage held both of them in his.

Why didn't he simply carry a placard advertising his suspicion of Butrus Dabir? Gage thought, angry with himself as he strode along the mosaic path back to the mansion. He had all but announced his concern to Princess Nadia just now. How much more unprofessional could he be?

He told himself he had wanted to find out how much she knew, but honesty made him accept that there was an element of jealousy, as well. She had thought herself unobserved, but Gage had seen her dancing attendance on Dabir since this gathering began, acceding to the man's every whim, never speaking up for herself. Couldn't Dabir see the strain around her lovely dark eyes every time she was treated like an empty-headed decoration?

Evidently not. Dabir had looked insufferably pleased with himself. Gage could swear the man heaped indignities upon Nadia for the sheer satisfaction of lording it over a member of royalty. Not that their relationship was any of Gage's affair, but he couldn't help pitying Nadia once she married Dabir, if the man was this dictatorial toward her now.

Gage's investigation into Dabir's past showed that he wasn't as high-born as was generally believed. He had been raised in a family of bluebloods, but Dabir himself was only the nephew of the man usually taken to be his father. His origins were far more modest, his real father having been killed in an accident in the oil fields while serving the Dabir interests. His mother had died in childbirth, so conscience probably drove the Dabirs to take Butrus in and raise him as their own, Gage concluded. Had the young Butrus resented being an object of charity? It would explain his driving ambition, which extended to marrying a princess.

Looking around at the lavish estate and thinking of his

assigned quarters with their antique furnishings, ancient mosaic floors and valuable artworks, Gage had to admit that Butrus had succeeded spectacularly. A royal marriage would seal his emancipation from charity case to second-most powerful man in the country.

Knowing the man's unbridled ambition and the unsavory types he associated with, Gage had had to restrain himself from hauling Nadia away whenever he saw her with Dabir.

Gage froze in his tracks. When had he stopped thinking of her as a potential accomplice of Dabir's? He had no more proof of her innocence than he did of Dabir's guilt, although he still hoped to find evidence during the house party.

He had established that none of the guests he'd met up to now were linked to the Brothers of Darkness, although Gage was so convinced this party was a front for a meeting of that group that he could smell it.

The sessions he'd attended had been exactly what they seemed—tedious discussions aimed at drafting a modern preamble for the Tamir constitution. Dabir had even sought Gage's opinion once or twice. But Gage was sure this was only a cover for more sinister activities. Did the princess know what they were, or was she as much in the dark as Gage himself?

In his experience, suspects were guilty until proved innocent. He would have to beware that Nadia's hypnotic attractiveness didn't blind him to reality. Once was enough to be taken in by a woman's beauty and charm.

He stepped out of the way of a maid carrying a tray of drinks and sweetmeats along the path. She smiled shyly at him before continuing on her way, as did he.

Tahani—his mind supplied the name automatically. Taking refreshments to her mistress at the ornamental lake.

One of the glasses on the tray would soon be cupped in Princess Nadia's fine-boned hands, he thought. Jealousy flashed through him, white-hot and searing in its intensity. He wanted to be that glass. Hell, he wanted to hold her more than he had wanted anything in a long time.

He almost laughed out loud at the foolishness of his thought. A glass held in her hands, indeed. What if she was in league with Dabir? She would also share responsibility for Conrad's death. Would Gage want to hold her then?

Yes, he would, he thought, mortified. He would hate her and probably himself, as well, but he would want her no matter who she was or what he discovered she'd done. Why else seek her out so persistently?

Telling himself the contact was part of his investigation didn't make it the truth. Finding evidence of Dabir's culpability was likely to indict her or clear her, as well. Spending time with her wouldn't make any difference to Gage's report to King Marcus.

Gage wished he could promise himself that he would stop seeing her, but knew he couldn't. Something about the princess attracted him like iron filings to a magnet. Pity that a princess of Tamir couldn't just have an affair and be done with it. Making love to her might be one way to get her out of his system.

The heat pouring through him at this idea made it seem unlikely. In any case, being who and what she was, a love affair was out of the question. Talking to her alone was difficult enough. Taking her to bed without benefit of a wedding ceremony would probably get him beheaded.

He massaged the back of his neck as if feeling the kiss of cold steel. Conrad used to joke about men losing their heads over women. Gage knew he would have to watch himself if he didn't want it to become a literal truth.

Chapter 7

The dinner was a dignified affair, held in the Great Hall, which was lit by torches, their stuttering flames creating giant dancing shadows that made Nadia feel distinctly uneasy.

Her traditional costume would have looked more at home in such a setting than the Grecian-style gown she had chosen to wear. The flowing dress of opalescent blue silk had long sleeves that ended in peaks over her hands. Seed pearls embellished the high collar and were sewn around the hem of the long skirt, the precious pearls having been Tamir's wealth before the discovery of oil.

Like the other guests, her feet were bare and sank into the sumptuous Shirazi carpets piled one on top of the other as carelessly as if each one wasn't worth a king's ransom.

Nargis had dressed her black hair into a shining cap of curls threaded with more pearls and miniature gold coins, which tinkled as she glided across the room to where Butrus waited for her.

He wore a superbly cut white dinner jacket, its snowy perfection suggesting that this was the first time he'd worn it.

She knew that wasn't unusual for Butrus. He frequently wore garments only once before passing them on to his servants. One of them had told Nargis, who had inevitably shared the information with her mistress.

Nargis had thought Butrus's behavior splendidly magnanimous. To the princess, it seemed more as if her fiancé needed to prove to himself that he could always have more of whatever he wanted. Was marrying her a further expression of this need?

So what if it was, she reproved herself. She had her own agenda for agreeing to marry him. Wasn't she trying to finally win her father's approval by accepting his choice of husband for her? If she also gained more freedom as mistress of her own domain, so much the better. It was only proper that they both gained something from the match.

As she reached him, Butrus stood and held out his hand to help her to a seat beside him on one of the cushion-strewn divans at the head of the long low table. "You look enchanting tonight, little one," he said, adding close to her ear, "However, I miss the veil. So mysterious, so provocative."

"So medieval," she murmured under her breath.

"Excuse me?"

"I said the hall looks so medieval tonight. I feel as if I've been transported back to ancient Arabia."

He gave her a gratified smile. "Exactly the impression I wanted to create. I've arranged a banquet fit for the sheiks and sheikas of old."

Butrus would favor the old traditions, she thought, suddenly glad that he wasn't in line to the throne. If he were ruler of Tamir, he would probably insist on every woman being veiled from head to toe. She gave a slight shudder at the thought.

Butrus probably thought he was being astonishingly liberal by allowing the women to share the same table as the men. Not so long ago, they would have been sequestered behind rugs and hangings. In many countries, they still were, she thought with another shudder.

She watched with interest as the guests took their places
at the long banquet table. She had seen some of them going
to the meetings Butrus had dissuaded her from attending. One
group of men, wearing western dress, was unfamiliar to her.
They looked foreign, possibly American, she thought, her
curiosity piquing.

"Who are those people?" she asked Butrus, who had
turned to speak to the man on his left.

Turning back to her, he gave a dismissive wave of his
hand. "No one you need concern yourself about, little one.
Foreign business associates I deemed it politic to invite."

To Nadia, they looked more like the shady types she'd
seen in the souks, watching warily from the narrow doorways
of shops or talking furtively with others of their ilk in back
alleys. Hardly the kind of men she would have expected Butrus to welcome to his estate.

Still, as he'd said, they were not her concern and for once
she was glad. None of them looked like the sort of person
she wanted to associate with.

Then there was Gage Weston.

She realized she'd been studying the unsavory-looking
group to avoid letting her gaze come to rest on Gage, but he
was impossible to ignore for long. Almost a head taller than
most of the other men, he radiated an air of assurance that
had her wondering about his true nature yet again.

He was seated between two of Butrus's associates, and was
deep in conversation with one of them, so she could look her
fill for the moment. She was troubled by how much she
wanted to.

Unlike many of the foreigners, including the unsavory-
looking ones she saw squirming in obvious discomfort, Gage
had no difficulty relaxing on the low divan. He had one knee
raised, the other tucked under him, one arm resting easily
atop the raised knee. He had also pulled up his right sleeve,
evidently aware of the local custom of using only the right
hand for eating.

How easily she could imagine him in the flowing robe and

headdress of the desert, enjoying the same meal on rugs spread on the sand as he leaned against a camel saddle, the smell of brushwood and cardamom coffee tangy in the night air.

He looked up and caught her studying him. In a gesture that brought color rushing to her face, he lifted his hand and touched the fingertips to his lips, the message unmistakable. He was reminding her of how he had kissed her hand beside the lake this afternoon.

As if she could forget. Maybe there was some merit in being segregated behind rugs and hangings, she thought as she felt warmth suffuse her. She refused to look away, which would reveal how much his gesture had discomfited her.

Picking at her food was not an option, lest she give Butrus the impression his hospitality was lacking, but the sight of so much food being served made her sigh inwardly. To a Tamiri, hospitality was not a favor to a guest, but an obligation. Providing only enough food for the invited number would be shameful. What if one of them brought friends, or travelers arrived unannounced?

No one could accuse Butrus of neglecting custom, she thought as the servants carried in immense silver trays piled high with everything one could possibly want. The centerpiece was a bed of rice topped with a whole roast lamb. Around this radiated dishes of tomatoes, pigeons in wine sauce, a stew of chicken, figs and honey, the finely ground wheat dish called couscous royale with more stew, this one of lamb with vegetables, chick peas and raisins. There were also pastries of meat, onions and eggs, and stuffed vine leaves, many of the recipes originating in the elegant days of the Caliphates.

The guests murmured a prayer of thanks and soft-voiced compliments to Butrus on the size and appetizing look of the feast, then deftly began to dip pieces of flat bread into the stews and sauces, tearing loose portions of the roast lamb and kneading helpings of rice into neat balls with their fingers.

She tried not to watch Gage, but found herself drawn to him, mesmerized by the skillful way he handled the food, unlike many of the foreigners who looked frustrated as rice cascaded from their inexperienced hands.

There was little conversation; it was mostly reserved for the leisurely drinking of coffee and mint tea before and after the meal. Occasionally a guest spoke to a servant standing behind the diners to request a glass of water, which was quickly brought from outside the hall. But otherwise, the only sounds were soft music and of the enjoyment of the food.

For a moment Nadia found herself wishing her people practiced the dinner-table conversation she had encountered during her studies abroad. Anything to distract herself from her awareness of the man seated halfway down the table, where she couldn't avoid seeing him every time she looked up.

She solved the problem by simply not looking up. When she couldn't restrain herself any longer, she found Gage watching her with a kind of wary interest, as if he suspected her of something and was waiting for her to betray herself.

Nonsense, she told herself. He had no reason to suspect her of anything, unless it was showing unseemly interest in him, a man she shouldn't have exchanged words with, much less allowed a closeness the thought of which made her burn inwardly.

The meal seemed endless and she was relieved when people began to drift from the table to the courtyard, where servants waited with urns of warm water, soap and towels. Stooping over a brass ewer, Nadia washed her hands with the soap as a servant poured warm water for her, then dried her hands on a towel held out by another servant.

"Nice touch," came a soft voice behind her. "You'd never guess this place has more bathrooms than bedrooms."

She steeled herself to ignore Gage, who had followed her out to the courtyard, but his touch on her arm made this impossible. He had also washed his hands in the traditional way and was drying them when she turned. "Do you enjoy playing desert queen?" he asked.

"The theme of the evening was Butrus's choice," she said coldly, hoping her tone would deter Gage.

No such luck. "Your intended provided enough food for an army. What happens to all the leftovers?"

He wasn't giving up, she realized, knowing that at some level, she didn't really want him to. His attention made her feel vibrant and desirable, the responses humming through her like the strings of a sitar plucked by an expert. As an engaged woman, she should be ashamed of such feelings, she reminded herself, but to no avail.

"The members of the household will eat their fill, and what remains will be shared with the poor," she explained, the neutral subject leaving her feeling less safe than it should.

She felt glad that Butrus had already retired to the salon where coffee and mint tea would be served and incense burned for the pleasure of his male guests. He wouldn't appreciate her spending time with Gage, however innocently. And she wasn't sure herself how innocent she could claim to be, given the turbulent state of her thoughts.

Gage nodded. "Good economy, handed down from when food was scarce and couldn't afford to be wasted."

She gave vent to a sigh of frustration. "Mr. Weston, why do you persist in speaking to me when you know it's wrong?"

"Why shouldn't I speak to my hostess?"

Because he wasn't content to speak, she knew. He liked to stand close, to touch. She liked it, too, but didn't want to like it, not from him. "Because you confuse me," she admitted.

"Myself, too," he surprised her by saying. "You're an intriguing woman. A princess, an artist, as well as beautiful and beguiling. A powerful combination."

"Enough," she commanded, more shaken than she wanted him to see. "You should join the other men. Butrus will be wondering where you are."

"Where will you be?"

Where she invariably ended up, she thought in annoyance. With the other women, discussing fashion and shopping, although such subjects held only limited interest for her.

"I shall be where I am supposed to be," she snapped. She muttered the leave-taking, which was half a blessing, and moved determinedly away, somehow aware that he stood where he was for a long time. She steeled herself not to look back.

As she'd expected, she was bored by the conversation within a few minutes and had to work to stop her thoughts from drifting to Gage in the men's salon. She pictured him drinking bitter coffee out of the tiny Spode cups the servants refilled from a brass coffeepot, which mysteriously, never seemed to run dry. Was he holding out his hands to receive a few drops of aromatic attar to perfume his skin? Breathing in the fragrant incense of sandalwood burned in a wooden urn on a four-footed brazier set on the floor in front of him?

Stop this, she commanded herself less than successfully. What Gage did was of no concern to her. She should more properly imagine Butrus doing these things, but couldn't make her thoughts turn to her fiancé. What was the matter with her?

"Your Highness looks feverish. Are you well?" the wife of one of Butrus's guests asked in a tone of concern.

Nadia thought quickly. Iriane was the woman's name, and she was the wife of one of Butrus's lawyer friends. "I am well, thank you, Iriane, just…distracted," she admitted. What an understatement that was!

The woman chattered on about how wonderful the evening had been, what a thrill it was to participate in such a night. Nadia listened with only half her attention, giving what she hoped were appropriate responses, all the while wondering how soon she could gracefully escape.

Her reprieve came soon afterward, when she heard Butrus personally showing out those of his guests who were not staying the night. The process required much hand shaking and compliments on the excellence of the dinner and the occasion in general. As host, Butrus waved these aside as no more than the guests' due and gave the blessing/leave-taking she had earlier offered Gage.

Except that he hadn't left.

Without quite knowing how, she knew he was standing in the shadows when she emerged from the salon to make her way across the colonnaded courtyard to her sleeping quarters. Needing a few minutes to herself, she had sent Nargis and the other attendants ahead to prepare the room.

At first she thought Gage was waiting for her, and her heart did an uncomfortable double beat, until she saw the silver device almost concealed in his palm. He was talking quietly on a cell phone and didn't hear her soft-footed approach.

"Dani, me darlin', you're a wonder to be sure," Nadia heard him say in a teasing imitation of an Irish accent. "If you can get that information to me overnight, I'll love you even more than I usually do."

Nadia felt her heart solidify in her chest like a lump of concrete. Somehow she had thought…she refused to allow the thought to blossom in her mind. Gage had meant nothing by his attention and his effusive compliments. How could he? He already had a woman called Dani waiting at home for him.

An aching sense of longing gripped Nadia. She hated that she had made a complete fool of herself, letting him touch her and whisper sweet nothings to her, for that's all they had been. Nothing.

Just as well the only witness was herself, she thought savagely. She hadn't told Tahani about Gage's tender touch, not because of the shame she should have felt, but because she had wanted to savor the moments she had spent with him, going over and over them in her thoughts like a lovestruck adolescent.

Served her right for mooning over a strange man when she was promised to Butrus, Nadia lectured herself. The pain didn't lessen, but she welcomed it as her just desserts.

"Take care of yourself, darlin'. We'll talk in the morning. Sweet dreams," Gage said, retrieving her attention as he flipped the phone closed.

At her slight movement, his head snapped up. The air fairly crackled as he cranked up his energy level to a new level of alertness. "Fancy meeting you here," he said, the softness of his tone belying his tense stance. "How long were you standing there listening?"

"I wasn't listening," she denied, then said, "All right I was, but only to the last part of your conversation, and not intentionally. Was there a reason I shouldn't?" Such as remaining in ignorance of the woman in his life? she added to herself, wondering why the thought made her feel so angry.

"No reason," he said, his pose still arguing with his denial. He seemed to realize it, and rested one shoulder against a marble pillar. "I was just…checking on things at my office back home."

"Your wife works for you?" Nadia asked, wanting him to know she had heard enough to be aware of the other woman's role in his life.

In the shadows his eyes narrowed with puzzlement. "My wife? Oh, you mean Dani."

His lover, then. Nadia subdued a fresh wave of jealousy, finding it annoyingly hard to do. "I'm surprised she didn't accompany you to this posting," she said.

"Unlikely, since rock bands aren't a favorite form of entertainment in Tamir."

Nadia was confused. "What has a rock band to do with anything?"

"Dani O'Hare is the lead singer of an up-and-coming group known as DaniO. She'd be the last person to think of joining the diplomatic service. Too conservative. No room for women with six-inch platform shoes and spiky purple hair. She's more like—" he thought for a moment "—my protégé, although she'd laugh herself silly if she heard me call her that." He sobered. "I found her sleeping in my office doorway one rainy winter night. She was eleven and her mother had kicked her out because she didn't get along with her new stepfather. The mother refused to accept that the stepfather was an abusive bully to anyone smaller than himself. When I found her, Dani only weighed about seventy pounds wringing wet, and she was covered in bruises.''

"So you took her in."

"What else could I do?"

"Allowed the appropriate authorities to care for her," Nadia said.

He gave a hollow laugh. "The appropriate authorities were responsible for her fix in the first place. Soon after her mother remarried, Dani ran away. She was returned to the family home because the appropriate authorities thought it was the best place for her."

His eyes were warm as he spoke about the girl he had rescued, Nadia noticed. She felt slightly ashamed of her earlier thoughts, when it was obvious that Gage looked on Dani almost as a daughter.

She touched a hand to her own raven locks. "Does she really have purple hair?"

"This month, anyway. Last month it was green, as I recall."

And her father thought *her* hair style was daring. Nadia's mouth curved into a smile. "She sounds like an interesting person."

"Funny, she said the same thing about you, Princess."

She would not let herself feel pleased, Nadia vowed. Hadn't she learned her lesson yet? Gage's life had nothing to do with her. She would never meet Dani, nor did she need the young woman's approval. Or Gage's, for that matter. "I'm glad you enjoyed discussing me with her," she said stiffly, and made to move past Gage.

He stepped between two pillars, blocking her path. "I wasn't discussing you, so there's no need to take that regal tone of disapproval. I merely told her I'd met a fascinating member of the royal family, who happened to have painted one of my favorite paintings."

"What you do is your own affair. It isn't my place to approve or disapprove of your actions."

He gave a low growl of impatience. "Save that submissive stuff for Butrus Dabir, Princess. He may enjoy it, but I don't."

Unable to pass him without stumbling through the garden beds, she had little option but to stand her ground. "I have no idea what you're talking about."

"Don't you? I've seen you with Dabir. You can't tell me all that 'yes sir, no sir, three bags full, sir' is the real Nadia Kamal."

"I don't see—" she began.

"That it's any of my business?" he supplied, then rubbed his hand tiredly across his face as if the long festivities had taken their toll. Or was there another reason? She recalled that he had asked Dani to report to him with some information he needed. What about? Instinct warned her not to ask.

"You're right, I spoke out of turn. My apologies, Princess," he said in a curiously flat tone.

She couldn't resist. "Now who's being submissive?"

He straightened and she could almost hear his mind reject such a notion. "You think so?" he said with dangerous precision, and then moved closer, almost rearing over her.

Her mind reeled. Dear heaven, what had she invited? "I didn't mean…"

He ignored her halting attempt to apologize, continuing his relentless progress until her back met cold, unyielding marble. "What was that about submissive?"

Chapter 8

As her awareness sharpened to almost painful intensity, Nadia knew she had several choices. She could scream to summon one of the guards patrolling the boundaries of the estate, aim her knee where it would do the most damage or force her way past Gage and run to her quarters.

None of the choices was as compelling as letting him kiss her.

She had known it would come to this from the moment she first saw him slumped behind the wheel of his car on the road to Marhaba.

Her country's tradition held that people's fates were often written in the stars. Was Gage's kiss an example, or was she merely trying to excuse her own outrageous behavior by blaming fate?

She had little time to wonder as his mouth pressed against hers, warm, demanding and infinitely exciting.

The faint tang of sandalwood incense clung to his hair, and he tasted of the cardamom coffee he had recently drunk.

His jaw felt rough against the smoothness of her cheek, the touch provoking her to match his ardor with her own.

Without conscious intention and with no idea where the instinct came from, she linked her hands around his neck, pulling his head down. She felt a slight resistance in the muscles of his neck, as if he questioned the wisdom of his actions, then he bent his head and deepened the kiss.

Her breath became shallow and she parted her lips to gain breath, but only succeeded in allowing Gage's teasing tongue entry to her mouth. She gasped as he made the most of the opportunity to explore, making her light-headed.

Or was it the heady touch of skin to skin, so rare in her experience, that made pleasure spiral through her, deliciously close to pain? She fought to silence the inner voice warning her that this was wrong and just clung to him, glorying in being held close and aroused so wantonly.

She had thought herself in love before, but Gordon had been no more experienced in such matters than she was. The blind leading the blind. Gage was far from blind, and where he was leading her didn't bear thinking about. She only knew that she was ready to follow him anywhere, if only this wonderful sensation could be allowed to continue.

It couldn't of course, and she should have been glad that Gage had the strength to end it for both their sakes. She felt a terrible sense of loss when he stepped back, swaying a little as if paying a price for his restraint.

"Dear heaven, Nadia," he said, his voice raspy. "I didn't mean to do that."

It was the first time he had used her name without adding her title, or calling her "Princess" in a mocking tone. Added to the intimacy they had just shared, she felt like a fishing vessel cast adrift by a storm tide and had to steady herself by resting a hand against one of the cool marble columns.

Afraid that she would sound as shaken as she felt, she pressed a finger to his lips. "If there is fault, it is mine, also."

He shaped his mouth around her finger, his tongue moistening the tip until her insides cramped in response. She tore her hand away, shocked that such a slight touch could have such a powerful effect on her. It went against all her common sense.

He dragged his fingers through his hair. "Maybe we are equally to blame. But it doesn't excuse me taking advantage like this."

She allowed herself a slight smile. "I didn't exactly—what would you English say?—put up a fight."

His shaky smile answered hers. "True. Why didn't you?"

"Why did you feel the need to kiss me?"

"Touché. We both did what we wanted. So where do we go from here?"

"To bed," she said simply, then blushed as she realized how he was bound to take that. "Our own beds," she amended. "We must never speak of this moment again."

The command was directed as much at herself as at Gage, and was accompanied by an aching sense of emptiness. She not only wanted to speak of it, but to dream of it and, God help her, to repeat it. But she could not and hope to live with herself. She was a princess with responsibilities and duties, engaged to be married. Her life allowed no room for such self-indulgence.

No room for passion. Or love.

With a cry of despair, she pushed past Gage and fled along the mosaic path to her quarters.

Long after he heard the door close behind her, Gage stood in the colonnade, anchoring himself to the marble pillar as he had seen her do. The cold stone was little comfort after the warmth of holding the princess in his arms. He could still feel her lips pressing against his and hear her gasp of response as he plundered her mouth.

She had acted as if his touch electrified her. With her limited experience, it probably had, although he could hardly take all the credit. He was pretty sure he was the first man to kiss her in such a flagrant fashion. In her society men and women rarely mixed, much less touched, unless they were husband and wife. She probably couldn't conceive of making love purely for pleasure.

Was he the loser for living in a more permissive society? he wondered. In his home country of Penwyck not so many years ago, a look or a touch had been considered as romantically daring as they were in Tamir today. Like so much of the world, his country's morality had moved with the times. Now anything went, and experiences had to become ever more intense to achieve the same level of piquancy.

He indulged himself in a sigh. He wouldn't want to lead a cloistered life, were it even possible. But he did envy Nadia her innocence. His roomy four-poster was going to seem cold and empty tonight, and he wondered if hers would feel the same.

The next morning brought no new information from Dani. As soon as he'd returned to his suite, Gage had e-mailed her photos of the new arrivals, which he'd snapped covertly during the banquet with a camera the size of his thumb, but so far Dani had no news for him regarding the identity of the subjects. She'd promised to keep digging.

He knew they had connections with the American underworld, as Dani had confirmed. What he needed now were clear links between Butrus Dabir and the Brothers of Darkness. All he'd gotten so far were more suspicions.

King Marcus wasn't going to be thrilled when Gage reported in. Well, that made two of them, Gage thought. His need to bring Conrad's killers to account burned like a flame inside him, driving him through this mission, although he wanted nothing more than to be gone from Tamir and its palace intrigues.

And its beautiful princess?

He'd lain awake for a long time pondering that one. After one bad experience, he'd resolved to remain coldly professional and keep his feelings out of his missions. He'd even managed to relegate his need to revenge Conrad's death to a part of his mind where it wouldn't affect his ability to function.

What was it about women in need that touched him so deeply? The last time he'd allowed a woman to reach him, he'd come to regret it. He hated to think he was in danger of doing it again.

Nadia was hardly in need. She had everything a woman could want. Except freedom. She was beautiful, talented, strong. Everything in him rebelled against seeing such a woman under the thumb of a man like Dabir. At least, that was the reason Gage gave himself for caring so much. His concern for Nadia had nothing to do with the way her jasmine scent haunted him and her taste lingered on his mouth, he assured himself.

At breakfast Butrus Dabir was the image of the genial host, inquiring repeatedly after Gage's health and how well he had slept after the lavish banquet. As was expected, Gage repeated his effusive compliments about the food and the presentation, although they risked sticking in his throat along with the honey pancakes he was served.

He didn't know if he was glad or sorry that Nadia preferred to eat breakfast in her quarters. Facing her across the table, not knowing which side she was on, was going to be hellishly difficult when his mind insisted on replaying the sensation of her lips on his and her arms tight around his neck.

He forced the image away and concentrated on what he had learned during the banquet. The group of newcomers he'd noticed the previous night who, he'd managed to learn, had arrived at the estate only the previous afternoon, were nowhere to be seen.

During the conversation he'd carefully orchestrated, his dinner companions hadn't been able to tell him anything about the group other than that the men were American. They were obviously close to Butrus Dabir, judging from the warm welcome they had received upon arrival. Since warm welcomes were a feature of Tamiri life, Gage didn't read too much into that.

He thought back to his conversation with Nadia. Gage hadn't lied to the princess about Dani's role in his life or her involvement with the rock band, but he had carefully omitted mentioning how good she was at tracking down information.

He didn't blame Dani for finding nothing. These people were experts at covering their tracks. Gage decided that his best hope was to keep his eyes and ears open when the newcomers joined Dabir's meetings and try to pick up on something more.

Easier said than done, he discovered as he washed his hands after the morning meal and prepared to join the others.

At the door to the conference chamber, Dabir placed a hand on his shoulder. "I have monopolized your time long enough, my friend. You have been most patient with our deliberations when I know that your main interest in Tamiri affairs is in trade."

Gage felt as if a loathsome spider had crawled onto his shoulder. He barely kept the reaction from showing on his face. "Not at all, old chap," he said, all British bonhomie. "When the new preamble to the constitution is unveiled, I shall feel I have played some infinitesimal part in its development. It is a singular honor to have the privilege of watching a master legal mind at work."

He tried to sidestep Dabir and enter the room, but the burly attorney managed to get in his way, looking smugly pleased, although he said, "You give me far too much credit. My role in our history is a mere footnote. You are the one who struts the world stage, dispensing diplomacy on behalf of your great country."

Gage nodded his thanks, wondering where all this was leading.

He soon found out.

"Only a short drive from Zabara is the Black Rock Souk. Located at the top of the famous Zabara cliffs, it is a beautiful and very active center of day-to-day trade."

Dabir wanted him to go shopping? Gage's skepticism must have shown on his face, because Dabir clapped him on the shoulder again. "There is no better place for a man of your interests to study Tamir trade at its grass roots. Trust me, my friend."

Knowing he wouldn't trust Dabir to count the small change in his pocket, Gage managed a stiff smile. "Sounds splendid. I'll make a point of visiting this souk right after the meeting."

"There's no need to trouble yourself further with our tri-fling affairs. Today we discuss matters of purely local inter-est. My dishonor would be great if, as my guest, you should be bored. I would be delighted to place a car and driver at your disposal, so you may avail yourself of a visit to the souk this morning."

In short, the talks were none of Gage's business, but it would be impolite to say so directly, much in the manner that a Tamiri would say he'd think about a deal in which he had no interest, rather than insult his guest by saying so out-right. In return, a good guest was expected to take the hint and not press the matter.

Gage decided to be a good guest for the moment. "Splen-did idea. I'm sure I'll find the souk educational. But I'll take my own car, thanks."

His host frowned. "You must permit me to provide you with a car and driver. If you were to get lost or suffer any ill effects at all, I would never forgive myself."

"The responsibility is mine alone," Gage insisted, resist-ing the urge to clench his fists over the excess of politeness. He had no intention of accepting the offer of car and driver and thus placing himself so completely in Dabir's hands. Get-ting lost was far preferable to ending up dumped over a cliff with his throat cut.

After a few more effusive compliments and not-at-alls were exchanged, Gage was left alone, wondering what he was going to do now. Since trade was his cover story rather than his area of expertise, he felt disinclined to visit this souk, but didn't see how he was going to get out of it.

In the main courtyard two black Bentleys waited, their uniformed drivers energetically polishing imaginary specks off the showroom-bright surface. Gage saw Nadia approach the first car, surrounded by her chattering attendants and obviously bound for the same shopping expedition. Dressed in a buttercup-colored *galabiya* threaded with gold over matching wide-legged pants, with a wisp of white scarf fluttering around her shoulders, she looked as fresh as a spring day.

He felt his interest quicken. Maybe the day wouldn't be a total loss, after all. He strode up to the women and performed a polite salaam, greeting them in deliberately woeful Arabic.

The two younger ones, duplicates of one another, giggled and covered their faces with their hands. Nadia winced, but smiled politely and returned his greeting. Not by a blink of her lovely dark eyes did she show that Gage meant any more to her than any of her fiancé's associates, two of whom were waiting with their wives, obviously intending to join the expedition.

If Gage hadn't caught the fluttering of a pulse at Nadia's throat, he might have convinced himself he'd imagined kissing her last night.

"I trust Your Highness will prevent this foreigner from making too many blunders at the souk today," he said, switching to English.

Nadia's face remained impassive. "Nargis is a capable bargainer. I depend on her utterly. You'll be delighted to assist Mr. Weston, won't you Nargis?"

Looking pleased, the attendant hovering beside the princess stepped forward and threw herself immediately into her assigned task. "The main thing to remember is not to buy anything at the first shop you enter. Go to several, drink the coffee you are offered and get a feel for the value of the item you are interested in, then return to the first place you visited and begin to bargain in earnest."

Gage let his look tell the princess that there was only one item of value to him here, and he wasn't going to find it at the souk. She looked away, pretending not to notice, although he was sure she had.

"Come, we must be on our way," she told her attendants. To Gage she said pointedly, "Your car has been brought around for you, and the rest of the party is ready to go."

Watching Gage move with obvious reluctance toward his car, Nadia released a breath of relief. For a moment she'd thought he might insist on traveling in their vehicle. It was bad enough to have him stand so close to her that she could smell the lingering traces of the attar he had shared with his host last night, the scent reminding her of how shamefully she had succumbed to the temptation of Gage's kiss.

After leaving him in the colonnade last night, she had slept little, and wondered if he had been as disturbed by their encounter as she was. He did remember it, she gathered from the volatile look he'd given her when he approached. But he hadn't had to endure the pangs of guilt that had plagued her. She deserved every one of them, she had told herself as she tossed and turned. She had wronged her fiancé, and it was only proper that she suffer for it.

Unfortunately most of her regrets were in her head and refused to reach her heart. There, she felt only a soul-deep yearning to know more of Gage's attention, to find herself once more in his arms, his hungry mouth claiming hers.

She looked up to find Nargis regarding her speculatively. Although her attendant said nothing, Nadia could almost hear the other woman's earlier accusation that Nadia was thinking about "this man who isn't Butrus, who makes your cheeks glow and your eyes shine." And Nargis would be right. The problem was, Nadia had no idea how to stop.

Chapter 9

Driving along the road to Black Rock Souk always made Nadia nervous. The bazaar, built on the ruins of an ancient trading center, was perched atop one of the highest cliffs in the region and could only be reached by a narrow road carved out of the side of the cliff.

On one side of the road rose a wall of rock that felt as if it could come crashing down on the car at any time. Even so, it was easier to fix her gaze on the cliff wall than to look at the other side, where the road sheared away in a dizzying drop to the sea, pounding the rocky shore far below.

At one point their driver had to slow almost to a crawl as a massive, yellow power shovel-tractor chewed chunks out of the cliff to widen the road ahead of them. Nadia saw more yellow vehicles parked along a new dirt siding they had gouged out of the cliff to keep the main thoroughfare clear while they worked.

"It's about time something was done about this road," Nargis commented, clutching a handful of scarf to her face although their car's air-conditioning system kept the choking dust from reaching them.

Nadia looked back. The car occupied by the other guests had almost disappeared in the dust churned up by the road-work machinery. She couldn't see Gage's car at all, although she told herself she hadn't been looking for him. In any case, he was well able to take care of himself.

"Do you have much shopping you want to do?" she asked her attendants to distract herself.

Nargis gave her the sort of look usually reserved for a backward child. "There is always shopping to be done, my princess. A new dress, a headscarf, some jewelry, gifts for friends."

For Nadia, shopping was something she did when she needed something, not a pursuit she found pleasurable, as well Nargis knew. She brightened. "I may buy some art supplies so I can paint the swans, as well as sketch them."

Nargis made a tongue-clicking sound of disgust. "Art supplies. What about the beautiful things you will need for your wedding?"

"Mother is taking care of everything to do with the wedding."

More tongue clicks. "She is not the one being married," Nargis said acerbically. "You might take a little interest in the proceedings, my princess."

Nadia traded looks with Tahani, knowing she understood. "Oh, but I do. I assure you I'm taking as little interest as I possibly can." She saw Tahani duck her head to hide her smile. On either side of Tahani, Thea and Ramana adopted bookend looks of confusion.

Muttering her disapproval, Nargis subsided against the butter-soft leather seat and said no more about wedding preparations, much to Nadia's relief.

Suddenly a new idea occurred to Nadia. "I know what I'll shop for—a gift for Father to commemorate his long tenure on the throne."

Her attendants approved of this, she saw as they burst into

an excited discussion of possibilities. Their suggestions ranged from gold and precious stones to daggers, Tamiri pearls and fine carpets, all of which would be available in abundance at the souk.

None of them were what Nadia had in mind. "I shall purchase new tools and order a special piece of marble to make a bust of the sheik," she announced.

The attendants stared at her, all but Tahani looking aghast. "But, Princess, surely you don't want to be carving statues now, when you are soon to be married?" Nargis asked.

Nadia read between the lines. What Nargis meant was that *she* didn't want to prepare the princess for her wedding day by picking chips of marble out of her hair and scrubbing the dust of the studio off her skin, as had happened the last time Nadia embarked on a major new work.

"Indeed I do," she said happily. "This bust will be the most special gift I have ever given my father."

"I think he would prefer grandchildren," muttered Nargis under her breath.

Nadia pretended not to hear. Her mind was already racing ahead to the bust she intended to create. At the Black Rock Souk she knew of a shop that specialized in supplying marble of all kinds, more usually for floors and columns. They were bound to have a piece that would suit her needs. In addition, she would need new chisels, hammers and bolsters, and sketching materials to make a preliminary plan. Oh, this would be wonderful!

She was so preoccupied that she hardly noticed when they crawled along the stretch of road she usually found most alarming, where the edge looked as if it might crumble at any moment, and there was barely room for one car to pass in either direction. They had reached the souk before she had finished outlining the new project in her mind.

Black Rock Souk was the largest of the Tamiri marketplaces, built according to traditional design and extended many times throughout the centuries. Bridges and staircases connected the older clifftop section with the newer sections, although even they were a century old by now. It was hard to tell old from new, because both featured intricate Tamiri architecture, Arabesque granite floors and spectacular sky-lights, as well as lovely murals on the walls.

In the old section, men gathered in coffee shops to play dominoes and cards, or waited on benches outside a tradi-tional hairdresser, talking to while away the time.

One wing of the souk was reserved for gifts and electronic wares, while the other housed gold, gems and jewelry shops. Nadia knew there were more than six hundred shops arranged along the winding alleyways and atop the steep stone stair-cases. New merchants seemed to be opening stores all the time.

The upper floors were the most popular with tourists and offered antiques, fine carpets, Tamiri jewelry, curios and ar-tifacts. On the lower floor could be found gold, precious stones, rosewood furniture and household items. A special section offered textiles and bridal wares, garments, cosmetics and leather goods. Here, there were also stores devoted to particular designers—Versace, Chanel, Tiffany and Gucci—which Nadia's sisters adored. Nadia was happy to replenish her store of jasmine perfume blended especially for her and stored inside an exquisitely handcrafted bottle.

She was surprised at how quickly she became caught up in exploring the lower floor. She even found herself enjoying inspecting some of the bridal wares, as bolts of exquisite textiles were unrolled before her, accompanied by thimble-size cups of coffee.

For once she was happy to follow Nargis's advice and refuse to buy at the first few shops they visited, although privately she thought the custom unnecessarily time-consuming. Left to herself, she would probably buy the first thing she saw that suited her needs and be on her way. As it was, she couldn't resist buying a dress she knew would be perfect for her sister Samira, without inspecting the dozen more that Nargis recommended.

"You would take all the pleasure out of the experience,

my princess,'' Nargis said reprovingly as they left the shop. She gestured ahead of them. ''At least your fiancé's guests take my advice.''

Nadia felt her heart catch as she automatically looked for Gage ahead of them, forgetting for a moment that he wasn't the only one of Butrus's guests to join the shopping excursion. And indeed, Nargis was referring to a married couple Nadia had barely spoken to. They shook their heads and lifted their hands as a merchant tried to thrust a Shirazi carpet upon them. From where she stood, Nadia saw that it was an imitation.

Stepping out of the shop with the merchant on their heels, the couple gave the princess's party a helpless look. Nargis stepped between the merchant and his victims, remonstrating with him in voluble Tamiri until he rolled up the offending carpet and returned to his shop.

Nargis turned away the couple's thanks, insisting she had done nothing, but Nadia heard her attendant give them a few more shopping tips before they plunged once more into the heart of the bazaar.

''Maybe you should go with them,'' the princess suggested.

Nargis shook her head. ''They were wise enough not to be taken in by the carpet seller. They will be all right.'' She looked at her mistress keenly. ''Were you, perhaps, expecting to see one of your fiancé's other guests, my princess? When I pointed them out to you, you reacted as if you had been stung by a bee.''

''You're imagining things.''

''No doubt. Shall I imagine your reaction this time, when I tell you that Mr. Gage Weston has just entered the shop of the gold merchant we are to visit next?''

Forewarned, Nadia was able to stop herself from reacting so obviously this time, although she couldn't slow the racing of her pulse or stop her hands from growing moist. ''I have no idea what you're twittering about,'' she said to Nargis in her most regal tone.

The attendant gave her an assessing glance. "As Your Highness wishes." She lifted the embroidered hanging separating the gold merchant's shop from the busy alleyway and bowed slightly as Nadia passed her. Thea, Ramana and Tahani had paused to inspect a display of gold trinkets outside the shop.

"He is a most attractive man, your foreigner," Nargis said for the princess's ears alone.

Nadia shot her a sharp look. "He is not *my* foreigner. From the way you're going on about him, one might think you were the one stung by the bee."

Nargis let the curtain drop and spread her hands. "Alas, the bee of passion is unlikely to sting me, my princess. I am not such a beautiful flower as you, to attract men so easily."

"Maybe you're better off," Nadia said thoughtfully. Since Gage Weston had come into her life, she had known nothing but confusion. Allowing him to kiss her last night had only deepened her mental turmoil.

She knew she was letting him assume far too much importance in her life. That was what came from leading such a proscribed existence. Probably any man would have caused the same havoc within her, had they met under similar circumstances.

Or so she tried to tell herself.

One look at Gage, reclining easily on the cushions that edged the shop floor, his arm resting on a padded, boxlike affair, was enough to convince her of the folly of this idea. A coffee cup looked absurdly delicate in his masculine grasp, and Nadia couldn't help remembering how those same hands had felt holding her last night.

He uncoiled from the floor with all the grace of a hunting tiger. The slight smile curving his generous mouth suggested that he was remembering, too. She met his gaze directly, refusing to let him see how unsettled she was by his presence.

The gold merchant, Mr. Khalid, also sprang to his feet as soon as he recognized the princess. He bowed low. "This is a great honor, Your Highness. Let me make you comfortable.''

She was shown to cushions opposite Gage. As soon as she and Nargis were comfortable, the merchant clapped his hands and a servant materialized from the rear of the shop to offer her one of the small, bell-shaped cups that held a tablespoonful of very spicy coffee. She drank and answered polite inquiries about her father's health, her own health and the health of everyone in the royal household, then in turn inquired about Mr. Khalid's well-being and that of his children.

Throughout the ritual, she was aware of Gage relaxing on his cushions, watching and saying nothing. He didn't seem impatient with the performance; indeed he was enjoying it she saw, when she studied him covertly from beneath lowered lashes.

No doubt visiting the souk was a novelty for him. England had its share of marketplaces but none as rich and varied as the Black Rock Souk, not only for the breathtaking choice of wares, but also for the timelessness of the shopping experience.

While studying abroad, she had been bewildered to visit English stores and to see price tags for the first time. Such an idea was totally alien to her experience. How could prices be negotiated if they were already written down? For once Nadia found herself agreeing with Nargis, who believed such an outrageous concept allowed no room for the delicious art of haggling, which the merchants enjoyed as much as their customers. According to the attendant, the cut and thrust of arriving at precisely the right price to suit both parties was what made shopping the adventure it was.

Nadia wasn't as enthusiastic as her attendant and often found herself wishing every transaction didn't have to take quite so long, but she had to agree that the process had its pleasant moments.

The coffee ritual began again when Tahani, Thea and Ramana joined them. Nadia's cup was refilled twice from a brightly polished brass pot. At last she shook her empty cup and said, "Bass—enough." The server then collected all the cups and departed, one hand looking like a chandelier from the cluster of cups hooked onto his fingers.

Only then did the merchant bring out trays of gold wares for the women and Gage to inspect. As the agreed bargainer for the group, Nargis recoiled in horror every time a price was mentioned. Gage looked amused, but went along with the process, Nadia was pleased to see. Nargis would have been highly affronted had he contradicted her at any stage.

Nadia found her eye drawn again and again to a necklace made of heavy gold links in the shape of the Greek key pattern. At the center of the chain was a tiger's head the size of her thumbnail, the eyes made of gleaming emeralds. She had never seen anything to compare with it.

Had she been alone, she would have paid Mr. Khalid's price, but she didn't wish to incur Nargis's wrath a second time. When the attendant signaled, Nadia took a last regretful look at the necklace, then followed the group out of the shop. After a moment's hesitation Gage shrugged and followed them.

Mr. Khalid pursued them along the footpath until Nargis managed to convince him that no one in her entire life had ever offered her such inferior wares at such inflated prices. Seemingly cowed, the merchant returned to his shop.

"Wasn't she a bit hard on him, considering we'd accepted his hospitality?" Gage asked Nadia in a low voice.

"In Tamir hospitality is not considered a favor, but an obligation. By the time this day is done, you will have drunk many cups of coffee or tea and probably bought very little."

"Sounds like an expensive way to do business," he observed. "I was hoping you would buy that tiger necklace. It looked superb on you."

Nadia felt her face grow warm. She had seen him watching as the merchant placed the necklace around her throat and had also caught the nod of approval he gave, as if the combination pleased him. "If I had agreed to buy it so quickly, Nargis would have had my head on a platter. I already succumbed to impulse and bought a dress for Samira. Two impulses in one day are more than Nargis can cope with.''

"Tough lady, your Nargis."

"She has served my family well for many years, and has only my best interests at heart."

As if to prove the point, Nargis moved closer to the princess, her frown disapproving of the whispered conversation between her and Gage. "We will visit three more gold merchants, then we will return to Mr. Khalid and purchase the tiger necklace."

"Wouldn't it have been easier to buy it the first time around?" Gage asked innocently.

He might as well have asked Nargis why she made a habit of breathing, Nadia thought, restraining her smile with an effort. Her attendant drew herself up. "If you seriously intend to improve trade relations between your country and ours, Mr. Weston, you will do well to observe how things are done here."

He made an elaborate salaam. "My apologies, Mistress Nargis. My words were ill chosen and I withdraw them. I shall listen and learn."

Mollified, Nargis let out the breath that had puffed up her chest and addressed Nadia. "Come, we have many more merchants to visit."

She wasn't exaggerating, and by the time Nargis was satisfied they'd made enough comparisons, Gage's head was spinning. He was ready to call for time-out when Nadia announced they would stop for refreshment at one of the many cafés crowding the souk.

To Gage, one café looked much like the other, but Nadia insisted they patronize a particular one, which evidently had links to her family for generations back. The food was certainly good, Gage thought. They ate spicy roast lamb carved from a giant vertical spit, with flat bread and fragrant sauces, followed by honey-drenched baklava, the meal washed down with springwater, which he found a welcome antidote to the copious amounts of coffee he'd drunk that morning. The beverage may have been served in tiny cups, but they added up.

Afterward Nadia announced that she intended to order the marble and hammers for her new work.

"I'll forgo the tiger necklace and have those, instead," she said.

Nargis made a face. "Butrus will not appreciate seeing you on your wedding day wearing marble and hammers."

"Perhaps not, but my father will be thrilled with his gift."

The princess had spoken. Nargis fell silent but kept up a moody sulk all the way to the marble seller. Only Tahani showed any interest in this stage of the proceedings, Nargis and the twins remaining outside to rest on wooden benches. Gage accompanied Nadia and Tahani into the shop, wishing he could convince Tahani to stay outside, as well.

When the merchant brought out the coffee cups and brass pot, Gage had to work at looking pleased, not sure he could handle much more caffeine. He wondered if that was the source of Nadia's dazzlingly bright eyes, then decided the credit was hers alone. She was easily the most engaging and lively woman he'd ever met.

If he hadn't been preoccupied with what was going on back at Butrus's estate, he would have enjoyed the shopping expedition, if only for the pleasure of watching Nadia. She was enough to distract any man, especially as she was now, engaged in a quest that commanded her full attention.

After they had drunk coffee and exchanged the required small talk, the merchant automatically turned to Gage. "I am honored to be asked to supply marble to the royal palace, Your Highness. My grandfather, may he rest in peace, supplied marble to the princess's grandfather, may he rest in peace. May I be permitted to ask, how many columns are we discussing?"

Nadia sketched a foot-square cube in the air. "One piece, about so large."

The merchant hid his disappointment well, but still insisted on honoring Gage with a title. "Your Highness, I understand why you would wish to order a sample—"

"It isn't a sample. It's for a sculpture of my father, Sheik Ahmed," Nadia said in a voice with an edge that Gage thought the merchant would do well to heed. Although the merchant had recognized the princess on sight, he obviously didn't know her very well. Addressing his remarks to the male in the party was probably automatic, but wasn't going to get him anywhere with her.

"I think you'd better talk to the princess," Gage advised, keeping his voice low.

The merchant looked flustered but did as bidden, eventually promising to supply a piece of marble of the size and quality she required. The stone would be shipped to the palace without delay.

When Nadia began to discuss chisels and hammers with the expertise of a stonemason, Gage saw his chance and excused himself from the discussion. He didn't think she saw him leave, so caught up was she.

Slightly breathless, he returned to the party just as she and Tahani emerged from the marble seller. Nargis and the twins rose as one, and rejoined them.

"Did you get everything you needed?" he asked.

Nadia inclined her head. "Of course, *Your Highness.*"

For a moment alarm bolted through him. Had she discovered the truth about him? The sparkle in her eye told him she was only mimicking the marble seller. He concealed his relief behind a shrug. "What can I say? The man recognizes quality."

"The man recognizes another man," she snapped.

He caught her wrist. "Hey, it was hardly my fault."

She looked coldly at his hand, but he didn't release her. "I note you didn't mind."

The pulse he felt racing under his fingers was a potent reminder of how he had made her feel last night. How she had made *him* feel. He pulled his hand away as if burned. "I told him to talk to you, didn't I?"

Her face gave nothing away, but he saw her rub her wrist as if feeling something similar. "Precisely. You had to tell him to."

"I don't make the laws, Princess." If he did, she wouldn't be surrounded by attendants and they would be miles from here, lying on a beach somewhere, sharing an intimate meal and then… He snapped himself out of the reverie. Nothing of the sort was going to happen, and as long as he didn't know how much she knew of Dabir's affairs, it never would.

The thought left him feeling edgy and unsatisfied, in no mood for more shopping and, saints forbid, more coffee.

Nadia evidently agreed. She directed Nargis to locate the rest of their party and have the cars fetched for them. While the attendant was gone and the others window-shopped, Gage slipped a velvet box into the princess's hands.

She looked at it in confusion. "What is this?"

"I guessed you wouldn't have time to go back for it, so…" He left the explanation hanging as she opened the box. Inside was the tiger necklace.

She closed the box with a snap, her expression clouded. "You bought me a gift. Why?"

He wasn't sure. He still didn't know which side she was on, and he had almost no control when he was around her, breathing in her heady jasmine scent. Why he should feel motivated to give her anything was beyond him. But he did.

"You remind me of a tigress," he said, explaining to himself as much as to her. "Outwardly you're subservient to the males in the pride, but you're actually the huntress who takes care of everybody."

She gave him a look that said she didn't like being known more than she wanted to be. "You presume a great deal, Mr. Weston."

"That name again. In my country, once two people have kissed, they're usually on first-name terms."

Her hunted glance found Tahani and the twins, but they gave no sign of having heard. "I thought we agreed not to speak of that," Nadia hissed.

"You agreed not to speak of it, Princess. Yet today you've spoken of it with every look."

"Then I shall try not to look at you."

"The way you're not looking at me now?"

His huskily voiced challenge made her lift her long lashes and face him, as he had intended. His loins tightened as he felt himself drowning in her lambent gaze. Her lips curved into a reluctant smile. "You are an impossible man, Gage."

Better. Now all he had to do was prove that she was one of the good guys, deal with Butrus Dabir and whisk her away from all this, so he could taste more of the passion he knew simmered beneath that compliant exterior.

Which of the Herculean tasks would he find most difficult? he wondered. He wasn't sure he wanted to know the answer, but was afraid he already did.

Chapter 10

A few minutes later Nargis returned, shepherding the other members of the party. The petite, black-haired attendant was frowning. "A thousand apologies, but your car is proving difficult to start, Your Highness."

The man Nargis had rescued from buying the fake carpet stepped forward. "Please take our car, Your Highness. We can wait until the second car is fixed."

Before she could answer, Gage offered, "I'd be delighted to drive the princess back to the estate in my car—with her attendant, naturally."

Nadia schooled the turmoil out of her expression. "Thank you, but I'm sure my car will be ready soon. I don't mind waiting a little longer."

"Not afraid of riding with me, are you?" he asked her in an undertone.

She bristled, furious that he could think she was afraid of him when she had an entire army at her command if she so wished. Not that she needed one to handle such a presumptuous man. To prove it, she said through gritted teeth,

"Rather than inconvenience my fiancé's guests, I shall accept your offer. Tahani will attend me."

Nargis looked as if she would prefer to accompany her mistress, but Nadia quelled her with a fierce look. Bad enough to have to ride in the same car with Gage, without having Nargis reading omens into every word that passed between them.

She saw Gage's mouth twitch as she said as regally as she could, "Come, Tahani."

She swept ahead of him to the waiting Branxton, but somehow he reached it before her, opening the rear passenger door for her with all the aplomb of a professional chauffeur, although no servant would dare look at her so boldly as she brushed past.

At least he had the sense not to expect her to ride in front, Nadia thought. It was unthinkable for her to travel beside any man not her husband. Equally unthinkable for her to be alone in the car with him. So why did she feel a faint sense of disappointment that Tahani was sharing the journey?

She needn't have worried. Tired after the long shopping expedition, Tahani began to nod off almost as soon as they were under way.

"Looks like you wore out the hired help," Gage said, watching them in the rearview mirror.

She glanced at Tahani. "She told me she was troubled by bad dreams last night and didn't get much sleep." Nadia didn't add that the maid's dreams had worried her or that Gage himself had figured in them. He didn't seem like a man to believe in what he couldn't see, feel, taste or touch, so the premonitions were unlikely to impress him.

"I didn't get much sleep, either," he admitted. "Guess I don't need to tell you why."

She pursed her lips. "Dare I hope that your conscience was troubled?"

He shook his head. "Not a bit, Princess. Was yours?"

"It should have been."

"Which doesn't answer my question."

She summoned her voice with difficulty, unable to be less than truthful. "No, my conscience wasn't troubled. But my mind was uneasy." She had been kept awake last night, not because she felt guilty for having kissed Gage, but because she *hadn't* regretted it.

In truth she had wanted much more and had lain awake long into the night suffering from a bad case of frustration. Her penance for being disloyal to Butrus. Unfaithful was more accurate. Not only had she lost herself in Gage's embrace and enjoyed it, she had craved more of his attention. What kind of wife would she make when it took so little to turn her thoughts away from her duty?

"Don't look so troubled, Princess," Gage said softly, his gaze darting from the winding cliff road to her and back to the road again. "Lots of people succumb to a moment of curiosity. It doesn't mean you're beyond redemption."

"Perhaps not where you come from." And probably not in Tamir. It was Nadia herself who was letting the moment of weakness disturb her, mainly because she knew it was becoming far more than a moment. Every time she was near Gage, her thoughts turned in directions they shouldn't be going.

Could she really blame her response on curiosity? If it had been, surely the kiss would have satisfied her. Instead, it had set up a hunger that was becoming a fever in her blood.

She saw Gage's smile reflected in the mirror and thought she saw a tinge of sadness there. "You'll marry your attorney and have lots of kids," he said, "and look back on this as a test that you passed with flying colors."

He didn't sound happy, she noticed, her spirits lifting in spite of herself. "Do you enjoy wreaking havoc in people's lives?" she asked, well aware of how much havoc he wreaked in hers.

"Only the ones whose beauty takes my breath away."

Did she really do that? Heat radiated through her, although she tried to subdue it. "You mustn't say such things. And you can't give me gifts, either. You must take back the neck-lace.''

''Sorry, the style wouldn't suit me at all.''

She wished he wouldn't mock her. ''Is there no one in England you could give it to?''

''Fishing, Princess?''

''No!'' She knew her denial sounded forced. ''You mentioned your sister...''

''If I start giving Alexandra jewelry, she'll think I've lost my mind.''

Nadia tried to tell herself she didn't care that there was no other woman in his life, but her feeling of elation argued against it. ''What kind of gifts do you give her?''

''Horse-riding gear, painting equipment. She's an artist like you.''

''And a sportswoman, from the sound of it.''

''She was part of the British equestrian team at the last Olympics.''

The pride in his voice was unmistakable. ''What about your parents? What do they do?''

He hesitated. Somehow she sensed it wasn't because he needed to give the hairpin turns his full attention. She could almost hear him trying to decide what to tell her. Why? Was he afraid the truth would repel her? She didn't care if his father was a street sweeper and nearly said so, until she stopped herself, not wanting to betray any more interest in him than she had already.

As the road straightened a little, he said over his shoulder, ''My father advises our government on policy.''

Hardly a street sweeper, so why the hesitation? She wished she could shake off the feeling that Gage was being secretive. ''Like Butrus?'' she said.

''Hopefully with a little less self-interest.''

''You don't like Butrus, do you.''

She saw his fingers tighten around the steering wheel. ''Why do you ask?''

"You never mention him without sounding disapproving."

"Has it occurred to you there could be a good reason for that?"

Thinking of what the reason might be, she turned away, feeling her cheeks heat. They were approaching the steepest part of the road, she noticed. Her attention had been too focused on Gage for it to register before.

She remembered that Tahani's dream had concerned a road and cliffs, although she had been unable to specify where they were. Nadia became aware that Gage's attention had become totally fixed on the driving. The rigid set of his back and neck told her something was wrong.

"Aren't we going too fast?" she asked, fear gripping her as she saw the cliff face hurtling past much, much too close.

He didn't take his eyes from the road. "I don't want to alarm you, Princess, but you'd better brace yourself. We don't seem to have any brakes."

Tahani was awake and upright now, the car's swaying movement disturbing her doze. She looked at Nadia with wide frightened eyes, "Are we going to die, my princess?"

Gage heard her. "Not if I have anything to do with it. Hang on."

Gage knew his confident words belied the empty sensation that had hit him when he felt the brake pedal sink all the way to the floor without affecting the car's speed.

Instinct made him pump the pedal rapidly several times to try to build up brake-fluid pressure, but it was useless. Praying, he downshifted to the lowest gear and groped for the parking brake, easing it up. Just as well he kept a hold on it, because the car skidded into a four-wheel slide that took them perilously close to the crumbling shoulder. He had to spring away from the brake and put all his muscle into keeping the car from becoming airborne.

Loose stones skittered away from their wheels as he wrenched the car out of the careering dive at the last second.

Then he braced himself for the screech of tortured metal as he deliberately sideswiped the stone of the cliff side.

Sitting closest to that side, Tahani screamed and scrambled to the center of the seat, hunching away from the stone fragments peppering her window. "What is he doing?"

Struggling for calm, Nadia wrapped her arms around her attendant and friend. "I don't know, but I trust Gage."

"I'm using the friction of the cliff against the car to scrub off some of our speed," he ground out, steering against the stone again. Metal screamed and stone chips rained on the car. They slowed a fraction. Not nearly enough for Gage's liking, and he wasn't sure how much more of this the car could take before the body ripped open like a sardine can.

"The roadwork," Nadia remembered. "We shouldn't be far from it."

He nodded grimly, wondering if they would last that long. In the corner of his mind that wasn't fully occupied with keeping them alive, he had to admire her courage. The princess must be as terrified as her maid, but she was the one comforting Tahani and assuring her that Gage would get them out of this if anyone could.

He wished he shared her confidence.

Two more encounters with the cliff slowed them a little more. There was no time left to lose. Gage's arm muscles screamed with the effort of keeping the car on the road, instead of letting it launch itself into the space over the rocky shore.

With each catapulting turn his shoulders felt as if they would be wrenched from their sockets. It was becoming a race to see which would come apart first, car or driver.

Nadia's life and that of her attendant were in his hands, he reminded himself. It was his fault the princess was in the car with him. If he hadn't persuaded her to let him drive her home, she would be safely back at the souk. He wasn't about to let her die as long as he had breath left in him to prevent it.

He set his teeth against the pain in his arms and shoulders, and fought the car with everything in him, and a bit more besides. He couldn't have said how far they'd hurtled down the mountain. At each turn he expected to meet someone coming the other way and thanked providence when the road remained clear. How long could their good fortune hold?

The emptiness of the road started to make sense when he saw a blur of yellow filling his vision. Automatically he rode the brake pedal, then cursed himself for the futile gesture. They had reached the roadwork. If he ploughed into the giant machine blocking the road ahead, they were all finished.

Seconds before impact seemed unavoidable, he spotted the red-earth furrow of track off to the side, which the workers had gouged out to give them somewhere to park their machinery so they wouldn't obstruct traffic.

Saying a prayer to the gods that protected intelligence operatives, he steered for the side track, slewing past the machine close enough to hear the driver let loose with a string of colorful Arabic expletives.

"I'm with you there, pal," Gage muttered. The tires clawed for purchase on the earthen surface, the incline of the track further slowing them. Ahead was one of the yellow machines, the cabin empty this time.

Just as well, because they were still moving fast when the Branxton plowed into the yellow monster, coming to a shuddering stop that Gage felt in every muscle in his body. He slammed against the seat belt with bruising force, but wasted no time releasing it and swinging around. "Are you two okay?"

White-faced, Nadia fumbled for her own seat belt. "We're all right, thanks to you."

The attendant was slumped across Nadia. "Tahani?"

"She fainted when we were about to hit the yellow machine, but her seat belt saved her from harm."

As they spoke, Tahani began to stir, her eyes turning luminous as Nadia assured her they were all still alive. Gage heard her mutter a prayer of thanks and added his own. Nadia continued to murmur encouragement, and Gage was pleased to see a little color seep into the women's faces.

He needed all his strength to open the damaged door and climb out. Nadia was struggling with her door and smiled her appreciation as he grappled it open for her. Relief swept through him as he saw she was uninjured. He reached in and lifted her out, reveling in the feel of her living body in his arms. She gave a cry of surprise, but clung to him as if to reassure herself that he, too, was in one piece.

He had a momentary glimpse of a different scenario, one in which he cradled her lifeless form and her eyes were closed forever. The vision had come so close to being a reality that his heart almost stopped.

She was having similar thoughts, he saw, as her arms linked around his neck and she held on for dear life. Dear life. Suddenly it was more than a trite phrase.

Her huge eyes looked moist, but she didn't give in to tears and even managed a brave smile. "You saved my life. Thank you," she said in a husky voice.

He glanced at the car. "I still have to work out why it needed saving." Brakes sometimes failed without warning, but he couldn't shake off the suspicion that there was more to it this time. Dabir had insisted Gage go to the souk. While he was inside, Dabir could have arranged to have the brakes tampered with, ensuring that the culprit couldn't be connected with him.

Nadia shivered. "You think this wasn't an accident?"

"I don't know, but I intend to find out."

Sorely tempted never to let her go again, he made himself set her on her feet, leaning against the car, while he assisted Tahani. The attendant was quivering like an injured puppy. She had recovered from her faint, but was still paler than Gage liked. Shock most likely, Gage concluded. He knew just how she felt.

Men in coveralls raced toward them from the road-making machine, shouting and gesticulating. Gage had never felt so weary, but forced himself to face them, groping for the right words in Arabic to assure them this wasn't his idea of a joke.

"The car's brakes failed," he repeated, wondering if he was using the right expression. His Arabic wasn't bad, in fact, it was pretty good, but right now he was barely staying upright and his thinking processes were far from reliable.

Nadia levered herself away from the car and addressed the men. Immediately they came to a sort of ragged attention, murmuring her title in amazement. Gage could see them wondering how on earth their princess had come to be hurtling down a cliff at a million miles an hour with this incoherent foreigner.

He pulled himself together and reached into the still-steaming car for his cell phone. Like its owner, it had taken a beating during the rough ride, but looked to be functional. Unfortunately he wasn't, and he couldn't make his fingers hit the right keys to put through a call for help.

Nadia's fingers gently closed around his, closing the phone at the same time. "It's all right, Gage. The other cars will pass by soon and see what has happened. In the meantime, the workers have said they will summon help for us."

"For you, anyway." He wasn't sure they'd have been so enthusiastic about helping him after he'd slammed into one of their multimillion-dollar machines.

Folding chairs were brought and placed in the shade of a canvas awning the workers had rigged up between machinery and cliff for their own use. Gage was too keyed up to sit, but he helped Nadia and Tahani to the chairs and gratefully accepted the cool water that was offered. The drink washed away some of the dust and bile clogging his throat, although he needed both hands to hold the cup steady.

The car was a mess. Looking at the crumpled side, scraped down to bare metal but still essentially intact, he made a mental note to stick to Branxtons in the future. He had rented this one when he arrived in Tamir because he owned a couple of similar models back home in Penwyck. He was going to have some explaining to do when the agency saw what he'd done to this one. But they were alive. He'd settle for that, for now.

On a sudden inspiration, he located the foreman of the team and took him aside for a few private words. The man took pity on his inadequate Arabic. "My friend, you've had a great shock. We can speak English if it's easier for you."

"Thanks. Right now, any language feels beyond me. I want you to do me a favor. I'm willing to pay well."

The man shook his head. "You have saved the life of our princess. Any service I can do in return is my pleasure, although I can think of nothing that would repay the great debt we owe you."

Impressed by the love and devotion Nadia inspired in her people, Gage nodded, knowing he wasn't far from feeling the same way himself. It was reassuring to find he wasn't the only one falling under her spell. At the same time, he hoped he would never have to shake the faith of this man and others like him by unmasking her as a traitor.

He rubbed his hand over his jaw. "Do this one thing, and we'll call it even. As soon as we're gone, check the car over and let me know what you find."

The foreman looked at the damaged car in disbelief. "You think someone tampered with your car to try to harm the princess?"

"Not her. She hadn't planned to be in the car. Her own broke down."

"Then someone wished to do you harm. Why?"

"If it was deliberate sabotage, I can think of a few reasons. But first I need answers."

The foreman clapped him on the shoulder. "You shall have them, my friend. Where can I reach you?"

Gage gave the man his number at the British Embassy. "If you can't contact me, you can leave a message and someone will make sure I get it."

"Consider it done."

By the time Gage returned to the princess's side, the rest of their party had caught up and she was explaining what had happened. Nargis and the twins threw up their hands in horror, exclaiming over their lucky escape.

"It was Gage's doing. He saved our lives with his skillful driving," Nadia said, reaching for his hand to pull him into the circle.

He saw Nargis's disapproving look go to their joined hands. She could worry about morality even now? Well, to hell with that. Nadia's hand in his felt good. He tightened his grip, his frown daring the older attendant to interfere.

Summoned by the workmen as soon as they recognized Nadia, another limousine arrived soon afterward, dispatched from Butrus's estate. Rather than scandalize Nargis too much, Gage helped Nadia and her attendants into the spacious rear compartment and climbed into the front seat beside the driver. He had never felt so bone-weary in his life. He let his head drop back against the leather headrest and closed his eyes.

Watching him through the glass partition separating them, Nadia felt her heart squeeze into a giant fist. She felt as if the jolting ride had bruised every part of her body, but none ached as poignantly as her heart. She knew she was verging on shock, and her judgment was impaired, but she felt more drawn to Gage than she had ever been to any man.

She had thought herself in love before, but nothing compared to the strength of her feelings for this Englishman, with his forward manner and powerful kisses. She had never been overjoyed about the prospect of marrying Butrus, although she had been resigned to doing her duty. Now she felt sick inside, as if some part of her that had only newly awoken would shrivel and die the day she exchanged wedding vows with Butrus.

What was she thinking? She was a princess of Tamir. Her life was devoted to duty. There could be no room in it for the sort of foolish love she was afraid she was starting to feel for Gage Weston.

No, she wouldn't allow it. In any case, he didn't return her feelings. Kissing her wasn't the same as loving her. His society put far less store by kisses than hers did. Just because the feel of his lips was imprinted on her own and she ached to feel his arms around her again didn't mean he felt the same. In time he would return to his own country and forget her. She should try to do the same where he was concerned, although it was amazingly difficult to contemplate.

"I dreamed of this road," Tahani said in a tremulous voice, startling Nadia out of her reverie. "I saw us hurtling down the cliff, barely missing the edge. I should have stopped you from getting into that car, Your Highness."

Nadia covered the girl's hand with her own, noting that Tahani's fingers were icy. "I won't permit you to blame yourself for something you couldn't control. You had a dream that could have meant anything. It's only now the drama is over that you see it as an omen."

Nargis looked affronted. "Omens are not to be taken lightly. I wish you had listened to Tahani, my princess."

Nadia gave a weary sigh. If she had listened, would she have refused to travel with Gage? She doubted it. She wasn't much good at making predictions herself, but she would stake a lot on her future being intertwined with his. Wishful thinking? she wondered. More like something about him that kept him in her thoughts constantly. Maybe that would change once she was married.

She fervently hoped so, hating to think she would have to endure a lifetime married to one man while dreaming of another.

Chapter 11

Butrus Dabir was pacing up and down Zabara's main court-yard when the convoy pulled in. As soon as Nadia's driver opened the door for her, he rushed to her side. "My dear, are you sure you're all right?"

"Perfectly, thank you, Butrus," she assured him, but her pallor contradicted her assertion.

"A doctor is waiting inside to check you over. Those dolts working on the road told me you weren't injured, but I couldn't rely on their word."

The princess gave a faint smile. "Those dolts saved our lives, along with some brilliant driving on Mr. Weston's part."

Dabir's eyes became lethal slits as they slid over Gage. "Then you and the roadworkers have my gratitude for saving Her Highness's life."

Butrus didn't sound especially grateful, Nadia thought. He sounded—she searched for a suitable description—upset to see Gage. She shivered, reminded that Gage thought the brakes might have been sabotaged. Surely Butrus couldn't have had anything to do with it, could he?

Nadia tried to persuade Gage to let the doctor examine him, but he insisted he was fine. He didn't look fine, she thought worriedly. Steering the runaway car at breakneck speed down such a tortuous road must have drained him. She knew she would have bruises from neck to thigh from being jolted around, as well as where the seat belt had cut across her when they ran off the road. What injuries had Gage suffered?

The rigidity with which he carried himself suggested how close he was to collapse, although he would probably never admit it. She couldn't help thinking about the crumpled, stripped metal along the side of the car. The slightest miscalculation on Gage's part, and they would have crashed into the cliff face or soared helplessly over the edge to their deaths.

Where had he learned to drive like that? Not in any diplomatic corps she knew of. As she allowed herself to be steered inside where a female physician waited to examine her and Tahani, she wondered again about his background and his true purpose in Tamir.

Gage waited until she was safely handed into the doctor's care before he turned in the direction of his suite, wanting nothing so much as a hot shower and a stiff drink.

His host had other ideas. "I would like to speak with you in my study, Gage."

He didn't say "right now," but Gage heard it in his voice. Dabir sounded like the headmaster at the prep school Gage had attended as a boy, only this time, instead of shivering with apprehension at the summons, he felt utter loathing.

He masked the feeling with a perfunctory smile. "I wouldn't think of sullying your presence in this condition. Permit me to shower and change first."

"This will only take a moment."

In a country where a guest could do no wrong, Dabir wasn't playing by the rules. Gage decided to go along for now, wondering how much Dabir knew. Could the attorney possibly have learned his real identity? Today's near miss made him think it was possible. But how had he found out? And how much of the whole picture did the other man possess?

He followed Dabir across the courtyard, their footsteps loud on the mosaic tiling. A servant opened a heavy carved door into a sparsely furnished chamber that led to a larger chamber. Dabir's office, Gage guessed.

He hadn't been in here before, and his swift assessment missed nothing. The sophisticated computer equipment, satellite-communication devices and other paraphernalia of the modern office contrasted with the ornate wall hangings, mahogany furniture and Persian carpets overlying one another with the lavishness of merchandise in a souk.

The carpets were edged with cushions and armrests, but Dabir gestured toward an upright chair in front of the massive desk. "Sit."

No polite chitchat? Just "sit"? Too shell-shocked to do anything else, Gage sat. Dabir chose to pace.

"You sounded surprised to see me still in one piece," Gage said.

Dabir wasn't to be drawn out so easily. "Relieved, yes, but hardly surprised. Why should I be?"

Gage crossed his arms and tried to appear relaxed. "I thought you might not be expecting me back."

Dabir affected a shrug. "Your fate is in the hands of the Almighty. Today your life was spared. Tomorrow, who knows?"

A threat or simple local philosophy? Gage was too tired and bruised for verbal sparring. "If you have something to say to me, just say it, Dabir."

The other man's expression hardened. "Very well. Have you any idea what you just did?"

"Saved the princess's life?" Gage asked, striving to play the British diplomat to the hilt.

Dabir whirled on him. He was wearing a hand-tailored suit,

so there was no robe to swirl dramatically, but it was implied in his movements. "Had she not been in your car, her life would never have been put at risk in the first place."

"I wasn't the one who cut the brake lines," Gage snapped.

That stopped Dabir. "Are you suggesting someone sabotaged your car?"

"I'm not suggesting it. I know it." He didn't, but Dabir's reaction was making him more convinced all the time. Was Dabir so shaken because Nadia had been in the car and his attempt on Gage's life—if such it was—had almost killed the other man's ticket to power, as well?

Dabir looked convincingly shocked. "Why would anyone do such a thing?"

"I thought you might have some idea."

Dabir slowed, looming over Gage. "You are a guest in my house. I do not like—or accept—any insinuation that I am somehow involved in your misfortune."

"Then I withdraw the suggestion," Gage said smoothly, knowing he didn't sound in the least repentant.

"Why was Her Highness traveling with you?" Dabir demanded.

"Her car refused to start."

"So you gallantly offered to drive her home."

Gage nodded. "That's about it."

"There was nothing more to your offer than simple courtesy?"

Now who was implying impropriety? Gage stood up, exhausted, and tired of having Dabir loom over him. They were evenly matched in height, although Gage was broader of shoulder and probably fitter.

He gained a little satisfaction from seeing Dabir shrink away from him. "What's really bothering you, Dabir? That your fiancée isn't as devoted to you as you'd like? I understood yours was to be a marriage of convenience." Mostly Dabir's, but Gage managed not to add that part.

"Our marriage plans are none of your concern."

"Then why are you letting a little thing like my giving the princess a ride bother you so much?"

"You don't understand Tamiri ways. A woman driving with a man who isn't her husband is inviting scandal. If she is royal, the potential for scandal is much worse."

"Even if her maid goes along for the ride?"

"It is still unseemly."

Gage raked a hand through his hair and his fingers came away caked in dust. Dabir's preoccupation with appearances was getting to him. Didn't the man realize his fiancée had come within a hairbreadth of being killed today? That didn't seem to bother him half as much as having her flout convention by riding with Gage.

"Look, Dabir, I've had a day out of hell. My car's a crumpled mess stranded halfway up a mountain. It's only by the grace of that Almighty of yours that Nadia, Tahani and I aren't in the same state. We can continue this discussion later if you insist, but right now, I'm going to take a shower."

Only when he saw his host's eyes darken did Gage realize his mistake. By referring to the princess so familiarly, he had fueled Dabir's suspicions about them. He decided it didn't matter. If the man already suspected him of being interested in Nadia and wanted him dead, the extra ammunition wasn't going to make much difference.

Dabir inclined his head in a parody of graciousness. "I see no need to discuss the matter further. I think we understand each other."

Gage knew his gaze was as cold as his adversary's. "No doubt."

"After sustaining such a shock, I understand that you would wish to take your leave tomorrow. Go in peace."

Gage remembered a line his partner had often used: "Don't go away mad." Implied was the tag line "Just go away." Gage heard it now in Dabir's words. He allowed himself a moment of frustration. The conference was finally becoming interesting. He was convinced that the meetings up to this point had been window dressing. With the arrival of the underworld types, Gage felt certain Dabir was settling down to the real business of the conference.

Since he could see no way to prolong his stay and learn more, he gave the expected response, "Peace be with you, too." At least, until he had enough evidence to hang the man.

Dabir pressed a button on his desk and a servant appeared silently, prepared to escort Gage back to his suite. So he wasn't to be allowed the freedom of the estate any longer. That meant he would probably be watched until he left. No problem. If Dani learned anything, she knew better than to tell him so in plain words. That left the foreman and whatever he uncovered from Gage's car. With luck, that message wouldn't reach Gage until he was safely back at the British Embassy.

He decided to relax and enjoy being alive.

Nadia was resting on a chaise longue in the shade of a colonnaded veranda when she saw Butrus approaching. He waved away her attempt to get to her feet. "Please stay where you are. You must be exhausted."

She set aside the magazine she'd been looking at without really seeing it. "I am tired, but the doctor says there is no lasting damage."

"Praise be. How is your maid?"

"Tahani is fine, too. She's gone to her room to rest."

Butrus frowned. "Leaving you alone?"

"It was my wish. I needed time to think, to deal with what happened today."

Butrus pulled up a chair close to Nadia. "I understand. It was a most unfortunate accident."

"According to Gage, it may not have been an accident."

"He has proof?"

She shook her head. "Not really, but he seems fairly confident."

Butrus's smile vanished. "Mr. Weston is a little too confident about many things. It is fortunate that he is leaving us tomorrow."

Nadia struggled to keep her disappointment to herself. She should be glad, she knew. She was finding Gage far more attractive than was proper, and she suspected Butrus knew it. All the same she couldn't help asking, ''Was it his idea to leave?''

''Does it matter? I imagine he is needed at the British Embassy.''

''He didn't say anything to me about having to go so soon.''

Butrus took her hand. ''Much more of this, little one, and I shall fear that my presence alone is insufficient to make you happy.''

Instead of the expected reassurance, she said, ''You must agree, you have been preoccupied with your business affairs lately.''

Her fiancé sighed. ''Regrettable, but necessary. I shall make it up to you as soon as my guests leave.''

''Those men who arrived yesterday?''

He nodded. ''They are only here for one more night. We had much business to discuss today.''

''What kind of business?''

''Nothing you need worry about. You have had enough excitement for one day.''

She shifted restively. ''Hearing about your discussions will help take my mind off…what happened.''

He spread his hands wide. ''We talked of many things, mostly international affairs.''

''This morning I heard you tell Gage that your discussions would concern purely local matters.''

Angry color washed up Butrus's neck into his face. ''What we spoke about is none of Gage Weston's concern.''

Or hers, she heard, although he didn't say it. Butrus knew that she had a brain and opinions of her own and couldn't be relegated to a decorative role in his life. ''Those men look more like criminals than businessmen,'' she insisted. ''I can't imagine what you have in common with their type.''

Butrus reined in his temper with a visible effort. ''In my

work, it is sometimes necessary to deal with people other than one's own kind.''

"Then you don't like them, either?"

"Liking them is not the issue. The important thing is that I can deal with them when I must." He stood up. "They will only occupy me for another few hours, then I can devote my time to you. Your father agreed to allow you to come to the estate because he thought you needed the rest. He will never forgive me if I return you in worse condition than when we arrived.''

Fueled by the knowledge that Butrus and her father had made plans for her without consulting her, she felt her impatience grow. She had thought the invitation was Butrus's idea alone. "Surely where I go and what I do is up to me."

"Of course. Before today's misadventure, I thought you were enjoying your small vacation.''

"I have enjoyed myself. The souk was wonderful.''

He smiled indulgently. "Did you buy a great many new clothes and jewels?''

She shook her head, deciding not to mention the tiger necklace, which she intended to return to Gage as soon as she could. "Nargis and the others bought clothes. I ordered the most wonderful piece of marble.''

He frowned in confusion. "You bought marble? Whatever for?''

Didn't he know even now that her passion for painting was equaled only by her enthusiasm for sculpting? "I intend to make a bust of my father as a gift to celebrate his long tenure on the throne.''

He regarded her as if she'd lost her mind. "Wouldn't you rather commission such a piece? I know an artist who—''

"I know an artist," she said, modulating her voice with an effort. "As do you—the one you're about to marry.''

"I understood that after our marriage—''

"I'd give up all this foolishness?'' she supplied for him. "If I did, you wouldn't want me, because I'd be unbearable to live with.''

He took her hand. "You are far too beautiful to be unbearable, my dear. We'll work this out, I have no doubt."

She had plenty of doubts but didn't voice them. "Let's hope so." Extricating her hand from Butrus's hold, she got to her feet. "I think I shall go to my suite and rest, after all."

"Excellent idea," he commended her. "This has been a difficult day for you."

She looked away. "More than you know." Almost getting killed had a way of sharpening one's thoughts, she had discovered. She wondered if Butrus had any idea of the direction hers were heading in. She would petition her father to release her from the engagement when she returned to the palace.

She had thought she was prepared to marry Butrus, but his persistent refusal to understand her filled her with misgivings. More worrying still was his involvement with men she was sure were criminals. Nargis had heard that the Americans were linked with a crime syndicate in that country and had reported that another servant had overheard them plotting. Although Nadia didn't encourage Nargis to relay gossip, this time she had listened with alarm. Why was Butrus entertaining such men? His evasiveness had only added to her unease. She was sure her father didn't know or approve.

"I'll see you at dinner," Butrus said.

She hesitated, reluctant to sit at the same table as his guests. "Will you forgive me if I don't join you tonight? As you say, it has been a difficult day. I'll have something brought to my room."

Butrus seemed almost relieved by her decision. "It's probably wise. Rest well, little one. I'll see you tomorrow."

As she made her way to her suite, she found herself wondering how Gage would choose to spend the evening.

The object of her thoughts had retired to his suite, citing his need to prepare for his departure the next day. In truth he felt as if he had gone several championship rounds in the boxing ring. The last thing he felt up to was sitting cross-legged on a divan for hours, drinking coffee and making polite conversation with Dabir and his guests—when he would have preferred to get his hands around the man's throat.

Why was he so antagonistic toward Dabir? In the intelligence field, Gage had dealt with all kinds of people, good and bad. Where Dabir was concerned, all he had were suspicions. Not enough to feel so violently inclined toward him.

Gage suspected the real reason for his antagonism, and its name was Nadia Kamal. He was starting to hate, really hate, the thought of her marrying a man like Dabir, sharing his bed, bearing his children, when the man didn't deserve to breathe the same air she did.

Looking down at his hands, Gage saw they were tightly clenched and made an effort to unclench them. Dabir wasn't worth the expenditure of so much energy. There was a better solution. Find proof that he was the traitor in the Kamal ranks and solve both his problems at once. Sheik Ahmed would hardly want his daughter to marry a traitor.

After he finished packing, Gage had a servant bring a tray of cheese, fruit and pastries, as well as a jug of chilled water to his room so he could graze at his leisure. Afterward he spent a long time standing under the steaming spray of a shower, letting the hot water unknot his aching muscles.

"Nice set of bruises, Weston," he told his reflection. Tomorrow he was going to be an interesting shade of black and blue from neck to hip. He had just finished zipping up a pair of chinos but was still bare-chested, when his cell phone rang.

He slung a towel around his shoulders and picked up the phone, flipping it open in the same movement. "Dani here," came the unceremonious greeting.

"Darlin', you've no idea how good it is to hear your voice," he told her. "How's your dear father?"

It was their agreed code for "Do you have any information for me?"

"He's not at all well," she said, sounding cheerful for someone with such news.

No news yet, Gage interpreted. "Is he still in the hospital?" he asked.

"I'm afraid so. He's in intensive care."

Intensive care meant Dani was still investigating and would report back as soon as she had more news.

Disappointment swamped Gage. He had hoped Dani would be able to link at least one of Dabir's recent arrivals to the Brothers of Darkness. "At least your father's in good hands," he said, trying not to communicate his disappointment.

Dani heard it, anyway. "I'm sorry not to have better news."

"Not your fault. How are your brothers holding up?"

Dani had no brothers. She would know that Gage was asking after the organization. "Quiet for the time being, thank goodness. I thought one of them was in those holiday snapshots you sent me yesterday."

Gage felt his tension increase. "And was he?"

"No, he only reminded me of my brother. I'll show it around and see if the rest of the family sees the resemblance."

"Good girl." Dani was telling him she wouldn't rest until she had identified all the men in the photos Gage had e-mailed to her.

"How are things at your end?"

"I'm living the diplomatic high life, rubbing shoulders with royalty." Almost getting killed, he was tempted to add but didn't. No sense alarming Dani when there was nothing she could do. "I'm returning to the embassy tomorrow," he finished.

"I thought you were staying for another few days."

"Let's say I wore out my welcome."

Her musical laugh lifted his spirits. "Next time keep your roving eye to yourself."

Dani was closer to the truth than she knew, he thought as

he ended the call. Shoving his open suitcase to one side, he threw himself onto the four-poster and linked his hands behind his head. Was Gage being asked to leave because Dabir suspected his real mission, or because he didn't want Gage anywhere near his bride-to-be?

If Dabir knew who he was, Gage was sure he wouldn't have been allowed to leave the man's office alive. That left Nadia. Had the lawyer somehow found out about the kiss they'd exchanged last night and sabotaged the car to get Gage out of the way? It would explain Dabir's shock at hearing that his plan had almost killed Nadia, as well.

Gage wondered if he should have told Dani the truth. If anything happened to him, she would know his demise was the result of foul play.

And do what? Come racing to Tamir to avenge him? Forget it, he instructed himself. Allowing Dani to do research for him was one thing. Involving her in the dangerous side of his work was another.

He hadn't wanted her to be involved in any of it, but she had insisted after overhearing him and Conrad planning a mission together. With her contacts in the rock-music scene all over the world, some with dubious connections of their own, she had proved more adept at ferreting out information than Gage liked. Since he hadn't been able to stop her from getting involved, he had tried to keep her out of anything remotely risky, starting with limiting the people who knew she had anything to do with him.

Nadia knew, he thought, sitting up with a jolt. What sort of fool was he, telling her about Dani's role in his life, when the princess herself was still a suspect? Putting himself in danger because he was attracted to Nadia was one thing, but if he had endangered Dani because he couldn't control his hormones, he would never forgive himself.

Chapter 12

He jolted awake to find the room lit only by the spill of moonlight from the window. Some nightmare, he thought, rolling to his feet in a swift movement that brought a stab of pain. His ribs felt as if they'd been used as a trampoline.

Snapping on a light, he poured himself a glass of the now-tepid water at his bedside and sat on the edge of the bed to drink it. In the nightmare he'd been riding a magnificent filly that had bolted toward the edge of a cliff, jerking awake as the horse gathered herself and leaped into the void.

No need to wonder where that dream came from, he thought. The runaway horse had been his mind's way of dealing with the runaway car. Then he remembered reading that in some schools of dream theory, runaway horses were also powerful sexual symbols.

"That's what you are, frustrated," he told himself, getting up and peering in the dresser mirror to finger a bruise blossoming on his cheek. Time he wrapped up this mission and headed home to Penwyck, where he could find a nice woman of his own kind, a woman who wasn't promised to a lowlife like Butrus Dabir.

The thought was oddly unsatisfying, not because Gage didn't have his pick of women back home. One of the advantages of being a duke, even if you didn't use the title, was its attractiveness to the fairer sex. In Gage's experience, half the women he knew would kill to be able to call themselves a duchess.

One or two of them he liked enough to imagine bestowing the title on them.

He wasn't exactly in his dotage, but he wanted to have children while he was still young enough to keep up with them. So why hadn't he done anything about it?

Because liking a woman wasn't enough, he thought, repressing a sigh. He was an idealist, who wanted the whole brass band and fireworks of being in love. He wanted to put stars in his woman's eyes and feel them in his own. To make vows about "till death do us part" and mean them with all his heart. He was probably setting himself up for a lonely future, but he couldn't change how he felt, and didn't really want to.

Restless and uncomfortable, he began to wish he'd taken the princess's advice and consulted her doctor, after all. She could have prescribed a painkiller and maybe something to help him sleep. It was too late now. He didn't have as much as an aspirin in his luggage, and he was so wide awake he felt like jumping out of his skin.

It was the aftereffect of the brush with death, he knew. Going back to sleep didn't appeal after coming as close as he had to never waking up at all. So why try? He reached into the suitcase and put on the first shirt he grabbed, tucking it into his jeans with decisive movements. He thrust his wallet into his back pocket, pulled a pair of ripple-soled moccasins on his bare feet and he was ready, although he couldn't have said for what.

He prowled to the door of the suite and listened, hearing the restive stirring of the guard posted in the hallway. He would have to use the other exit. Luckily the terrace off his living room was only a dozen feet off the ground, with lawn underneath. He waited but saw no sign of another guard, so he climbed over the balustrade and jumped.

He swore aloud as the landing made his bruises sing a song of pain. Instantly he melted into the shadow of the building and waited, but no challenge came. He was free to walk off some of his restless energy.

The direction was decided for him when he saw another figure gliding along the moonlit path leading to the swan lake. Recognizing the figure, he felt a grin play across his features. So he wasn't the only one being kept awake by their near miss.

He tracked her silently, in no hurry. Once, she stopped to listen, looking around as if sensing his presence. By the time she turned in his direction, he had become one with the bushes beside the path. He saw her shrug and continue on. He counted a couple of heartbeats before following.

It came to him that she could have her own reason for being out here. He would feel like a complete fool if she was meeting someone else, or was on some errand for her fiancé.

She had almost reached the filigreed metal pavilion when she spun around. "Who's there? I know someone's following me. Show yourself before I scream for help."

Gage stepped into a pool of moonlight and held up his hands. "No need to scream, Princess. Not that anyone would hear you from here. But it's only me, your faithful stunt driver."

She clutched a hand to her chest. "Gage, you scared me out of my wits."

She sounded remarkably in possession of them, he thought. He had heard that the princess had been schooled in self-defense and wouldn't have been surprised if she had decided to get in some practice on him. She looked more than capable.

"I didn't mean to frighten you," he said, lowering his hands.

"And I'm not usually so nervous. I'm still feeling jumpy, after what happened."

He moved closer. In the moonlight, the contours of her

face were outlined like the lines of a classic sculpture. She was dressed in a long, lemon-colored robe that rustled with her movements. Moonlight reflected off the gold embroidery at her throat, wrists and hem. She swayed a little in the light breeze, as a swan called to its mate in the reeds at the water's edge.

Without conscious intention, he put an arm around the princess's shoulder and urged her into the shelter of the pavilion. She felt fragile but strong, as if she possessed an inner core of steel. Candle lanterns and matches stood ready on a side table. He crossed to them and lit a couple, hanging them from brackets on the pavilion walls. Soon the dancing flames filled the structure with soft golden light.

Nadia had seated herself on one of the velvet-covered divans that edged the pavilion. She leaned back. "I couldn't sleep."

He resisted the temptation to sit beside her and took a seat opposite. "Me, neither. Rough day, huh?"

She opened her eyes and nodded. "Not the sort I'd care to repeat. I told Butrus you thought the car had been sabotaged."

"Let me guess—he didn't believe it. What other explanation did he suggest?"

"None. He was more concerned that I was in the car with you."

"Were you? Concerned, I mean?"

She pulled some cushions toward her and arranged them as an armrest. "I shouldn't have agreed to ride with you."

"Because of the danger?"

She dropped sooty lashes over her night-dark eyes. "Certainly because of the danger." Suddenly she lifted her head and looked directly at him. "You are the most dangerous man I have ever met, Gage."

He found the statement curiously encouraging. If she had known who he really was, she would never have risked such a betraying admission. "Most men would take that as a compliment," he said.

"It wasn't meant as one."

"I don't mean to frighten you," he said.

"You don't, not in the usual way. But you upset many of my beliefs and customs. Tamir society is orderly, predictable."

"And I'm not," he guessed.

"Not in the least. You remind me of Gordon."

Gage wished he knew whether that was good or bad. "Who is Gordon?"

"Was," she corrected gently. "Like you, he was English."

In the sudden softening of her tone, he heard what she wasn't saying. "And you were in love with him."

Without the intimacy of the flickering lanterns keeping the balmy night at bay, and the fact that they had nearly died together this day, Gage doubted she would have continued. Now she nodded. "He was a man of great talent and sensitivity. We met while I was out painting and arranged further meetings without anyone knowing what was really going on. As far as anyone knew, he was teaching art to me and my sisters. They helped me to keep our secret."

Gage found his insides clenching involuntarily as he imagined what this Gordon might have taught Nadia. He reminded himself she was speaking in the past tense. "What happened to him?"

"One day my father caught us together in my studio and ordered Gordon to leave Tamir. I heard no more of him until I saw a television news report that a foreign visitor had drowned while swimming off a treacherous stretch of our coast. Even before they identified Gordon, I knew it was him."

"You think he killed himself?"

She shook her head. "I think he was so distraught over being forced to leave that he took less care than he should, and drowned as a result."

"But you blame yourself."

She turned brimming eyes to him. "Why shouldn't I? Had we never met, he might still be alive today."

Again Gage was thinking of himself. "I wonder if he

would agree with you. You know what they say about it
being better to have loved and lost, than never to have loved
at all?''

She drew her knees up and wrapped her arms around them,
the robe pooling over her slippered feet. ''I've tried to tell
myself that, but my heart doesn't agree. Although seven years
have passed and the pain has receded, the guilt lingers. I
don't expect you to understand.''

''Why shouldn't I?'' Gage asked, wounded that she should
credit him with so little feeling. ''I know how it feels to lose
someone you care about and to feel responsible.''

She regarded him with renewed interest. ''Someone you
loved?''

''Not in the same way you loved Gordon. I lost my friend
and partner, Conrad Drake. We were closer than brothers.''

He watched her carefully, but she gave no sign that the
name meant anything to her, other than as someone Gage
had cared about. Her response strengthened his conviction
that she was unaware of Dabir's true nature. Gage knew he
needed to believe in her innocence, but right now, he couldn't
make himself believe anything else.

Her eyes were huge with empathy. ''I have two brothers.
Losing either of them would be like losing a part of myself.
Why do you feel responsible for Conrad's death?''

''He got into some trouble in America. I wasn't there to
help him.''

The harshness he couldn't screen out of his tone brought
Nadia to her feet. She crossed to his side, the aura of her
distinctive perfume fogging his senses. ''How long ago did
you lose your brother-of-the-heart?''

''A few months ago.''

She touched his arm. The lightest of caresses, meant to
communicate her understanding of his loss. Instead, he felt a
sense of arousal that only made him feel worse.

''Not enough time for the grieving to stop,'' she said.

He placed his hand over hers. ''Does it ever stop?''

''Perhaps not, but it becomes bearable with time.''

''For you, too?''

She nodded. "At one time I thought I would never feel whole again. Now I do. We must accept the will of the Almighty and go on."

"Conrad would have agreed with you. He was a great fatalist."

"And you?"

"I'm with Dylan Thomas when it comes to raging against the dying of the light."

"So you don't see yourself going gently?"

He gave a sharp laugh. He might have known she would recognize the quote. "Hell, no. When the time comes, I'll have to be dragged kicking and screaming every step of the way."

Her fingers curled around his, her no-nonsense artist's fingernails teasing his palm. "Now I understand why you fought so hard for our lives today. I haven't had the chance to thank you properly."

Before he knew it, she had bent down and found his mouth. The kiss should have been a thank-you, sisterly and chaste, but he couldn't help himself. He had to have more.

He got to his feet and wrapped his arms around her, putting into the kiss all his love of life and thankfulness that he had been able to preserve hers for her. And for him.

Nadia felt her head spin as Gage deepened the kiss. What on earth had possessed her to kiss him, when there were far more suitable ways she could have shown her appreciation? She had known she was playing with fire the moment she crossed the pavilion to his side. Had she hoped he would take control of the situation and give her what she craved in her most secret heart?

This.

The night, the stars, the call of the swans, all combined to create the most magical backdrop she could possibly imagine for a kiss. Held in Gage's strong arms, she felt at once peaceful and caught up in the most exquisite turmoil. How could she feel both at once? Somehow he made it possible.

His lips roved over her face, her eyelids, her forehead, tasting every inch of her as if he could never get enough. As

his questing mouth returned to hers, fire tore through her, the
flames consuming what was left of her reticence. They had
nearly died today. But for Gage's skill and fast thinking, she
wouldn't have the choice of whether to kiss him or not. She
wasn't sure she had the choice now.

Her senses swam and she let her head drop back. He trailed
a line of kisses over her exposed throat, his tongue gently
lapping at the fast-beating pulse and sending it into orbit.

"Oh, Gage," she breathed, panting with the exhilaration
he made her feel.

"Am I going too fast for you?" he asked. "Should I
stop?"

She almost panicked, fearing that all the unbridled emotion
was on her side—until she saw the answering fire in his eyes.
"Please don't stop. I couldn't bear it, not now."

He threaded his fingers through her hair. "I don't think I
could, either." He cradled the back of her head in his palm,
his gaze clouding. "This wasn't why I followed you here."

"Does it matter?"

"It matters to me. I have strong principles against moving
in on another man's woman."

Her heart raced in instant objection. Was he going to aban-
don her, after all, in the name of principle? "You're wrong,"
she said huskily. "I may be engaged to Butrus, but I don't
belong to him."

"Engaged will do," he said unsteadily, and moved as if
to release her.

She clung to him. "You don't understand. The marriage
is my father's wish. I agreed to it to please him. Today I
realized I can't go through with it. I intend to tell my father."

Gage lifted her hand and grazed her knuckles with his
teeth, sending shivers of sensation rebounding through her.
"Sheik Ahmed won't like that."

"Neither will Butrus, but they'll have to accept my decision."

"Won't they ship you off to a harem, or something?"

"I don't care. It would be better than marrying a man I
don't tr…love."

She saw Gage's interest sharpen. "You were going to say you don't trust Butrus, weren't you?"

She looked away, but he caught her chin and gently turned her to face him. The compassion and caring she saw in his gaze was almost her undoing. "Yes," she whispered.

He slid his thumb along the line of her jaw. "Why not?"

It was hard to think straight when he did that. She made the effort. "According to Nargis, those men who arrived to meet with Butrus are American criminals. He won't say why they're here or what connection he has with them. This...this isn't the first time he's had dealings with such people. I'm afraid he may be involved in something bad. He may be betraying Tamir."

"He was keen enough to get us out of the way before the meeting began," Gage added thoughtfully. "In fact, we were nearly put out of the way permanently."

"Oh, Gage." Her throat closed as she remembered how close they had come. She slid her hands around his back. He felt so strong, so alive. The steady beat of his heart reaching her through her robe was like a celebration of life. Tremors rippled through her and she never wanted to let go.

"Have you told anyone your suspicions?" he asked.

"How can I? My father would think I was trying to discredit Butrus as a suitable husband."

"And are you?"

"That would go against all I have been taught about my duty," she said, drawing herself up. "I would rather face my father's wrath directly than try to undermine his confidence in Butrus without just cause."

Gage's hold tightened. "I'm sorry for suggesting it. I needed to know."

"Why?"

He debated how much he could safely tell her. "Some of us in the...diplomatic corps suspect Dabir, as you do. We would like to find proof of any illicit activities on his part before he harms your country's interests." It was the truth, as far as it went.

He saw her lovely eyes narrow. "I thought there must be more to you than meets the eye. Are you some kind of spy?"

"Sure," he said in a low-pitched Scottish brogue. "The name's Weston, Gage Weston."

She took a swipe at him. "Be serious. Someone tried to kill you today. Could it be because of your interest in Butrus?"

"Possibly."

"Gage, you must stop this before you are hurt or killed. Tell the police about your suspicions and let them handle this."

"Doesn't Dabir serve as your minister of police?"

She understood immediately.

He felt a shiver take her and held her closer. "Don't be frightened, Princess. Whatever can be done is being done. As long as you're not involved, you're safe." Dabir wasn't going to risk harming the person who could bring him ultimate power. His horror at today's near miss was proof enough.

Gage's use of her title had been mocking before. Now he said it like a caress, and her blood heated to fever pitch in response. "I don't think I want to be safe," she said on a heavy exhalation of breath.

"What do you want?"

She shuddered again. In her society what women wanted was rarely a consideration. Being expected to articulate her needs so boldly filled her with confusion, but she saw that Gage really wanted to know.

"I want you," she said in a voice barely above a whisper, knowing she had never spoken more truly in her life.

"Are you sure?"

The churning inside her made her wonder, but she said firmly, "I've never been more sure of anything."

When he didn't seem shocked, she became bolder. "What do *you* want, Gage?"

He took so long answering that she wondered if she had miscalculated. At last he said unsteadily, "You know I want you."

She was heartened to see that he was as uncertain about

this as she was, although she suspected their reasons were very different. For all her thirty-five years, she was still hopelessly inexperienced. Her only taste of seduction had been with Gordon, and theirs had been such a whirlwind affair that she wondered now if the forbidden nature of the liaison had made it seem more intense than it really was. These days she had difficulty remembering what he had looked like.

She would never feel that way about Gage. Every sharply delineated line of his ruggedly handsome features was imprinted on her mind. Ten years from now she'd be able to paint him from memory and no one would doubt the subject's identity.

She knew well the source of Gage's uncertainty. Her royal status made many people feel uncomfortable around her. Normally she did all she could to make them feel at ease. Now she wished desperately that she could cast aside her crown for this one night and come to him as an ordinary woman.

"I know this isn't easy…" she began hesitantly.

Questions sprang to his eyes. "What do you mean?"

"Can't you try to forget that I'm a princess? Treat me as you would any woman. It's what I want, honestly."

She was puzzled by the laughter infusing his expression. She drew herself up angrily. "I don't see what's so funny."

He caught her hands in one of his and lifted them to his mouth, kissing her fingers. "I'm not laughing at you," he assured her.

"Then what?"

"You think I'm worried because you're royalty?"

"It has a way of coming between me and other people."

"Not this time." His dark warm gaze lent weight to the assurance. "If you must know, I was worried about…consequences."

She felt her cheeks heat and was grateful for the shadows cast by the flickering lanterns, shielding her embarrassment. "I see." She couldn't keep the defeat out of her voice. How could he satisfy the aching need vibrating between them without the risk of pregnancy?

He couldn't, and she wasn't so much of a rebel that she would take such a risk. When she had a child, it would be loved and wanted and welcome in the world, not conceived in moonlight with a man she might never see again.

She half turned away, a thick knot of despair filling her. "I'd better return to the house."

He caught her by the shoulders and spun her back. "I have some protection with me in my wallet, but I don't want you getting the wrong idea."

"I'm sure it's all right," she said stiffly. What was the matter with her? A moment ago she'd been plunged into despair because she thought he couldn't make love to her. Now she knew he could, she was as nervous as a serving girl about to cope with her first royal banquet.

Watching her, Gage wondered if he was going crazy. He wanted to make love to Nadia more than he had ever wanted anything. Yet something held him back. Despite her belief, his reluctance had nothing to do with her royal status. She didn't know it, but his blood was every bit as blue as hers.

It was Nadia herself who terrified him. She was younger in experience than her years. He gathered she'd only known one man in her life, and he wasn't too sure how far that had gone. She was bound to have dreams of what love should be like. Gage hated the thought of disappointing her.

He touched her cheek. How flawless her skin was. How dark and compelling her eyes. Surely if he shared with her all that was inside him, it would be enough. It had to be. He didn't know how to give more than all he had.

Chapter 13

Not giving himself any more time to think, to doubt, he swept her up into his arms. She lay as lightly as thistledown, laughing as she linked her hands around his neck. "There's no need to carry me, Gage."

He smiled down at her lovely face. "You wouldn't deny a man who nearly died today this simple pleasure, would you?"

"When you put it that way..."

For pure enjoyment, he swirled her around the pavilion, delighting in the way the moonlight kissed her raven hair with silver and turned her skin to silk. One jeweled slipper went tumbling to the floor. She kicked the other off and wiggled her bare toes, which were painted an opalescent pink. "This feels amazing."

"It does, doesn't it?" He kissed her gently and placed her on the divan, gathering cushions to support her head. His heart thudded with anticipation.

Lying against the cushions, she looked every inch a fairy-tale princess, her diffident expression part of her charm. He reminded himself to take things slowly, give her time to adjust to this new experience, to him.

She smelled of jasmine, roses and something else, a faintly musky scent that tantalized his senses, challenged his self-control.

Nadia had never before been so conscious of a man's appraisal. In her society it simply wasn't done for a man to gaze so openly at a woman. Husbands and wives might do so in the privacy of their boudoir, but in the open air and the moonlight, far from the forbidding eyes of a chaperon, it was unthinkable.

She knew she should feel ashamed for letting Gage look his fill, for encouraging his attention by stretching her arms over her head so that the swell of her breasts was outlined by her yellow robe.

Instead, she felt womanly and alive, desirable and wanton, cherished and beautiful all at the same time. She told herself she had no need to be nervous. She had invited this and she wanted him with all her heart. She knew he would be careful.

Knowing that didn't stop the nerves from leaping inside her, constricting her breathing and making her heart pound. Anyone would think this was her first time. In a sense, it was. She and Gordon had had so little time to explore, to touch, to discover each other. Of necessity, their lovemaking had been quick and furtive, not at all satisfying because of the fear of being found out. Why didn't she feel that fear now?

Because the man was Gage. How could she be afraid of anything when he was strong enough and sure enough for both of them?

Keeping one leg on the floor for balance, he knelt beside her on the divan and leaned over her. The heady male scent of him washed over her as his mouth found hers.

This kiss was different. Deeper, more giving but more demanding. He teased her lips apart, sending spirals of need eddying through her as he explored with tongue and teeth, tasting, nipping, enticing, until she felt drugged by desire.

The night air whispered against her legs as he slid her robe up her body. She felt herself go rigid. Years of conditioning urged her to deny him such intimacy, to cover herself and escape.

"It's all right, my princess, I won't hurt you," he said softly, feeling the tension coiling through her. "I won't do anything you don't want me to do."

She summoned the strength to allow his touch and was glad when she heard him murmur, "Beautiful, so beautiful." She began to relax, to open to him.

Suddenly his muttered oath made her eyes widen. He was seeing her bruises from today's helter-skelter ride, bending his head to kiss each one in turn. "My poor princess."

She didn't feel like a poor princess. She felt like a queen as he kissed each faint blemish. She was almost glad they were there, so delightful were his ministrations. When he returned to her mouth, she gave a sigh of pure satisfaction.

He seemed to have all the time in the world, losing himself in her kiss as if that alone could satisfy him. She fervently hoped not, because she could feel building within herself such a volcano of need that she could burst into flame at the slightest spark.

His clever hands were everywhere, stroking, teasing, as if he was blind and exploring her by touch alone. Each gentle caress brought new shivers of pleasure until she was a mass of them, floating, dreaming, drifting, wanting.

Over and over he murmured her name. Not her title this time, but her name, as if it was the most beautiful name imaginable. She found herself repeating his name until the fragrant night air sang with the wonderful sound of it.

More words poured from him, reassurances, although she needed none now. For the first time in her life she understood why such words were called sweet nothings. They meant nothing of consequence, but they were so very sweet.

When her English became insufficient for the words she wanted to say to him, she used beautiful, poetic Arabic, calling him the sheik of her heart and other ancient endearments.

She wasn't sure he understood all the words, but his kisses and caresses told her he understood what she meant.

Touch became their common language, and she began to wonder how she had communicated without it for so long.

When Gage undid the fastenings of her robe and let it fall away, she felt no fear or shame, only intense pleasure at being so blatantly appreciated. His mouth became more eager to explore, and she arched beneath him, barely able to stop herself from crying out for sheer joy. He undressed her lovingly and she helped him, eager to remove all barriers between them.

Feeling sublimely desirable, she pulled his shirt out of the waistband of his pants, her fingers busy on the buttons, wanting to look and touch her fill of him, too. When she saw the mottled stripe the seat belt had seared across his chest, she drew a gasp of dismay. She skimmed her fingers over the mark. "Does it hurt very much?"

"The bruise? No. This waiting? Pure agony."

He reared back long enough to strip off the shirt and toss it to one side. His remaining clothes followed, and she had her wish. Only one barrier remained.

He was not eager to cross it, taking endless time to bestow more of the delicious kisses that pushed her to the brink of endurance, on her mouth, her breasts, even those most secret places that made the color flood her cheeks even as she readied herself to receive him.

She was aware that he retrieved something from his pants pocket and heard his labored breathing as he put on the protection he had assured her he would use. In the next moment passion tore through her like fire. Her breathing sounded loud in the night air, but she didn't try to hold back. She was where she most wanted to be, and nothing else mattered. It came to her that Gage was awfully skilled at this, knowing exactly where to touch, to kiss, to arouse. She decided not to care. His skill was his gift to her, and her very inexperience was the offering she gave him in return, allowing him the pleasure of showing her how wonderful it could be between a man and a woman.

Higher, higher, he took her until she felt as if she had left the earth and was floating in the night air, the magic carpet of her culture's mythology becoming real as she was carried aloft.

How could anything feel more wonderful than this?

Amazingly it was possible, she discovered as Gage eased himself over her. He came to her gently, so gently that she wanted to beg him to be strong, to assure him she was strong, too. He made her strong, even as he weakened her with passion. The heat, the momentary pain that made her gasp with shock was nothing compared to what waited beyond the pain.

She could hardly believe one could experience such pleasure and live.

She wasn't at all sure she had lived until Gage's mouth on hers told her so. His heart pounded in time with hers, and his hand felt damp as he stroked her hair, holding her through the tremors rocking her.

Holding her, stroking her hair away from her forehead, Gage could hardly believe what had just happened. Because of who she was, he had known she wouldn't have much experience and had driven himself nearly insane trying to pace himself to her needs. But he had never expected to be her first. The privilege both humbled and exalted him beyond belief. Just as she was, she was a man's dream, but this... He felt his eyes swim with the wonder of it.

The lantern light danced over her body, making him want to touch her again, take her to heights beyond her wildest dreams. Too soon, he cautioned himself. Give her time to recover.

But this time she was the one exploring with hands and mouth, pulling his head down to her and molding herself against him until his restraint became ragged and his breathing shallow.

"Not yet, you need time," he murmured, pulling away from her mouth.

She shook her head, her hair making a soft halo around her face. "There is no time, not for us. This night may be all we have."

A pang gripped him. She was right. They may never have more than this precious moment in the moonlight. He wanted more, and was astonished at the intensity of his desire. Afraid it might make him savage when she deserved better, he forced himself to be careful, although he wanted to plunge into her sweet depths and carry her to heights undreamed of in her imagination.

In the end the carrying was mutual. Ancient instincts guided her to touch him and move with him until he was no longer sure who was teaching whom, the experience melding into a feast of pleasurable sensation until they were both utterly spent.

The candles had sputtered low by the time he brought her back to earth, or she brought him. Or both. He only knew breathing had never been such an effort, and his heart felt as if it would beat right out of his chest. But she looked happy. Satisfied, like a cat curled into itself after a surfeit of cream.

He had given her that.

She had given him so much more. He had never known it could feel like this, be like this. How could he leave her, now that he knew what they could be to one another?

He dropped butterfly kisses on her brow. Her eyes fluttered open and her lips curved into a smile. "Wonderful," she said dreamily.

He kissed her open mouth, tasting her. "You're wonderful, my princess."

She smiled teasingly. "More wonderful than any woman you've ever known?"

He affected an innocent look. "There has been no other woman like you." True enough. None like her.

She touched a finger to his lips. "I believe you."

He closed his lips around it, drawing the finger into his mouth, taking delight in her gasp of response. When she pulled away, he said, "You surprised me tonight."

"In what way?"

"I thought Tamiri princesses led sheltered lives."

"We do."

"Then who do I thank for your education?"

She smiled, taking his meaning, and touched the back of her hand to his cheek. "You."

"Not—" what was the name of her first love? "—not Gordon?"

"You should know better by now."

He did. Whatever had passed between her and the other man, they had never really made love. Gage decided not to take too much satisfaction in his own part in her awakening. Pride was a sin even in his culture. Better to humbly appreciate the gift she had given him.

Trouble was, he didn't feel humble. He felt like a giant killer, and he knew she was the reason. "You're bad for me," he murmured.

Her dark brows came together in an expression of concern. "Was I such a disappointment?"

"The very opposite. I've never known a woman like you. You make me feel more of a man than is good for me."

She sat up, shaping herself to the curve of his arm. "I'm not sure I understand the problem."

"The problem is, I have to leave tomorrow. Today," he amended, noticing for the first time the faint fingers of dawn creeping across the sky. "How can I leave you now?"

"If it is in our stars to be together, we will be together. For now, we will both do what we must."

"And that makes you happy?"

She shook her head, resting it against his shoulder so that her silken hair brushed his chest. Her face was hidden from him, but he heard the thickening in her voice. "What would make me happy would be to go with you, but we both know I cannot."

"When will I see you again?"

"At the palace, when you become again Gage Weston, diplomatic attaché."

"By then you'll be Her Royal Highness, Princess Nadia."
The untouchable princess. How could he stand it?

"We can't change who we are, Gage."

He could and did. He wondered what she would think if
he revealed his true identity.... But too many other lives were
involved. He couldn't put them at risk to satisfy his own
desires. "You could run away with me." Even as he said it,
he knew it wasn't an option.

She knew it, too. "I would be turning my back on my
family and my country, never welcome here again."

"That's why I would never ask it of you. But I can dream,
can't I?"

"As can I," she said. "You gave me a wonderful dream
tonight, Gage. Let's not tarnish it with regret for what we
can't have."

He tightened his hold on her and rained kisses on her up-
turned face. "Whatever I may feel about tonight," he assured
her, "it will never be regret."

That came later, as he was stowing the last of his belongings in his suitcase. He picked up the crumpled shirt that had
spent the better part of last night on the floor of the pavilion.
Unable to stop himself, he lifted it to his face, smelling her
jasmine perfume in the folds. His heartbeat quickened and he
let the shirt drop, closing the suitcase and wishing he could
do the same with the memories.

He hoped Nadia had been able to return to her suite safely.
Having more experience of getting in and out of places un-
detected, he'd had no trouble climbing the balcony and letting himself into the room. As far as the guard outside his
door was aware, Gage had never left.

Nadia had told him that she had slipped away by pretending to go to the kitchen for a cool drink. Her sleepy servants
hadn't protested when she assured them she could manage.
The rest had been easy. But if any of them, that nosy Nargis,
for instance, had monitored how long she was away, she
might have some explaining to do.

Nadia was a strong independent woman, Gage reminded himself. Strong enough to be suspicious of Butrus Dabir. As his parting gift to her, Gage had asked her not to share her suspicions with anyone else. She hadn't understood at first, and he'd had to remind her that Dabir was the most likely suspect behind the sabotage of the car.

"Why would he do that?" she had asked.

"Someone may have reported our first kiss."

"He would kill you for that?" Nadia's tone had revealed that she knew as well as Gage did that Dabir was capable of such an action. If he suspected that Gage had made love to Nadia, who knew what would happen.

The thought that he had put her in danger to satisfy his own needs made Gage furious with himself. No matter how extreme the temptation, he should have kept her at arm's length for her sake and his, until he had sorted out this whole mess. Once Dabir was safely behind bars, then maybe Gage could justify getting involved with Nadia.

It was too late now. He was already involved with her. He not only had to find enough evidence to convict Dabir, he had to protect Nadia, as well. He fought the impulse to barge into her suite and take her away to safety right now. That was one sure way to get both of them killed.

As long as Dabir thought she knew nothing, she was safe. Gage had to hang on to that and start working with his head, instead of his heart. Not easy when he kept thinking of her in his arms, remembering the heaven they'd shared.

A sudden flash of the bruises marring her perfect body had his hands clenching into fists. Dabir would pay for every one of them, Gage promised himself. Not today, but as soon as Gage could arrange it.

Chapter 14

Three days later Gage was still no closer to bringing Dabir to account. He'd learned little more from Dani about his host's American visitors and established no definite links to the Brothers of Darkness.

He looked at a message lying on the desk he ostensibly occupied at the British Embassy. He had underlined the three words: "Brake lines cut." The note was signed Hamad, the name of the foreman of the road-construction gang.

No news there, Gage thought, feeling his mouth twist into a grim smile. Hamad hadn't found any clues as to who the perpetrator was, but then Gage would have been surprised if he had. Dabir was proving annoyingly efficient at covering his tracks.

Arranging to retrieve the car and smoothing things over with the rental agency had taken time Gage would have preferred to use to further his mission. When he reported back to King Marcus, the king had sounded frustrated at the lack of progress. That made two of them, Gage thought. As much as Marcus wanted the traitor in the Kamal household caught,

Gage wanted Conrad's killer more. Neither of them looked as if they'd get satisfaction anytime soon.

He looked up as his godfather, Sir Brian Theodore, walked into the office. At sixty the British ambassador was an imposing figure, still strikingly good-looking, with a lion's mane of black hair, silvering at the temples.

From Gage's desk the ambassador picked up a bullet between thumb and forefinger, and examined it before returning it to Gage's desk. "Still contributing to international relations, I see," he said in his clipped British accent.

Gage fitted the magazine back into the gun he'd just finished cleaning and grinned. "In my own way, Sir Brian. It's good of you to let me use the embassy as my cover."

"Your father would never forgive me if I hadn't." The ambassador's ties to Gage's family went back to before Gage was born. His wife, Lillian, was from Penwyck, and was a cousin of Gage's father. The ambassador frowned. "I don't know what Sheik Ahmed will make of King Marcus hiring you to investigate his family."

"He won't know until it's over. Then I imagine he'll thank King Marcus for uncovering the viper in his nest."

Sir Brian nodded. "You're probably right, provided you can find enough evidence to convict this viper."

Gage had already shared his suspicions with his godfather, who had turned out to be no fan of Dabir's. Sir Brian's greatest concern was that the attorney would gain sufficient power to take over control of Tamir, ruining what Sir Brian called "a perfectly good country" in the process.

Sir Brian saw Gage's gaze flicker to the royal palace framed in the view from the embassy window. "You're not getting personally involved in this case, are you?"

Gage pulled his gaze back with an effort, aware of a strong reluctance to do so. Nadia was home now, behind one of those carefully screened windows. He hadn't been able to see her again before leaving Zabara, and he felt as if some crucial part of himself was missing. "What makes you ask?"

"Lillian noticed it at dinner yesterday, actually. You know

how women pick up on these things. She thinks you're becoming attracted to Nadia Kamal.''

Not by a flicker did Gage let his expression betray him. ''Lillian is a romantic.''

''Then she's wrong about you and the princess?''

Gage saw no point in dissembling. Along with his father, his godfather was one of the few people in the world with whom he could be honest about who he was and what he did. ''She isn't wrong,'' he said heavily.

Sir Brian sat down opposite Gage and steepled his hands on the desk. ''Have you considered that Nadia could be in league with Dabir?''

''I've considered it. She isn't.''

Sir Brian's eyebrows lifted. ''You have evidence?''

''I don't need evidence. I know Nadia.''

''I won't ask how well. Just be careful. Dabir won't give her up easily.'' The ambassador picked up the note from Hamad and frowned. ''You already know how far he's prepared to go to secure his future within the royal family.''

Gage still had the bruises to prove it, as his godfather was well aware. He and Lillian had been horrified when they heard about Gage's near miss. ''I know,'' he said shortly. ''I won't take any unnecessary chances.''

The ambassador stood up. ''It's the necessary ones Lillian and I worry about.''

''Thanks, but there's no need. I know my job.''

''Does King Marcus know how fortunate he is to have you on his side?''

Gage holstered the gun, easing his specially tailored jacket over the top. ''I'm only on his side to catch whoever killed Conrad. Then it's up to Marcus and the sheik to sort out their own politics.''

Sir Brian's mouth softened. ''A lot of people would believe you, but not me. You'll do whatever you can to help secure a lasting peace in this part of the world. Even as a boy, you took it upon yourself to broker agreements between your friends, occasionally cracking heads if that's what the situation required.''

''Are you telling me I haven't changed much?''

''These days you broker more agreements and crack a few less heads. It's called growing up.''

Gage grinned. ''Or an increasing sense of self-preservation.''

Sir Brian sobered. ''Quite possibly. Just don't let your personal feelings get in the way of this mission.''

''About Conrad?''

''About everything.''

His godfather meant Nadia, Gage knew. It was good advice. All Gage had to do was remember to take it.

In her apartment at the royal palace, Nadia curled her feet under her on the divan, watching Samira try on the dress she'd bought for her at the Black Rock Souk. She had felt strange not buying anything for their younger sister, Leila, but then, she had married a Texas oilman, Cade Gallagher, and gone to live in America. It was impractical to exchange small gifts on impulse, the way they had done when Leila lived at the palace. From her sister's letters and phone calls, Nadia knew that Cade would give Leila the moon if he could. What would it be like to be the focus of one man's desires?

She wasn't fooling herself that Gage Weston felt like that toward her. To him, she was forbidden fruit. Now that he had made love to her, he probably wouldn't want to see her again, even if it was possible. It wasn't, of course. Nadia's father would never permit a man like Gage to court his daughter. The sheik would be horrified if he knew what they had already done.

For herself, Nadia had no regrets. Twinges of conscience, yes, but no regrets. The hours she had spent with Gage remained in her mind like a glimpse of paradise. If she never knew such sublime pleasure again in her lifetime, at least she had known it once, and that was more than many women experienced.

Or so she tried to make herself believe. Only, the ache inside her told her that she would give a great deal to know such ecstasy again. To see Gage again. She found her gaze straying to the window, to where she could see the British Embassy in the distance. Was he there now? Was he thinking of her?

Chiding herself for behaving like a lovestruck adolescent when she knew there was no future in it, she forced her thoughts back to reality. "I knew that dress would be perfect for you the moment I saw it," she told Samira, pleased with the way the color emphasized the sparkle in her younger sister's eyes.

Samira twirled in front of the mirror. "I suppose it's too much to hope you bought something gorgeous for yourself."

Nadia hid her smile. "Of course I did."

Samira bounced to her side. "Where is it? What color is it?"

"It's a glorious shade of coral pink."

"Long or short? Formal or casual? Let me see."

Nadia laughed. "I can't because it hasn't been delivered yet. It's a piece of marble I plan to sculpt into a bust of our dear father."

Samira's face fell. "I might have known. Honestly, Nadia, you'll be the only bride in the kingdom to be married with marble dust in your hair."

"Nargis said much the same thing. She thoroughly disapproved of my buying marble, instead of gowns and jewels."

"You did buy some jewelry, though," Samira said. She gestured to where a jewel case sat on Nadia's dresser. "That's new since you came home. Aren't you going to show me what caught your eye?"

Trust Samira to spot the case. "It was a mistake. I mean to send it back."

Samira's keen glance caught the flush of color Nadia was unable to hide. "It was a gift, wasn't it. From Butrus? Surely not from another man." She swirled around the room, chanting, "Nadia has a secret admirer."

"Stop it. I don't have any such thing."

"A lover, then. You *do* have a lover. I can see it in your eyes."

"You're fishing, and I'm not going to tell you anything if you keep needling me."

Samira picked up the jewel case from atop the dresser. Nadia had left it there, intending to return it to Gage. She should have done it by now. Why hadn't she?

Before Nadia could say anything to dissuade her, her sister opened the box. "It's magnificent," Samira said on a sharply indrawn breath. She lifted the tiger necklace from its velvet nest and held it up to the light. "Whoever your admirer is, he must care for you very much to give you such a stunning necklace."

"He saw me try it on in a shop in the souk. He thought he was doing me a favor by buying it for me, not knowing how shocked Father would be." Not to mention Butrus, Nadia thought uncomfortably. She was sure her fiancé had tried to kill Gage because he knew Gage had kissed her. What might happen if he knew about the necklace or the hours Nadia had spent in Gage's arms beside the swan lake didn't bear thinking about.

"Then there is a man involved," Samira concluded. She replaced the necklace in its case, replaced it on the dresser and sat down beside Nadia. "You have to tell me the rest now."

"You're as bad as Nargis when it comes to gossip."

"This isn't gossip. It's my sister's happiness."

Nadia passed a hand over her eyes. "If you really care about my happiness, you won't ask me anymore."

Samira took her hand. "This sounds really serious. What are you going to do?"

Nadia was afraid her expression revealed the truth to Samira, who knew her better than most. "It is serious, and I haven't decided what I'm going to do. Until I do, I'd rather you didn't say anything about this to anyone."

"Of course I won't," her sister said. Her eyes narrowed. "This doesn't have anything to do with why you were nearly killed on the cliff road, does it?"

Nadia clasped her hands together. "It might."

Samira looked shocked. "You don't think Butrus…"

"I don't think anything. Please, we mustn't discuss this anymore." She looked around as if the walls themselves might have ears.

Samira saw the look. "You don't think someone's listening to our private conversations, do you?"

"I don't know anymore. All I know is I can't marry Butrus. I simply don't love him."

"You've never loved him, but you were committed to marrying him. What has happened to change your mind?"

Nadia got up and paced to the windows opening onto a screened balcony from where she could observe the comings and goings in the palace gardens. She knew there was only one figure she hoped to glimpse among the fountains and flower beds, because she had been watching for him since returning from Zabara.

But Gage was nowhere in sight.

She wondered what Samira would say if she knew that Nadia was half in love with the English diplomat. He made her feel things she had never experienced before, made her yearn for a life beyond the palace walls, beyond even Tamir's borders. Like the eagle in her paintings, she had always wanted to stretch her wings and fly. Gage was the first person to make her feel that was possible.

She knew that making love wasn't the same as being in love and hoped she wasn't confusing the two. What he had made her feel was so wonderful it would be easy enough. Since returning to the palace, she had felt different, as if the doors of a new world had been opened for her and there was no going back.

Her conscience should have troubled her, but instead, she

yearned for more of Gage's touch. He was in her thoughts as she lay in her solitary bed at night and when her attendants woke her to a new day. In between, he haunted her dreams.

She couldn't sketch, couldn't paint, could barely manage to eat properly. Already her mother had expressed the hope that her daughter wasn't coming down with something. How long before her father noticed and demanded to know the reason?

Soon she would have to tell him that she couldn't marry Butrus. The sheik's wrath would come down on her head as never before. He might even carry out his threat to exile her to a harem miles from anywhere. After what she had experienced in Gage's arms, she knew she could live with that more readily than with a man she didn't love.

"Why is life so difficult?" she asked Samira. "Leila dreamed of going to America and seeing Hollywood and Rodeo Drive and Texas. It happened for her. You dream of someone so secret you won't even share his name with me. What's wrong with wanting what we don't have?"

At the mention of the mystery man occupying her thoughts, Samira shook her head, her dark hair cascading around her face in a satin curtain, hiding her expression. "There's nothing wrong with dreaming. It's wanting the dreams to turn into reality that causes problems."

"And for that reason, we shouldn't dream?"

Her sister put a hand on her arm. "Nadia, what's the matter? You've always had big dreams, bigger than either Leila or me. But you were always a realist when it came to your life. What happened at Zabara to change you?"

Gage happened. Since she couldn't very well tell Samira so, Nadia gave an enigmatic smile. "Coming close to death has a way of revealing what is important in life." It was the simple truth, perhaps not the whole truth, but enough to satisfy her sister.

Samira nodded thoughtfully. "I think I understand. And I hope you achieve whatever this important thing is. When will you tell father you can't marry Butrus?"

Nadia gave a slight shudder. "I should tell him soon. Mother already suspects that all is not well between Butrus and me, so I may tell her first. She has a way of charming father into seeing things her way, without actually contradicting him."

"The perfect wife. Do you think we'll ever be that perfect?"

Nadia knew she hadn't a hope. She was far too outspoken and independent to let a man think he ran things, while getting her own way through guile. She didn't really think her mother did that. Alima was quite capable of speaking her mind when she thought it was warranted. But she knew her place, something Nadia doubted she ever would. "You might, but not me," she told Samira with a rueful smile.

Nargis chose that moment to bustle in, reminding them that it was time to prepare for dinner. Nadia knew the private moment with her sister was at an end. She didn't dare express her thoughts so openly in front of Nargis. They would be all over the palace in a day. She didn't blame the attendant for taking pleasure in gossip. Nargis had few other joys in life. But Nadia had no wish to be the focus of that gossip. Not when her desires were so new and tender—and so unlikely to be fulfilled.

The ringing of the phone on his desk pulled Gage away from the embassy window. Night was falling and lights were springing on all over the city, turning the royal palace into a fairy castle. Which window was Nadia behind? he wondered. What was she doing now? Probably being fussed over by that dragon lady of a maid. Nargis. And the beautiful twin servants who hardly ever said a word.

He reached for the phone, having to fumble with it before getting a hold of it, so distracted were his thoughts. He made an effort to concentrate. "Weston."

"You sound as if you're a million miles away," came the laughing response.

He felt something inside himself loosen. "Dani, me darlin' girl, how are you?"

"Don't change the subject. What were you thinking about when you picked up the phone?"

"You're much too young to understand."

"Nineteen is hardly young these days, oh, ancient one," she teased. "But I get the message. Butt out of your love life."

"Exactly," he said, cursing inwardly as he realized he'd been neatly trapped into confirming her suspicion. He was glad the embassy phones were secure, the lines being swept regularly for bugs and protected by state-of-the-art encryption systems. It meant he could talk openly to Dani for once. "How's your own love life?"

He imagined her shrug. "You know me, wedded to my music."

And gun-shy when it came to relationships, he knew. Hardly surprising, considering her experience of family life to this point. He wasn't setting much of an example himself, come to that. "No one on the horizon for you yet?" he probed gently. "Not even that drummer with the eye patch?"

To anyone who didn't know Dani as well as Gage did, the hesitation would have been imperceptible. "Nothing I want to talk about yet."

The yet gave him hope. "When you're ready to talk, I'm here," he reminded her.

"Same goes for me," she said. "By your reckoning, I may be just out of the cradle, but I know a thing or two about life."

More than he wanted her to know. "I'm a long way from the cradle and I'm still learning, but thanks for the offer, darlin'. Now tell me, to what do I owe the pleasure of this call?"

He heard papers being shuffled. "I've found out some interesting stuff about that orphanage you told me about, the one where the doctor and the princess hang out together."

"They don't hang out together, at least not in the way you make it sound."

"Gotcha." Dani sounded triumphant. "I knew from the way you spoke about her that the princess was more than a lead in this case to you."

First his godfather, now Dani. Was everybody in the world pairing him with Nadia? He must be losing his touch. "You're imagining things."

"Whatever you say, boss. But she must be affecting your thinking processes. You still haven't asked what I've discovered."

He *was* losing his touch. "What have you discovered?"

"You won't like it."

"Dani…"

She heeded the warning in his voice. "I took the list you e-mailed me of people working at the orphanage and ran it through your computer. One of the women, Sitra Wahabi, rang alarm bells. Her maiden name is Salim."

Gage's mind leaped ahead. "Any relation to Jalil Salim, aka Kevin Weber, confirmed Brothers of Darkness agent?"

"None other than his sweet little sister," Dani supplied.

Gage frowned at the phone. "I didn't know Salim had a sister."

"He kept his family in the background. After he was caught, she must have decided to go into the family business."

Kevin Weber's real name and connection to the Brothers had been established when he was captured in America by Max Ryker Sebastiani, a nephew of King Marcus's, and his bounty-hunter partner, Cara Rivers. Gage remembered the details from reading the files on the case before he came to Tamir.

Disappointment stabbed through him. "So the orphanage does have a connection to the Brothers." He hadn't known how much he wanted the opposite to be true until he felt the bile rise in his throat. Did Nadia know about the connection?

"Unless Sitra is a sweet innocent and you're completely misjudging her."

In Gage's experience, it was unlikely, given the octopus-like spread of the Brothers' influence. The more hotheaded younger members even used the octopus as their secret symbol, which Gage felt was extraordinarily appropriate. "We can't be sure of anything until I can find more evidence," he said.

"Your princess friend may not know about the connection," Dani said, reading his mind. "It doesn't mean she's involved."

Gage's grip on the phone intensified. "It doesn't mean she's innocent, either."

"Until proved guilty at least."

"Yes." Gage let his breath out in a gust. He had to grant Nadia that much. She might not know that the orphanage was a possible safe haven for the Brothers of Darkness.

And she might be in it up to her beautiful neck, along with her fiancé.

"What will you do now?" Dani asked as his silence continued.

He had always been careful to keep his protégé out of the active side of his work. Tracing information for him was one thing. She was damned good with a computer, better than Gage himself. And thanks to the traveling she did with her band, her network of contacts stretched all over the world. But he wasn't about to let her risk her life out in the field. "You know better than to ask. The less you know about my plans, the safer you'll be."

"Hey, take care, man. You're all I've got."

He forced a smile into his voice. "What about Patch, the drummer?"

"Okay, maybe you can be replaced in time. But not easily."

Did Nadia feel the same way? Had Gage already been replaced by an earlier allegiance, one that had motivated her to let him make love to her? Lord, he hated that thought. It

meant that all the time she lay in his arms, she had been
serving a cause he hated with everything in him.

All the sweetness and sublime passion would have been a
lie.

She had shared her doubts about Dabir with him. Did she
genuinely suspect her fiancé, or was that a clever ruse to
throw Gage off the scent?

"You still there?" Dani asked anxiously.

For all her worldly wisdom, Dani was still only nineteen
and had precious few people she could rely on. "I'm always
here for you, me darlin' girl," he said blithely. He had no
intention of sharing his personal heartache with her, although
he suspected she might be way ahead of him this time.

"Anything else you want me to do?" Dani asked.

"You've already done wonders. Now get back to that band
of yours and knock 'em dead in Heidelberg."

"Frankfurt," she corrected good-humoredly. "Our next
gig is in Frankfurt, but I'll be available daytimes if you need
me."

"I'll try not to let my concerns interfere with show business. The show must go on."

The phrase haunted him as they said their goodbyes and
hung up. No matter how he felt about Nadia Kamal, and he
was starting to suspect he felt a lot more than he admitted to
himself, he had a job to do.

He refused to accept that Sitra Wahabi's presence at the
orphanage was coincidence. He had to find out what she was
up to, and what role the orphanage itself played in the Brothers' schemes. If Nadia was implicated, not even his feelings
for her would be allowed to stand in the way of seeing justice
done. Later would be time enough to deal with the consequences to himself.

First he was going to pay another call on the orphanage.

Chapter 15

Getting in unseen and planting a listening device in the orphanage's infirmary was the easy part, Gage discovered. He'd done the deed the next morning while everyone was still sleeping. He hadn't counted on how hard it would be to listen to Nadia working with the children and not be able to see or touch her.

Maybe Dani was right and he was getting too old for this work, he thought as he sat in his car a short distance from the building, concealed behind a thick screen of bushes. Not surprisingly, the rental company was less than keen to entrust another car to him after what had happened to the last one. His godfather had come to his aid, assuring Gage that the ambassadorial limousine took care of his driving needs, so he was welcome to take their compact sedan.

Gage wished his own needs were as easily met. Listening to Nadia persuading little Sammy to let the doctor check him over, Gage found himself dreaming of her in his arms and had to direct his thoughts elsewhere fast in order to keep his mind clear.

He had to admire her skill with the child. By making a game of the checkup, she soon had Sammy chuckling and cooperating.

The examination apparently over, Gage heard a door slam, signaling the child's return to the play area. "You're good at this, Nadia," Gage heard the doctor say. "I've never had a more able—or lovelier—assistant."

Clenching his fists, Gage focused on Nadia's response. It was playful and sweet, not exactly encouraging, he heard with some satisfaction. Evidently she didn't return the doctor's obvious interest. Just as well, or Gage might have had to storm into the orphanage and tell Warren where to get off.

Now where had that thought come from?

He wasn't in love with Nadia, Gage told himself. He couldn't afford to be until he knew more about her role in Dabir's affairs. The assurance didn't stop him from remembering how wonderful she had felt in his arms. The scent of jasmine would forever remind him of how he had taken her to the heights of ecstasy.

No matter how he tried to keep some mental distance from her, he couldn't bring himself to regret the hours they had spent together beside the swan lake. Knowing he had been her first real lover was enough to make his heart pick up speed. The thought that she would always compare other men to him was little consolation. He didn't want to imagine her with anyone else. Didn't want her to be with anyone but him.

But he wasn't in love with her.

He sat through an hour of listening to more children coming and going, being reassured by Nadia as she cajoled them into letting Warren look after them. The doctor's easy familiarity with her had Gage gritting his teeth, especially when he heard Nadia respond in kind. Not that Gage was jealous. He was merely protective of the princess. Warren obviously needed a lesson in how to treat royalty.

In a pig's eye, he admitted to himself. He was jealous. The very sound of her voice, like a musical instrument played by a virtuoso, was enough to turn his insides to mush. On a sudden impulse he grabbed his cell phone and dialed, hearing the orphanage phone ring a couple of seconds later.

To avoid a feedback loop, he turned the monitor speaker off before Nadia answered. Satisfaction coursed through him as he heard her pleased response to his suggestion that he visit the orphanage later that day. She sounded as if she couldn't wait to see him.

That could have been because he had said he might know of a suitable adoptive family for Sammy, but Gage liked to think he was at least part of the reason. And he did know someone interested in adopting Sammy. Himself.

The more he thought about it, the more attracted he was to the idea of giving the little boy a home. Back in Penwyck Gage could provide a child with everything he would need, including a loving father. He was already thinking about staying at home more, concentrating on his investments while someone else took over saving the world. Which should give him ample time to raise a child as his son and heir.

A wife would have been nice, too, but seemed impossible. The one woman he would like to carry home to Penwyck was strictly off-limits. Gage could imagine Sheik Ahmed's response if Gage were to ask for his daughter's hand in marriage. Gage told himself he was only interested in what great parents they would make for Sammy, but couldn't hide from the truth—he wanted Nadia for himself.

He was still smiling as he closed the phone and turned the speaker on again.

What he would do if she turned out to be on the side of the devil, he didn't know. He could only pray it wouldn't come to that.

He shifted restively in the car seat, which was too small for his six-foot frame. He had adjusted the seat as far back as it would go, but he still felt cramped. Getting up and walking around wasn't an option. Too much chance of someone from the orphanage spotting him. He began a series of yoga breathing exercises designed to convince his body that he was comfortable and relaxed.

They were about as successful as telling himself that he wasn't in love with Nadia. Time he faced facts. He had fallen for her hard the day she stopped to help him when she thought he'd crashed his car on the Marhaba road. His feelings had only intensified since then. Making love to her had been an expression of his feelings, not the cause of them. Thinking of her and marriage in the same breath felt as natural as breathing.

Could he be in love with her and still do the job he'd come to Tamir to do? He had an awful sense that he was going to find out soon.

Nadia and Warren's voices began to fade, and Gage turned up the volume on the miniature speaker he'd positioned above the steering wheel. "Time for lunch," Warren was saying. Gage heard Nadia agree with the doctor. Her sigh had Gage clenching his fists again. She sounded tired. Was it the pressure of leading a double life between the orphanage and her royal responsibilities? He was conceited enough to hope he might be the one keeping her awake at night, but doubted it. There was no reason she should have given him a second thought since returning to the palace.

The infirmary door opened, closed, then silence. They had gone to lunch. Maybe it was time for Gage to do the same. He was reaching for the ignition switch when he heard the infirmary door open again, creaking a little as if it was being pushed slowly and carefully. He pulled his hand back and listened.

There was the sound of footfalls across the floor. Very light. Female, then. Nadia? Gage's sixth sense told him it wasn't. His intuition was confirmed when he heard the phone being dialled and a woman's voice said, "It's Sitra. You wanted to know when she came here again. She's been here all morning, but this is the first chance I've had to call you."

Gage couldn't hear the other end of the conversation, but he was sure "she" meant the princess. Sitra had to be Sitra Wahabi, sister of the terrorist, Jalil Salim. Gage sat forward, straining to hear more.

"No, he isn't with her this time," Sitra said. "As they passed me in the corridor, I heard her tell the doctor that he's coming here this afternoon. It seems he's interested in one of the children."

The woman laughed unpleasantly, chilling Gage's blood. Sitra had to be talking about him. Who was she informing of his impending visit? Butrus Dabir? Someone in the Brothers of Darkness? How had they caught on to him?

His mind raced. If Nadia hadn't betrayed him directly, she had probably done so indirectly. Gage's suspicion that Dabir had been having her followed cemented into certainty. It would explain how Dabir had known about their first kiss in time to sabotage Gage's car. Did Dabir know they had made love? Probably not, or Gage doubted if he would still be alive to ask the question. Dabir wasn't a man who would take kindly to being cheated on.

Gage was surprised to feel an unfamiliar flash of sympathy for the man. They didn't have much in common, but Gage knew if any man laid hands on his woman, that man's life wouldn't be worth living.

Sitra was speaking again. He made himself pay attention. "Just don't do anything inside the orphanage. We don't need police swarming around, finding out what else goes on here."

She hung up and then Gage heard her depart, leaving him gripping the wheel in fierce concentration. So he was to be ambushed when he left the orphanage this afternoon. His gut tightened in automatic response as he thought of all the ways they could disarm, then dispose of him. Not that he intended to sell his life cheaply, or at all, if it could be avoided. His veins sang with the adrenaline coursing through him at the prospect.

It was small consolation to be right about the place being used as a front for illicit activities. Given Sitra's connection with the Brothers, they had to be involved. What more-innocent venue could they hide behind than an orphanage? How did Dabir fit in with their activities? Gage decided he had to live long enough to find out.

A cold sweat broke out on his brow as another thought drove through him. Nadia was in there. Somehow he had to get her away before all hell broke loose.

She was going to see Gage again. Nadia hoped her elation wasn't too obvious, but she felt as excited as a child on the night before a birthday. Ever since he had made love to her at Zabara, her thoughts had been filled with him. How he touched her, how he held her and kissed her, the masculine scent of him that lingered on the yellow robe she had worn that fateful night.

When Nargis found the robe folded under her pillow, Nadia had pretended she had put it there by mistake, earning a curious look from the servant. In truth she had hoped to dream of Gage and the marvellous way he had made her feel.

She had been so preoccupied that she hadn't even started the bust of her father, although the coral marble had been in her studio for several days. Normally she would have been unable to stop herself from making preliminary sketches and staring at the marble until she could see the sculpture in her mind's eye. Then she would have started to chip away at the marble until the shape in her mind was mirrored in the stone.

Instead, she had mooned around her studio, making desultory sketches that were all of one face, one pair of hands, one set of penetrating eyes. Gage Weston's. Thinking his name filled her with anticipation.

"Better eat your lunch before it gets cold," Warren urged, drawing her back to reality.

She looked at her plate. Today Sitra had cooked spinach stew with chicken pieces and rice, one of the children's favorites and usually Nadia's, too. Today she had little appetite. "I'm not very hungry," she confessed. "Sammy will help finish my portion, won't you, Sammy?"

Sammy didn't need a second invitation to help himself to her lunch. Warren jokingly called him a bottomless pit, but Nadia was aware the child had known many days of hunger after his mother died of a heart attack while hanging out washing. His record showed that the boy had been alone in the house for a week, eating whatever he could find and open from the cupboards, before he was brought to the orphanage. There was no sign of his father.

She hoped that Gage really did know someone who could adopt the child. She tried not to play favorites. All the children were worthy of love and attention, but she couldn't help being seduced by Sammy's cheeky charm.

She had a sudden vision of herself, Gage and Sammy as a family, and felt her cheeks grow warm. Nothing of the sort was likely to happen, so she might as well stop fantasizing about it.

"I hope you're not coming down with something," Warren said, giving her what she called his doctor's look.

She mustered a smile. "With the medical care available here, how could I?"

"Nevertheless, you look a little flushed."

"I'm fine, honestly." She would be even better after Gage got here.

Supervising the children's hand washing and helping the other women to settle them for an afternoon nap took enough of her attention that she was able to avoid checking the front gate every few minutes to see if he was approaching.

So successful was she that he was able to come up behind her in the play area, where she was collecting the children's toys, without her being aware he'd arrived.

"Gage, you startled me!" she said, spinning around, her arms full of toys. She was afraid her expression must have given away how glad she was to see him.

If so, he didn't react. "It's good to see you again, Your Highness."

She shot a concerned look around them, but no one was within earshot. Why was he being so formal suddenly? "You mustn't call me that now. To everyone here, I'm plain Addie," she said.

Nadia couldn't be plain if she tried, Gage thought. He assumed that the *galabiya* she wore belonged to her maid, who was probably standing in for her mistress right now. The white dress, embroidered with dark-blue cornflowers, fell over flowing pants caught at the ankles with more embroidery. In it Nadia looked heartrendingly beautiful. The delicate color of the traditional gown made her dark eyes shine like stars, and set off her high cheekbones and full lips so that he ached to kiss her right here and now, and to blazes with what anybody thought.

It took almost more willpower than he possessed not to take her in his arms, but he dared not. Not if his plan to get her away safely was to have any chance of success. If she had the slightest notion of the danger facing him, he was sure she would refuse to budge. That left him only one option. Somehow he had to convince her that she had been no more than a memorable one-night stand to him.

"Very well, Addie, then," he said, keeping his tone cool. "You must get quite a kick out of slumming here, pretending to be an ordinary person."

Her shocked gaze shot to his face and her arms tightened around the toys. "I beg your pardon?"

His gesture took in the humble surroundings. "You have to admit, this place is a long way from the royal palace. It must be a novelty for you to spend a few hours here, knowing you have all that luxury waiting for you back home."

She drew herself up, looking every inch a royal princess, although the hurt and puzzlement in her expression was heart-wrenching. "It is a contrast certainly. That's why I come, to remind myself that there are many people in the world less fortunate than I, and to do what little I can to redress the balance," she said.

He nodded. "The rich can afford to be charitable."

She frowned. "This isn't charity, Gage. It's a choice. I work here because I love the children." She piled the toys into a wooden chest and closed the lid carefully. "I thought you, of all people, would understand."

He retrieved a stuffed camel from beneath a potted palm and handed it to her. "Why me, of all people?"

"Because you and I...because we..." Color suffused her face and she stumbled over the obvious explanation—that she had allowed him to get closer to her than any other person.

"All we did was have sex. It doesn't have to signify anything," he said, keeping his tone neutral, although he longed to tell her that she had made far more impact on him than he could possibly have made on her.

"What are you trying to tell me, Gage?" she asked as calmly as if he hadn't just wounded her to her core.

He took her arm and stepped into the shade, towing her with him so they were both shadowed by the wall of the building. Hugging the toy camel, she looked so young and vulnerable that he almost betrayed himself by giving in to the urge to kiss her. He released her arm. If he kept hold of her, he *would* kiss her, and he wasn't at all sure he'd be able to stop.

"After that night, I realized that you might read more into it than I wanted you to. Women do that, I know."

Her face remained impassive, her voice cold. "Do they?"

"It's different for men. With us, sex doesn't have to be about love. More often, it's merely an expression of physical desire, without any strings attached."

"Go on," she said levelly.

"I don't expect you to understand."

"Oh, but I do," she said, all chill regal fury and splendor now. "You decided it would be—what did you call it?—a novelty to sleep with a princess. Something to boast about to your men friends when you return to England. You hadn't expected to be my first, and now your conscience is troubling you, so you've come to apologize."

He raked a hand through his hair, torn between being relieved that she had swallowed his lie and wishing desperately that it hadn't been necessary. "Something like that," he agreed, feeling as low as he'd ever felt in his life. Only the awareness of what awaited him outside the gates of the orphanage prevented him from telling her the truth.

"Then you've wasted your time. No apology is necessary.

I am a grown woman and I knew what I was doing. Has it occurred to you that I might also have found the experience a novelty?''

He hadn't expected that. ''I hadn't considered such a thing,'' he admitted frankly, aware of a stab of discomfort. Hurt pride? Their situation didn't entitle him to it, he thought as he pushed the feeling away.

''Perhaps it's time you did. I am to be married within a few weeks. One night with you was a last fling for me, as you say, with no strings attached. You can return to your own country with a clear conscience, knowing that both of us got what we wanted from the experience.''

He was fairly sure she was lying to save face and decided he owed it to her to go along. ''No hard feelings on either side?''

''None at all.''

He couldn't help himself. ''All the same, I am sorry, Prin…Addie.''

Abruptly she thrust the toy camel into his hands. ''I hadn't realized the time. It's late and I must be getting home. If you want to discuss an adoption, you'll have to do it with Warren. Goodbye, Gage.''

The toy was still warm from her hands and he found himself caressing it as he watched her walk swiftly to her car, which was parked to one side of the courtyard. The faintest hint of her perfume lingered in the synthetic fur and he inhaled deeply. Be careful what you wish for, he thought. He had wanted to send her away as fast as possible, and he had done so. He had also made her hate him.

He tried to tell himself he was relieved when she drove out of the gates at a less-than-moderate speed. All he felt was an aching emptiness at seeing the joy in her face turn to misery in the space of a few minutes, knowing he was the cause.

''Nice work, Weston,'' he said to himself. What came next? Taking candy from babies? He carried the camel to the chest and placed it among the other toys, feeling as if he closed the lid not only on the contents, but on something good in his life that he might never find again.

He had moved his godfather's car so it was parked well away from the orphanage gates, where it couldn't be missed if someone came looking for him, but where he could be sure the children weren't in any danger. Now he braced himself to walk back to the car, knowing that there was very little chance he would reach it before Sitra's friends intervened.

He almost welcomed the prospect of some action to burn off the distaste he felt at the way he'd been forced to treat Nadia. *They* were responsible—Dabir, the Brothers of Darkness, all the forces of evil that contaminated everything that was good in life. They were responsible for the death of his friend, Conrad, and for making Gage put the despair on Nadia's face. He looked forward to evening the score.

Chapter 16

She did not care. She did not care. She did not care. Nadia repeated the mantra to herself as she drove away from the orphanage. She considered herself a modern woman. That meant she could enjoy Gage Weston's lovemaking without requiring a happy-ever-after, couldn't she? He obviously could.

Her fingers tightened around the steering wheel. No love, no strings, he had said. Well, what had she expected? A marriage proposal? A declaration of undying devotion? In her experience, living happily ever after only happened in fairy tales.

She still intended to ask her father to release her from her engagement to Butrus. Gage had left her one legacy. He had shown her that she couldn't commit to a loveless marriage. The sheik would be furious, and she regretted the hurt she knew she must cause him. Butrus would be even angrier, but if he was involved in shady dealings, as she suspected, it served him right. For herself, she would rather endure the storm of their wrath for a time, even if it meant spending her future alone, with only her art for company.

Her thoughts were so busy that she almost drove past the field where she had left Tahani and Mahir, her driver. She looked around at the empty landscape. Surely this was the right place. In her confusion, she could have been mistaken.

Adjusting Tahani's scarf over her head, she put on her dark glasses and got out of the car, walking across the field in bewilderment. Her foot kicked a small object, and she stooped to pick up a tube of bright red paint, which she studied for a moment before slipping it inside her *galabiya*. This was the right place, but why would Tahani have left before they could change places again?

Her heart almost stopped. Something must have happened to her father or mother and the palace had sent someone to find her, taking Tahani back to the palace in her place. Her parents were visiting the island of Jawhar, inspecting a new oil field. There could have been an accident. Nadia stumbled back to the car. She had to return home quickly.

But there was no sign of a problem at the palace. Removing the scarf and glasses, she was recognized at once, although the guard looked bemused to see her behind the wheel and unescorted. She didn't feel inclined to explain. "Where is Mahir?"

"Mr. Dabir sent a car to fetch you. I saw it return a short time ago with Mahir and…and you, I thought, Your Highness."

"Obviously it wasn't me," she snapped, her nerves stretched to breaking point at hearing that Butrus was behind this. "Can you not tell the difference between me and Tahani?"

The man turned beet red. "Of course, Your Highness." But he had been fooled, she saw, although she took little satisfaction in the knowledge. Nadia had used her trick once too often, and today she was to pay the price.

"Is everything all right with my mother and father?" she asked.

"Certainly, Your Highness. Before I came on duty, I saw a news broadcast that showed that your father's inspection of the oil fields on Jawhar is going well."

Her apprehension grew. If nothing was amiss, why had Butrus had Tahani brought back to the palace? Their deception must have been discovered. Nadia's heart was beating double time as she gave her car into the care of a servant and made her way to her apartment.

"How good of you to pay us a visit," Butrus drawled as she let herself in past a saluting guard.

He was seated at the desk in her living room, his fingers drumming on the leather surface. On the sofa sat a white-faced Tahani, visibly trembling.

Nadia ignored Butrus and went to the attendant. "Are you all right?"

Tahani nodded, biting her lip to hold back tears. "Mr. Dabir sent a car for you, and they insisted I return at once. I wanted to wait for you."

Nadia took her friend's hand. It felt icy in hers. "It's all right. You did the right thing." The only thing, if Butrus's implacable expression was any guide.

Tahani brightened a little. "Thank you, Princess."

"You can go now. Please fetch cool drinks for me and Mr. Dabir."

With alacrity, Tahani jumped up from the sofa, giving Butrus a wide berth, Nadia noticed, as she headed for the door. The princess waited until the door closed behind Tahani, then turned her attention to her fiancé. "What is the meaning of this intrusion?"

He folded his arms and glared at her. "I thought you could tell me. Quite the adventuress, aren't you, little one?"

"I have no idea what you're talking about."

His dark brows arched. "No? Then why was your servant disguised as you, painting at your easel, while her mistress was nowhere to be found?"

"I had an errand to run."

"What could possibly be so urgent that you had to go in person, rather than send your maid?"

She stood up. "Why don't we stop playing cat and mouse, Butrus. Say what you came here to say."

He stood up, too, and moved to stand over her, his closeness daunting. She refused to back away. "Very well. I've known for some time that you have a habit of changing places with the maid and going off on your own for hours at a time."

Horror made her skin crawl. "You had me watched? How dare you do such a thing to a member of the royal family?"

"Oh, I dare." He reached into the jacket of his impeccably tailored suit and pulled out a handful of photographs, dropping them onto the couch beside her. "You forfeited any protection due your royal status when you assumed the guise of a humble maid. No one could blame me for treating you as such. Look at you!"

He was referring to her simple attire and disheveled state after her stint at the orphanage. She drew herself up, refusing to look at the photographs. "One does not have to appear royal to *be* royal."

"But one does have to maintain certain standards. You can hardly be said to have maintained them today."

"Are you worried about my actions or my image?" she asked wearily.

He placed his hands on her upper arms. "Since we are to be married, both are of concern to me."

She glared at him. "Remove your hands from me. We are not going to be married."

She had not intended to be so blunt, but Butrus had left her no choice. His attitude confirmed what she had long suspected—that as his wife, she would be no more than a chattel to him, her royal status a convenience that would be ignored when they were alone. She would tell her father of her decision as soon as he returned.

Butrus's grip tightened to bruising force as he urged her

to her feet. "That's where you're wrong, my princess. We are going to be married, and soon."

She caught her breath. "You can't make me marry you."

"No, but your father can. Once he hears what you've been up to…"

She felt the color rush to her face. "You wouldn't tell him." Her father would be devastated by her behavior, especially when the tale was slanted to show her in the worst possible light, as Butrus was sure to do.

Butrus's eyes lit with purpose. "Not unless you force me to."

"He will never take your side against his own daughter."

"Once he sees these photographs, you'll be lucky to claim that status."

She made herself look at them, horrified when she saw that the photographer had captured her in Gage's arms the first time they had kissed under the colonnade at Zabara. The odd lighting suggested some kind of security camera or infrared device, but there was no mistaking the scene. There were more pictures of her changing places with Tahani, driving alone in her car and, worst of all, entering the orphanage at Marhaba.

"How did you get these?" she asked, her throat so tight that speaking was an effort.

He grinned, running his hands along her arms from wrist to elbow. "Changing your tune a little, are you? As you should. I've had you followed for some time, but saw no reason to interfere in your activities until now."

Until it was beneficial to him, she interpreted. She pulled free of him and moved away, feeling cold in spite of the day's warmth. "I'm surprised you would want to marry a woman who has so dishonored herself," she said, her voice dripping sarcasm.

He chose to ignore her tone, taking her words at face value. "I'm glad you agree that your behavior is dishonorable, my princess. I confess, I did think of baring my soul to your father. No woman has been stoned for immoral behavior in

Tamir for centuries, but Sheik Ahmed might be persuaded to revive the custom if the transgression is sufficient. You must agree, your transgressions are more than sufficient.''

She shook her head, refusing to entertain the vision of herself being so punished, although her blood chilled at the very thought. ''You sound like someone from the Dark Ages, Butrus. My father would never condone such a thing.''

Butrus began to gather up the photographs. ''Shall we put his response to the test when he returns from Jawhar tomorrow?''

''No, wait.'' She couldn't let her father see the photos.

Butrus paused, the photos fanned in his fingers like a hand of cards. The one of Gage kissing her was uppermost, she noticed. Remembering how special he had made her feel, she couldn't bring herself to regret the moment. She only regretted that Butrus had found her out. What sort of woman did that make her? Was Butrus right about her lack of morals?

No, she thought defiantly. No matter how sordid Butrus made this look, she cared about Gage, even if he did not return her affection.

She loved him.

The realization left her thunderstruck. She had thought herself infatuated with him, driven to find out what his lovemaking was like, but never in love with him. Now she made herself face the truth. From the moment she had set eyes on him, he had begun to capture her soul.

That he had thrown her feelings in her face didn't stop her from having them, any more than she could stop the sun from rising in the morning.

Did Butrus know that she and Gage had made love? If he did, nothing on earth would have stopped him from seeing her punished as cruelly as he could devise, she knew. Apparently he did not know, not yet.

''What do you want from me?'' she asked.

The gleam of satisfaction fired his gaze. ''What I've always wanted from you—membership in the most exclusive club on earth, the royal family.''

"Power and prestige mean so much to you that you would marry me, knowing how I feel toward you?"

"You don't understand, do you? You've always had power, always had people rushing to do your slightest bidding. Yet you throw it all away to pretend to be less than you are. You would not be so eager to do so if you knew what it's like to be truly less than others."

She clasped her hands together. "You're right, I don't understand."

A timid knock interrupted them. At Nadia's distracted command, Tahani entered with a tray containing two glasses of chilled fruit juice and a plate of sweetmeats. The glasses rattled as she edged past Butrus and placed the tray within Nadia's reach. "Thank you. You may lay out my clothes for this evening," Nadia told her.

Tahani gave her a grateful smile and disappeared into the bedroom, closing the door carefully behind her.

"That's what it's like to be less than others," Butrus said, gesturing toward the closed door. "It means being at the beck and call of your betters, jumping when they say jump and being terrified of making the slightest wrong move."

Nadia refrained from pointing out that it was Butrus who had caused the other woman's fear. "You sound as if you speak from experience," she said, knowing it was impossible.

He crossed to the tray and picked up one of the glasses, drinking deeply before returning his attention to her. "Bitter experience," he confirmed. "The man you know as my father is really my uncle. He took me in when I was orphaned as a small boy."

Her hand went to her mouth. "I had no idea."

"I don't want your pity," he said savagely. "I had enough of that as a child. Pity and condescension, always aware that I wasn't a son of the house, but a charity case, taken in on sufferance."

"Your father...your uncle's behavior never suggested he thought less of you than his natural children," she said, striving to think of a time when she had noticed any discrimination between adoptive father and son. Butrus's family had socialized with hers often enough that she would have noticed some difference. She could remember none. In fact, she had occasionally thought his adoptive father favored Butrus over his other children. Couldn't Butrus see that?

Apparently not, because he shook his head. "Perhaps not to you. To me, the difference is always there."

"In you, not in your family," she insisted. "Can't you see, you're fighting phantoms. You don't want to marry me. You want to marry what I am. That makes your actions worse than those you attribute to your father."

He swept the glasses off the tray onto the floor, making her jump. "You will not judge me. As my wife, you will do my bidding and put a glad face on it. Understood?"

"I will never lie with you willingly," she said in a low tone, more shaken than she wanted him to know.

He gave a guttural laugh. "No matter. Unwilling can be even more exciting."

She couldn't stop a shudder from rippling through her. After the joy she had found in Gage's arms, how could she resign herself to the travesty of a marriage Butrus meant them to have? She would rather die first, and she let her resolute gaze tell Butrus so. "Even though my heart belongs to another?"

Butrus looked as if he would like to kill her there and then. She saw his hands actually flex and reach out for her before he brought them back to his sides. When he spoke, his voice was as rigidly controlled as his pose. "When I saw the photo of Weston kissing you, I told myself you had been coerced by him. You have not tasted a man's love yet—that boy, the art teacher, was barely a man—so it is natural for you to be curious about such things. And a man from the West has little compunction about despoiling such innocence as yours. I have decided to forgive you."

Knowing she was flirting with danger, she could not keep silent. "I don't want your forgiveness, Butrus. I was not coerced, nor a victim of curiosity. I am in love with Gage Weston."

Butrus's expression turned to stone. The coldness in his eyes froze her blood as he said, "Then you are in love with a dead man. Weston is already being hunted by my agent."

She stared at Butrus, aghast. "You were the one who tried to kill Gage before by sabotaging his car brakes, weren't you?"

His mouth thinned. "Unfortunately I was unsuccessful. This time there will be no mistake. He sealed his fate by touching my woman."

"How many times must I tell you I'm not your woman, and never will be? If you harm Gage in any way, I won't rest until you are made to pay."

Butrus was not as discomfited as she thought he should be. "Without proof that I had anything to do with it, who will believe you? I'll deny we ever had this conversation."

Suddenly everything fell into place. Appalled, she remembered Gage's determination to convince her that their lovemaking had meant nothing to him. Had he found out that Butrus meant to have him killed and decided to remove her from harm in the only way he could—by driving her away?

How could she have fallen for his scheme? Her body had known, if her mind had not, that their lovemaking had meant more to him than a casual experiment. He had been willing to sacrifice their love to save her. She had to get to him.

As soon as she gained her feet, Butrus motioned her to sit again. "Whatever you are planning will be too late to save Weston. By the time you can reach him, his body will be lying in a ditch and my agent will be on his way to claim his payment."

She felt her eyes brim and she blinked furiously. She refused to accept that Gage was dead. "I can't believe you would stoop to paying someone to do murder."

''Believe it. I have done worse, and doubtless will again in the future. It is not your concern.''

This time she would not remain seated. ''It will certainly be my father's concern after I tell him what you are.''

''Are you sure he does not know?''

Horror overcame her. She and her father had had their disagreements, but he would never endorse Butrus's crimes. Her father could be hard, but he was just and he always upheld the law. ''No, he isn't like that.''

''Of course he isn't. So I undertake the causes he cannot support publicly, using ways and means not open to him to achieve his aims.''

''You're mad. My father would never condone what you're doing.''

Butrus gave an ugly sneer. ''How prettily you defend him, my princess, for all the good it will do either of you. Sheik Ahmed benefits from my actions, therefore he is a party to them by default, at the very least.''

Her head swam with the effort to make sense of Butrus's ramblings. He had taken her father's lack of objection for approval, convincing himself that the sheik supported his actions, when the sheik knew nothing of what his adviser was doing. When he learned the truth, Butrus's reign of terror would be over, she knew.

''How are you going to prevent me from telling my father what you've told me at the first opportunity?'' she demanded.

''The guard at your door is one of my men. He is under orders to see that you remain in seclusion here for the next few days. By the time you are recovered from your...indisposition, Weston will be long dead, and our wedding will be only days away. Any hysteria you exhibit will be blamed on prewedding nerves.''

The thought of being unable to save Gage turned her heart to lead. Was her fate always to have her love snatched from her by the cold hand of death? How could she go on living, knowing that Gage was lost to her forever, the last words they shared a repudiation of the love she was sure he felt for

her? Why else had he tried so hard to drive her away, if not
to keep her from harm?

"My parents will never take your word over mine," she
said bitterly.

Butrus patted his jacket pocket. "I still have the photographs as a last resort. Once Sheik Ahmed sees them, he will
think you are accusing me to deflect censure from yourself.
He will be happy to expedite our marriage in order to have
such a troublesome daughter off his hands."

"You really mean to go through with this, don't you?
Even though it means I will hate you for the rest of your
life."

"That is a long time," he said equably. "Ample for me
to change your opinion of me."

"Never. You will have to drag me to the ceremony, for I
shall not go any other way."

"Not even knowing that your dear Tahani will be standing
in the wings with a knife pressed to her throat?"

Butrus knew she would never let anything happen to Tahani to save herself, and his smug expression told her he
knew he had won. "Cheer up," he added, as if he had not
spoken of murder and mayhem the way other people discussed the weather. "When you are my bride, I shall build
you the finest studio, where you can dabble in your art to
your heart's content."

"With bars on the windows," she threw at him.

Her anger rolled off him. "That depends entirely on how
you behave." He consulted his watch. "Much as I would
like to stay and discuss our plans for the future, I must go. I
have an appointment to keep with your beloved's killer."

"Butrus, wait. Why must Gage die? I could tell Father that
he accosted me and forced me to kiss him. He would be
banished from Tamir instantly, never to cross our borders
again." Bleakness gripped her at the thought of never seeing
him again, but at least he would be alive.

Butrus favored her with a wintry smile. "I wish I'd
thought of that. It would have been far less trouble. But I'm

afraid you're too late. His body should be discovered within the hour, the victim of an unfortunate robbery. Since your family knows you were acquainted with Mr. Weston, they won't be surprised if you withdraw to your apartments and don't want to see anyone. Very sad, really. I wish there was something I could do to help you get over your grief.'' He brightened suddenly. ''Fortunately the prospect of our wedding will restore your mood.''

She grabbed one of the glasses lying on the carpet and flung it at him. He ducked and the glass shattered against a wall, the remaining juice spilling like blood over the costly drapery. ''I'll see you in hell before marrying you,'' she vowed.

His laughter mocked her. ''Princess, this *is* hell.'' The second glass exploded against the door, but he had already closed it behind him.

Chapter 17

The old fort that housed the orphanage had been built on a rocky promontory overlooking the town of Marhaba. Once, the fort would have commanded unlimited vistas over the surrounding area, but in modern times, greenery had grown up around the old stone walls, although the view was still spectacular from some parts.

Gage was in no mood to enjoy the scenery as he scanned the bushes for signs of an attacker. Every rustle of a bird made his nerves strain almost to the breaking point as he readied himself for anything. He knew that dealing with whoever was sent against him wouldn't be a picnic.

Too bad he hadn't brought his gun along on what he'd believed would be a simple surveillance exercise when he left the embassy this morning. A weapon would have gone a long way toward evening the odds. But thinking that an orphanage wasn't the place to bring a loaded weapon, he had left it behind. He hoped his concern for the children's safety wasn't going to cost him too dearly.

He consoled himself with knowing that Nadia was safe.

The specter of her hurt expression as he convinced her she meant nothing to him haunted him, but at least she was back at the palace by now.

She couldn't know how much she really meant to him, couldn't be allowed to know, as long as it put her in danger. Every time he imagined her here dealing with this, he felt himself break out in a cold sweat. He wasn't afraid for himself, but he was terrified for her.

He continued walking back to where he had left the car, trying not to betray his tension in his movements. Thinking of Nadia was a welcome distraction. When had she started to mean so much to him? When he kissed her beneath the colonnade at Zabara, he decided. She had been so uncertain, yet she had kissed him back with surprising enthusiasm.

In spite of his unease, a warmth spread through him. He'd never come across such a wondrous mix of worldly wisdom and inexperience before. She charmed, delighted and challenged him in a way no other woman ever had. By the time they made love, she had already found a place in his heart.

His sense of well-being evaporated. By now she was probably cursing his name and wishing she'd never set eyes on him. Even if he lived through the next few minutes, and he intended to do his level best, she would probably never speak to him again.

A rustling sound in the bushes just ahead and to his left drove all other thoughts out of his mind. He kept his pose relaxed, kept his feet tracking, while fixing every shred of his attention on the source of the sound.

Not birds this time, something far larger, moving stealthily toward him. Whoever it was had waited until Gage was out of sight of the orphanage entrance, not out of consideration for the children, but to ensure the minimum number of witnesses.

He braced himself.

The man who confronted him belonged to one of Tamir's hill families, judging by his wide shoulders and swarthy complexion. A head taller than Gage, he wore his people's tra-

ditional outfit of coarsely woven shirt and loose pants tucked
into leather boots, with a wide sash around the waist, hear-
kening back to a Tamir of a century before.

Gage had a split second to absorb this information before
the man was on top of him, large hands reaching for his
throat.

Gage leaped aside, slashing the side of his hand down on
the man's shoulder with all his strength. The blow glanced
off the muscle as if he'd merely patted the big man on the
back.

No picnic, he reminded himself, dodging out of the path
of the man's bull charge. His adversary had the advantages
of weight, size and blood lust. All Gage could do was try to
exhaust him, hopefully before he finished Gage.

Head down, the man charged at him again. Gage twisted
in the air and landed on his feet, getting in a rabbit punch to
the back of his attacker's neck. The man staggered, shook
himself as if momentarily groggy, then came back at Gage,
his eyes fiery with the desire to exact payment for the blow.

Some distant part of Gage's mind calculated the odds of
getting out of this alive and found them depressingly stacked
against him. No matter. He had beaten the odds before. He
would do so again.

This brute was the reason Nadia never wanted to see him
again, he thought, goading himself to fury. A haze of red
darkened his vision. This man and whoever had sent him
were responsible for Gage's being forced to hurt her, and for
the pain in his own heart as a result.

He stopped dodging and moved in, looking for an opening.
The mountain man swung at him. Gage ducked and came
back with his hands locked together, slugging at his adversary in double-handed blows that should have been lethal but
seemed merely to increase the other man's fury.

Another pass and Gage caught only a handful of shirt for
his trouble. He found himself staring at the man's shoulder
where the ripped fabric had exposed a symbol that made
Gage's blood roar.

"You're one of the Brothers," he ground out as he and the man circled each other. He knew that the younger, more hotheaded members of the Brothers of Darkness had adopted the tattoo of a black octopus as their personal symbol, but had never seen it on a living person before now.

Most of the men wearing that tattoo had been in the morgue.

"What of it?" the man demanded, seemingly disconcerted that Gage had recognized the symbol. As the shoulder muscles of its owner twitched, warning Gage to brace himself for another rush, the creature seemed to writhe with an evil look of purpose.

Keep him talking while you formulate a strategy, Gage told himself. "This is a mistake. I'm one of you," he said, fighting his distaste for the admission, even if it was a pretense to buy himself some time.

The big man blinked his confusion but for the moment held off on another charge, giving Gage a few precious seconds to slow his laboring breath.

"Prove it. Show me the sign."

Gage thought fast. Did he mean the tattoo or some other code signal used between members of the Brothers? Since he didn't have a clue, he rode another hunch. "I'm working undercover for Butrus Dabir."

The look of confusion changed to blind rage. "Now I know you lie. Dabir himself hired me to kill you."

With a bull roar, the mountain man charged, locking his great arms around Gage's ribs, squeezing tighter and tighter until Gage felt as if he was in the grip of a boa constrictor. He felt his ribs start to give way under the relentless pressure. Black fringed his vision, and his lungs screamed for air. The octopus writhed close to his face, its tattooed death's head mocking his fight to breathe.

He—would—not—give—in—to—such—evil.

Desperately he brought his knee up, finding his target unerringly. He felt a grim satisfaction as his attacker's arms fell away and the man doubled over.

The sudden release of pressure on his ribs brought a new burst of agony, but Gage staggered for a moment until he got his feet centered under him. Determinedly he advanced on his attacker, the pounding in his temples and the ache in his ribs driving him on. The big man was trying to pick himself up when Gage drove his head back with a right to the jaw.

"This is for Nadia," he snarled as he sent the man doubling over again with a blow to the midsection.

As he moved in to finish the job, he caught the gleam of metal and dodged the blade barely in time. He should have known the man would come armed. Gage had not so much as a dinner knife on him, while the stiletto being waved in his face looked wickedly purposeful.

He weaved out of its deadly reach. The man wasn't as vanquished as he'd encouraged Gage to think. He came up remarkably easily and balanced on the balls of his feet, jabbing the air in front of Gage's face.

Trying to buy himself some time, Gage retreated behind a pile of boulders, but the mountain man followed him, stalking him, confident that his knife gave him the upper hand.

Gage allowed him to think so, not at all sure that his attacker wouldn't turn out to be right. Think, he ordered himself. That's what his training for this work had taught him to do. Too bad his training hadn't anticipated such unequal odds.

He kept retreating until he reached the bushes where he'd waited this morning while he listened in on the activities at the orphanage. Was it only hours ago? It felt like an eternity.

Backing the clearing, he remembered, was a rock wall hidden by greenery. He stepped out into the middle of the clearing, noting the tracks of his own tires from earlier in the day. By a miracle he was in the right place.

As if directing traffic, he held up his hands, flexing his fingers toward himself, inviting the other man to come at him. If he had judged the situation accurately, the rock wall should be only a couple of yards behind him.

The giant obliged him by rushing in for the kill. Head down, blade extended, he never saw the rock wall until he drove headlong into it, Gage stepping out of his path at the last second. Then the crunching sound of bone against rock jarred Gage's senses. The mountain man went down.

Moving in cautiously, Gage felt for a pulse. The man still lived. Good. He was only a hired gun, and Gage had never meant to kill him.

For a moment during the fight, he had wanted to, he thought grimly. Thinking of the distress this man's cohorts had caused to Nadia had made Gage furious enough to kill. Even now, as he thought about the hurt he had inflicted on her this morning, Gage had to struggle against the urge to keep going until the man was not only defeated but dead.

She was worthy of much nobler impulses, he told himself. He stripped away a length of the pliant strangle-quick vine clinging to the cliff, using his attacker's own knife to cut the thing to size. He used the vine to bind the attacker hand and foot, before slicing another chunk off the man's shirt to use as a gag when he came to.

Propping the man's trussed body against the rock wall, Gage dropped to the ground beside him and waited.

Only then did he allow himself to take stock of the injuries he'd collected from the pounding. His ribs weren't broken but were severely bruised by the man's boa constrictor grip, and every breath hurt. Something wet dripped into his eye. He touched the spot tentatively and his finger came away red. Mountain Man must have nicked him with the knife without his noticing.

Gage pressed a handkerchief to the spot until the bleeding stopped. Considering the size of his attacker, Gage counted himself lucky to be the one sitting up.

As soon as his breathing slowed enough to make movement less arduous, he levered himself to his feet and headed for the car. A bottle of tepid water lay on the front seat and he took a swallow, then poured some on to the handkerchief and swabbed the knife wound. Squinting into the driving mirror, he was glad to see the injury felt worse than it looked.

By the time he returned to the clearing, the mountain man was awake and pulling at his bonds. "The more you strain, the tighter they'll get," Gage warned him. The vine he'd used for rope wasn't called strangle-quick for nothing. Under strain the fibers kept contracting until there was no give left.

If looks could kill, Gage would be dead where he stood. "Why didn't you kill me when you had the chance?" the man demanded

"That may be how the Brothers of Darkness do things, but not how I work. As long as you tell me what I want to know, you'll be allowed to live."

The man spat on the ground. "I'll tell you nothing."

Gage flicked the knife against the octopus tattoo on the man's shoulder. "This thing offends me. It ought to be surgically removed." Pressing just deeply enough to make his point without breaking the skin, he traced the tattoo's outline delicately with the blade.

In spite of his bravado, the man shrank away from the deadly blade. "Butrus Dabir will kill me, anyway."

"Not if I let him think you're already dead. You'd have time to escape back to the mountains before he finds out the truth."

The man tossed his head. "You think I'd be safe there? The Brothers are everywhere."

Like the tentacles of their chosen symbol, Gage thought. "Then I'll turn you over to the police and you can ask for protection in return for giving evidence against the Brothers. It's your problem, not mine. All I want to know is where and when you're supposed to report to Dabir and collect your payment for this job."

The man hesitated, weighing whether it was better to die now at Gage's hands or later at Dabir's. Deciding that later at least offered him a fighting chance, he let out a whistling breath. "I am to meet him in the alleyway behind the Old Souk in Marhaba in one hour."

Gage's sigh mirrored his captive's. "All I needed to know."

The man offered his bound hands. "Untie me now."

"Not until I've settled with Dabir. Until then, you're my insurance policy. Don't worry, I won't forget where I parked you."

The man began to protest, but Gage wadded up the piece of shirt he'd souvenired and used it to silence any further objections. Gage knew the man's best hope for life was to throw himself on the mercy of the police. He planned to tell them where to find him and also suggest they pick up Sitra Wahabi for questioning, but not before he confronted Dabir.

He finally had the link he'd been searching for between Dabir and the Brothers of Darkness. King Marcus was going to be very pleased with the news when Gage eventually shared it with him.

First there was Dabir's complicity in the murder of Conrad Drake. Before he died, Conrad had left a clue to his killer in the letters DOT he'd scratched in the dirt. Gage had followed the killer's trail to Tamir and found the Octopus—the Brothers' symbol. That left only D for Dabir. For once, Gage wished he was the vigilante type, who could mete out his own brand of justice without waiting for the law to act. He wasn't, but Dabir didn't know that.

Before handing Dabir over to the authorities, Gage intended to give the other man a taste of the suffering he had put Conrad through at the last. First he had to track down a traditional hill-family costume. Since he was meeting Dabir at the Souk, that was as likely a place as any to find what he needed.

Tahani watched her mistress pace. "A thousand apologies, Princess. When the car came for me—for you—I tried to make the driver wait, but he insisted Mahir and I were to return to the palace immediately. With your father and mother away, I thought something must be wrong with them. I had no idea what was to unfold."

Nadia rested a hand on her attendant's arm. She was sure when Butrus posted the guard on her apartment, he had forgotten that Tahani was in the bedroom, preparing the princess's clothes for the evening. The irony wasn't lost on her. He had objected to being treated as an inferior by his family, yet he was the one who had treated the servant as if she didn't exist.

The princess smiled at her attendant. "It's all right, Tahani. You did the right thing. The fault is mine for thinking I could change my situation."

"You have changed it, my princess. The children at the orphanage adore you. Your paintings command high prices."

"Because they are sold for charity, not because of their artistic merit," Nadia said on a deep sigh. She wished Tahani would stop fretting and allow her to think. She knew the other woman was distressed. Butrus's anger had shaken the princess, too, more than she was letting Tahani see. But she was more terrified for Gage. If she was too late to save him— and a tight fist of pain closed around her heart at the idea— she could at least make sure Butrus paid for his crime.

"I'm going out," she said resolutely.

Tahani was on her knees, collecting the last of the glass fragments and placing them on the tray. She stood up. "But the guard..."

"Did he pay you any heed when you came and went before?"

"Of course not, my princess." Her tone said she would have been surprised if he had.

"Give me a moment."

Nadia took out a palm-size tape recorder she often used to capture her thoughts about future works of art. Going into the bedroom, she recorded two messages, rewound the tape and returned, handing it to Tahani. Then she made Tahani stand still while her long hair was tucked out of sight under one of Nadia's beautiful scarves. Nadia was staking a lot on the guard's not noticing her clothes, but they didn't have time to change.

As she pushed a last strand of Tahani's hair under the scarf, the princess felt her attendant trembling. "All will be well," she assured her, wondering in her own heart if anything would ever be well again.

Tahani fumbled in her *galabiya*. "Please take this, my princess."

Tahani held out a jeweled knife in a carved leather scabbard. It was the sort of knife one would use to peel fruit or whittle a piece of wood, but the sight of it heartened Nadia. "Thank you, I shan't forget your loyalty," she said. tucking it into her own garment. Then she pulled a scarf over her head, shadowing her features.

She bid Tahani stand near the window with her back to the door, then opened it a little, balancing the tray in her free hand. As instructed, Tahani played the tape Nadia had made.

"Guard, kindly come in here."

The man looked around the crack, ignoring Nadia's downcast head. "I'm sorry, Your Highness. My orders are to remain outside until Mr. Dabir returns."

Nadia saw her maid's hand go to the tape again and heard her second message. "Kindly permit my maid to fetch refreshment for me. The first she brought was unacceptable."

The man must have heard the shattering glass, because Nadia saw him nod from under the fringe of her lashes. She adjusted the scarf over her hair and kept her head down as she carried the tray past him. He was so intent on watching Tahani's back that he barely gave Nadia a glance.

She kept her head down until she was out of his sight, then set the tray on the nearest table and ran the length of the corridor and across the courtyard to her car. A servant was cleaning it and looked astonished when she snatched the keys from his hand. But he was too well trained to intervene. As she got in and drove toward the main gates, in the mirror she saw the man resignedly gather the cleaning things.

Butrus was already out of sight. She pulled up beside the sentry box at the main gate. The guard was the same one she had passed on her return earlier. This time he looked less surprised to see her behind the wheel. "My fiancé forgot something," she said. "Did you see which road he took?"

"Mr. Dabir did not inform me of his destination, Your Highness, but he went right, along the main Marhaba road."

One way or another, that road seemed to lead to her destiny, she thought as she thanked the guard and drove on. Tears almost blinded her as she passed the place where she had first met Gage. She couldn't believe she would never see him again, never know the magic of his touch or the press of his lips on hers.

Would the outcome have been different if she hadn't allowed him to send her away this morning? She should never have believed his assertion that she meant nothing to him. In her heart she had known it wasn't true.

It had never been true for her.

Gage meant more to her than any man she had ever known, and she was sure she meant more to him. No man could have spoken to her, touched her, loved her so completely unless he cared. Now she might never know for sure.

If Gage had come to harm, Butrus would pay, she vowed as the turnoff for the orphanage slid past. A commotion up ahead made her frown. She soon saw what was happening. A farmer was herding cattle across the road and Butrus's car was stuck behind them, delaying him long enough for her to catch up. She stopped, not wanting him to recognize her car, although it was agony when everything in her wanted to race after Butrus and claw his traitorous eyes out. When the road cleared and he moved off again, she saw he was heading for the old town.

How long had he been following his own agenda while pretending to be serving the crown? Most of his life, if his story was to be believed. She had never known that he was adopted, or that he so bitterly resented his lack of status.

It would have made no difference to her if she *had* known, but she could see that Butrus would never believe her. He was too caught up in his quest to redress what he perceived as the unfairness of his lot. No amount of reassurance would make any difference to how he saw himself.

She thought again of Gage, so confident and self-assured. He had never let her royal status come between them. A sob welled in her throat, but she throttled it back. She would have time for tears later, when she knew what had happened to her beloved. For now, she concentrated on following Butrus's car.

Chapter 18

Marhaba's Old Souk had been built around the town's original customs house, and it still boasted the original massive wrought-iron gates. Alleyways led away from the building in all directions, their narrow cobbled stretches packed with furniture, wrought-iron wares, dusty coffeepots, wooden boxes and many more Arabian curios. Some of the alleyways were so narrow and shadowy they were lit by wrought-iron lamps even in full daylight.

The Old Souk had been the heart of the town many years ago and was one of the oldest in Tamir. The Gold Souk, a souk-within-a-souk, was still a center of local commerce, providing dowries for those families who still subscribed to the notion.

As he wove his way through the alleys, Gage's nostrils were assaulted by the scents of aromatic herbs, spices and incense, their purveyors assuring him they could be had for pennies. He shook off the hands clutching at him, importuning him to come in for coffee without obligation, and left the puzzled merchants wondering what sort of boor had no time for coffee and conversation.

He further offended the merchant from whom he bought the traditional mountain accouterments by paying the first asking price and refusing the man's offer of coffee. The merchant looked so offended that Gage wondered if he would be allowed to make his purchases at all.

Fortunately the man's instincts for profit won over his desire to see custom satisfied, although he muttered to himself in Arabic. Gage knew enough of the language to recognize that some of the words weren't normally used in polite company, and he summoned an equally earthy reply, silencing the merchant.

Sullenly, the man provided Gage with billowing cotton pants and a woven white shirt that would have done Errol Flynn proud. A scarlet sash and black boots completed the outfit, and Gage stowed his attacker's silver-handled stiletto into the sash, feeling better for knowing it was there. A white skullcap and scarflike head covering secured by a black band provided limited disguise potential, Gage found when he pulled the end of the scarf experimentally across his nose and mouth.

After his fight with the mountain man, Gage's own clothes were the worse for wear, so he felt no regrets about bundling them up and leaving them with the merchant.

His shopping expedition had left him barely enough time to find his way out of the maze of alleyways to the meeting point. Since his disguise was at best rudimentary, he decided to stick to the shadows and let Dabir do most of the talking to begin with.

The attorney was late. Gage fingered the handle of the dagger, wondering what was keeping him. Then he heard a movement behind him and whirled to find Dabir entering the alley. The attorney's shoulders were hunched and his eyes darted everywhere until he spotted Gage waiting in the shadows.

Gage performed a deep salaam and dropped his voice into the low register. "Your will has been done, Mr. Dabir."

Dabir looked around uneasily. "Don't use my name here, Rukn."

So that was his adversary's name. Gage grunted an affirmative that seemed to satisfy Dabir.

"Did he give you any trouble?" Dabir asked.

Gage shuffled his feet. "No trouble, Mr....sir." He couldn't resist adding, "He fought like a tiger, sir."

"But you were able to subdue him?"

Gage jerked his head back in the direction of the orphanage. "His body lies well away from the road, behind a curtain of strangle-quick."

Dabir gave a satisfied nod. "No one would be foolish enough to look for him there. Good work." Gage tensed automatically as Dabir reached inside his jacket, but it was only to withdraw an envelope. Rukn's fee, he assumed.

He accepted the envelope without a twinge of conscience, knowing how much the orphanage could use the money. Holding it by its corner to preserve any fingerprints, he tucked it inside his shirt. He wondered if Rukn would have opened the envelope and checked the contents. Dabir didn't seem to notice the omission.

"You have more work for me, sir?" Gage asked in the same husky voice.

Dabir flicked a glance back the way he'd come, but the alley remained deserted, although with so much of it in shadow, it was difficult to tell. "How loyal are you to Sheik Ahmed?" he asked.

Gage gave a careful shrug. "I am loyal to my brothers."

The answer seemed to satisfy Dabir who nodded. "Good. These brothers of yours grow tired of waiting for power. The sheik is talking of instituting reforms that will endanger our plans. He's starting to listen too much to his headstrong daughter."

"The princess Nadia?" Gage asked, surprise making him

almost forget to disguise his voice. "I understand she is soon to become your bride. Will you not be able to control her?"

Dabir gestured savagely. "No one can control that one. After we are married, she will meet with an unfortunate accident and will no longer be able to contaminate the sheik's thinking. As his son-in-law, I shall console him in his grief and then guide his mind until he speaks for the Brothers without ever knowing he does so."

Gage's hatred of Dabir spiraled into blood rage as he wondered what kind of vicious instincts were needed to contemplate marrying Nadia, while planning to have her killed. His hands itched to close around the man's throat and squeeze the life out of him for daring to threaten the woman he loved.

Gage mastered his urge by assuring himself that Dabir wouldn't be permitted to harm one hair of Nadia's head as long as breath remained in his body to prevent it. With every word he spoke, Dabir was incriminating himself further. All Gage had to do was keep him talking until the police arrived, which should be anytime soon. Before setting off for Marhaba, Gage had called to alert them to pick up Rukn, and had suggested that a bigger fish could be caught if they raided the alleyway behind the Old Souk right about now.

"I'm not sure…" Gage began, thinking that even a mercenary would balk at assassinating a woman.

"Then become sure. Or I will find someone who is."

"I will become sure, sir." Abruptly Gage threw off the disguise and straightened to his full height, clearing the huskiness out of his voice as he said, "In fact, I'm sure now."

Dabir's face drained of color. "What the…? You!"

"I'm afraid your hired killer, Rukn, is the one lying in the strangle-quick, where the police should have found him by now."

"I have no idea what you're talking about. I know no one called Rukn."

"And the envelope in my possession doesn't contain cash covered in your fingerprints," Gage threw at him. "Between the money and the testimony of one who wears the symbol of the Brothers of Darkness, you're finished, Dabir.'' He pulled the dagger out of his sash and held it so the thread of light penetrating the alleyway glinted off it.

Dabir's throat convulsed as he saw the blade. Evidently it was one thing to order someone to be killed, and quite another to be faced with the possibility of one's own demise. ''What are you going to do?'' he asked, sounding strangled. He had flattened himself against the ancient stone wall as if he needed its support to remain upright. His expression was hunted.

''What I'd like to do and what I will do are, unfortunately, different matters,'' Gage said. ''Gutting you like a fish has a certain appeal, but I promised the police I would hand you over to them in one piece.''

''So what happens now?''

Gage made a show of examining the deadly blade. ''We wait. In the meantime, you can tell me about Conrad Drake.''

''That name means nothing to me.''

''How many men did you order to their deaths in America?''

He saw the dawning of recognition in Dabir's eyes, masked by a thin-lipped smile of contempt. ''His death was his own fault. He tried to join the Brothers and failed on his first mission.''

Gage let his knife settle on the other man's throat, wondering how much pressure would be needed to sever the jugular. Only a little more than he was exerting now. Only a little.

Reluctantly he eased the blade back. Whatever Dabir had done, the law would judge him, not Gage Weston. ''He didn't fail. He took five members of the cell he'd infiltrated with him,'' he said.

Dabir's eyebrows arched as he tried to make his breathing shallow enough to avoid contact with the knife. ''Infiltrated? What was this man to you?''

''My partner, my best friend, you could say my brother. Like me, he was working deep undercover for King Marcus of Montebello. The king asked us to find who, in Sheik Ahmed's circle, could have betrayed Prince Lucas and my partner. Before he died, Conrad left a message that led me to Tamir and to you. You're tied in with the American criminals who operated through that same cell of the Brothers of Darkness. It doesn't take a genius to know who was reporting to whom.''

Dabir shook his head, stopping the motion as he felt the press of cold steel against his skin. ''You have nothing that would stand up in a court of law. All I have to do is deny everything.''

''No doubt. But I'm just as happy to see you convicted of a charge of conspiracy to commit murder. And that will stand up in court when your hireling, Rukn, testifies that you sent him to kill me. Either way, you're finished.''

He saw the same certainty reach Dabir's eyes, but felt no shred of pity. The man deserved everything that was coming to him. In Gage's mind his crimes included the murder of Conrad Drake. It didn't matter what was read out in court.

Suddenly Dabir laughed. ''I suppose you think you've won.''

''I don't think it, I know I've won.''

''Then you sacrifice the most important prize of all. If I don't return to the palace within two hours, your beloved princess will die. I left one of my men guarding her, with orders to kill her if he doesn't receive my coded assurance that all is well.''

This time it was all Gage could do not to drive the blade home. His hand trembled with the need, but he dared not, as long as there was a chance that Dabir was telling the truth. ''What makes you think I care what happens to her?'' he asked carefully.

''I know you are in love with her. I had her followed all the time we were at Zabara. You were photographed kissing her in the colonnade.''

''A kiss doesn't have to signify love.''

''A man knows when another man desires his woman.''

"In this case, you're right. I do love her. But she was never
your woman and never will be once she hears that you intended to marry her, then have her killed as soon as your
position in the royal family was secure."

A gasp of shock brought Gage's head up, and a hint of
jasmine reached his nostrils. Joy ripped through him as he
realized that Nadia wasn't at the palace, under threat of death.
In the same moment, his joy was engulfed by stark terror that
she was here, where he couldn't guarantee to protect her.

He peered into the shadows in time to see a slight figure
duck out from under a wall hanging. A moment later he saw
Butrus give a start of recognition. "Nadia."

Making her way alone through the souk, Nadia had felt
horribly exposed, although she had drawn her scarf over her
face to avoid recognition. She was unaccustomed to being in
such a crowded public place without Nargis, Tahani and the
twins. Every time she was jostled, she was filled with apprehension, aware of the curious glances she drew from men as
she scanned the alleyways for any sign of Butrus.

She had seen him leave his car and enter the labyrinthine
complex. In the short time it had taken her to find somewhere
to leave her car, he had disappeared. How was she ever going
to find him and bring him to account for what he had done
to Gage?

She was alerted by the sound of a man's voice, one so
dear and familiar that tears sprang to her eyes. Gage. He
sounded as if he had a heavy cold, and his British accent had
been replaced by a rough Tamiri dialect, but she was sure it
was him. He was alive and very nearby. She lifted her head,
trying to determine where the sound had come from.

He was only a few feet away, separated from her by what
she had taken to be a solid wall, but was actually a thick old
carpet hung from a line.

She froze, listening hard, her joy turning to ashes in her
mouth as she heard Gage say in the low unfamiliar voice,

"The princess Nadia? I understand she is soon to become your bride. Will you not be able to control her?"

Her heart solidified in her chest and she brought her hand to her mouth to keep from screaming. Had Gage's courtship been nothing more than an elaborate scheme to see her dead and Butrus ruling by her father's side? The possibility made her sick to her stomach, the words buzzing in her mind, beyond any possibility of denial. Her mounting horror drowned out Butrus's reply. Her thoughts whirled so fast that the rest of the conversation went by in a blur of sound.

After a few minutes she straightened. She was not going to let them get away with this. She wasn't sure what she could do, but she was determined to make Butrus and his charming accomplice pay for their treasonous plans.

She pulled out Tahani's knife, discarding the scabbard. As a weapon, it wasn't much against two grown men, but it was all she had. Taking deep breaths to slow the rapid beating of her heart, she ducked under the carpet into the alleyway. The deep shadows protected her, and her dancer's skill enabled her to move on silent feet until she was within sight of Gage and Butrus.

Relief shimmered through her, cool and sweet, as she saw that Gage held a knife to Butrus's throat. The two couldn't be in league, after all. But what had Gage meant about controlling her, and why was he dressed in the costume of the hill people? She forced herself to remain still and listen.

The more she heard, the more appalled she became at the thought of how close she had come to entrusting her future to Butrus Dabir. He was responsible for the death of Gage's best friend and partner. How many other crimes had he committed in his quest for power and glory?

Bad enough when she thought he suffered from a sense of inferiority because of what he believed he had lacked as a boy. She had never dreamed that his aspirations had led him to join the Brothers of Darkness, one of the most feared and hated organizations in her country's history.

Her heart ached for poor King Marcus of Montebello. He

was her brother's father-in-law, and she knew how badly the king had suffered while his son was missing. All the time Butrus had been paying lip service to concern for the king, he had been helping the people who had tried to kill Prince Lucas.

In the shadows, she pressed her hands together to stop them from trembling. She had sensed all along that Gage was more than he seemed. Now she knew he was some kind of secret agent, charged with finding the traitor in her family. She felt confused, on one hand pleased that he had unmasked Butrus, but on the other wondering how much of his love for her had been part of his cover story.

"She was never your woman and never will be once she hears that you intended to marry her, then have her killed as soon as your position in the royal family was secure."

This time she couldn't restrain her gasp of shock and saw the two men turn toward her.

She moved out of the shadows. In the instant that Gage's attention was distracted, she saw Butrus slam the blade away from his throat and heard the dagger clatter to the cobblestones. Before she had time to react, Butrus had grabbed her and spun her around to put her between him and Gage. Butrus's arm pressed painfully against her windpipe. "If you really love her, you'll stay where you are," he ordered Gage.

She saw Gage freeze. She could have wept for knowing she had helped Butrus to turn the tables. "Never mind me," she urged. "Do what you must." Then Butrus's hold tightened, silencing her.

She increased her grip on the knife and jabbed it upward, hearing her fiancé's grunt of surprise as the small blade penetrated his sleeve. "You little…"

She used the moment to twist free and held her knife between them. "Hurry, Gage," she implored.

In the narrow confines of the alley, he maneuvered around her, but desperation made Butrus quicker. He slammed Nadia against the wall and tried to shoulder past Gage to make his escape. Gage shot a foot out and tripped the attorney, who fell heavily. He made a strange rattling sound and lay still.

"Stay there," Gage ordered Nadia, and went to Dabir, rolling him just enough to see what had happened. The stiletto had landed between two cobblestones with the blade pointing skyward, spearing Dabir through the heart when he fell. Gage let his inert body fall back. The police would have no difficulty working out how Dabir had died. Gage was torn between relief that it was over and regret that he wouldn't have the satisfaction of seeing the man brought to trial.

A whimpering sound brought his head around in time to see Nadia sliding bonelessly down the stone wall. Cursing, Gage went to her, collecting her in his arms. Had she realized what had happened to Dabir and fainted?

Her eyes fluttered open. "I think something's the matter with me," she murmured, her hand against her breast.

Gently Gage pried her fingers loose and felt his heart turn to stone in his chest. When she had been thrown against the wall, the knife she had wielded against Dabir had slipped. The jeweled handle now protruded from her breast, and a tide of scarlet was spreading outward from it.

"No, Nadia, dear heaven, no," he moaned, feeling as if the blade had pierced his own heart. "Don't do this to me. I love you. I can't live without you."

He saw her sweet beautiful mouth turn up in a gentle smile. "I love you, too," she said faintly, and slipped into unconsciousness.

Careful of the protruding knife, Gage compressed a handful of her gown against the wound, pressing hard, but unable to stem the spreading red tide. Moments later he heard the wail of sirens coming closer. Too late, he thought in anguish. He cradled the princess in his arms, rocking her gently backward and forward in a grief too soul-deep to be borne. He was still holding her when the sirens stopped.

Chapter 19

Nadia swam up toward the light. Although she was deep underwater, she felt no urgency to breathe. The crystalline water felt warm and welcoming, as if she was being cradled in loving arms.

She felt blissfully happy and knew why. Gage had told her he loved her and couldn't live without her. It was a dream of course, too beautiful and magical to be real, but oh, what a wonderful dream. She thought she had told him she loved him, too, then she had slipped underwater and drifted there for a long, long time.

Now some instinct told her it was time she returned to land. She started to swim toward the light, her strokes fluid and unhurried. Never had she known such lightness and joy. Her *galabiya* floated around her, pinpoints of phosphorescence clinging to the fabric like fairy lights.

"I think she's coming around," came a strange voice. She felt her eyelids being lifted back and a pinpoint of light shone in them. The hands were gentle.

She opened her eyes and the light was lifted away. She

was lying in a high narrow bed in an unfamiliar room. The walls and ceiling were white, but against them were banked huge vases filled with red roses. Their glorious perfume surrounded her, bringing a smile to her lips.

A woman dressed in white was bending over her. Then the woman was moved aside, and Gage leaned over her, taking her hand. "Nadia, thank goodness."

He exchanged a few words with the woman in white, and Nadia heard a door close as she was left alone with Gage.

His voice sounded strained, she noticed, and his eyes were red-rimmed. "Where am I?" she asked, her voice husky.

Gage heard and cradled her head in one hand while he lifted a glass to her lips with the other. She swallowed a few drops of water, and the rasp in her throat lessened. "Thank you."

He eased her head back to the pillow, letting his fingers trail through her hair as though touching her was a minor miracle. "You're in the hospital," he told her. "You were injured and you collapsed in the alley at the Marhaba Souk."

Memory came rushing back, displacing her sense of tranquility. She looked at Gage with wide unhappy eyes. "Butrus?"

"He's dead," he told her. "I'm sorry."

Now she remembered seeing her fiancé fall and land on the dagger he had knocked from Gage's hand. "It's hard to feel sorry," she said. "I had no idea he bore me and my family such ill will. My father was always good to him, yet he repaid us by collaborating with the Brothers of Darkness. How could he do such a thing?"

Gage caressed her forehead. "Many reasons can motivate a man to side with the forces of evil. Power, greed, the need to feel bigger than he is, are all reason enough if you want them to be."

She nodded. "Butrus told me his uncle adopted him. He never felt equal to the other children of the household."

Gage's face took on a faraway expression. "I knew someone in the same position. He never knew his father, and his mother died when he was a child. He was farmed out to aunts and uncles, then we became friends at school and my family adopted him. We grew up together as close as brothers.''

"Your friend, Conrad Drake?" she guessed, remembering what she had overheard in the alleyway.

Gage seated himself on the side of her bed. "You heard what I told Dabir?"

"Not everything, but a lot. I gather you hold Butrus responsible for the death of your friend."

"Without a trial, I'll never have all the facts, but the evidence is there. Prince Lucas of Montebello identified one of the Americans Dabir met with at Zabara as belonging to the Brothers who held him prisoner in America. They kept their affiliations well hidden. If Lucas hadn't identified the man in the photos I sent to King Marcus, we still wouldn't have the link."

"You've been busy," she said dreamily, "for a minor English diplomat."

He smiled self-deprecatingly. "You're entitled to know that I'm neither English, nor a diplomat. The British ambassador and his wife are my godparents, and they kindly allowed me to use the embassy as a base, but my home is in Penwyck and my business...well, I think you know what that is by now."

She nodded, finding she didn't mind as much as she thought she would. Unlike Butrus, Gage hadn't deceived her for his own benefit, but to ensure that justice was done. She felt her eyelids grow heavy. "I forgive you," she murmured.

She was aware of the woman in white returning and checking her over, a doctor, she knew now, but her eyelids felt so heavy she could no longer keep them open.

Gage watched her slip into sleep, pleased to see how peaceful she looked. Her color was back to normal, and the pulse he felt under his fingers was strong and steady. He curled his fingers into hers, before bending and dropping a light kiss on her slightly parted lips.

After the rigors of these last horrible few days, he felt as

tired and battered as he ever had, but he didn't care as long
as she was all right.

When he thought she had been fatally wounded, he had
thought his own heart was going to stop. Cradling her, watching the crimson tide seep through her gown and knowing
there was nothing more he could do, he had fought back tears
of anguish, which had threatened to become a flood if he
gave in to them.

He had not wanted to give her up to the care of the police
and ambulance attendants who had arrived at the scene.
When the paramedics told him she was only slightly injured,
he hadn't believed them.

"No one bleeds that much from a slight injury," he had
insisted, knowing that his control was a hairbreadth from
snapping.

Not until one of the paramedics had taken Gage to the
ambulance and shown him the tube of paint that Nadia's
knife had ruptured did Gage start to believe she might live.
He had no idea what she was doing with a tube of red paint
tucked in her *galabiya,* but he thanked God that it was there.
When Dabir threw her against the wall, the paint had absorbed most of the impact of the knife, so she was only
slightly wounded. Gage had been right all along. She had
fainted from the shock of Dabir's revelations and seeing him
fall on his knife.

"The princess is exhausted," the doctor had assured Gage.
"We will hospitalize her to treat the shock and the minor
wound, but she will recover quickly."

After the police had confirmed his identity, he was allowed
to ride in the ambulance with Nadia, and they agreed to take
his statement at the hospital later. They would need to talk
to the princess, too, but Gage could see they were prepared
to await her pleasure. There were some advantages to being
royal, he thought. He didn't mind as long as it meant he could
be with her.

When next Nadia opened her eyes, daylight streamed into
the room. Gage was asleep in a chair at her bedside, she saw,

her heart filling with joy at the sight. During the night she had drifted in and out of awareness as doctors watched over her. She had known that Gage was there, a reassuring figure, willing her to recover.

His prayers had worked. She felt strong and well, and relieved beyond measure that Butrus hadn't succeeded in subverting the throne of Tamir to the will of the Brothers of Darkness. Thinking of how close he had come made her shudder. If she had forced herself to do what she thought was her duty and marry him, she would have been helping him to further his devilish aims.

Never again, she thought resolutely. From now on, she would be true to herself first. She had no illusions that Gage would sweep her off her feet. He had said he loved her, but that was in the heat of battle with Butrus. In daylight he would probably feel otherwise. They were from different backgrounds. Her father would never allow her to marry Gage.

She felt a smile start. Old habits died hard. She had just finished deciding to be true to herself, and already she was worrying about what her father would and wouldn't permit her to do. After all, he *had* allowed her sister Leila to marry an American just weeks ago. She might just tell her father that she was going to visit Penwyck. The former British colony was reputed to be a beautiful place. If she and Gage were to meet there, who knew where it could lead?

"You look pleased with yourself," Gage observed.

Her thoughts had been so busy, she hadn't seen him stir. "I was thinking of my future," she said. "Thanks to you, I have one to look forward to." She didn't add how largely Gage himself figured in her dreams.

He stretched and stood up, then padded to her bedside to take her hand. She felt some of his strength flowing into her. "Don't thank me. You were the one who attacked Dabir with the knife." He picked up a distorted piece of metal from the bedside table. "Thank God the blade went into this tube of paint, instead of into you."

She nodded, remembering. "I found it in the field where I'd left Tahani painting. Butrus had sent a car and taken Tahani and my driver back to the palace. Until I stumbled across the tube of paint, I thought I was in the wrong place."

"Picking up the tube probably saved your life."

Her hand went to her breast. The knife had pierced her *galabiya*, fatally she'd thought. She was pleased to find only a small dressing over the place and murmured a prayer of thanks.

Gage heard her. "Amen to that. But I wish you'd found another color besides red. When I held you in my arms, I thought you were bleeding to death."

"Would blue paint have made you believe that royalty is truly blueblooded?" she asked, hoping to defuse the tension she saw in his face and posture.

He leaned over and gathered her into his arms, being careful to avoid hurting her. She almost sighed with annoyance, wanting him to be anything but gentle. She wanted to be crushed against him, to feel his mouth hungry on hers and to hear him say he loved her now, when he knew she wasn't dying.

He didn't say it and she became aware that his embrace was stiff and awkward. She pulled back a little, looking at him anxiously. "What's the matter, Gage?"

"Your parents are due to visit at any moment."

She frowned. "I thought the sheik was still away." He and her mother were inspecting the new oil field on the island of Jawhar.

"They returned as soon as they knew you were hurt. They were here earlier, but you were still asleep, so they went out for some air. They'll be back any moment."

She gripped his arm. "Stay with me, please."

"Your father isn't very happy with my clandestine activities."

"I'm happy with you," she affirmed. "I want you to stay."

"You're certain?"

Another thought made her frown. "Is Tahani all right?"

"She's a little shaken by what happened to you, but she's fine. The police arrested the guard who was working for Butrus."

She chewed her lower lip. "Butrus had photographs of us."

"I know. I found them on him and destroyed all but one."

"To use as blackmail against me?"

"To remind myself of what a lucky man I am to have known you."

Past tense, she noticed with a stab of anguish. He sounded as if he was preparing to leave. What else had she expected? Declaring his love when he thought she was engaged to another man or dying was one thing. Saying it now would probably be more of a commitment than he wanted to make. Although she had prepared herself, the thought plunged her into the depths of despair.

Reading the unhappiness in her expression, Gage touched a hand to her cheek. "Don't worry, Princess. All will be well."

She had said the same thing to Tahani, and look what had happened. Then she had no more time to brood, because her mother and father entered the room. Sheik Ahmed looked astonished to find Gage there, but made no comment. Her mother was too busy gathering her into a loving hug.

"My dearest child, I was worried out of my mind. Are you all right?"

Nadia returned the hug. "Yes, Mother, I'm fine. It's good to see you both."

Sheik Ahmed moved closer to the bed and took her hand. "It's good to see you awake, my daughter. From what the police told me, we almost never saw you again."

Nadia's look included Gage. "Mr. Weston saved my life, and saved Tamir from Butrus's schemes."

The sheik's cool nod acknowledged Gage's role. "Since arriving in our country, Mr. Weston has been rather active, he tells me."

A doctor who had followed the ruler and his wife into the room bustled around the spacious suite, rearranging the comfortable chairs for them. Alima declined hers, preferring to perch on Nadia's bed and cling to her hand as if to convince herself that her eldest daughter was really safe and well.

Sheik Ahmed thanked the doctor curtly, his tone suggesting dismissal. The doctor took the hint and left.

"Gage has told me why he came to Tamir," Nadia said to her father. "He had nothing but our best interests at heart."

The sheik's lips thinned. "Mr. Weston and I will discuss this again later, Daughter. It is not your concern."

"But it is my concern," she insisted, a now-or-never feeling driving her to throw caution and years of royal education to the wind. "I want you to know that when I marry, it will be for love."

The sheik looked as if she wasn't telling him anything he hadn't suspected—and dismissed. "Love has little to do with making a good marriage. Your mother and I married for family reasons, and they were sufficient."

Nadia saw Alima's face dimple and knew that love had crept into her parents' relationship over the years. She was sure her father felt the same, although he would never admit it. She took a deep breath. "Your way was appropriate for your generation. I am of a new generation, and I wish to live my life differently."

"I told you so," Gage said, folding his arms and resting his back against the wall, his gaze soft on her.

She looked at her father in confusion. "What does he mean?"

"While you were asleep, Mr. Weston asked me for your hand in marriage," the sheik said. "He asked me not to tell you until you indicated that you wanted the same thing." He looked over his shoulder at Gage. "I think we may take this as an indication."

"Sounds like it," Gage said equably. He sounded insufferably pleased with himself.

Feeling as if she had been outmaneuvered, Nadia felt her face heat with annoyance. "So the two of you have already settled my future?"

Gage nodded. "Pretty well."

"Without bothering to consult me?"

"Uh-huh."

"That is how men decide matters," the sheik added loftily.

Nadia retrieved her hand from her mother and gesticulated in anger. "Men! Always men! What they want, think, decide. Can't a woman decide for herself what she wants and whom she will marry?"

Gage seemed unmoved by her tantrum. "I thought she already had."

"Is Gage wrong?" her father asked.

She subsided against the pillows. "No," she said sulkily. "But it would have been nice to have my opinion considered."

"Your opinion was considered," Gage said, moving closer. "Why do you think I asked Sheik Ahmed to withhold his news until I knew how you felt?"

As marriage proposals went, it had to be the strangest one in the history of Tamir, she thought. Then it came to her that she didn't really mind if it meant she and Gage could be together for always.

"I admit I wasn't pleased when I heard why Gage had come to our country," the sheik continued. "I had started to believe that relations between us and King Marcus of Montebello had reached a new level of understanding. Finding that the king had secretly arranged to have our family investigated hardly seemed a step in the right direction."

"I wish there had been another way, too," Gage agreed. "Your father now accepts that there was no other way to uncover the traitor who was working against your family's interests."

Alima touched a hand to Nadia's cheek. "You're not too distraught about Butrus, are you, child?"

Nadia shook her head. "I shudder to think of the havoc he could have caused Tamir if he'd achieved his aims."

"That isn't going to happen now," Gage said. "You're safe, and so is the peace process between your country and Montebello."

The sheik rose to his feet, adjusting his headdress and *'iqual,* and gathered his wife up with a look. "We'll leave you to rest now, Daughter. Your sister and attendants will visit later. They have been beside themselves with worry and will be relieved to hear that we found you looking so much better."

Alima placed Gage's hand into Nadia's. "Keep her safe for us."

His glowing expression was answer enough, but he said, "Believe me, I will." If it cost him his life, Nadia read into his expression.

Thinking of how close they had come, she tightened her fingers around his and sent her father a radiant look of gratitude. "Thank you for giving us your blessing, Father." Then a frown creased her brow. "Although I don't understand how you can be so pleased that I wish to marry a commoner of another country and faith."

The sheik's look went to Gage. "He is not as much a commoner as you think, my child. Tell her, Gage."

Gage shuffled his feet and looked uncomfortable. "It's true I'm from Penwyck, but from the royal part of it, although I don't use the titles much."

"I'm pleased to present His Grace, Gage Weston, Duke of Penwyck," the sheik said with a satisfied smirk. "As for his faith…"

"We share the same beliefs," Gage said quietly.

She blinked in surprise. "But you have godparents."

"An honorary role. The Theodores are long-standing friends of my father's and consider themselves my godparents. I have known them so long that I regard them in that role, too."

Alima clapped her hands in delight. "I must return to the

palace. There is much to be done to plan another royal wedding feast.''

Nadia didn't even try to mask her distress. The thought of her wedding reception being turned into a royal circus was not to be borne. "Mother…," she said warningly.

Alima gave her a wicked smile. "Permit a mother her pleasures, child. I promise to make the feast last no longer than a week."

Nadia collapsed against the pillows, knowing when she was being teased. "You are impossible, but I love you both."

Her mother stroked her brow. "As we love you, too, Daughter."

Although they might frustrate and anger her beyond belief, Nadia had always known her parents loved her. She felt blessed to hear it spoken at long last. Murmuring a prayer of leave-taking over her, the sheik left with his wife in tow.

"They're quite a couple, aren't they?" Gage asked. He got up and snapped the lock closed on the door. They were finally, blessedly alone.

"You should have told me you were a duke," she said reprovingly. "How many other secrets have you kept from me?"

"Only one," he said with a seductive smile. "How much I truly love you. I doubt if even your parents have any idea."

He pulled her into his arms and found her mouth with a certainty that took her breath away. Just as well the medical staff had unhooked her from the monitoring equipment over her bed while she slept, because the heart monitor would have gone crazy, she knew. She could feel her pulse racing and knew the cause was far from medical.

"I love you, too," she whispered, linking her arms around his neck. How strong he felt. The prince of her heart, now and for all time. "For a moment there, before my parents arrived, I was afraid you were preparing to leave me."

"I was," he confirmed, his kiss silencing her indrawn breath of alarm. "I knew how I felt about you and I had your father's blessing. But I wanted to be sure you felt the same way. As you must know by now, I'm not your average royal, and I have my own ideas about equality between men and women.''

He was giving her a gift greater than anything she had ever dreamed of receiving—the right to choose her own destiny, she thought on a swell of joy so great it was almost more than she could bear. Her eyes filmed with tears as she smiled up at him. "I have made my choice," she said huskily. "Wherever you go, whatever you do, I shall be at your side.''

His breath of relief washed over her and his arms tightened around her. Through the thin fabric of the hospital gown, she felt the powerful beat of his heart keeping time with hers. "In return I promise to love you and honor you as my wife and the custodian of my heart, for as long as we live.''

No woman could ask for more, she thought as his mouth claimed hers again. The kiss went on for a long time, flooding her with desires both sacred and primitive, making her hope that their wedding would take place soon. She chided herself for her impatience. She and Gage had the rest of their lives to be together. "I never thought I could be so happy," she said.

"Nor I, my darling princess," he said, sounding as impatient as she felt. "There's another person who will be even happier, if you feel as I do.''

"Who?" she asked, puzzled.

"Little Sammy. I'd like us to adopt him," Gage suggested.

She knew her cup of happiness was brimful. "I can think of nothing more wonderful.''

"Other than to provide Sammy with a houseful of brothers and sisters," Gage said.

She laughed. "My parents would consider that my royal duty." At the same time, she knew that doing her duty had never appealed to her more.

Epilogue

Nadia felt a buzz of excitement as she took her place beside Samira in the small room concealed from her father's council chamber by a beautifully patterned screen. The palace had many such hideaways. They had been used for centuries by the women of the household to observe palace life without being exposed to the eyes of strangers.

"I was delayed by yet another journalist seeking an interview," she told Samira in an undertone. Since her release from the hospital the previous week, Nadia had been besieged by the world media, fascinated by the story of her adventure and enchanted by her romance with the handsome duke from Penwyck. They hadn't been told the half of it of course, and Nadia had been amazed that her father had allowed her to speak to the media at all. Had he sensed her determination to emancipate herself once and for all, and decided to give her more leeway in order to head off a family crisis?

Her father was a realist, she knew. Before he died, Butrus

had accused Nadia of influencing her father to institute reforms. She was starting to hope it was true.

She smiled warmly at Alima, seated on her sister's other side with her dutiful attendant, Salma, behind her. Their mother was also intent on watching the proceedings.

Alima gestured to the chamber below, which was filling rapidly with delegates to the conference being held to improve relations and trade between Tamir and their neighbors from Montebello. "Look, King Marcus has arrived."

Nadia had no trouble spotting the distinguished monarch. In his sixties, he was still lean and broad-shouldered, his white hair making him look every inch the elder statesman. With her parents' approval, the king had impressed her by calling on her the day before to apologize personally for his role in having her family investigated. Since his actions had led to her and Gage meeting and falling in love, she had seen little need for his apology. Instead, she thanked him, much to the king's pleasure.

Samira nudged her gently. "Your Gage makes a handsome conference chairman, doesn't he?"

Pride and love brightened Nadia's features as she watched Gage take his place at the table. As a member of the royal house of Penwyck, and thus considered impartial, he had been seen as the ideal person to mediate the conference. "Of course."

"Not that you're biased," Samira teased, her sparkling eyes reflecting Nadia's happiness.

Nadia gave her a "who, me?" look and settled to listen to the proceedings.

Her attention was distracted by Nargis bustling in. "Your Highnesses, Sheik Ahmed commands your presence in the council chambers."

"Now?" Such a thing was unheard of in Nadia's experience.

Nargis nodded. "He wishes you to act as his advisers." The attendant also sounded disbelieving.

Nadia looked at Samira, then back to Nargis. "Are you sure he said adviser and not observer?"

"Yes, my princess. He has reserved seats for you directly behind him."

Catching Nadia's questioning look, Alima shook her head. "You two go. I am happy here with Salma for company." Her message was clear. She would do as she had always done, share her thoughts with their father behind the scenes.

Nadia needed no second invitation. Her heart swelled with pride and not a little nervousness as she and Samira slipped into seats behind her father in the main conference room. A ripple of surprise had traveled around the room at their arrival, but Nadia lifted her chin. This would not be the last time a woman of Tamir served in such a capacity, if she had anything to say about it.

Across the table King Marcus smiled a welcome, as did the king's principal adviser, Desmond Caruso. He was standing in for the king's son, Prince Lucas. Evidently the prince was still recovering from his long ordeal. If *she* had crashed her plane, lost her memory and been held hostage by the Brothers of Darkness, she would probably need some recovery time, too, Nadia supposed.

Lucas's cousin, Desmond, had grown up in America, not knowing he was a member of Montebello's ruling family until he was nineteen, she recalled.

Beside her, she felt Samira stir and looked at her curiously. Her sister's eyes were fixed on Desmond. In them Nadia saw the same sparkle she felt in her own whenever she looked at Gage.

Surely Desmond couldn't be the man that made Samira look so enigmatic whenever love was mentioned, could he? Glancing at her sister's vivid expression, Nadia began to wonder. But she had no more time to consider the question, because Gage was calling the conference to order.

His warm look washed over her, suggesting that he approved of her presence. Had he noticed that she was wearing the tiger necklace he had given her? The slight upward curve of his mouth told her he had and was pleased.

She listened intently, offering her father a suggestion when invited, finally feeling as if she was contributing something to her country's future. The time flew past, and soon Gage announced they would break for coffee.

"It feels strange, being here among the men, doesn't it?" Samira whispered as they sipped their coffee. "I could get to like it, though."

Nadia already liked it, and she said so. She felt her spirits lift further as Gage drifted to her side, her father with him. "Thank you for your contributions this morning, my daughter," the sheik said.

Gage's look of love spoke more eloquently than words.

"Thank you for allowing me to voice them, Father," she returned, her tone adding, *at long last.*

The sheik nodded as if he had heard what she didn't say. He took a sip of cardamom-scented coffee. "I have reached a decision concerning your future."

She bristled automatically, but he smiled to disarm her fears. "The choice is yours and Gage's of course, but I have been talking with Ambassador Theodore, and the time is ripe for Tamir to send our first ambassador to England."

Gage, of course, she assumed, as he gave her a knowing smile. The prospect of living in England as the ambassador's wife was attractive, although she couldn't subdue a feeling of disappointment. Was her involvement today nothing more than a token because her father knew she wouldn't be living in Tamir for much longer?

The sheik must have seen the disappointment on her face, because he continued, "How does Madam Ambassador sound to you, Daughter?"

She almost choked on her coffee. "*Madam* Ambassador?" Instinctively her gaze flew to Gage.

He nodded approval. "Sounds pretty good to me."

She could hardly believe it. "You...you won't mind?"

"Why should I? I can operate as well from England as from Penwyck."

"What about Dani, your protégé? Won't she mind you living in England? I was looking forward to meeting her."

He looked pleased. "Dani spends more time traveling around the world with her band than she does in Penwyck, so you'll meet her soon, no matter where we're based."

"Then I accept the appointment with pleasure, Father."

"I thought you might," the sheik said dryly, but his eyes shone with satisfaction as he swept Gage off to consult with King Marcus. Nadia couldn't wait to share her wonderful news with Samira, but her sister had slipped away. Casting her gaze around for her, Nadia almost bumped into Desmond Caruso.

"A thousand apologies, Your Highness," he said formally.

She studied him with interest, certain that he was the man who had caught her sister's eye. He had inherited the dynamic looks of the Sebastiani family, with raven hair, chiseled features and a cleft chin that made him look like a film star. Personality fairly radiated from him. So Nadia was at a loss to explain the unease she felt around him. "The fault was mine for not looking where I was going," she said, struggling to mask her reaction.

He didn't seem to notice. "Are you enjoying the conference?"

She nodded, hoping he didn't know that this was the first time she had served her father publicly in such a capacity. "If it leads to better relations between our two countries, I will be delighted."

He nodded. "That's what we're here for."

A servant refilled their coffee cups from an ornate brass pot. Nadia saw Desmond trying to survey the crowd without her noticing. "Are you looking for someone?"

He dragged his attention back to her. "Forgive me, Your Highness, but I thought I saw your sister, Princess Samira, at your side a few moments ago."

So the attraction was not one-sided, Nadia thought, reading

a certain desperation in the young man's expression. She tried to feel happy for her sister, wondering why she found it such a challenge. "She will return shortly," she assured him. "When she does, she will look for me."

"Then I hope you won't mind if I remain at your side until she returns," he said, his interest unmistakable. He seemed irritated when an aide discreetly attracted his attention. "Excuse me one moment," he said, and turned to the man.

She sipped her coffee, not wishing to eavesdrop, but the aide's voice carried to her ears. He was saying something about a Miss Ursula Chambers from America insisting on speaking with Desmond. Evidently she was refusing to hang up until he came to the phone.

Concern for her sister made Nadia anxious. Did this Chambers woman have a claim on Desmond's affections? Nadia hoped not, because she knew only too well the look she had seen on Samira's lovely face. Since falling in love with Gage, Nadia saw the same expression on her own face whenever she looked in a mirror.

She let her gaze wander over the crowd, pretending disinterest, but listening carefully as Desmond said, "Give Miss Chambers my regrets, but tell her we have nothing to say to each other and I would prefer her not to telephone me again."

Whatever might have been between Desmond and this woman was over now, Nadia gathered. Seeing Samira crossing the room toward them, Nadia allowed herself a sigh of relief. Her sister's happiness meant as much to her as her own. She would hate Samira to give her heart to Desmond, only to have it broken.

Desmond's face lit up at Samira's approach, although Nadia noticed that the smile didn't quite reach his eyes. She decided now was a good time to slip away and find Gage, leaving her sister and Desmond alone.

She hated to think that Desmond might be an opportunist who had decided that a royal princess was more useful to him than this American woman he had refused to speak to, but the suspicion refused to go away.

It was none of her concern, she told herself firmly. In Gage she had found the other half of her soul, and happiness beyond her wildest dreams. Samira deserved the chance to work out her destiny in her own way.

Seeing Gage beckoning, Nadia murmured a prayer that her sister would find a love as all-consuming as hers. A tall order, given that Nadia's cup of joy was full to overflowing. But as she well knew, with love, nothing was impossible.

* * * * *

Possessed by a passionate sheikh

The Sheikh's Bartered Bride by Lucy Monroe

After a whirlwind courtship, Sheikh Hakim bin Omar al Kadar proposes marriage to shy Catherine Benning. After their wedding day, they travel to his desert kingdom, where Catherine discovers that Hakim has bought her!

Sheikh's Honour by **Alexandra Sellers**

Prince and heir Sheikh Jalal was claiming all that was his: land, title, throne…and a queen. Though temptress Clio Blake fought against the bandit prince's wooing like a tigress, Jalal would not be denied his woman!

Available 19th September 2008

www.millsandboon.co.uk

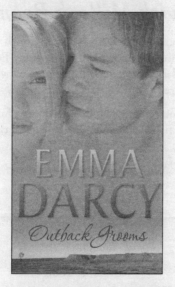
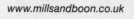

Celebrate 100 years of pure reading pleasure with Mills & Boon®

To mark our centenary, each month we're publishing a special 100th Birthday Edition. These celebratory editions are packed with extra features and include a FREE bonus story.

Plus, you have the chance to enter a fabulous monthly prize draw. See 100th Birthday Edition books for details.

Now that's worth celebrating!

September 2008

Crazy about her Spanish Boss by Rebecca Winters
Includes FREE bonus story
Rafael's Convenient Proposal

November 2008

**The Rancher's Christmas Baby
by Cathy Gillen Thacker**
Includes FREE bonus story *Baby's First Christmas*

December 2008

One Magical Christmas by Carol Marinelli
Includes FREE bonus story *Emergency at Bayside*

Look for Mills & Boon® 100th Birthday Editions at your favourite bookseller or visit
www.millsandboon.co.uk